PRAISE FOR
SHARKY'S MACHINE

"Compelling...The complete thriller."
—*Newsweek*

"A suspense-jammed feast."
—*San Diego Union*

"Excellent."
—*The Houston Post*

"Classy, kinetic, awesome...Tough...Colorful à la Wambaugh."
—*Kirkus Reviews*

"Fast, furious, sensational."
—*Publishers Weekly*

"A perpetual motion narrative. If *SHARKY'S MACHINE* omitted any action thrills, I can't think what they are."
—*John Barkham Reviews*

By William Diehl
Published by Ballantine Books:

SHARKY'S MACHINE
CHAMELEON
HOOLIGANS
THAI HORSE
27
PRIMAL FEAR
SHOW OF EVIL

SHARKY'S MACHINE

William Diehl

BALLANTINE BOOKS • NEW YORK

For my first editor
Linda Grey
who opened the door for me.
Her warmth and kindness made it easy;
her brilliance made it better.
With my gratitude

Copyright © 1978 by William Diehl

All rights reserved under International and Pan-American Copyright Conventions. Published in the United States by Ballantine Books, a division of Random House, Inc., New York, and simultaneously in Canada by Random House of Canada Limited, Toronto.

No part of this book may be reproduced or transmitted in any form or by any means, electronic or mechanical, including photocopying, recording, or by any information storage and retrieval system without the written permission of the publisher, except where permitted by law.

For permission to quote from copyrighted material, the author gratefully acknowledges the following:

ANDREW SCOTT, INC. for permission to use the lyric excerpts from "Centerpiece," quoted on p. 185. From "Centerpiece," lyrics by John Hendricks; music by John Mandel. Copyright © 1959 and 1976 by Andrew Scott, Inc. Used by permission.

SPACE POTATO MUSIC LTD. for permission to use the lyric excerpts from "Midnight at the Oasis," quoted on p. 206. From "Midnight at the Oasis," by David Nichtern. Copyright © 1973 and 1974 by Space Potato Music Ltd. Owner of publication and allied rights throughout the world. Used by permission.

ISBN 0-345-40239-1

This edition published by arrangement with Dell Publishing, a division of Bantam Doubleday Dell Publishing Group, Inc.

Manufactured in the United States of America

First U.S. Ballantine Books Edition: December 1995

10 9 8 7 6 5 4 3 2 1

Acknowledgments

To these special people for their love, encouragement, and support before and during the writing of *Sharky:*
to my mother and father; to my children, Cathy, Bill, Stan, Melissa, and Temple; to Carol, Temp, and Julie; to my dear friends, Marilyn and Michael Parver, Carole Jackowitz, Mardie and Michael Rothschild, Leon and Judy Walters, DeeDee Cheraton and Ira Yerkes, Arden Zinn, and Larry and Davida Krantz for "The Nosh"; to three generous and indulgent editors from the past, Al Wilson, Howard Cayton, and especially Jim Townsend; to Delacorte's Helen Meyer, a legendary woman; and my new friends Ross Claiborne and Bill Grose for their dazzling enthusiasm; to my editor, Linda Grey, whose warmth and kindness made it easy and whose brilliance made it better;

but most of all, to my dynamic and unerring agent, and devoted friend, Freya Manston, who made it all come true.

*Our deeds will travel with us
from afar,
And what we have been makes us
what we are.*

GEORGE ELIOT

PROLOGUE

Northern Italy, 1944

It had been dark less than an hour when Younger and the two sergeants finished loading their equipment on the three mules and prepared to head north toward Torbole and the rendezvous with La Volte. The young captain was excited, his eyes flashing as they smeared boot black on their faces. He was like a football player just before the first whistle blows, charged up, fiery with nervous energy. Harry Younger was perfect for this kind of cloak and dagger stuff; it was like a game to him. You could almost hear the adrenaline pumping through his veins. When they had the mules ready, Younger took out his map one more time and spread it on the side of an ammo box strapped to the flank of one of the mules and held his flashlight close to it. He went over the details once more and everybody nodded.

The paisanos stood back from the group and smoked American cigarettes and said nothing.

When he was finished, Younger smacked his hands together and then ran one hand through his crew cut several times and pulled his cap down over his head. Then he took Corrigon by the arm and led him away from the group, off by himself.

"How ya doin', buddy-boy?" he asked Corrigon.

"Four-o," Corrigon said, but there was an edge in his voice.

"Sure you're okay?"

"Yeah, yeah, fine, sir."

"You're not gonna choke up on me, are you, chum?" Corrigon smiled. "I wouldn't dare," he said.

"That's m'boy. Look, it's a piece of cake, Corrigon. I've done this, shit, half a dozen times. You been in here for two days, right? Not a sign of a fuckin' Kraut anywhere around. Don't think about what might go wrong, think about how simple it's gonna be."

"Yeah, sure," Corrigon said. *Will you knock off the pep talk, for Christ's sake!*

"I'll make you a bet. I'll bet we all come outa this with Silver Stars. I know this La Volte, see. He's got every fuckin' paisano guerrilla in north Italy up his sleeve. It'll be a little Second Front, up here. They'll kick the Krauts in the ass and we'll be across the Po before Christmas."

"Yeah, right, right." Corrigon tried to sound enthusiastic.

"You know why I picked you for this end, Corrigon? Hunh? Because Pulaski and Devlin there, they been sluggin' it out all the way since Anzio. If anything goes wrong, we're between you and the Heinies, if there *are* any. And we been in here now two days and not a sign, not even any recons overhead. Hell, buddy, God lost his galoshes in here. Nobody's gonna bother us."

Corrigon was beginning to feel a little better. *You oughta be a coach,* he thought. *You'd have the whole team playin' with broken legs.*

"Feel better?"

Corrigon nodded. "I'm okay, Captain. Believe me."

Younger laughed, his all-American smile flashing through the blackface. "What the hell am I pumping you up for? Look, two days, we'll be back in Naples. I'll swing a seven-day pass for all of us out on Capri and the drinks'll be on old Bud Younger."

"You're on," Corrigon said.

Younger slapped him on the arm. "Don't break radio silence until you're set up. You won't hear from us unless there's trouble. When you're ready, give us a call and we'll be back at you. We won't be a mile away from you when they make the drop."

"Right."

Younger walked back to Pulaski and Devlin and said, "Okay, let's saddle up." They started off to the north into the black night.

"See you in a couple hours," Younger said jauntily and then the darkness swallowed him up. Corrigon didn't move for a couple of minutes. He felt suddenly lonely. Fear tickled his chest. Then finally he turned to the two paisanos and swung his arm and they started off toward the lake. Fredo led the way with Sepi bringing up the rear, a tight little group walking almost on each other's heels. In less than an hour they reached the bluff overlooking di Garda. They lay on their stomachs on top of the ridge and Corrigon could hear the wind sighing across the lake and feel its cool breeze on his cheeks. Somewhere down below, a hundred yards away perhaps, water slapped against a shore.

"Garda," Fredo whispered, pointing down the opposite side of the slope. "Yeah, *si*," Corrigon whispered. It would have been nice, he thought, if just one of these

eyeties could say something in English besides "cigarette" and "chocolate." But then, why should he com-
plain? The only Italian he knew was "fig-fig" and a
couple of cusswords.

Typical army. Three guys behind the German line
and they can't even talk to each other.

Corrigon took out his binoculars and scanned the
darkness. Here and there small diamonds of reflected
light shimmered on the rough surface of the big lake. A
wave of fear washed over Corrigon and then it went
away. He reached into the breast pocket of his field
jacket, took out the rice-paper map, and spread it on
the ground beside him, holding a tiny penlight over it.
Fredo looked at it for a moment or two and nodded
vigorously, smiling with a row of broken teeth, and
pointing to a spot on the northeast shore of Lago di
Garda. It was almost exactly on the perimeter Younger
had laid out for him.

"Phew," Corrigon murmured with relief.

"Buono?" Fredo asked. Corrigon nodded. *"Si,* very
buono. Uh, the flares, uh, la flam, flame, uh . . ."

"Ahh, si," the guerrilla answered and nodded again
as he reached into the khaki duffel bag and took out
one of the railroad flares. He was a nodder, this Fredo.
The flare was eight inches long with a short spike attached to one side and a pull fuse on the bottom. There
were twelve in the bag. Fredo and his companion, Sepi,
knew exactly what to do. They had been rehearsing all
afternoon, ever since Captain Younger had dropped in
and made contact with La Volte. Fredo tapped Corrigon's shoulder and pointed down at his wrist.

"Ten to eight," Corrigon said.

Fredo puzzled with it a minute and then smiled
again. "Den, den," he said, wriggling ten fingers in the
corporal's face.

"Yeah, right, *si,* ten more minutes." He pointed to

the duffel bag and then down the hill toward the lake and Fredo and Sepi moved out without a sound. Corrigon listened for a full two minutes and heard nothing. They were good, no doubt about that, like cats tiptoeing on sand.

He snapped open the khaki cover on the radio and cranked it up, then spoke softly into the headset.

"Spook One, this is Spook Two. Do you read me. Over."

The radio crackled to life, much too loud, and Corrigon quickly turned the volume down. Sweat broke out in a thin line across his forehead, smearing the black shoe polish on his face. His hands were wet. And they were shaking.

"Spook One to Spook Two. Reading you loud and clear."

"Spook One, we're set up. No trouble so far," Corrigon said.

"Roger, Spook Two, and we're affirmative also. Any signs yet?"

"Negative. We got"—he looked at his watch again—"seven minutes."

"That's roger and we're in synch. Out."

"Out," Corrigon said and cradled the headset. He was lying on his stomach, chewing unconsciously on his thumb, wondering what the hell he was doing there, when he heard a sound beside him. An electric shock of fear shot through his chest and he reached for his .45 and turned on the penlight. Fredo grinned back at him.

Corrigon sighed with relief. "All set? Uh, okay?"

"*Si*, oh-kay."

He snapped off the light and lay with his eyes closed, listening. He thought, What the hell am I worried about? It's a fairly simple operation and these guys do it all the time. The sector was isolated; no major roads anywhere near. Why would there even be any Germans around? He began to relax.

At first it was hardly a sound. It was a low rumble, like distant thunder, then it built, growing into the deep, solemn throb of four engines, coming in from the south.

"Now," he whispered sharply and Fredo and Sepi were gone. The roar grew and then burst overhead, so low he could almost feel the slipstream of the B-24 as it passed overhead.

Pop, pop, pop, pop, pop, pop, one after another the flares sizzled to life as Fredo and Sepi ran along the two lines they had set, pulling the fuses, marking a twenty-yard strip between Corrigon and the lake. Corrigon threw the shoulder strap of the radio over his shoulder and ran down the hill after them. The plane wheeled hard and started back down the run toward him, its engines whining at full speed. It was then Corrigon realized the wind wasn't coming off the lake at all. It was coming from behind him, blowing streams of smoke from the flares out over the lake.

"Holy shit!" he cried aloud. The plane was almost on top of them, roaring down the lakeside. He was vaguely aware of the engines backfiring as he slid the radio off his shoulder and knelt beside it, frantically cranking up the generator.

"Spook Two, this is Spook Two to Angel. Go around, go around, the wind's . . ."

Too late. The bomber rumbled overhead. A second later he heard the faint *jump* as the first chute opened, then another and another . . .

It was then that Corrigon became painfully, terrifyingly aware that he had not heard the engines backfiring. It was gunfire. Gunfire from Spook One's position half a mile uplake.

There were flashes jarring the black sky, the rapid belch of a German burp gun, a faint agonized scream, the hollow crack of a grenade. Fredo and Sepi, etched in the ghoulish red glare of the flares, turned sharply and ran back down the line, kicking over the flares and throwing sand on them.

The first parachute, a gray ghost with its heavy load swinging below it, plopped into the lake. It sank immediately.

"Spook One, Spook One, what the hell's going on?" Corrigon yelled into the radio.

"Bandits, we got band . . ."

An explosion cut off the transmission. Fire swirled up into the black sky and vanished. Then a machine-gun chattered, no more than twenty yards away, and Fredo, running, leaped suddenly into the air. His back arched. Tufts flew from his ragged jacket. He fell on his face, arms outstretched in front of him, rolled over on his back, and lay still, his feet crossed at the ankles. Sepi turned and started back toward Fredo.

"No!" Corrigon cried. It was too late. The machine-gun chattered again. Bullets stitched the ground around Sepi's feet, snapping his legs out from under him. He screamed and fell, skittered along the ground, started to get up to his knees, and was blown back into the air, dangling for an instant like a puppet, then dropping in a heap as the earth around him burst into geysers of death.

There were still flares burning behind Corrigon, but there was no time to bother with them now. Farther up the shore more explosions rent the night, more flames licked the sky. A burst of gunfire tore the radio to pieces. Corrigon veered, started running, hunched over, toward the safety of darkness. He slung the tommygun under his arm, firing several bursts behind him as he ran. He was almost to the top of the hill, almost outside the shimmering red orbit of the flares, when he felt something tug at his shirt, felt fire enter his side, boring deep and burning his insides.

He staggered but did not fall, dove to the ridge, and rolled over the top as a string of bullets chewed up the crest of the hill behind him. Pain flooded his body, seared his lungs, filled his chest.

"AHHHH, G-O-D D-A-A-A-M-N!" he screamed and crawled back to the ridge, laying the tommygun on the ground, pulling it against his cheek. Below him, shadowy figures moved toward the remaining flares. He squeezed the trigger. The gun boomed in his ear, shook him, jarred the pain deep inside him, but he kept firing and screaming. One of the figures whirled and fell, then another. A third turned and ran back toward the darkness, and Corrigon swung the gun, saw the bullets strike, saw the figure dance to his death. He kept firing, raking the three bodies until the barrel was so hot he couldn't hold it anymore. He struggled to his feet, pulled the rice-paper map from his pocket, and stuffed it in his mouth, feeling it dissolve in saliva as he started to run.

He did not know how long he ran, only that each step was worse than the last and the pain in his side seared deeper with each one. Vomit flooded his mouth; he spat it out and kept going. His mind wandered back in time and seized on an old chant from his Boy Scout days, "Out goes the bad air, in comes the good. Out goes the bad air, in comes the good," and it became a cadence that kept him going.

Darkness gobbled him up. He tripped, staggered, fell, felt cruel stones bite into his knees, and ignored them. "Out goes the bad air, in comes the good," lurching back to his feet and running on. "Out goes the bad air, in comes the good," running through a black void with his eyes closed and then he smacked headlong into a wall and his forehead burst open like a tomato and he bounced backward and landed in a sitting position and madness seized him. He pulled his .45 automatic from the holster and in a rage fired over and over again at the wall, and then for no reason at all he started to giggle. Sitting there with his side shot apart and his head split open and a pistol jumping in his hand, lost in the middle of an alien land and alone, totally alone, with death snapping at his ankles, Corrigon laughed and the laughter turned to sobs. Once more he got to his feet, felt the wall, staggered along it to a corner and, turning, felt the gritty rust of a latch. He lifted it and went through the door, and leaned on it, closing it behind him.

Silence. And it was blessed. He felt for his penlight, but it was gone. Then his fingers touched the cold metal of his Zippo lighter. He took it out, snapped the flint, and held it high over his head. He was in a shed of some kind, abandoned except for spiders busily weaving webs in the corners. He walked to the opposite side of the small room and sat against the wall, facing the door.

The pain in his side hit him in waves, subsiding, then washing back through him and subsiding again. He heard himself groaning and he snapped the carriage on his .45 and ejected a bullet into his lap and put it between his teeth.

You're crazy, Corrigon, crazy as shit, sitting here in the dark actually biting on a bullet.

But it helped and finally, as he leaned against the wall trying to make peace with the fire inside him, he passed out.

When he regained consciousness, he was bathed in sweat, the bullet still between his teeth. He looked at his watch. Ten-o-five. Two hours.

Then he heard the voices. Low, cautious. At least two of them, talking rapidly. He strained to make out words. The beam of a flashlight filtered through the cracks of the shed. They were nearer now, at the door. He heard the latch lift from its rusty hook.

Corrigon sat straight up. He held the .45 in both hands and aimed it at the door and waited, biting down hard on the bullet, blinking the sweat out of his eyes. The flashlight beam fell on his face. He squeezed the trigger and the pistol plinked. Empty.

Corrigon's shoulders sagged. He lowered the gun to the floor and spat out the bullet and raised his head toward the ceiling, closing his eyes and waiting for it to come.

The flashlight beam lowered and picked out the gun.

"Americano," a voice said.

"Si," came the answer.

"La ferita è molto sanguinosa. E gravemente leso."

"Ummm," said the other one.

"E morto?"

"No."

"Buono."

Buono? That was *good.* What were they saying? Something about blood, death. A jumble of words he could not understand.

One of them was very close now, leaning over him. Then he said, very slowly, "You are lucky, *amico.* That the gun was empty. I would not want to kill you."

Corrigon opened his eyes.

The Italian lowered the flashlight and in its reflection, Corrigon could see the two men. The man who had spoken to him was tall and lean with gray hair and a jawline like granite. The other one was younger and shorter and had shoulders like a football player.

"My name is Francesco. *Capisce? Francesco."*

Corrigon managed a feeble smile.

"Hi, Francesco," he said in a voice hoarse with pain and exhaustion.

"That is Dominic. He does not capisce English."

"No capisce," Dominic said and smiled from embarrassment.

"That's okay, I no capisce Italiano."

"E ufficiale?" Dominic said.

"He says, Are you an officer?" Francesco said.

"Shit, I'm a goddamn corporal."

Francesco turned to Dominic. *"No. Sottuficiale."*

Dominic shrugged. Then he held up a tommygun. *"Abbiamo udito colpi e trovato una mitragliatrice."*

"We heard the shooting and we found this gun on the hill."

"I think it's mine," Corrigon said, then: "Who are you?"

"Farmers."

"Not partisans?"

"Non siamo guerriglieri, ma siamo simpatizzanti." Dominic said.

"He says, we are not guerrillas, but we are sympathetic to the Americans."

"Grazie."

Everybody nodded.

"Do you know La Volte?"

Francesco looked puzzled. *"La volte?* The fox. What is that?"

"Shit," Corrigon said, "I'm too tired to go into it."

Dominic said, *"I tre altri sono morti."*

"Si," Francesco said and, turning to Corrigon, told him, "the other three Americani are dead. I am sorry."

"Ah, Jesus."

"Pray for yourself. It is too late for them. What are you called?"

"Corrigon. Johnny."

"Buono, Jah-nee," Francesco said and he took a dagger from a sheath in his boot. Corrigon's smile vanished and he stiffened. "Easy," Francesco said, "I must cut the shirt. There is much blood."

Corrigon lay back and listened to the blade slicing through the cotton shirt. He felt a finger probe his side and it exploded with pain. He decided to think of something, of Major Halford calling him in, giving him the pep talk, telling him Harry Younger thought he was ready for a mission. "It's really fairly simple," Halford had said, "just drop in, make the connection, supervise the drop and get out." *Sure, nothing to it, Major. Like falling into a bear trap.* And Younger, all full of piss and vinegar, dreaming about all the broads lining up to rub his Silver Star. Only now it would be a Purple Heart. Posthumously.

And where was the big shot La Volte when all the shooting started?

"Hey, Jah-nee," Francesco said. "You are lucky. It just went in one side and out the other." He whistled softly through his teeth. "Just like that, eh, paisan? Lots of blood, but it could be worse."

He reached into a first-aid kit on his belt and took out a small cylinder and a bandage roll. "You have how you call it, uh, a nose cloth, *capisce?*"

"Handkerchief?" Corrigon asked.

"Si, si."

"Back pocket, left side."

Francesco took it out, tore it into two strips, and made patches of them. He sprinkled gray powder on the entry and exit wounds. "Penicillin," he explained. Then he and Dominic bound up the wound.

"Our town is Malcesine. About three kilometers. Can you walk?"

"How far's that?"

"Two miles maybe."

"I'll do an Irish jig for two miles to get outa here," Corrigon said.

The two Italians helped him to his feet. The pain

swelled back through him, but he clenched his teeth and tried to ignore it.

"Tough guy, eh, *amico?*" Francesco said.

"Yeah, sure, tough guy, that's me," he groaned. I'll tell you what I am, he thought, I'm a simple, dumb, dogface, eighty-two-dollars-a-month-plus-combat pay corporal from Clearfield, Pennsylvania, and I used to drive a delivery truck for my brother-in-law's brewery and it makes about as much sense me being here as it would to put army shoes on a fucking French poodle but I ain't *so* dumb that I buy that shit about you two being farmers when you have knives in your boots and penicillin on your belts but I'm not gonna argue with anybody right now so let's stuff all the Dick Tracy bullshit and get the lovin' hell outa here fast and maybe, later on, when we can put our feet on the table over a little pasta and vino somebody will tell me what happened back there and why everything went to hell so fast.

But Corrigon hurt too badly and was too tired to think much more about it. All he knew for sure was that Captain Harry Younger and Sergeant Joe Pulaski and the other noncom, Devlin, were dead and Major Halford's operation had bought the farm. And right now four million dollars in gold was lying on the bottom of Lake Garda.

Hong Kong, 1959

The morning sun blazed off the wings of the plane from Tokyo as it banked sharply over the edge of the bay and began the long descent to the runway that jutted out over Victoria Harbor. In the back of the crowded DC-6 tourist section the stewardess, a beautiful Oriental woman who spoke flawless English, picked up the interphone and began her final announcements:

"Welcome to Hong Kong. In a few minutes we will be landing at Kai Tak Airport terminating PanAm flight twelve. Hong Kong means 'Fragrant Harbor.' The city is divided into several districts. At the front of the plane on your left is Kowloon Peninsula. Kowloon means 'Nine Dragons' and was named eight hundred years ago by the boy-emperor Ping, who believed that dragons lived in the eight mountain peaks surrounding the harbor. His prime minister reminded him that there were really nine dragons, since the ancient Chinese believed that all emperors were dragons. The modern section at the tip of the peninsula is Tsimshatsui, the modern shopping center of Hong Kong harbor.

"Hong Kong island is at your immediate left and beyond it is the South China Sea. On the far side of the island is the harbor of Aberdeen . . ."

The man in the dark gray suit in seat 19B tuned her out. He took off his sunglasses and pinched the bridge of his nose. He had been flying for almost twenty-one hours with only three stops and his eyes and neck ached. Although he felt cramped in the tourist section, it was safer, less conspicuous than flying in front, where the passengers somehow seemed nosier and quicker to strike up conversations. Tourist section provided anonymity.

He took out the passport and checked it one more time. It identified him as Howard Burns of Bridgeport, Connecticut. It was a good alias, one he had used sparingly. Only Casserro knew about it. The passport was over a year old and well-used. He had told Casserro, "Get me something with a little mileage on it, nothing new," and as usual old Chico had come through.

The man who called himself Burns was of medium height and slender with a few gray streaks in his close-cropped black hair. He was dressed inconspicuously in a business suit and wore dark glasses, and he had slept most of the way from Tokyo, awakening once to eat a warm snack. His food had been cold when he got it, but he ate it without complaint to avoid attracting attention to himself.

He shook off the effects of the arduous trip and, reaching into his suit jacket pocket, took out a small pill which he casually swallowed without water. The amphetamine was mild, just strong enough to get his juices running again. Then he settled back and began ticking off details in his mind, hitting only key words: Peninsula Hotel on Kowloon Causeway. George Wan, Oriental Rug Company, phone 5-220697. Star Ferry to the island. Causeway Typhoon Shelter, Wharf Three. Twelve noon. Brown and tan Rolls Royce.

Simple. No wrinkles. He settled back, feeling secure as the plane bumped down and taxied to the terminal. He moved casually through customs, his only luggage a small carry-on bag with a change of shirt, socks, and underwear and toilet articles. No pills, not even aspirin. Once inside the terminal he went to the money exchange and traded five hundred dollars for twenty-five hundred Hong Kong dollars. Then he went outside and found a taxi.

The drive to the Peninsula Hotel took only fifteen minutes. The manager, a short, stubby Oriental in a silk brocaded cheongsam, checked him in and presented him with an envelope.

"You have a message, Mr. Burns. I believe it is a package. May I have the porter get it for you?"

"I'll do it myself," Burns said in a flat, brittle voice.

The manager rang a bell and the porter appeared and followed Burns across the lobby to the cluttered office of the concierge, where a small, middle-aged woman sat reading what appeared to be the morning paper. Burns tore open the envelope and removed a receipt and a key. He gave the receipt to the woman and received a new attaché case, which he refused to let the porter carry.

His room was on the fifth floor. It was old and elegant and faced the harbor. Across it, like a jewel shining in the morning sun, was the island of Hong Kong.

"Very nice," he said and got rid of the bellman with a tip.

He sat on the bed and unlocked the case. Inside were

a long-barreled .22 pistol equipped with a silencer, a nylon cord four feet long, and a pair of latex surgical gloves. In the pocket at the back of the case were six bullets and a physician's envelope containing two pills. There was also a roll of cotton swabbing.

Excellent, Burns said to himself. So far nobody had missed a beat. Burns put on the surgical gloves and then removed the cylinder and silencer of the gun and checked it with the precision of a toolmaker, examining the barrel and firing pin before reassembling it and dry-firing it twice. It was clean and freshly oiled, although not new. Satisfied, Burns loaded the six bullets into the cylinder and replaced the gun. Then he took out the nylon cord and, wrapping it around both hands, snapped it sharply several times. He doubled the cord, tied a squareknot midway between the ends, and put it back. He put one of the pills in his suit pocket and placed the other back in the envelope, took off the gloves and dropped them in the case, locked it and put it in a drawer.

He checked his watch. Eight forty. He opened the carry-on bag and from his leather toilet kit took out a small travel clock. He set it for 11:15, then called the operator.

"I'd like to leave a call for eleven fifteen, A.M.," he said. "That's two and a half hours from now."

"Yes, sir," said the operator, "eleven-fifteen A.M."

Then Burns loosened his tie and lay back on the bed, folded his hands across his chest and fell immediately to sleep.

At 11:25, Chan Lun Chai closed his antique shop, put a sign on the door announcing that he would be back in ten minutes, and stepped into sweltering Cat Street. Shimmering heat turned the crowded confines of

the old Morlo Gai shopping district into dancing mi-
rages as he threaded his way through the crush of
Chinese nationals, tourists, and sailors, toward the
phonebooth half a block away.

A heavy-set Englishman, overdressed for the heat,
his tie askew, and sweat pouring into his shirt collar,
was bellowing into the phone while his wife, who was
almost as tousled as he, waited outside the booth with
her arms full of packages.

Unperturbed by the heat, Chan stood nearby, studying the window of a jade shop. He was short and wiry, a
man in his mid-thirties, dressed in the traditional black
mandarin jacket and matching pants. Only his glasses,
which were gold-rimmed and tinted, seemed out of
place.

Finally the Britisher left the booth fuming. "Really!
They say you can't make reservations for the Chinese
Opera. Have you ever heard of such a thing? No reservations at the opera!" They trundled off through the
crowds toward Ladder Street.

Chan stepped into the booth and looked at his watch.
It was exactly 11:30. Seconds later the phone rang. He
answered in a slow, quiet, precise voice:

"Royal Oriental Rug Company."

"May I speak to Mr. Wan, please?" The voice on the
other end was sharp and irritating, like the sound of
firecrackers exploding.

"Which Mr. Wan?" Chan said.

"George Wan."

"This is George Wan speaking. May I help you?"

"This is Mr. Johnson."

"Welcome to Hong Kong, Mr. Johnson. Did you get
the package?"

"Excellent. Everything's satisfactory."

"I am pleased," Chan said.

"How about tonight?"

"It is all arranged."

"Good. I should be back to you in three hours. Maybe four."

"I will be here. May I suggest the sooner the better. It may be difficult, locating the object you seek."

"I understand," Burns said. "I'll try to call back by two-thirty."

"*Dor jeh*," Chan said, "which means 'thank you.' *Joy geen*." And he hung up.

The shower and shave did not help much. Burns still felt sluggish, his senses dulled by time lag and lack of sleep. After talking to Chan he went into the bathroom and took the pill from his pocket, popped it in his mouth, and washed it down with a full glass of water. He was hardly out of the room when it hit him, a dazzling shot, like a bolt of lightning, that charged through his body, frazzling his skin. He felt as though he were growing inside his own shell, that his muscles and bones were stretching out. He became keenly aware of sounds, the hum of the elevator and the muffled roar of a vacuum cleaner behind a door somewhere. His entire body shuddered involuntarily as he waited for the elevator.

Leave it to the Chinks, Burns thought. Whatever it is, it's nitro, pure nitro.

By the time the Star Ferry was halfway across the harbor, he felt ready again, his eyes bright and clear, his reflexes quivering like rubberbands stretched to the limit. He got out of the cab and let the hot breeze tickle his skin, watched the concrete skyline of the Central District draw closer. The buildings seemed to soar, telescoping up from their foundations and dominating the two mountain peaks at either end of the island. His heart was thundering and he felt a keen, familiar sense of anticipation and his penis stirred between his legs.

Without thinking, he began rubbing his hands together. The exhaustion that racked him was jarred, splintered, purged from his body, like torn pieces of paper thrown to the wind. He got back in the cab.

The driver moved expertly off the ferry and down through the crowded slip, blowing his horn and ignoring the catcalls and shaking fists of the crowds of pedestrians. He turned left onto the Causeway, a wide boulevard, and then drove swiftly, due east toward the shelter, passing through Wanchai, the garish night-club colony with its neon signs exploding invitations to the mid-day trade, and away from the skyscrapers of the Central District. A minute or two later the driver leaned his head back toward Burns but kept his eyes on the highway.

"Typhoon Shelter ahead, san. You have a place?"

"You know sampan three?"

"*Hai.*" The driver nodded.

"*Hai*, that's 'yes'?" Burns asked.

"Yes, *hai.*"

"How would you say 'no'?"

"*Um.*"

"*Um*, hunh? *Um, hai, um, hai,*" Burns repeated several times and began laughing and patting his knees like a drummer keeping rhythm with the words. Abso*lute* nitro!

The taxi turned off the Causeway and wound down a curved road toward the waterfront. The Typhoon Shelter was a triangular cove protected on the inland sides by tall concrete abutments. The driver stopped. Burns got out and looked down at the harbor. The cove was choked with sampans. Hundreds of the small flat-bottom boats bobbed in the water, their mid-sections protected by hoods made of rice mats, their pilots standing at the tillers in the stern, beckoning to the tourists and calling out prices. Several of the sampans had woks in the bow and chests filled with beer and soft drinks, like floating delis. The wind carried the smell of cooking fish and shrimp up to the abutment.

Burns was overwhelmed by the sight. This was the China he had envisioned.

The driver stood beside him and pointed to a wharf directly below them at the bottom of the concrete stairs. Sampans hovered around it.

"Sampan three," he said.

"Great. What I owe you?"

"Seven dollars," the driver said.

Burns gave him eight and said *"Dor jay,"* and the driver, smiling at his awkward attempt to say thank you, bowed and replied *"Dor jeh,"* and was gone.

Burns walked to the eastern wall of the shelter and waited. At 12:05 a brown and tan Rolls, polished like a mirror, pulled up. The man who got out was tall and beginning to show the signs of overeating. He wore a white linen suit and a flowered sport shirt open at the collar. His receding hair was blondish and he wore a thick mustache and dark blue sunglasses. He walked with a cane of finely polished teak with an ornate dragon's head handle carved out of gold. The man stared down toward sampan three for several moments and then descended the concrete stairway. The Rolls drove away.

Burns waited for a full ten minutes, watching the roadway leading to the stairs and scanning the entire abutment. When he was sure the man had not been followed, he too went back to the stairway and down to the wharf.

The big man stood on the pier, haggling with an ancient and toothless crone who stood at the rear of one of the boats. A small child sat at her feet playing with an empty soda bottle. They appeared to be arguing.

"Gow, gow," the woman yelled in a voice tortured with age.

The big man shook his head. *"Tie goo-why. Laok."*

The old woman glared at him with anger. *"Laok. Laok! Hah! Um ho gow gee aw!"*

The big man laughed. Burns stepped up behind him and said, "Why fight with the old crone? There's plenty of other boats around."

The heavy-set man jumped and turned quickly, startled by the words. He stood close to Burns and the two men stared at each other for several moments. Finally the big man smiled, very vaguely, then said, "She is telling me I am cheap, to stop bothering her. It is a game we play, *senhor.* She wants nine dollars, I offer six. I pay her seven and tip her two." He spoke with an accent that seemed part Spanish, part German.

"Gay doa cheen," the old woman yelled, *"um goy?"*

"Chut," the large man replied.

She grumbled. She looked wounded. She chattered and pointed to the child. Then finally she motioned him aboard.

"Are you taking a sampan?" the large man said. "Perhaps we can share a ride."

"Sounds okay to me," Burns said.

The big man offered his hand. "I am Victor DeLaroza."

"Howard Burns." They shook hands.

"I am going to the Tai Tak," DeLaroza said. "It is the finest floating restaurant in the city."

"What a coincidence," Burns said. "So am I."

"Excellent. Are you a visitor?"

"Yeah," Burns replied.

"Well, perhaps I will be able to recommend some dishes." DeLaroza took seven Hong Kong dollars from his pocket and gave it to the woman. She counted it and glared at him. *"Aw tsung nay,"* she muttered. DeLaroza laughed. "She says she hates me. When I tip her, she will tell me she loves me."

Burns stepped into the sampan and walked to the seat in the mid-section. He was hunched over and walked with his hands on the sides of the tenuous skiff, and he turned cautiously before he sat down. DeLaroza followed, walking upright with ease and sitting beside him.

"You do that like a champ," Burns said to him.

"*Ho!*" the old woman cried out and cackled.

"She tells me 'good'," DeLaroza said. "I was like you at first, overly cautious. She is the oldest of the old. *Jung-yee Pau Shaukiwan*, the grandmother of Shauki-wan."

"What's a Shaukiwan?"

"Shaukiwan is the Chinese settlement, a floating village around on the southeast side of the island. You have never seen greater poverty."

The old woman stood at the rear, moving the scull with arms as thin as twigs, expertly guiding the sampan around the hundreds of other boats and moving it toward the open water of the harbor. Ahead of them, to the west, was a great three-story junk, its pagodalike awnings stretching out over the water and its garish red and yellow trim gleaming in the sun.

"That's Tai Tak," DeLaroza said. Behind him the baby started banging the empty bottle on the bottom of the boat.

"Hell of a place to babysit," Burns said. "What happens this thing, you know, dumps over?"

"She and the child will probably drown. He is her grandson. She watches over him while her daughter works in one of the whorehouses in West Point, the old city. When he is a little older, they will sell him."

"Sell him!" Burns was shocked. "Sell their own kid?"

"It will be better for him. He will be sold to a good family, possibly even British or American."

"Jesus, don't they have any feeling for the family?"

"Life is harsh on the harbor," DeLaroza said, and then, "I almost bought the boy myself."

Burns turned to him and stared for a moment at one corner of his sunglasses. Burns never looked anyone directly in the eye. Then he looked back at Jung-yee.

"It's all right, you can speak freely. She does not understand English."

"You're crazy," Burns said flatly.

"A little, I suppose."

"You got pretty fat and sassy there, uh, uh . . ."

"Victor. V-i-c-t-o-r. I am Victor, you are Howard."

"Yeah. Anyway, you learned a lot out here, only a coupla years, too."

"You haven't changed much at all," DeLaroza said.

"Yeah, well, a little gray hair maybe. Fifteen years is a long time, right? I wouldn't recognize you. Not at first anyway. The weight, the hair. You done something here too, around the eyes."

"It is called a stretch. They pull the skin tight to the ears on both sides. Gets rid of the wrinkles. I do not have the proper bone structure for a face lift, but . . ." He let the sentence dangle.

"The accent's good too, pal," Burns said. "Now what's this about buying the kid? Some kind of guilt thing?"

"No, loneliness. And pride. I am building an empire and there is no one to carry on the line. When Victor DeLaroza dies, then what?"

"So what, that's what. When you die, who gives a damn?"

"They have a saying here. If a dragon smiles on you, you have luck. If two dragons smile on you, you have love. And if three dragons smile on you, you are immortal."

"Quite the philosopher there, ain't you, Vic, old boy? Well, goes with the new look. We got a saying too. You can't take it with you."

"Exactly. That is my point."

"You got a lotta time. So far the dragon's been pretty good to you."

"So far only one dragon has graced me."

Burns did not answer immediately. DeLaroza took out a cigar, snipped off the end, and lit it with a small gold lighter. He puffed it until the end glowed evenly. Then he turned abruptly to Burns, offering him one.

"I don't smoke. That a real Havana?"

DeLaroza nodded.

"I got a lotta pals, business pals, right?, gonna drop millions down there, that fuckin' Batista runnin' out like that. Castro's closing up the casinos, now the word's out he's gonna take them, just *take* 'em."

"Castro is an enigma."

"I don't know about that," Burns spat out. "He's a goddamn Commie thief is what he is. We oughta go in there, blow the whole dingo outa the pond with an A-bomb, you ask me. Start over."

Burns's sudden vehemence startled DeLaroza. Then just as quickly the American's mood changed and he started to laugh. "You hear about Castro going to a costume party. Stuck out his tongue and came as a hemorrhoid." He laughed even harder at the foul joke and the old woman, caught up in his gaiety, laughed with him. "Listen to that old crone," Burns said and laughed even harder. DeLaroza puffed on his cigar. "Anyway," Burns continued, "you got the golden touch, Victor."

"We may be expanding again," the big man said.

"How's that?"

"It is becoming more and more profitable to manufacture products out here in the Orient—Hong Kong, Singapore, Japan. Then assemble them in the States. There are certain tax advantages."

"You thinking of opening up something in the States?"

"It's obvious to me now. In another year or so it will be obvious to many."

"Well, you got the instincts there, Victor. I'll give you that. Fifteen years, you ain't made a mistake yet. I thought you were nuts, movin' out here from Brazil. What did I know?" He paused, then added, "Don't you ever wanna stop, sit back, listen to the grass grow, drink a little vino?"

"Not yet. The bigger it becomes, the more challenging it is. We may have to go public. It is all becoming too big for one man. Too cumbersome."

"Sell out, then."

"Perhaps. Get out of all this, try something new, different. Something small."

"Look, I don't care, see? I mean you do what you do. That's your end of it, I got no complaints, no complaints at all. Me, I'm here to do what I do, see? I figure, you used the Pittsburgh drop, it had to be something serious. I got here in three days, pal. Think about it. Had to get things set up, a passport, like that. I was twenty-fucking-one hours on the plane. I don't even know what day it is, flying up and down and around, across datelines, that kinda shit. You know what? I was on Wake Island for four hours, can you beat that? I went out, looked at the monuments and all. I never been this way before, Europe but never over here. For all I know, I get back, it's gonna be the day before I left. You just be careful, that's all. You get too greedy, you'll be like the monkey, you know, kept puttin' his paw in the jar, bringing up a peanut, finally he puts it in there, grabs a whole fistful of peanuts and he can't get the fist out and he won't drop the peanuts and you know what. He got the old blasteroo, that's what."

"I shall keep that in mind."

"So what's the problem? What am I doin' here?"

Burns was beginning to sweat. He took off his coat and draped it over his lap."

"You remember Halford, the major in Firenze?"

Burns thought for a moment.

"Vaguely."

"He was in charge of Stitch. Tall man. Very straight, tough. Very smart."

"Yeah, sure I do. The paisanos called him, what was it?"

"Gli occhi di sassi. Stone eyes."

"Right. A very suspicious man. He didn't believe shit. What an asshole."

"You know him. Four days ago I saw Halford, on a restaurant like the one out there. In Aberdeen Harbor. He is a colonel now, a full colonel."

"Is that what's got you goin'? Hey, I hardly recognized you and I was *looking* for you. Is that what this is all about?"

"He recognized me. I am sure of it."

"Ah, c'mon."

"We were not five feet apart. I was paying the check and I turned to leave and he was just sitting down at the next table and we stood there and stared at each other and I swear, for a moment he almost said something. Then I got out, very quickly. But as we were pulling away in the launch I looked back up and he had come outside. He was at the rail, watching me."

Burns said, "Humh."

"I have been terrified ever since. It is frightening, to be afraid to walk on the street. My company is in Mui Wo, on the island of Lantau, to the west of here. Only occasional tourists come over there, to visit the silver mines. And yet I have been afraid to go outside. Today, coming here, my stomach hurt. I sat in the back seat of the car looking out the window, looking at every face."

"Take it easy."

"It has been a nightmare."

"So far you did everything right. You didn't try anything. No phonecalls. Didn't try to get a line on him, right? Nothing to set anybody off?"

"No. I followed the plan. I contacted you and waited."

"Okay. Good for you."

"There is a danger. He may have reported it to someone."

Burns said nothing. He stared straight ahead, his brain clicking off the options, the odds. Finally he said, "Okay, we got to go on the assumption he didn't. I mean if he did, it's too late anyway. So we got to figure he's here on vacation, okay? Was he in uniform?"

"Yes."

"Okay, nine, ten to one he's on a furlough. So it's a fluke. Maybe he got a little shot, see? Thought to himself, Hey, I know that guy. But it's fifteen years. You changed a lot. What were you then, anyway? I don't see him putting it together. I don't see that at all. Maybe, if anything, he's probably still trying to put his finger on it."

Burns thought some more.

"Thing is, if he's on vacation, he's too busy having a good time. He's outa the element right now. He's thinking, maybe. Maybe even he's touched it around the edges. But it's a long shot, he made you. I promise you. What we gotta do, we gotta locate him fast and then . . ." He snapped his fingers and smiled. DeLaroza stared at him and a chill passed through him. Burns went on:

"Okay, okay. You relax, see? You forget it. We have

a good lunch, you go back over there to whatever, Mooey Pooey, whatever you call it, lay low another day. By tomorrow it'll be over. You don't worry, see? This is my end of it. This is *my* business. I'm glad you didn't panic. Anytime there's trouble, I handle that. What I don't want, I don't want amateurs fallin' in the soup, know what I mean?"

"Yes. Thank you."

"Forget it. My problem. It's done. Besides, I may be needing to call on you one of these days. I may have to make a big withdrawal."

"What happened?"

"Well, you know, this and that and the other thing. Some friends of mine, *used* to be friends of mine, they may have tumbled on to our little freelance thing down there in Brazil. It could be just I've got the butterflies like you. But just in case . . ."

"How much?"

"I dunno. Couple hundred thousand maybe."

"It will be no problem, my friend."

"Good. One more thing. About Halford. I want a good description. And I'm gonna need money, Hong Kong dollars."

"How much?"

"I dunno yet. Could be, maybe fifty thou Hong Kong. How late can you do business with the bank?"

"Up to six is no problem at all. It will come out of the box. The president of the bank and I are friends. We play golf together."

"Ain't that sweet? Six is okay. I'll probably need to make the tap about five. Deliver it to my hotel. In a shoebox, wrapped up like I bought some shoes, had them delivered. You call me at five, I'll give you the tally. Where's the bank?"

"Right around the corner from the hotel. The China

Bank, behind the old Supreme Court building just before you get on the Star Ferry in Kowloon."

"No problem. You ain't five minutes away."

"Right."

"Okay, how about Halford? What's he look like?"

"His full name is Charles David Halford and he is a full colonel," DeLaroza began, and then described the military man.

"That's beautiful. Look, you can forget it, okay, Victor? Now, what are we gonna have for lunch?"

"Well, I would suggest starting with shark's fin soup and then either the Shanghai crab or empress chicken . . ."

At 2:30, Burns made his call from a public phone booth in the lobby of the Excelsior Hotel, directly across the causeway from the Typhoon Shelter. Chan answered.

"Royal Oriental Rug Company."

"Is Mr. Wan there?"

"Which Mr. Wan?"

"George."

"This is George Wan."

"It's Johnson again."

"Yes sir. Do you have the information yet?"

"Yeah. An eagle colonel, U.S. Army, name of Charles David Halford. H-A-L-F-O-R-D, Halford. Six-one to two, hundred-eighty pounds, white hair cut short, one of those curled-up type mustaches. I'm guessing he's down from Tokyo or maybe the Philippines. I don't think he's here permanently. That's all I got."

"It is enough."

"I was planning, I'd like to be outa here tonight, know what I mean? Can it be handled that quick?"

"I feel certain, if there are not complications. Call

back each hour. If there is no answer, I have nothing to report."

"That's fine, just fine. Did you make the shipping arrangements?"

"Uh, yes, uh, you understand, there is a risk in moving the object about. There will need to be an additional charge for, uh, packing and insurance."

"Of course. You get too greedy, I'll let you know. *Dor jeh.*"

"*Dor jeh.*"

There was no answer at 3:30. At 4:30 the line was busy and Burns began to get nervous. Another hour would be pushing the bank deadline. He waited a minute and tried again. The phone rang several times before someone answered.

"*Jo sun,*" a high, whining voice said.

"Is this the Royal Oriental Rug Company?" Burns asked.

"*Um ying gok yun,*" the voice said.

Jesus, he can't speak English, Burns thought.

"George Wan? You know, George Wan?" he said, speaking the name slowly and distinctly.

There was a disturbance on the other end, a flurry of Chinese words spoken in anger and then:

"This is George Wan. Hold a moment, *um goy.*" Then he heard him snap out a stream of Chinese, followed by another flurry. Finally: "I am sorry. This man was using the booth for business calls. I had a small problem with him. Is this Mr. Johnson?"

Burns paused. Then: "Where do you work?" His voice was flat, harsh, and suspicious.

"Royal Oriental Rug Company. It is George Wan, believe me."

"Okay, what've you got?"

"The eagle colonel Halford is with military intelligence. He comes from Korea by way of Tokyo and is on rest leave. It required many calls. I had to prevail on a friend in Japan in the Yakuza and . . ."

"Forget the road map, okay? I don't care where he came from, how he got here, all that. You got to understand, George, you and me we're in the same business. You don't have to jack up the price with all these details. All I want is essentials."

Wan paused, then he said, "Yes. Halford is at the Ambassador Hotel on Nathan Street in Kowloon. Everything is arranged for tonight."

"You got the shipping thing set up?"

"*Hai, nin.*"

"I'm changing signals a little. It'll be two."

"Two?"

"Yeah, two."

"But I don't understand, who . . ."

"Think about it, George. You can figure it out. I said I wanted shipping *and* insurance, see?"

This time the pause was longer. "That could make things very difficult for us, Mr. Johnson. It will really not be necessary to . . ."

Burns cut him off. "Look, you come over on my turf, you got a job to do, we do it your way. This we do my way. What happens afterward, that's your problem. Whatever it's worth, okay?"

"I see," Wan said. "It will take a moment . . . uh, the price will . . . uh, I will have to ask sixty thousand Hong Kong dollars."

"That's a little high, but I ain't arguing. You know where to pick it up?"

"*Hai.*"

"Five-thirty, it'll be there. Now, where do I go?"

"You have something with which to write?"

"I don't write anything down. You gimme the details once, I'll give it back to you word-for-word."

"It is a place known as the House of the Purple Azalea in New Kowloon . . ."

Colonel Halford had fallen asleep on the balcony outside his room. He was still weak from dysentery. His nerves were shot. He was burned out. And even though his mental and physical condition were improving each day, it was easy to drift off in the hot afternoon sun.

As usual, he dreamed.

Violent nightmares.

The dreams were never the same, but they were alike. Unrelated scenes, spliced together into subliminal nonsense rhymes.

Fragments of fantasy and reality, leaping back and forth through time.

He was in Italy. An olive grove, standing beside a long conference table under the trees, talking to a group of American and Italian officers, but the words were gibberish, like a record played at triple speed, and he was interrupted by the sound of trumpets, and then bells, and sticks beating on pans. Everyone began to run so he ran too, blindly through the grove, past great numbers of soldiers lying dead on the ground, out of the grove to the rim of a high, steep hill and there, looking down, saw hundreds of North Koreans charging toward him and there was gunfire and explosions and men fell all around him screaming but the bullets passed through him and he felt nothing and then the Koreans reached the crest of the hill and ran past him as though he were invisible and he picked up a gun and fired over and over again but it was impotent. He ran after them, back to the conference table and now there were Americans and Italians and North Koreans standing at the table, judging him, pointing all around him to the bodies of the soldiers swinging from tree limbs. And he looked at them and he knew them but he could not put names with their faces and when he tried to speak to them, the words that came out of his mouth were foreign to him.

He awoke in a sweat. For a minute it was difficult for him to breathe. He stood up and took several deep breaths and stood watching the sampans and junks gliding lazily through the harbor. Below, the street was alive with the sounds of civilization and he began to relax.

He tried to ignore the dream, to concentrate on other things.

He thought about the man he had seen on the floating restaurant the other day and tried to place his face. He was sure he knew the man. Perhaps from Honolulu when he was stationed at Pearl. Or from the days in Tokyo, before Korea. But the mental walls were still there, separating Halford from his subconscious.

He began to think about tonight. Perhaps he should not have accepted the invitation. The last time, in Tokyo, he had been embarrassed. The young girl had tried so hard, been so understanding and, ultimately, comforting. He was not sure that he wanted to risk so soon again the anguish of an emotional need he could not satisfy physically.

When he had left Tokyo for Hong Kong and terminated his three-month, twice-a-day therapy with Captain Friedman, it was like cutting an umbilicus. Friedman had recommended the four-week leave. "Get out of here, try some of the things we've been working on," he had told the skeptical Halford. "Look, it's going to be like going to camp by yourself the first time. Scary, but exciting. You're going to be okay, Charlie. Thing is, don't be afraid to *try*. Remember what Bishop Chamberlain said in the seventeenth century: 'It's better to wear out than rust out.' "

An hour out of Tokyo old fears had begun chewing at his gut again, but he owed it to the doc to at least try. And he had to admit, in two weeks things had improved.

Then there was Kam Sing, who had gone to such trouble contacting his cousin here, arranging "something special" for him. Yes, tonight he would have to try again. For months, Kam had been a faithful collaborator in Korea and he could not risk insulting the man who had become his friend.

He went into the bathroom and splashed water on his face and then fixed himself a Scotch and started to dress for dinner.

———

Burns had time for only an hour's nap before the phone jarred him awake.

"Seven forty-five, Mr. Burns," the hotel operator said.

"Dor jeh," he said.

"Dor jeh."

A moment later the alarm went off. He closed up the travel clock and put it in the toilet case. The pill had worn off and he felt even worse than he had that morning. His mouth was fuzzy and his eyes burned. He took a quick shower, shaved, and put on a clean shirt, clean socks, clean underwear, and threw his dirty clothes in the carry-on bag. He took the attaché case out of the drawer, examined its contents once more, and went down and checked out. Then he walked two blocks on Nathan Street to the Imperial Hotel and took a cab to the airport. There he checked the bag, confirmed his reservations on the 11:45 P.M. flight to Tokyo and then took another cab to the House of Eagles on Min Street.

He had to hand it to old George Wan. The place was no
more than ten minutes from the airport. The House of
Eagles was a flashy third-class night club which, were it
not for the sign in both Chinese and English, could have
been in Miami or North Beach or on Sunset Boulevard.
The decor was early joint, imitation leather, fake silk
drapes, candles in used wine bottles. Three of the five
girls were Caucasians and the bartender looked like an
ex-sailor from Brooklyn. The place was almost empty.
As Burns sat down at the bar one of the Oriental girls
walked up to him and ran her hand across his neck.

"Are you from Hong Kong?" she asked.

"Nope."

"Ah, American. *Aw chung-yee may gock yun.* That
means 'I love Americans.' "

"Not tonight, I got plans."

"Plans can be changed."

"Maybe tomorrow I'll come back."

The girl's smile vanished and so did she. Burns ordered a glass of plain soda water and asked where the
bathroom was.

The restroom was filthy. Soiled paper towels littered
the sink and floor, and the entire room seemed coated
with grime. Burns entered one of the two booths and
locked the door. He opened the attaché case and took
out the surgical gloves and put them on. He loosened
his belt, lowered his pants, and tied the cord around his
hips using a simple bow-knot, then pulled his pants
back up and buckled them. The knot was directly under
the zipper. He took the other pill and put it in his suit
pocket and put the cotton swabbing in one of his pants
pockets. Then he took out the pistol and checked it
once more before reaching around to his back and slipping it in his belt.

He buttoned his coat and flushed the toilet and went
back to the bar.

The glass of soda was waiting for him. He slipped the pill into his mouth and washed it down with soda water. The rush was almost instantaneous. His body seemed to vibrate with electrical charges. Life surged back into his feet, his hands, his fingertips. New strength flooded his worn-out body, adrenaline pumped through his brain. His eyes began to clear. The sounds in the room amplified, were crisper, more distinct. With the rush came an anticipation so keen that he began to fantasize as he mentally ticked off the steps he was about to follow.

He looked at his watch. It was 9:20, time to go. When he got up to leave he was aware for the first time that he had an erection.

———————

The house on Bowring Street sat back from the road among hundreds of dwarf azaleas, an old Chinese one-story mansion, weathered and ancient, its tiled pagoda roof scarred by the years, its azaleas, perfectly shaped, blooming in small step terraces down to the curb.

The house was deceiving, for it was shaped like a U and only the south wing faced Bowring. A wall circled the entire block. It was nine feet high and had a single opening, a mahogany door nine inches thick with brass hinges embedded in the wood. The door had no latch. It could be opened only from the inside with a special key. The top of the wall was littered with broken glass.

Behind it was a garden almost three hundred years old, a garden that was weeded and trimmed and pruned every day and was so immaculately manicured that it was rare to find even a single blossom on the ground. A small stream curved through it with benches at intervals where lovers for the evening could sit and talk or perhaps just touch each other. Each of the interior rooms of the house had a frosted-glass panel that opened onto the garden.

In the front of the house, over the door, a lamp hung from an ornate brass serpent that seemed to curl from the wall. There were no other lights. The windows of the house had been blacked out for years.

The place was as still as a painted landscape.

Halford stood in front of the house for several minutes after the taxi left. He smoked a cigarette and walked to the corner and back. The old fears gnawed at him and the sounds of Min Street beckoned him away from the house. But something else drew him to it, something Captain Friedman had said to him early in their therapy, a quote from Spinoza: *So long as a man imagines he cannot do something, so long as he is determined not to do it; then it is impossible for him to do it.*

Finally he went up the cobblestone walk and rang the bell.

The door was opened almost immediately by a woman, an ageless and splendid Chinese woman, tiny but erect and commanding, her graying hair pulled tightly away from a face that was unwrinkled and smooth as a rose petal. She was elegantly dressed in a formal cheongsam and wore a tiara of small, perfectly shaped diamonds. If she was startled by Halford's gaunt appearance, by the sunken eyes peering from black circles and the caved-in cheeks, she did not show it. She bowed deeply to him.

"Welcome to my house," she said. "I am Madame Kwa. You must be Colonel Halford. We are honored by your presence and thank you for being so punctual."

"After twenty-four years in the army, madame, I doubt I would know how to be late."

"You forget time here, Colonel. At the House of the Purple Azalea there is no time, only pleasure."

She ushered him into a small room in the south wing. The lights were low and soothing and the room was decorated with antiques from several Chinese dynasties.

They were gold, teak, and silver and the furniture was deep and soft, covered with satin and linen. There was music somewhere, as elusive as an old memory, and the imperceptible presence of perfume. She brought Halford a drink, offered him opium, which he refused, and seated him facing a wall covered by a scarlet silk curtain.

"And now, Colonel," she said, "permit me to introduce my young ladies to you."

The lights in the room lowered and went out. The silk curtain drew back on soundless runners. Behind it was a plate-glass window and behind that, darkness. Then a spotlight faded in and a young woman sat in its glow. Her hair was woven in a pigtail that hung over one shoulder and she looked out through the glass with narrow almond-shaped eyes that were the deepest brown Halford had ever seen. She wore gold slippers trimmed in white and a white mandarin sheath split almost to the hip. On her left arm, over the bicep, the numeral 1 had been tattooed in bright colors. She smiled.

"This is Leah, the number one girl," said Madame Kwa. "She is nineteen years old and was trained in geisha houses before she came to me. She has perfected the Twenty-one Pleasures of the Chinese Wedding Night and she speaks English, French, Portuguese, Japanese, and three dialects of Chinese, and can recite more than a hundred love poems, including those banned by the cabala priests of Israel . . ."

One after another, the lights illuminated the women of the house, each a beauty in her own way, each with some special love secret from the ages, each with her number tattooed in small colorescura numerals on her arm. Halford's fears evaporated. He was entranced. He was aware of old stirrings, old needs. But he was waiting now for one girl in particular, because the cousin of

Kam Sing had told him as he was leaving the cab, "Wait for number nineteen. Kam Sing says the number is very special. You will understand."

And now Halford understood, for the light revealed a young woman whose beauty stunned the Colonel. She was small and delicate, her skin the color of brushed leather and hair coal-black, hanging straight to her waist. She looked not at him, as the others had done, but at the floor, and Halford was drawn to her instantly.

"This is Heth," Madame Kwa said. "She is special to all of us. She is only eighteen and she came to me when she was nine from deep in old China. She speaks Chinese and Japanese and some phrases of English. She has observed the mysteries of love from all the other ladies and she has mastered the ancient secret of the String with Twelve Knots. It is said that her tongue is like the wings of a butterfly."

Halford was moved by the obvious vulnerability of this beautiful creature and by the sadness in her enormous eyes.

"Yes," Halford whispered, "it must be her."

Madame Kwa smiled. "You have made the choice of the wise men," she said. "The gods will envy you."

"How do I talk to her?" Halford asked.

"It will not be necessary. She will communicate with you, Colonel, and you will have no trouble understanding."

Burns stood in the shadows at the end of the alley watching the house on Bowring Street. He had disposed of the attaché case in a convenient storm sewer. He waited until he was certain the street was empty and then crossed swiftly to the mahogany door, which was propped open by a stick.

He moved the stick, stepped quickly through the door, let it click shut behind him, and stood with his back against the wall, waiting until his eyes were accustomed to the darkness of the garden. It was empty. He moved swiftly across the stream and stood in the shadows under a cherry tree thirty feet from the corner room of the north wing of the house. Again he waited.

The room was small and comfortable, its floor covered with a llama rug, its walls decorated with yellow and red striped satin. It contained a large wooden tub big enough for two people and a massage table covered with a mat of goose feathers. Beside it was a smaller table covered with urns of oils, powders, and creams. There were no lights, only scented candles.

Heth led Halford by the hand to the room and she slid the door shut behind them.

"You wait," she said in her tiny, melodic voice.

She walked across the room to the door leading into the garden. But a foot or two from the door she stopped. Her hand reached out and, like a hummingbird poised before a honeysuckle bush, it fluttered for a fraction of a second before it found the door and slid it open.

Halford was stunned. Now he understood her vulnerability, the sadness in her incredible eyes, why Madame Kwa had said, "She is special to all of us."

Heth was blind.

"You see," she said turning in his direction, "garden."

Emotions he had forgotten swept over him, desire, feeling, longing. He walked across the room and held her face between his fingertips.

"Yes, I see," he said gently. "I see for both of us."

Heth smiled and her fingers moved over his body, as soft as cobwebs swaying in the wind.

Thirty feet away, Burns watched from the shadows, saw Halford framed in the doorway, watched as he touched the girl's face, saw her respond, her fingers moving over his body, the buttons on his shirt opening as if by magic as she removed his clothing.

The girl was great.

She led Halford to the tub and her hands moved down, unbuckling his belt, unlacing his shoes. She knelt before him and removed his shoes and pants and, reaching up, slipped her hands inside the waistband of his shorts. Her fingertips flirted with him, touching and yet not touching. She finished undressing him, leaning forward and breathing softly on him, letting her lips brush against him. She began an almost imperceptible chant in Japanese. She touched his face, felt the rigid line of his jaw, his quivering lips, and slipped two fingertips inside his mouth, tapping his tongue. Her own tongue fluttered over his chest and sucked at his nipples. She took his hand in hers, helped him undress her, guided them over her breasts, her stomach, and down to hair as soft as rabbit's fur.

His fears vanished. He was hypnotized, overcome by a sensuality more complete than any he had ever known. His manhood was restored.

Burns moved silently across the garden and stood near the door, heard her soft chant, the sounds of water splashing, the murmur of soft laughter. He took the cotton swabbing from his pocket, wrapped a strip around one hand, held it in place with his thumb, and slipped on one of the surgical gloves. He repeated the action with the other hand. He unzipped his pants and took out the nylon cord, wrapped it several times around each hand, and tested it again, pulling it taut. The knot

was centered perfectly. He eased himself to the door
and looked in.

They were out of the tub. Halford lay on his back on
the table, facing away from Burns, who stood watching,
behind him.

Heth covered her hands with warm oil and began
massaging Halford, her strong fingers kneading the
muscles in his legs and chest. She stroked his arms and
placed them at his sides. Then she got up on the table,
straddling him, settling down on him, moving against
him, leaning over him. Her butterfly tongue teased his
stomach, moved lower, and her mouth enveloped him.

Halford was unaware of the new presence in the
room, an obscene presence moving stealthily across the
llama rug, the nylon cord dangling between latex-
sheathed fists.

But Heth was aware. Her keen ears amplified each
creak in the floor, the rustle of clothing, a different
rhythm of breathing in the room. She reached out to the
smaller table. Her fingers found a short silk string with
twelve knots tied in it, each about an inch apart. She
slipped her hand under Halford and began to insert the
string. Halford, lost in fantasy, hardly felt it. His pulse
was hammering, his breath was labored and quick.

The tempo increased. Faster. Faster. Faster.

Halford gasped. His blood, charged with lightning,
surged through his body. His head rose off the table.
His body went rigid. At that moment Heth ripped the
string from inside him and Halford cried out. He exploded.

As he did, Heth dropped her legs over the side of the
table and clamped them under it. Her arms enveloped it
and she grasped one wrist with the other hand.

Halford was caught in a human vise.

Burns dropped the nylon cord around his throat. His
hands snapped apart.

The knot in the cord bit deep into the hollow in Halford's neck. Ecstasy turned to pain. His temples erupted. His breath was cut off, trapped in his throat. His tongue shot from his mouth.

Burns snapped the cord again, tighter this time.

Halford began to shake violently. Spasms seized his body. It began to jerk against Heth's. She tightened her grip. He tried to scream, but the cry was crushed in his throat. He looked up, saw the grotesque inverted face above him. He tried to utter one last word, a syllable, distorted and guttural, which died in his mouth:

"Wh-a-a-a-r-r-ghh . . ."

And then his windpipe burst. He shuddered convulsively. His breath surged from him like wind squealing from a punctured balloon.

He went limp.

Heth released her death grip. She lay across Halford's body, her arms and legs dangling over the sides of the table. Tears burned her cheeks.

Burns stepped back, unwound the cord from one hand, and pulled it free. He dropped it on the table beside Halford's body. Sweat bathed his face. His breath came in short gasps.

The girl struggled to a sitting position. She cried soundlessly.

Burns reached behind him and took the pistol from his belt. The girl made no move. She was looking toward him but not at him. It was then that Burns too realized she was blind, understood what Wan had meant when he had said it would not be necessary to kill two. There was no way the girl could identify him. He hesitated for a fraction of a second but then, like a programmed machine committed to one last act, he stepped behind her and held the pistol at arm's length an inch from her head. She followed the sound, turning her head, as if to look back over her shoulder.

"The door," he said in his brittle voice. She took the bait, turning back instantly.

The gun jumped in his hand, thunked, and her head snapped forward. He held her hair in his other hand and pulled her head instantly back up. *Thunk*. He lowered her across Halford's body.

Burns laid the pistol beside the nylon cord, walked quickly out of the room, crossed the garden, and went out through the gate. He stripped off the gloves, wrapped them in the cotton swabbing and walked back down the alley toward the storm sewer.

A moment after the door clicked shut, two figures emerged from the shadows of the garden and entered the room.

———

Burns was the first passenger on the plane. He walked to the rear cabin, found a pillow, sat down, buckled his seat belt, and settled back. By the time the flight for Tokyo roared down the runway and eased into the night sky he was deep in an untroubled sleep.

III

Atlanta, 1975

The face was malevolent, its mouth wrinkled and shriveled with age and frozen in an evil leer, its taunting eyes flickering feebly as they stared through the window of the pub. Outside a cold fall wind raced across the courtyard that separated the two-story shopping mall from the mirrored skyscraper, sweeping leaves before it as it moaned through the open plaza. They skittered along the pavement, dancing past the grinning apparition and swirling away into darkness.

A few blocks away the chimes of the cathedral began tolling midnight, striking the last seconds of Allhallows' Eve. Pursued by the clock, ghosts and goblins, saints, sinners, black magicians, and lords of the underworld raced across the moon-mad sky, and fire-eyed birds darted to the safety of skeleton trees. The last chord sounded. The piazza was quiet. A blanket settled over the city. Devilment ended. Halloween was over.

But not quite.

Evil muses were still at play, concocting one last monstrous trick.

The door of the pub called Kerry's Kalibash opened and a man in a scarred leather jacket stepped out into the chilly night air, carrying with him briefly the sounds of merriment, of laughter and music and ice rattling in glasses. The door shushed shut behind him. The man was tough-looking, with gray hair and dull eyes. He stood, shoulders hunched, and stared across the plaza at the twenty-story building, watching the blinking lights of a jet jog across the mirrored façade. It was a stunning structure, floor after floor of mirrored windows reflecting the distant skyline. The man turned as he stared up at the penthouse where lights glowed mutely.

He had followed the woman there. Somewhere in this building was the man he had wondered about, hated, for thirty years. As he watched, there was a movement in the shrubs near the pub behind him. A figure moved quietly and quickly along the wall, but the man in the leather jacket heard nothing. The sound was lost in the wind. He seemed hypnotized by the soaring building, by the kaleidoscope reflected in its face, by the bullet-shaped elevators that shot up and down the outside wall. A couple left the pub, laughing and wrapped in each other's arms, and walked toward the parking lot.

The hidden figure froze against the wall. *Son of a bitch*, he thought, *too open, too dangerous. Not neat and planned like Hong Kong. But it had to be done now*.

The couple vanished into the parking lot. The figure moved again. He came straight toward the back of the man in the leather jacket. As he approached him he raised his left arm. He was holding a pistol with the ugly black cylinder of a silencer attached to the end of the barrel. The gun was only a few inches from the back of the man's head when the gunman said softly:

"Corrigon."

The man in the leather jacket whirled and stared straight into the barrel of the pistol, now only two or three inches from his eye. A strange look crossed his face, a crooked grin of recognition and relief.

He saw the weapon only an instant before it flashed, before he heard the curious little *pwuit* the silencer made, before he felt the brief, fiery pain tear into his head, rip through his brain, and explode against the back of his skull.

His fingertips went numb. Then his hands. Then his arms. He lost the feeling in his legs and feet. His mouth filled with bile. He was falling and didn't know it. Streaks of light cascaded down toward him from the building, showering past him like antic stars. Then they diminished and died. He heard a scream, a tight and anguished cry trapped in an agonized throat. Then all was darkness and silence except the relentless wind crying across the open plaza.

The last thought the man in the leather coat had was that the scream he heard was his own.

BOOK ONE

1

At 5:25, Sharky pulled his battered Volkswagen into an alley two blocks off Peachtree and a block behind the bus station and parked near a Dempsey Dumpster. He was five minutes early.

The cold December wind swirled dust along the alley and rattled litter against the buildings. It had dropped ten degrees since the sun went down. Sharky's heater was shot and one of the windows would not close all the way. He breathed on his hands to keep them warm.

At 5:30, he got out of the car and stood with his back to the door, stamping his feet. He buttoned the top button of the plaid lumber jacket. Dirt hit his eyes and mouth and filtered through his beard.

"Shit," he muttered, leaning forward and shaking the dust from the thick growth on his face, then turned sud-

denly toward the rear of the car. A newspaper whirled
from behind it and flattened against the Dumpster.

Sharky was nervous. He reached inside the jacket,
fingering the brown manila envelope stuffed into the
waist of his Levis.

No sign of High Ball Mary.

He kept his eyes moving. If High Ball were setting
him up, now would be the time. A quick shot on the
head here in the dark and High Ball would be six
hundred dollars richer. And there wouldn't be much
Sharky could do about it.

To his right, in the darkness against the building
across the alley, Sharky sensed movement. Then he
heard a low, deep chuckle.

"Whatsa matter, honk, got the chills?"

The son of a bitch.

"High Ball?" Sharky said.

"Who else, baby? Got the price?"

"Think I'd be freezing my ass off out here if I was
short? Let's get back in the car and deal, I've had
enough of this goddamn wind."

"I like it better in the open, man. Take a little taste o'
the lady here and you won't give a shit how cold it is."

"Bullshit. I'm gettin' outa the wind. You wanna
freeze your balls off, stuff your lady."

"*Ooo*-weeee, ain't we testy this evenin'!"

Sharky got back inside and turned the interior lights
on so High Ball could check out the car. He lit a small
A&C cigar and held his hands around its glowing end.

High Ball strolled across the alley, hands in the pockets of an expensive full-length fur coat. He was wearing
a wide-brimmed Borsalino snapped down over his forehead, yellow platform shoes, and cream-colored wide-
flare pants. He moved cautiously to the car, walking
around the far side, leaning over with his hands still
stuffed in the pockets, looking in the back seat. The

gold earring that had earned him his nickname, Mary, glittered in the light from the dome. Finally he got in.

"You think I got J. Edgar Hoover stashed back there?"

"That fairy's off, man. Where you been?"

"The ghost lingers on."

"Turn the fuckin' lights off, turkey. This ain't a god-damn floor show."

Sharky turned the switch and the lights died.

"I tell you, honk, I'm gettin' my coat dirty in this garbage can."

"It beats walkin'."

"You score with this shit, man, you can get yourself some uptown wheels."

"Where's the merchandise? I get nervous sittin' here."

"How about the green, baby? No green, no sheen."

"I ain't showin' you shit till I taste your stuff."

"Oh, ain't we mean!" Mary took a small glassine bag from his pocket and held it up by his fingertips. He shook the white powder in the bag. "Lookit here, tur-key, how 'bout that? And fifteen more where that came from. Sixteen grams, m'man, a generous o-z of super snow. A hundred trips to the mooooon. Cut it three for one at least. Forty-eight bags at sixty per . . . lessee, that's, uh . . ."

"Twenty-eight hundred and eighty geezoes, High Ball. Cut the bullshit and get it on. Open up." He felt the anxiety building in him as he wet his middle finger and dipped it into the bag, drew it away with several grains stuck to it, and tasted it. His jaw tightened from the bitter taste. Good shit.

A car entered the alley at the far end and rolled slowly toward them.

"What the fuck's this?" High Ball growled. Fear and anger flooded his eyes. "What the fuck we got here?"

"Cool it, for Chrissakes. It's just a car."

"Crank up and move someplace. Too crowded here."

The car moved past them.

"Man, you're on a string," Sharky said.

"Fucker's stoppin'."

The car stopped, then backed up, pulling up in front of the Volkswagen and boxing it in. A large figure got out and loomed in the darkness, moving toward Sharky's side of the car.

"I'm takin' the train, turkey," High Ball snapped. Sharky could feel the tension crackling in the air.

"Stay cool, okay? I'll handle it."

"You ain't holdin', man. I can't stand a toss."

"I said I'll handle it."

The large man appeared at the window on Sharky's side, a flashlight in his hand. Light flooded the interior of the car.

"Goddamn," High Ball snapped.

"What the hell . . ." Sharky started to say, then his eyes met those of the fat man at his window.

Tully! Jesus Christ, that stupid shit!

Tully's eyes met Sharky's.

"Sharky!" he bellowed, "Jesus, I didn't . . ."

"Shut up!" Sharky yelled.

"Motherfucker!" High Ball screamed. "You wired me, you motherfuckin' goddamn pig!" The glassine envelope flew out of his hand. White powder billowed like a cloud in the interior of the car. Mary was already going out the door. Sharky grabbed his collar, but the black man twisted away and slid out sideways, landing on the balls of his feet, a small pearl-handled .25 caliber revolver appearing suddenly in his fist. He was hissing like a snake. Hate turned his eyes red.

Sharky hit the door on his side with his shoulder and shoved hard. It flew open, knocking Tully backward into the street. Sharky rolled out as Mary fired his first shot. The gun popped like a firecracker and the bullet breezed past Sharky's cheek as he fell, and hit the rim of the door, whining off down the alley.

Mary was already halfway to the corner when Sharky bounced back on his knees and reached under the front seat, feeling the cold grip of his 9 mm Mauser automatic. He pulled it out and laid both arms across the front seat, steadying his gun.

"Freeze, Mary . . ."

Too late. The wiry black man slid around the corner, his Borsalino flying off into the gutter. Sharky leaped across the front seat, yelling back at Tully as he did.

"Call it in, call it in . . . you goddamn moron. He's headed south on Spring toward Harris."

Tully struggled to his feet, his face chagrined and confused as Sharky ran to the corner. Sharky stopped for a second and peered around. Mary, halfway to the next corner, slowed, aimed the .25, then realized it wouldn't carry that far, and cut diagonally across the street. A car slammed to a stop as he raced in front of it. Sharky went after him, cutting through the traffic. Cars screeched to a stop all around him.

Jesus, Sharky thought, *five thirty. The middle of rush hour. Neat. Real neat.*

The pusher reached the corner and turned toward Peachtree Street. He fired an off-hand shot across his chest as he ran. The bullet smacked a telephone pole eight feet from Sharky. Sharky kept going, closing the distance on the pusher, who was hampered by his cumbersome shoes.

Half a black away five-thirty traffic choked the main thoroughfare. Pedestrians crowded the street corners, waiting for buses. Mary was panicky. He had to get lost in the crowd or get some transportation fast. He ran into the thick of it with Sharky closing in. As he started across Peachtree a black Cadillac drove in front of him, so close it brushed him. He jogged in place for a moment, then ran around the rear of the Caddy and dove headlong across the hood of the Buick behind it, sliding up against the windshield and falling on his hands and knees on the other side.

The astonished driver slammed on his brakes as Sharky ran up, jumped up on the hood in a sitting position, and swung his legs around, dropping to the other side.

The light had changed. Traffic was moving out. On the opposite side of the street a city bus began to pull out into the free lane in front of it. High Ball threaded through traffic, ran in front of the bus, slammed his hand against the grill, and reached the door. He aimed his gun through the glass at the driver.

"Open up, motherfucker," he demanded and the driver opened the door.

Through the window on the driver's side, Sharky saw the wild-eyed pusher waving his Saturday night special in the terrified driver's face. Then Mary saw Sharky and fired a shot past the driver's nose. It smacked through the window and hit the street between Sharky's feet, ricocheting into the fender of a nearby car.

Sharky aimed his automatic at the dealer and Mary dove out of sight toward the rear of the bus. Sharky pulled out his wallet and holding it toward the driver, flashed his shield. He ran to the door. The driver pushed the handle and the door hissed open.

"On the floor," Sharky yelled and dove aboard. The driver rolled out of the seat as Mary fired another shot. It screamed off the chromium rod near the driver's seat and went through the windshield with a splat.

Inside the bus, pandemonium. Women and children screamed, dropped behind seats, spilled packages. An elderly woman sat speechless in her seat, clutching a shopping bag to her bosom, staring straight ahead.

Sharky leaned against the wall between the front stairwell and the first seat as Mary fired another shot. He was gasping for breath. It had all happened too fast. Now he was in a box. A Mexican standoff in a crowded bus with a madman loose in the back. High Ball hunched behind the wall separating the seats from the stairwell at the rear exit. He shoved on the door but it was activated by stepping on the bottom step while the driver pressed a release button in front. Mary kicked frantically at the door, then turned and fired another shot toward the front of the bus. More screaming.

"You goddamn pig motherfucker," Mary screamed, "I'm taking me some hostages! I'm killing me some fuckin' kids back here, you don't open the goddamn door."

Sharky took a fast peek over the divider in the front of the bus and ducked back quickly as Mary's gun roared and the bullet sighed overhead and cracked through the windshield. Everyone behind Mary was on the floor. There was no time to negotiate. Mary was in a killing mood and had to be stopped fast. Sharky had soft-nosed loads in his pistol. There was little chance they would go through the pusher and hit someone behind him. He had to take the risk.

Sharky reached over to the busdriver's coin changer and clicked a dozen tokens out of it. He knelt and threw them across the bus behind the driver's seat. Mary took the bait. He stood and fired two more shots into the driver's seat. As he did Sharky rose up, throwing both arms over the retainer, and squeezing off a single shot. It hit Mary in the cheek. The right side of his face burst open. Blood gushed down his face and onto his chest. The shot slammed him back against the wall at the rear of the stairwell.

The elderly lady, less than two feet away, continued to clutch her shopping bag and stare straight ahead.

Mary looked surprised. He shuddered as blood poured out of his face. He started to raise his gun hand again.

Sharky lowered his aim an inch or so and fired twice more. The automatic jumped in his hands. Two more holes appeared in Mary's chest, less than half an inch apart. He moaned, turned sideways, and fell on his knees on the bottom step, his hands between his legs and his forehead resting against the door. Sharky stepped over the driver, who was huddled on the floor with his hands over his ears, and pushed the release button. The door opened and Mary pitched out head-first.

Sharky opened the front door and jumped out.

Two uniformed cops were eight feet away, leaning across the hood of a Chevrolet, their service revolvers trained on Sharky.

"Hold it right there."

Sharky held his I.D. high over his head and strode toward the rear of the bus.

"Sharky, Central Narcotics," he yelled. "Get an ambulance."

"I said, 'Hold it right there,' " the cop yelled again.

Sharky threw the wallet at him. It bounced off the hood of the car and spun around, opened at his shield.

"I said, 'Call a goddamn ambulance,' " Sharky said and kept walking. He reached Mary's still form lying face down in the street and stood over him, his gun aimed at the back of the dope dealer's head. He slid the .25 away from the body with his foot, then slipped it under High Ball, and rolled him slowly over.

The dealer looked straight up at the dark sky. Blood rattled in his throat. The eyes turned to glass and rolled up in his head. Sharky stuck his gun in his belt and reached down, pressing his fingers into Mary's throat. Nothing.

One of the two cops was shouting into his radio mike. The other joined Sharky and handed him his wallet. "What the hell's going on?" he asked.

"I just retired a junkman. Better have your partner call the ME too."

People pressed in from all sides. Horns blared as the traffic built up. Inside the bus, passengers crowded to the windows, pressing their faces against the cold glass. The elderly woman suddenly opened her mouth and screamed over and over at the top of her lungs. A flash-gun went off, blinding Sharky.

"What the hell was that?" he yelled.

"Somebody took a picture."

"No pictures, goddammit! No pictures!" Sharky barked.

"Too late," the cop said.

More noise. More confusion. A siren was shrieking nearby.

Sharky leaned against the bus. He felt suddenly tired, disgusted, used up, sick to his stomach. "Ah, shit," he said, half aloud.

He leaned over High Ball Mary's body, his fingers feeling the coat lining. He felt the bags, then a zipper, and pulled it open. Inside, in small pockets sewn into the lining of the coat, were fifteen one-gram bags of cocaine.

He arrived at the station at 9:45, fifteen minutes before his appointment. Jaspers's secretary was a hard-faced, sour-tempered policewoman named Helen Hill, a competent officer turned mean after eight years tied to a desk. She was less than affectionately known in the House as the Dragon Lady.

"Sit over there," she snapped, pointing to a hard oak chair without arms. She glared at his scruffy exterior for a moment, then ignored him.

The outer office was spartan. Nothing to read, no pictures on the wall. The Dragon Lady got up once, poured herself a cup of coffee from an urn on a table near the door, and sat down again. She did not offer Sharky coffee, a drink of water, the time of day, or a kind word. Finally he got up and helped himself to a cup.

"Don't you ask?" the Dragon Lady growled.

"May I have a cup of coffee?" Sharky said with a mock smile. He sprinkled half a packet of sugar into the cup, stirred it with his finger, licked it off, and returned to his seat. The Dragon Lady ignored him. He slurped his coffee loudly and stared at her. She continued to ignore him. The minutes crawled by. Fifteen minutes seemed to take an hour, at least. At exactly ten o'clock the phone on her desk buzzed.

"Yes, sir? Yes, he is. Yes, sir." She hung up. "All right. You may go in now," she said, without looking at him.

He plopped the half-empty cup in the middle of her desk. "Thanks," he said, "for starting my day so cheerfully." She glared at him as he knocked on the door. A voice inside said, "Come."

Captain Jaspers was a tall, angular, emotionless man in his early fifties. A scar as thin as a fishing line stretched from in front of his left ear down to his jawline. His black hair was streaked with gray. Cold, dead eyes hid behind glasses set in gold frames. His attire was as rigid as a uniform, dark blue suits, white shirts, drab ties, black lace-up shoes. His Timex watch had a gray cloth band. He wore no other jewelry.

To Sharky's knowledge, Jaspers had no friends in the department. His only confidant was the new police commissioner, Ezra Powers. Jaspers was a ruthless officer with little regard for his men, a rigid and stern disciplinarian, quick to demote or suspend the men in Central District, which was his command. Five years earlier when Sharky was assigned to a blue-and-white, his partner had been Orville Slyden, who had been flopped from detective third grade to patrolman and given six-and-six, six weeks suspension and six weeks at reduced pay, for taking a handout. Later Slyden had been proven innocent, but Jaspers refused to restore him to rank. It was the captain's contention that anyone even suspected of such an infraction did not deserve to be a detective. It was Slyden who had given Jaspers his nickname, The Bat. "He's a fuckin' vampire," Slyden had said and the name had stuck, although nobody ever called Jaspers that to his face.

Jaspers's predecessor had been a thoughtful and highly respected man who had risen slowly and painfully through the ranks. He had committed suicide after learning he had terminal cancer. According to a persistent rumor of the House, Jaspers had loaded the gun for him.

The office was barren. A spotless desk with nothing on it but a telephone and a letterbox. A table behind the desk contained a police squawk box, nothing else. Two uncomfortable chairs. A single photograph on the wall of Dwight Eisenhower shaking hands with Jaspers, who wore the uniform of an army major. Neither of them was smiling. There were no ashtrays; Jaspers did not approve of smoking or drinking.

He did not look up when Sharky entered the room; he jabbed a finger toward one of the chairs and continued reading a file that lay in front of him. Sharky sat down. Another five minutes died. Finally Jaspers closed the cover of the file and took a newspaper out of his desk drawer. He held it up with a flourish for Sharky to read. Jaspers thrived on these little *dramatis momenta.* The headline read:

"UNDERCOVER COP KILLS DOPE
PUSHER ON CROWDED CITY BUS"

Beside the story a photograph showed a scruffy, bearded, and weary Sharky, gun in hand, leaning over High Ball Mary.

"I saw it," Sharky said.

"When you blow your cover, you certainly do it extravagantly," Jaspers said. His voice was a dry, brittle rasp.

"Well, I had a little bad luck."

"You had a *lot* of bad luck."

"The way it happened, I was—"

"I *know* the way it happened. Anybody who can read knows the way it happened."

"The story in the paper isn't quite—"

"I read your report, what there was of it."

"Yes, sir, uh, about that . . . Lieutenant Goldwald thought we should leave out some . . ."

"I know what Goldwald thought. I've already finished with Goldwald."

"Could I just give you my end of it? Sir," Sharky said.

"No. I know all I need to know. I know you went into this meet with, uh, what was his name? Uh . . ."

"Creech. Percy Creech. A/k/a High Ball Mary."

"Yes, Creech. You went in there solo. No back-up. No surveillance team. Six hundred dollars of department money in your pocket. You set up this buy with a very dangerous pusher and kept the details to yourself. A real grandstand play, Sharky. And then to get involved in a chase through the most crowded section of town. At rush hour. A shoot-out on a crowded city bus filled with women and children. Just what else would you like to add to that?"

"Everything was rolling smooth until that goddamn Tully . . ."

"I'm not interested in Tully," Jaspers snapped, cutting him off. "Tully was an accident. Accidents happen. You should anticipate, *anticipate*, problems."

Sharky's face began to redden.

"He's a moron . . ."

Jaspers cut him off again.

"Are you deaf?"

"Pardon?"

"Deaf. Are you deaf? I said I am not interested in Tully. Tully was a mistake. It's what happened *after* Tully that concerns me. You forgot everything. You panicked, forgot every regulation. You ignored the rules. Pro-*ced*-ure. There is pro-*ced*-ure to be followed." Jaspers sat back in his chair and stared across the desk at Sharky, who felt suddenly like a grammar school boy called before the principal. It was humiliating and Sharky could not abide humiliation.

"Look, do I have any say at all? I mean, do I get to tell my end of this?"

"Don't be insolent," Jaspers snapped.

"Insolent! Insolent, shit." He stood up and walked to the edge of the desk. Jaspers's face was scarlet with rage. "Lemme tell you something, Captain. I spent three months on that goddamn machine. Three months setting it up, kissing that miserable bastard's ass so I could make that buy."

"Sharky!" Jaspers roared.

"No, I'm gonna finish this. This wasn't any ordinary coke buy, y'know. Creech was leading me upstairs, to his man. We were talking coke in pounds. Pounds! He couldn't handle that big a thing; he had to go to the supplier. That's who I was after, High Ball's connection. I had to. It couldn't leak out, see. One leak—"

"How dare you?" Jaspers was enraged now. "What in God's name possessed you? A gunfight on a crowded bus."

Jesus, is that all that mattered? The bus? Sharky started to explain what happened. That he had taken a chance and looked at High Ball Mary, that everyone behind the pusher had dropped to the floor, that he was using soft-nose bullets. It wasn't some irresponsible snap decision; he didn't have any choice. But he said nothing. *What the hell, all The Bat cared about was the goddamn bus.*

"This kind of press is disastrous," The Bat was saying.

"Press? For Christ's sake, what was I supposed to do, kiss his ass and wave goodbye?"

"I ought to break you. For insubordination alone. I ought to give you six-and-six and put you back where you belong, in a blue-and-white on Auburn Avenue. You'll never learn, will you? You have no respect for anyone."

"Captain, look, it happened too fast. All of a sudden there we were on a bus full of Christmas shoppers and he was bonkers, totally around the bend, threatening to kill kids and all. I had a clean shot and I took it. What the hell else is there to say about it?"

"Three clean shots, apparently."

"Okay, I hit him three times. I didn't want to take a chance that maybe he squeezes one off and wastes some old lady on the way home to dinner. Or some kid. I took him out. Isn't that the way it's supposed to work?"

Jaspers drummed his desk with his fingers. He glared at Sharky. God, how he despised these young hotshots. Headline hunters.

"I don't want any more headline hunting," he said.

"That's what it's going down as, hunh? Headline hunting? Everybody's scared shitless of the papers."

"You've tried my patience with your insubordination, Sharky."

"Captain, I'm asking to be treated fairly. No more consideration than we give to some bum in the drunk tank, that's what I'm asking for."

"I'll give you hell and call it whatever you want to call it Right now you're about as useful to Narcotics as a paraplegic."

"I don't . . ." Sharky started to say something and

stopped. He stared at the cold eyes. The bottom of his foot began to itch. He tried grinding his foot into the carpet. The itch grew worse. He tried to ignore it. Tears began welling up in his eyes. *Christ*, he thought, *the son of a bitch is going to think he's got me crying*. Sharky sat down, unzipped his boot and pulled it off, frantically scratching the bottom of his foot. His big toe stuck through a hole in his sock.

Jaspers stared at him, appalled.

"What in God's name?" he stammered.

"My foot itches," Sharky said. "It's driving me crazy."

Jaspers threw the paper in the wastebasket. He stood up and leaned across his desk. "Put that shoe on," he said. "Put it on and stand at attention."

Sharky put his boot back on and stood up.

"I'll tell you what's going to happen, Sharky. As of eight A.M. today you are no longer attached to the narcotics section. As of eight A.M. you are in Vice."

Sharky looked at him in disbelief.

"Vice!"

"Vice. Report to Lieutenant Friscoe."

Sharky stared at him for several moments. He looked around the room, struggling to keep his own anger in check. "Sir, will you please just look at my sheet? I think I deserve that much. Eighteen months on the street, eighteen collars, all hard drugs. I dumped eighteen goddamn pushers, one a month, and fourteen got the basket. The DA knows . . ."

"Shut up."

"I beg your pardon?"

"I said, 'Shut up.' "

"Sure. Yes, sir. I'll just, uh, yeah, keep my mouth shut, sit over there in public library watching the freaks jack off."

"Somebody has to do it. You think you're too good for the Vice Squad, that it?"

"I got eighteen months out there. That's got to be worth something to Narcs. Even on a desk I can be a lot of help down there."

"You're lucky I don't send you over. I've busted better men than you for a lot less. I had the mayor on the phone half the night. The commissioner calling me at six thirty in the morning. What kind of a nut is he? everybody asks. I'm giving you a break. I want you out of sight for a while. No more headlines. No more grandstanding. *Out of my sight.* I don't want to pick up the paper and see your shaggy . . . my God, look at you. When's the last time you shaved? Had a haircut?"

"You, uh, there aren't a lot of dope deals on the make out there for guys in Brooks Brothers suits and Florsheims. Sir."

"Clean yourself up. Get a shave, a haircut, some decent clothes. Buy some decent socks, for God's sake. Friscoe wants a man for something he's got working and you're it. I don't know what it is, I don't care. But I want you to understand one thing. Do you understand the term *low profile?*"

"Sure. Of course. Yes."

"Sir."

"Sir."

"Fine. Because from now on the first order of business for you is to maintain a very, very, *very* low profile. L-o-w. Clear?"

Sharky nodded.

"Good. Now get out of here."

3

It was noon when Domino headed across the windy plaza toward Mirror Towers. The cathedral clock began tolling the hour and as it did she shuddered unconsciously. It wasn't the wind. Or the cold. It was something else, the reflection in the building of the street behind her perhaps. Or the chimes solemnly striking twelve.

She shuddered again. What was it her mother used to say? *Someone's walking on your grave.*

She shrugged off the feeling and entered the building, walking through its wide, stark lobby in the private elevator in the corner. The security guard stood at leisurely attention. He smiled and touched the bill of his cap.

"Hi, Eddie," she said brightly.

"Miss Domino," he said. "How's it going today?"

"Just great," she said as she stepped into the glass-and-copper bullet attached to the side of the building. Eddie unlocked the up button with a key and pushed it. Then he picked up a wall phone and pressed a button. "Miss Domino's on her way up," he said.

The doors of the elevator swished shut and it shot up the side of the building, stopping at the twentieth floor. Five miles away, the skyline of the city was a sparkling cluster in the haze.

The elevator opened on a reception room that was almost as stark as the lobby, except that the two-story ceiling was supported by a dozen Plexiglas pillars. The interior of each pillar was lit by a single spotlight recessed overhead. Within each was a single toy, and each of the toys was unique. Electronic toys, stuffed toys, toys that moved, that sang, that walked and danced and spoke by means of tiny tape loops hidden deep inside them. Each was the prototype for a production model and each performed its eerie function silently within the towering glass rectangles that dwarfed the reception desk at the far end of the uncomfortably quiet room. To Domino, the collection of dolls, animals, trolls, and other creatures was almost too real. She walked past them without looking, her heels echoing on the tile floor.

At the reception desk a husky Oriental man, his ice-cube eyes concealed behind heavily tinted glasses, was operating the complex pushbutton switchboard. Music whispered from a tiny transistor radio at his elbow.

She made a pyramid of her hands and bowed low from the waist.

"*Jo sun,*" she said.

The guard-receptionist stood up and repeated the gesture.

"*Jo sun, dor jeh,*" he said.

He pushed a button under the desk and a door slid

soundlessly open nearby. "He awaits you," he said and
she was gone.

She stepped into a lush botanical garden, a giant two-
story terrarium filled with rare plants and shrubs from
all over the world: dracaena sanderianas, maidenhair
ferns, dwarf azaleas, Chinese fan palms and amazon lil-
ies, saffron pepper trees, butterfly gardenias, and six-
foot ferns, all flourishing under an enormous sun dome.
In one corner a circular stairway wound up through the
foliage to the penthouse above.

She skirted the dense, moisture-laden foliage and
peered past the greenery, through a heavy window into
the office beyond. Pieces of Mayan and Chinese sculpture crouched under soft lights on Oriental rugs.

In the center of the office a man sat behind a broad
desk cluttered with curios, a large, heavyset man, bald
as a crystal ball, with a full red beard that was turning
gray. He wore gold-rimmed bifocals and his large hands
lay flat on the desk in front of him. He was wearing one
ring, on his left hand, a platinum and jade design that
covered one entire joint of his little finger. His silk mandarin shirt had three entwined dragons brocaded in red
and gold across the chest. He stared at her for several
seconds and then smiled and pushed the button that
opened the door between the greenhouse and his office.

She stopped several feet in front of his desk, stared
down at him, turned slightly, raised her chin, and
arched her back and glared at him over her shoulder.

Incredible, he thought.

She had high cheekbones and a full, almost arrogant
mouth. Her thick black hair was bobbed at shoulder
length and had been tousled just enough by the wind.
Her neck was long and slender and the hollow place in
her throat, between her collarbones, was as soft and
delicate as the petal of a flower. She was slender, long-

legged, narrow-waisted, and her breasts were as firm and as perfect as an artist's sculptured fantasy.

She wore a Halston dress, its simple, straight lines flattering every curve, every line, its muted rose-gray accentuating the shades of coloring in her skin, her hair, and her eyes. She was young. Haughty. Superior. Elegant. Untouchable. And totally desirable.

"Well?" she said and raised an eyebrow.

He leaned back in his chair and, with a flourish of his hands, said, *"Você é bela."*

She raised the other eyebrow and half closed her eyes. *"Muito obrigada."*

"Pardon me," he said. "Of course, you are fantastic. *muito prazer em revê-la."*

She looked perplexed and shook her head. "Now you lost me. You know how limited my Portuguese is."

"It means simply, 'I am glad to see you,' " he said.

"That's all, hunh? Just glad to see you?" She struck another pose. She unbuttoned the top button of the dress. Then the second. The dress opened slightly. He watched her breathe. She was superb. He had known women in every country, of every race, he had known legendary beauties, the whores of the world, and had once lived for a short time in a very famous house in Bangkok where he had made love to two, sometimes three women at a time. None of them could match her beauty, her intelligence, or her incredible talents.

He laughed out loud.

"Is something funny?"

"Just a thought," he said.

"I'll give you ten dollars for it."

He laughed harder. "What extravagance! It is not worth more than a penny."

She reached into her purse, took out a penny, and tossed it into his lap.

"There."

"All right. I was thinking, I have worked hard all my life; I have built corporations on every continent. I have made millions and millions of dollars, created cartels. I have done all this and I was thinking, I could have become just as rich running a whorehouse with you in Hong Kong."

She threw her head back and laughed until small tears appeared at the corners of her eyes. She walked close to him, her perfume flirting with his nose. He wanted to reach out, to touch her, but he did not rush things. She touched his cheek.

"Victor, you are the most fascinating man I have ever met," she said warmly.

"And the most generous?" he asked.

"Well," she said, "there was this gentleman from Kuwait . . ."

Victor DeLaroza scowled.

"He was extremely grateful . . ."

The scowl deepened. "Oh?"

"But not nearly as much fun as you are."

"Thank you."

"You're welcome."

"Did he ever take you to Paris for the weekend? Shopping?"

"No, he never did that."

"And did he ever arrange for the most famous couturiers in the world to open their salons especially for you?"

"No, he never did that either."

"Did he ever take you sailing on a Chinese junk?"

She was laughing again. She shook her head. "Unh unh."

DeLaroza leaned back and grinned. "You see, gratitude has its limitations."

"My gratitude to you has none," she said and reaching down, unbuttoned the top two buttons of his shirt, slipped her hands inside, and caressed his chest, her fingers pinching his nipples. He closed his eyes, reached out to run his fingers along her satin-sheathed thigh, but it was gone. She had already moved away, as elusive as a dragonfly. She crossed to the windows and looked back at him.

"And now you make toys," she said.

"You always say the word *toys* with a very patronizing attitude," DeLaroza said. "I do not just make *toys*. I create masterpieces. Do you know I once made a tiny Rolls Royce, it was a foot long, a perfect replica. The wheels moved, the pistons worked, the engine worked, even the radio worked. It was exact to the most infinitesimal detail. The gentleman I made it for sat on the floor in this office and clapped his hands together like a child when he came to get it. It cost twelve thousand dollars, a fourth of what the real thing costs. He paid for it in cash."

She shrugged. "Big deal," she said.

He mimicked her. "Big deal. That is all you have to say, 'Big deal'? It was a very big deal to him. And to me. Besides, everyone loves a toymaker. It carries with it a unique kind of respect. Who can fault a man who spends his life making children happy?"

The question hung in the air. Domino did not hear it. She was looking at the ground, twenty stories below, at two boys rough-housing in the plaza, their arms wrapped around each other as they battled back and forth. She shuddered again.

"Is something wrong?" DeLaroza asked.

"It's nothing. I just remembered something. It's really quite silly."

"It could not be that silly, to have such an effect on you."

"You remember the last time I was here? Halloween night?"

A small fear crept into his chest.

"Of course. I never forget one of your visits."

"As I was leaving, these two men were on the other side of the plaza. I saw them from inside the building. One was very drunk. He was so . . . so limp . . . and the other one was trying to get him in the car . . ."

DeLaroza was no longer listening. The fear grew and crept deeper into his chest. He pressed his knuckles together until they were white. *Good God*, he thought, *did she see something? Was this the beginning of blackmail?* His eyes narrowed for just a moment. Old paranoias swept over him, rising up again from the past, nightmare creatures nibbling at his heart. He suddenly felt cold and alone.

". . . Guess I just felt sorry for him. I had a feeling I had seen him before. He was wearing this old leather jacket, way out of style."

"Did you tell anyone about this?" DeLaroza asked casually.

"What's there to tell? That I saw a drunk being shoved into a car?"

"Then why does it bother you so?"

"I wish I knew. It's like . . . like some kind of instinct. I can't put my finger on it. Am I being silly? Do you think I'm silly?"

"I think," said DeLaroza, "that you are far from silly." He shrugged off the feeling. This was not the time to deal with it. "Look at you," he said, "when you came in here you were, uh—how do you say it?— *acima* . . . *high*. Up. Now you seem so sad."

She turned back to him and smiled again. "It's all gone. And you're right, I am up. What did you call it?"

"*Acima.*"

"*Acima.* That's me."

"And why? Do you have some special new trick for me?"

"No. It's something more selfish."

"So? Everyone has the right to be selfish at times. What is it?"

"I knew you'd understand. You particularly would understand."

"Hmm. What is this all about?"

She came back across the room and sat on the corner of his desk.

"Victor . . . I think I've fallen in love."

He stared at her for a moment, then said, "Think?"

"I didn't plan on it. It just sneaked up on me. It surprises me. But then, of course, I adore surprises."

"And you have not been in love before?"

"Oh, many times," she said and laughed. "But not recently."

"Then I am happy for you. And who is the lucky gentleman. It is a man?"

"Oh, yes, a very special man."

"Aha, and do I know him?"

"Of course."

DeLaroza took out a large Havana cigar and started to peel away the cellophane. He needed time to sort out his thoughts. He found her news upsetting. She took the cigar away from him, snipped off the end and lit it, twirling it between her fingers so it burned evenly. Then she handed it back to him.

"Obrigado," he said.

"You're welcome."

He took a deep drag and blew the smoke out slowly. His face had grown sad.

"Have I upset you?" she asked.

"No. I am concerned, not upset. You know, of course, that he is going to make his announcement Monday night at the opening of *Pachinko!"*

"Yes."

"To continue this love affair at this time could be very risky."

"Love affair?" she said. The words hung in the air as though she were listening to them in instant replay. She frowned.

"Well," he said, "call it what you wish. Infatuation?"

"Trite. Trite words and trite phrases." She was scowling at him.

DeLaroza chuckled. "Far be it for me to accuse you of being trite, my dear," he said.

"Thank you," she said.

"It is just that I know both of you so well," DeLaroza said. "I've known Donald for sixteen years and you . . . for two. . . ."

"Almost three."

"Yes, almost three."

His gaze moved past her, settling on the foliage outside his office. Three years. At their first meeting he had acted on what he thought at the time was an impulse. A very lucky one, he had come to realize, although totally out of character for him. The first time he had ever seen Domino she was standing in a fleamarket in Buckhead, staring intently at an antique Morris chair. A stunning woman, though her clothes were not quite right, her hair a little too long, and yet . . . And yet.

He had ordered Chiang to turn the Rolls around and go back. He had found her, still contemplating the chair.

"The chair is overpriced," he had told her. "You should be able to purchase it for half what they are asking."

She smiled at him. "I'm not very good at that kind of thing," she had told him.

"Then I shall act as your agent in the matter."

Her education had begun that day. Now even he had

to marvel at what Domino had become. And now, too, in retrospect, he understood that meeting her that day had not been mere impulse. Domino had fit his plans perfectly.

"Hello," she said.

DeLaroza looked back at her. "Sorry," he said. "I was thinking about the fleamarket."

She laughed. "I still owe you twelve dollars for the Morris chair," she said.

"I consider that one of my better investments."

"You were saying?"

"Uh . . . what was I saying?" He was slightly embarrassed that he had forgotten his point.

"You were saying that you know both of us very well."

"Oh, yes. Perhaps love was too strong a word. There is a need there, for both of you."

"Of course. I guess it really isn't fair to say we don't love each other. I love Donald. And I love you."

"You love power, my dear. It is your passion."

"Maybe I'm just turned off by the lack of it."

"My point is, after Monday night you will become a luxury Donald can no longer afford."

A half-smile played briefly over her face.

"You know I'm really surprised that you're sharing the spotlight of your beloved *Pachinko!*—even with the next president of the United States."

DeLaroza looked away from her. She was quite astute. *Pachinko!* was DeLaroza's grandest achievement, an amusement park like no other in the world. It had taken years to conceive and build it. But Donald Hotchins's announcement at the opening of the park was part of his plan. Even Domino was part of it. DeLaroza did nothing without a plan. He finally waved a hand in the air.

"It will be a delicate situation," he said. "I hope you

can handle it. I admit if anyone can, you can. But the Chinese have a saying: The peacock should not strut when the tiger is about. There will be many tigers about, waiting for him to make a mistake so they can devour him. It could destroy him."

"Then I'll have to be very clever."

"You can be that."

"I'm sorry. Am I hurting you? I wouldn't hurt you."

"Of course not. I know you would never hurt anyone knowingly. It is just that I seem to have—how do you say it?—bit off my nose?"

"Cut off my nose to spite my face. It's a stupid saying."

"Yes, but true. I will not see you again, will I? That is what you are really saying to me, is it not?"

"Of course I'll see you. We'll all be good friends."

"Not business acquaintances."

The remark stunned her, as if he had slapped her. "Is that what it's been to you?" she said. "I hoped it was more than just business. You're very special to me. Don't you know that?"

He watched the smoke curl toward the ceiling, swirling in and out of the pools of light from the recessed lamps. "Yes," he said finally, "I do." She reached out and touched his hand with her fingertips. "You are quite something," he said. "You have what we call in Brazil *beleza inexplicada*. A quality that cannot be described."

"Thank you."

"Does he know about you? All about you?"

"No. Is that really necessary?"

He shook his head. "But if he should find out?"

"Someday I'll explain it all to him."

"No, no, you will not, my love. It is a thing you will never be able to do. But that is your problem." Then:

"So this meeting was all for talk, eh? Conversation. I will be disappointed this last time."

She moved closer to him, so close he could feel her warmth. She leaned over him and her breasts touched his chest. She brushed her lips across his eyelids. It made him tremble.

"No," she said. "You're very special to me. You've been very good to me and I know what makes you happy, Victor. I want our last private meeting together to make you happier than you've ever been before. A very special night. Tonight you will come to my apartment at eight o'clock and I'll give you your farewell present, *mui bita?*"

"Yes," he said. "I understand." He sighed, staring at her open blouse, at the tinted edge of her nipples, feeling her perfume hypnotizing his senses. Her fingers moved lightly across his neck and drew his head to her, his cheek against her breast.

"And why are we waiting until tonight?" he asked, his voice trembling.

"Because," she said, and her voice was a husky, inviting, ageless whisper, "I want you to think about it. All day long. It will be much sweeter that way."

He closed his eyes, turning his head so her dress fell away from her breast, and he was tasting the tartness of her hardened nipple.

"You are a masterpiece," he whispered. "On Ipanema, you would steal the beach away from the sea."

"You should have been a poet, Victor," she said softly.

"You *are* a poet, my dear." But even at that moment the old fear crawled back inside him again and the horror of what had to be done was like an angry voice hissing in his ear. And he could not ignore it.

4

The Vice Squad was located deep in the bowels of the main station house, a windowless, airless, cramped, messy space hardly big enough to accommodate the sixteen men who called it home. It was a forgotten hole, away from normal traffic, a place nobody had to pass or see or contend with. Prison-gray pipes rattled overhead. The place was too hot in the winter and frigid in the summer.

Barney Friscoe sat in a closet of an office, a short, chunky lieutenant with eternal five o'clock shadow and thinning brown hair, dressed in chinos, Adidas, a Wings Over America tee-shirt, and a yellow windbreaker. His cluttered desk looked like a combat zone. As Sharky entered the cubbyhole, he stood up, peering over the reading glasses that were perched halfway down his nose and smiling in a row of crooked, off-color teeth. He offered Sharky a hairy paw.

"Welcome to Friscoe's Inferno," he said. "You're Sharky, right? One o'clock, right on time. I hardly recognize you without all that hair on your face. Grab a chair there, throw that shit on the floor. You had lunch?"

Sharky shook his head, nodded yes to the question, and moved a pile of debris from one of the two battered chairs in the small room.

"Jesus," Sharky said, "what'd you do to deserve this?"

"Dirtiest digs for the dirtiest squad. Oh, well, nobody gives a shit. We don't spend any time around here anyhow." He waved outside the office at the bullpen where half a dozen desks were jammed together in a space hardly big enough for four. On the corner of one was an antiquated coffeemaker. Sugar and powdered milk formed pools around it and a dirty communal spoon lay forgotten nearby.

There were two men in the outer office. One of them, a hard-looking black man in his forties with a deep scar over his left eye and streaks of gray in his tight-cropped afro, wore a tan corduroy three-piece suit. The vest was open and his tie was pulled down to his collarbone. He stared coldly at Sharky then turned back to a battered Royal typewriter and began pecking out a report with two fingers. The other, an older man built like a refrigerator, was on the phone.

"That's Livingston and Papadopolis out there," Friscoe said. "Livingston's the one with the tan."

"He got something against me?" Sharky asked.

"Not that I know of," Friscoe said. "The Bat sent your sheet down. Looks like you got the shit stick handed to you. That was a nice machine you had workin' there until that dimwit Tully fucked it up for you.

He was down here a while. You cut off his head, he wouldn't be any dumber than he is with it on."

"I've been told to forget it."

"Probably the best thing to do. What's gonna happen with Tully, Tully's gonna end with his toes up one of these days. He's too stupid to stay alive. It's still tough, y'know. Nobody likes to take the gas pipe when they been workin' a thing as long as you were. Anyways, I got something down here you can maybe get your dick into. So far what we got is odds and ends, see? Nothing ties together yet. But it's lookin' pretty good. Here and there."

"You're a little vague," Sharky said.

"Paranoid," Friscoe said.

"Oh," Sharky said and laughed at Friscoe's candor.

"What it is, every once in a while one of my boys turns up something sounds interesting. Not the usual stink finger, hands-up bullshit but something maybe we can make a little mileage outa. What happens, I don't wanna give anything away, see what I mean? What I don't want, I don't want Homicide or Bunco or some lace doily outfit workin' special for the chief stealin' my melons, okay? Fuck that shit. I figure it starts here, I wanna keep it here. The other thing, I don't make a habit, see, of goin' down to the DA with my dick in my hand. Unless we make a heavy case, we don't nail it down, I flush it. We got a machine goin' and we can't put it together, it goes down the toilet."

He slurped coffee and kept talking. Sharky found himself breathing for him.

"Just so's you know the territory down here, let me tell you, here's how I feel about Vice. I got sixteen years in, almost seventeen. I been on foot in the boondocks. Did a two-year trick in a blue-and-white. Had one partner snuffed out from under me and another one, he tried to drive through a warehouse wall, ended up in a wheelchair. I got out lucky with a bad back. I been in Bunco, six years in Robbery, I did a short tour in Homicide and I was in the IA for about two minutes before I ended up here."

Sharky laughed. He could just see Friscoe in Internal Affairs in his sneakers and sweatshirt, investigating complaints against his fellow officers.

"Internal Affairs," Friscoe went on, "I told 'em to stuff it. I got to deal with snitches every day. I'll be damned if I'm gonna snitch on my own, see what I mean?"

Sharky nodded. There was a rumor you could not even be interviewed for the IA unless you'd been born out of wedlock.

"Anyways, I personally don't give a rat's ass what the public does," Friscoe growled. "Some guy wants to stick his dick in a coffee grinder, who am I to argue, okay? It's his dick. Personally I got better things to do. I could care less some shirt salesman from Dubuque comes inta town, wants to pay out fifty, a hundred bucks to get laid, get a little head, shit, why not? Live and let live, I say, but it's where they put you. The Bat, the commissioner, the chief, whoever puts you where you are. Like I say, I got almost seventeen in, so I don't growl too loud. Mainly we got misdemeanors down here. Hooking. Pandering. Freak show. It takes a lotta time, effort, to make a misdemeanor case, okay? I mean, nobody's sucker enough if he pays some chippie fifty to gobble his pork, he's gonna show up in court and testify against her. He's gonna head for the hills first."

"So what's the answer?" Sharky asked.

"So we make a case against somebody for trickin' it's gotta be the cop makin' it and that means he had to make a deal and money had to change hands. What we really look for is felony. Extortion. A and B. Juvenile crimes. The worst. But it's rare. Mostly what we do, we answer complaints and do what we can to keep the streets clean. If we get a handle on something good, it's gravy on the potatoes. You want some mud? It's strong enough to play fullback for the Falcons."

"No thanks."

"Another thing. We got that fuckin' DA Hanson comin' up for re-election so he's got all the Baptists, the bluenoses, Billy Grahamers fired up right now. . . . The schmuck hasn't done anything but indict homos and jack-off artists for two years, but he's makin' a lot of noise right now so he'll look good to the PTA, that kinda shit. To listen to him, see, you'd think you can't take a breath of fresh air downtown without gettin' the clap."

Sharky broke up again, but Friscoe went right on, ignoring the laughter.

"Anyways Hanson is keepin' me busy just on routine, shakin' up the ladies on the street, bustin' the massage parlors, movie pits, hourly hotels. What I want, see, I want to zero you in on this thing we got a handle on, let you loose, see what you can do. I give you Arch—that's Livingston—and Papa and anybody you can dog-rob outa some other department. That's your whole army."

Sharky nodded. "I've heard stories about both of them."

"Whaddya hear, good or bad?" Friscoe asked.

"Both. Depends on who you listen to. The guys I listen to say they're in sudden death playoff with the best there is."

Friscoe beamed, obviously pleased. "Livingston there, he's got thirteen in. Best goddamn street cop in the House. He's cautious but lotsa smarts upstairs, right? College guy like you. Papadopolis, a hell of a cop. Papa doesn't give a shit. He'll stake out the governor's toilet you tell him to. Been shot three times; don't even remember where the scars are. And that's your machine. Oh yeah, one other thing. You gotta understand the politics of the House, see. All of us down here, in the cesspool here, we either don't know the politics, see, or didn't give a shit. Or maybe what it was, we were too hard-headed. That's what happens, you don't suck ass, play by the book, all that shit, you end up down here in the fuckin' leper colony. I been hearin' about you, the last two, three years. The word's been around the department head's on you, okay? Some say you're a hard-head. Others say you're dynamite on the street. Thing is, I give you maybe three, four years, you'll walk."

"To where? I'll have eight years in. Where the hell do you go after sinking that much time in the cops?"

"I dunno, but y'see, Sharky, you're too goddamn contrary to suck up to the system and too smart to live in it. I heard this morning, from this buddy of mine in IA, he calls me before I got a cup of coffee in me, tells me The Bat's getting ready to flop you out of detectives and give you a six-and-six. Even upstairs they figure you got a raw deal. I mean, the way I look at it, what do they want? Maybe you should've given the creep a ticket to Detroit and cab fare to the fuckin' airport, right? So I go up to see Jaspers and I tell him I gotta have some help and could I have you since I heard he was bustin' you outa the narcs. The Bat thinks it over a minute or two and finally says, 'Okay, but tell him to keep out of my hair.' And then he says something real strange. He says, 'Tell him to keep his shoes on in my office.' What the fuck was that all about?"

"My foot itched."

"And you took off your shoe and scratched it, that it?"

"Right."

"Bad form. Very bad form. You gotta understand about The Bat, about them all. Shit, look, it's a lotta

fuckin' crap protocol up there, see? That's what I'm
talkin' about. You're a third or second-grade detective,
you're a maggot to them. Takin' off your shoe, that
makes sense to you, but to a creep like The Bat, it's
death warmed over. That's what I mean, I see you
walkin' a coupla years from now. You gotta roll along
and take the punches, let the big shots grab the big collars, keep your face off the front page, don't make
waves. That kind of thing. Otherwise what happens,
you end up down here. Me, I should give a shit. Two
years I make captain, probably get assistant in charge of
Criminal Investigation, some nice job to go out on. Another two years I take my retirement and fuck it. But
you, you're gonna kick ass a lot and get kicked a lot.
It's what always happens you got a guy who's smart,
savvy, don't mind taking a chance or two now and
then."

"You sure paint a rosy picture."

"Truth. I deal in truth. What comes from bein' a Boy
Scout my younger years. Point is, see, it takes me a long
time to say something, but I'm glad to have you down
here, okay?"

"Thanks, Lieutenant."

"It goes for Arch there and Papa. Arch, he was the
first black cop on the force. And he didn't suck ass,
didn't eat any shit. The ones that followed him, they,
y'know, stuck their dick in the air see which way the
wind's blowin', kissed the right asses, moved on up
there. Fuckin' Uncle Tom shit, but Arch, he didn't bow
down nowhere along the line. So here he is, best fuckin'
street cop on the force bustin' hookers and library
freaks."

"What happened to Papa?"

"Papa was in Bunco workin' under a shitass name of
Shaushauser, a fuckin' Nazi. He's dead now. Rest his
soul, all that shit, but he had it comin'. Anyway Papa

brought down two, three big scams and this Shaushauser he takes the collars and even ends up with a citation. One day Papa has enough. He's in the locker room with Shaushauser and suddenly he starts playing handball, only Shaushauser's the ball. Bim, bam, bim, he takes the lieutenant off the wall a coupla times, ties his feet in a knot, goes about his merry business. Shaushauser goes to the hospital, Papa does a ten-and-ten, a year back in uniform, and then down here. That's what I mean about the system, Sharky. You can't beat the motherfuckers, so you either give in or walk. I see you walkin', all I'm sayin'. Anyways, it ain't gloryland here but it's better than what you had, you ask me. You know what they say—Fuck around with frogs you end up with warts on your dick."

"I think it's 'Lie down with dogs and get up with fleas.' "

"Right, just what I said. Now let's get goin'. Hey, Papa, hang up the phone goddammit, we got business. Arch, get your ass in here. We can't wait until the day after tomorrow you finish that report. And somebody bring the tape recorder. Let's put some goddamn wheels on this machine."

5

The man who arrived at one o'clock at the private suite in the Regal Hotel was short and unkempt. He needed a shave, his graying hair was frazzled and uncombed, his fierce gray eyes ringed with circles. He wore a pair of baggy slacks, a mismatched sports jacket, and his tie was a disaster. He carried a cheap plastic snapshut briefcase under his arm and a copy of *The New York Times* he had brought with him on the early morning flight from Washington. And he was hyper; energy vibrated around him. He sucked noisily on an empty pipe, walking in tight little circles waiting for someone to answer his knock.

His appearance was deceiving. Julius Lowenthal, former advisor to two presidents and a gnawing antagonist for a third, had once been described by a Pulitzer Prize-

winning journalist as having the appearance of a bur-
lesque comic and the mind of a Borgia.

One did not court Lowenthal's services; he offered
them. On this morning he was about to meet Senator
Donald Walden Hotchins, Jr.

He was greeted at the door by another political curiosity. Physically, Charles Roan was Lowenthal's alter
ego: a tall, husky, pleasant man with an ebullient personality, boundless energy, and a taste for three-piece
tailored suits. He was an open, buoyant man, unlike the
caged lion that was Lowenthal. As Hotchins's campaign
manager Charley Roan had overcome two major draw-
backs: he was a former All-American football player—
a jock—and he had been Hotchins's roommate in college. Sixteen years earlier, when Hotchins had chal-
lenged one of the strongest old-line machine politicians
in the state for governor, his appointment of Charley as
campaign manager had been regarded as a joke. Nobody
laughed anymore. Roan had been the architect of a remarkable success, had guided Hotchins through two
terms in the statehouse, a term as governor and finally
had helped him defeat the state's senior senator. It was
Roan who had discreetly let it be known to Lowenthal
that Hotchins needed him.

The suite was modest, a living room furnished with
comfortable but undistinguished hotel furniture, a bedroom with a king-size bed, and a small kitchenette.
Only a few of Hotchins's closest confidants knew he
maintained the suite. The senator was standing near a
window when Lowenthal entered the room. He smiled
and limped across it with the aid of a highly polished
shillelagh, a tall, lean, handsome man, well-tanned, with
blond hair and penetrating blue eyes. He was casually
dressed in flared slacks and a dark blue sports shirt. He
shook hands with Lowenthal.

"How's the foot?" Lowenthal asked.

"It's okay. Occasionally it acts up when the weather's bad."

Lowenthal smiled. "Can you run on one leg when the weather's bad?"

"He can run on his hands if he has to," Charley Roan said.

"I appreciate your coming," Hotchins said. "Do you think I'm crazy?"

"Sure I do," Lowenthal said. "Anybody who runs for public office is crazy. Anybody who runs for this office is mad as a hatter."

Hotchins smiled. "Okay, welcome to the tea party. How about some coffee?"

"Cream and sugar," Lowenthal said. "I stayed in the airport motel in Washington last night and sneaked out. I don't think anybody knows I'm here. Once the press finds out, the cat's out of the bag. I'd like to forestall that as long as possible."

"You can stay here. Nobody knows about this suite but a few of us. My press secretary, Pete Holmes, is at a luncheon. He'll be along in an hour or so. He's very good at handling the media."

"So I've heard."

"Well," Roan said, rubbing his hands together, "what do you think?"

"What do I think?" Lowenthal said raising his eyebrows. "What do I think about what?"

"I think what Charley means is, What do you think of our chances?"

Lowenthal stuffed tobacco into his battered pipe and lit it, almost disappearing in a nuclearean smokecloud. He waved the smoke away with a hand.

"I think if you can survive until the convention, once you've made the announcement, you've got a chance. I also think that is one big *if*."

"I'm not a pussyfooter, Julius," Hotchins said. "Are you interested in working with us?"

"That's why I'm here, Mr. Senator."

"Great. That's great!" Roan said and slapped his hands together. Lowenthal felt a moment of annoyance before remembering that exuberance was one of the prices one paid for youth. "I took the liberty of talking to Bob Fitzgerald at the National Committee yesterday," Lowenthal said. "I hope you don't object. I realize it was a bit unorthodox going ahead before we talked, but the timing seemed right to me. I operate on instincts, been living with them a long time. Usually don't take time to question them, I just go."

"And how does Fitzgerald feel about us?" Hotchins asked.

"Well, you got to remember that Fitz is an old party bull. He's been chairman of the NC for ten years. He's tough, probably the best machine politician this country's seen since Tammany. He's like an odds maker. He adds it all up and then he makes his bet."

"And?" Hotchins said.

"And he's still betting on Humphrey."

"Humphrey!" Roan bellowed. "Jesus Christ, he's already been whipped once. Does he want to hand the election to Ford?"

"The way he sees it, it's going to be a free-for-all in New Hampshire, Wisconsin, West Virginia, and all the early runners are going to burn out in the stretch. We're talking about a lot of money and a lot of endurance. Hubert can afford to wait it out until May, maybe even June, then jump in at the last minute after all the shooting's over and walk off with it."

"So," Hotchins said, "what it's going to take is a long-distance runner with a lot of money."

"That's it," Lowenthal said.

"And he's writing us off, right?" Roan said.

"He thinks Carter's going to be the man in the South. And he doesn't even give *him* a chance. He doesn't think either one of you has a chance nationally. Doesn't think you have the clout. You've stepped on too many toes. The insurance companies, the lobbyists, nuclear power. You've kicked a lot of ass, Mr. Senator."

Hotchins smiled. "And there's still plenty of kick left in my good foot," he said.

"But that's where the money is," said Lowenthal.

"We got the money," said Roan.

"We're talking big money. *Big* money."

"We have *big* money. And we have stamina."

"How about Carter?" said Lowenthal.

"Well, how about him?" Hotchins said.

"He's going to run. I talked to his people last week."

"We can take Carter," Roan said. "He hasn't got the charisma Hotch has."

"And he's soft on some key issues. I know Jimmy. We get along fine. I like him. But we can take him," Hotchins said. "We can beat him right here in the back room before he gets started. I guarantee it."

Lowenthal nodded. "I agree. I think you can. But you're going to have to beat him out of the gate and that means starting the race too soon. It's dangerous."

"He'll have to do the same. It's a question of who comes out first. And we're coming out next Monday," said Roan.

"Next Monday!" Lowenthal looked shocked.

"We'll lock the state before Jimmy gets out of bed," Roan said. "Then hit New Hampshire like the blizzard of '88."

Lowenthal shook his head. "You'll be on oxygen before spring," he said.

"No way," Hotchins said and the intensity of his retort surprised Lowenthal. "I can hop faster and farther than any of them can run on two legs. I've been training

for this for too long. Let 'em think we'll burn out. Let
Fitzgerald think so."

Lowenthal nibbled on his pipe. He was seeing a new
side to Hotchins. Tough. Obsessed. A man who did not
consider losing. Maybe he could do it. Maybe he just
had the fever to do it. He decided to try another approach, another test. "Let me put it this way," he said,
"You know how the National Committee works. They
control party finances. They can also play hell with the
convention, with delegates' votes, simply by screwing
with the convention rules. They browbeat, cajole,
threaten, blackmail, call in favors—there are a hundred
ways they can steal committed votes. You could go all
the way to the wire and see it vanish in a two or three-
ballot donnybrook."

"They tried it on Kennedy and got their ass handed
to them," Roan said.

"And Harry Truman," Hotchins added. "Talk about
stamina. He whistle-stopped Dewey to death. We can
do the same thing. To Carter, Udall, Frank Church,
even Humphrey if we have to. We know all this. The
question is, Do we need the committee?"

"Academic question," Lowenthal said. "We don't
have 'em, so why worry about it? Fitz'll fight you all the
way to the final ballot. I know him. I've been up against
him before. He wants a winner; that's the name of the
game this year. And he doesn't think you have a chance
in hell. Look, you're running, okay? You need money.
If you're a good party hack, they back you. If you're a
maverick, played by your own rules, voted against a few
big party bills—which you have—they run out of money
just when you need it. So you can forget the committee
for money *and* support. And it can get very lonely out
there if the party strongarms are against you. They'll
throw everybody in the party at you in the early prima-
ries. They may even quietly support some weak sisters

to split the vote, throw it into a runoff. Make you spend more money. And what Fitz is looking for is for you to run out of breath in the stretch. He plays for longevity. Longevity is what counts."

"We'll be waiting for him in New York come July," Hotchins said, with more than just confidence. The way he said it, it was a statement of fact.

Lowenthal shook his head and chuckled. "Well, if confidence alone could win it, you'd be on the way to Washington right now," he said. "But I must tell you, I don't agree with this plan to announce on Monday. Hell, at least wait until after the New Year."

"We can't," Roan said. "Carter's getting ready himself."

Lowenthal shook his head. "It's Christmas. Nobody gives a damn about politics right now."

"They will," Hotchins said.

"Damn, you're determined!" Lowenthal said.

Hotchins fixed himself a cup of tea and put half a spoonful of sugar into it. He stirred it slowly, looking at Lowenthal with his crystal blue eyes.

"What's your interest in me, Julius?" he asked.

Lowenthal smiled. "Plain and simple? You're a maverick and I like that, always have. I've been watching you for years. We believe in the same things." Then: "So much for idealism. Now we'll get to the bottom line. You have style. You have a hell of a war record. But the big thing is, I don't think Humphrey can beat Ford and I think you just might. Ford's the weakest incumbent president the Democrats have ever run against, but that doesn't mean he's a pushover. He can shake the Nixon thing. He's already done a pretty good job of that. My personal opinion is that a dark horse is going to take him. And they don't come any darker than you right now."

Hotchins and Roan both laughed.

"Besides," Lowenthal said, "maybe, just maybe, you could make one hell of a president."

Hotchins smiled warmly. Then he laughed out loud.

"I'll be a son of a bitch," he said. "That's one hell of an answer."

"Good," Lowenthal said, "now let's get to the nut-cutting fast. You got any secrets. Anything in the closet we ought know about? Any illegitimate kids, bad friends, vices that may upset the little old ladies in Nebraska?"

Hotchins smiled to conceal a tiny shock that hit him in the stomach. A picture of Domino flashed past his eyes. "Of course not," he said casually.

"We've been through this before," Roan said. "If there was anything, it would have been turned up by now."

"Not like this time. This time they'll be all over you—into your business deals, your war record, your family life. *Both* parties in the beginning. I don't want any surprises popping up at the last minute."

"What else?" Hotchins said, killing that conversation.

"What's your net worth?"

Hotchins thought about that for a few moments. "I suppose I'll show close to a million dollars when my CPA finishes the audit. But most of that's on paper. Investments, stock in trust to protect me from conflicts of interest."

"How much liquid?"

"Less than two hundred thousand dollars."

"Our credit position is very strong," Roan said. "We can tap several banks. I'd say we can raise a million, maybe more to start with."

"Not enough."

"What is enough?" Hotchins asked.

Lowenthal tapped dead ashes out of his pipe. Then he said, "Two million, minimum. It could go higher depending on how rough it gets. And no big contributors. It could hurt you later. It also could be illegal."

Hotchins stared at the lawyer. He had to be careful with Lowenthal. No matter how tough he might talk, Lowenthal was known for his integrity. It was one of the traits that gave him credence and had ever since he had first appeared on the political scene during the Kennedy campaign. But Hotchins was thinking, *Illegal?* It was only illegal if they got caught and he knew DeLaroza well enough to know Victor would never get caught. Hotchins's big concern was two million dollars. Was his finance minister prepared to raise that kind of money? He thought he knew the answer.

"We've got it," he said suddenly. "And without that son of a bitch Fitzgerald. I don't want his money. I don't want him until we get to New York. Then I want him with his hat in his hand, begging to get on board."

He limped to the window and looked down at the street, at the little people scurrying back to their offices and after-lunch Alka Seltzers. The voters. They *were* little people to him, humiliated by the routines of life, badgered by the banks and the mortgage companies and the institutions, running one step ahead of failure. His contempt for the common man was a deeply guarded secret, a flaw which could destroy him. And looking down at them he felt a deep rage that his future lay in their hands. But the emotion passed quickly.

"So it's Humphrey we have to beat," he mused aloud.

"Hubert's a fine man," Lowenthal said. "And a hell of a campaigner."

"He had his chance in '68," Hotchins said, and there was a snap to his voice, like a whip cracking. To Hotchins, he was a loser, a failure, like the little people below, a man who smiled in defeat and cried in public. Happy Warrior, hell. But he said nothing, for he sensed Lowenthal's respect for the Minnesota senator.

Lowenthal walked over to him. "Look, you got a lot going for you. You're handsome, honest, got a great record. You're a war hero; you left a foot in Korea and came back with the Distinguished Service Cross and a Purple Heart. You took a little nothing business and an SBA loan and parlayed it into a national franchise. You're a lawyer, a soldier, a businessman. Got a great family. Mr. Clean. And it's all beautiful and great. What it gets you, it gets you into the gate, period.

"After that, it's a balls-out race. What I can do for you, I can bring in some real heavyweights. Joe McGuire, Angie Costerone, John Davis Harmon. They'll come aboard if I'm aboard. I can work the demographics, tell you how to get the Chicano vote in L.A., the blacks and Puerto Ricans in New York, the Irish vote in Boston, the Polish vote in Chicago, deal with the unions, the city machines, the state hacks. We can do all that. But it won't mean a damn unless we come off big. You got to open up your campaign like a winner and run like one. When we announce we have to take the biggest hall in the state and fill it with the kids, the senior citizens, blacks, reds, yellows, greens, pinks, Wasps. We want bands and noise and, uh, what we can't do, we can't come out with *bupkus*. You know *bupkus?* It's Yiddish. It means nothing, zilch. A quiet noise. You sneak into this campaign and Fitz figures he's got you dead already. You come out big, with me and McGuire and the rest, it's gonna scare him to death."

Hotchins grinned. He was going to come out big, all right. That, he could guarantee.

Phipps Plaza was one of the city's more elegant shopping centers, located a few minutes from Victor DeLaroza's office, its parking lot three stories deep and un-

der the mall. At two that Thursday afternoon there
were only a few cars on the lower level. One of them
was a brown Rolls Royce which sat facing the exit
ramp, its motor mumbling softly.

Hotchins guided his Buick down the ramp and
parked beside it. As he got out of his car the rear door
of the Rolls swung open and Hotchins got into its elegant interior. DeLaroza was sipping a cup of espresso,
an enormous Havana cigar smoldering in his fist. He
grinned as the senator sat beside him and he pressed a
button in the armrest near his elbow. A window rose
silently between the front and back seats.

"Bom dia," DeLaroza said.

Hotchins shook his hand warmly. "I feel like I'm in
the CIA," he said, "sneaking around parking lots just to
have a chat. You should have come to the hotel. I want
you to meet Lowenthal."

"All in time," DeLaroza said. "I still put a high price
on my privacy. When it becomes necessary for me to
become a more public person, then I will deal with that
problem at the time. So, what is so urgent?"

"Lowenthal's in."

"Excellent, excellent!" DeLaroza cried.

"And he's bringing in McGuire, Casterone, and Harmon with him."

"Ah! Even better. That is splendid news. More than
you had hoped for, eh?"

Hotchins's voice became flat and hard. His eyes narrowed. "I was counting on it," he said. "Lowenthal is
like an ace in a poker game. Without help he could be
beat by a pair of deuces."

"An interesting analogy. And who are these deuces?"

"Fitzgerald and Humphrey."

"So, the National Committee has made its choice."

"Yes."

"It is no surprise, my friend, right?"

"No. And I like it this way," Hotchins said. "When the convention's over, we'll have Fitzgerald at our feet. That's what I want. I want them all to line up and kiss my ass."

DeLaroza's eyebrows arched as he listened to Hotchins's venom spill out. He said, "I am sure Fitzgerald is aware of this threat."

"Sure he is. They're going to fight us hard and dirty. That's all right. It'll make the victory that much sweeter. I tell you, Victor, I can taste it. *Taste* it." Hotchins's eyes burned with almost sensual delight as he spoke.

"Easy, my friend. Save that energy, it is a long time between now and July."

But Hotchins's ardor could not be stemmed. He had contained himself in Lowenthal's presence, not wishing to reveal his need. Now he let go, savoring what he felt was a sweet victory.

"I can feel it in my bones," he said. "Lowenthal's committed. He's excited, enthusiastic. And he's a brilliant tactician. Just what we need to go up against the committee. Now we can beat 'em, I know it. We can grind the sons of bitches under."

DeLaroza stared at the senator and puffed on his Havana. Somewhere within the immaculate framework of the Rolls an exhaust fan quietly sucked the smoke from the rear compartment.

"You remember a movie with Brando called *One-Eyed Jacks?*" DeLaroza said.

"Why? What's the point."

"You remind me of a one-eyed jack. The rest of the world sees only half your face. They see the veteran hero, the warm family man, charging windmills, tilting with the political machines. How many people ever see the other side, the hidden face of the jack?"

"Why, what do you see there?" Hotchins asked cautiously.

"A barracuda. A competitor with big needs, big hungers. It is what attracted me to you, Donald. That is why you will win. It will not be because of Lowenthal or Casterone or any of the others. You will win because you have an instinct for the jugular and that will surprise them."

Hotchins leaned forward in the seat, tense and suddenly uneasy. They had never talked this openly before. Finally he said, "Takes one to know one, right, Victor?"

"Oh, I am not a barracuda," DeLaroza said. "The barracuda is selective. It picks its victims to appease its appetite. I am a shark, Donald. I will eat anything that comes in my way."

"Sounds like a warning," Hotchins said.

"No. I want to make sure you are aware that I too have big appetites. And I also go for the throat."

Hotchins pondered the comment for a few moments and then laughed. "All right," he said.

DeLaroza laughed with him. He puffed on the cigar again, then said, "Now, what are the complications?"

It was Hotchins's turn to raise his eyebrows. "Complications? Who said anything about complications?"

"My friend, there are always complications."

Hotchins rubbed his hands together but said nothing.

"I would guess," said DeLaroza, "that it is money."

"You're a mind reader."

"Not really. The last thing one always discusses is the price."

Hotchins's blue eyes grew colder. He looked DeLaroza hard in the eyes. "The price is two million dollars."

The big man said nothing for a few minutes. He puffed on the Havana, savoring the taste of the smoke on his tongue, letting the smoke ease from his lips, watching it race toward the concealed exhaust vents. Then he said, "Is this Lowenthal's estimate?"

Hotchins nodded.

"He's low," DeLaroza said.

"Low?"

"Yes, low. According to our computer, it will take four point six million. That is, of course, considering all the variables. Possible run-offs, et cetera. Add on a ten percent contingency, over five million."

Hotchins chewed his lips. He looked out the window of the car, staring around the tomblike interior of the parking lot. A Honda pulled in and stopped and a hassled suburban wife lifted a crying child from the car, then dragged him along behind her toward the elevators.

"I know what you are thinking," DeLaroza said, "you are thinking how could Lowenthal make such a sizeable error. Correct?"

"It crossed my mind."

"It is simple. The last time he was involved in a campaign was '68. In '72 his man lost in the primary, *but* principle was involved. We cannot fault him there. The point is, it is eight years since he was involved in a campaign that went all the way. Inflation. New methods. The cost of television, newspaper advertising, all rising every day. Many things could account for the discrepancy. He is not an accountant. His political acumen is beyond value. With his friends, you have a package worth more than a million dollars. You probably could not buy them for that."

"You can't buy them at all," Hotchins said.

"I would tend to doubt that. It is naïve, but also immaterial. We have them, that is what is important." He paused, then mused aloud, "Five million dollars. A lot of money."

"Yes," Hotchins said. "Now we have some strong bank commitments and . . ."

DeLaroza held up a hand. "Donald . . . *Don*ald,

wait. I said a lot of money. I did not say too much money. You have relied on my financial advice for what—sixteen years now? Are you getting nervous because the price is going up?"

"It has to be done carefully," Hotchins said. "You know the rules of disclosure. If Fitzgerald can turn up anything—"

"Please," DeLaroza said, "do not tell the hunter how to load his gun."

Hotchins stopped. Then he patted DeLaroza on the knee. "Sorry," he said.

"The money is my problem," DeLaroza said. "There is this other thing."

"It can wait," Hotchins said quickly.

"No, I think not."

"It can wait!"

"No."

The muscles in the corners of Hotchins's jaw quivered, then grew rigid. The flat, hard tone returned to his voice. "It is personal, Victor."

"It is a dangerous thing now. Before it was merely risky. I could understand it. I know that kind of hunger. But . . ."

"It's still *my* business."

"I have never risked five million dollars on you before, Donald."

"Ah, so now I find out where the strings are."

"Have there ever been strings attached before?"

"No. But I knew there must be a price. Sooner or later there had to be a price. I guess now is as good a time as any to settle that."

"You are getting off the subject."

"This *is* the subject."

"You are getting angry," DeLaroza said.

"You're damn right. We're getting into my personal life—"

"You have no personal life anymore."

"Half the politicians in Washington have mistresses."

"Half the politicians in Washington are not running for president."

"Jesus!"

"Donald, we are friends. After all it was I who introduced you to the woman. I saw the need. Understood it. But now it must wait until after the election."

"You think she's going to wait around until after the election? Hell, you know her better than that, Victor. Besides, it's not just me, it's the idea of me that fascinates her."

DeLaroza nodded. "I am glad you realize that," he said.

"It would be a sign of weakness, asking her to sit in the wings until the election's over."

"My friend, when you are in the Oval Office, you will have anything you wish. Women will be at your call."

But I need her now, Hotchins thought to himself. "I'm not talking about women," he said, "I'm talking about her."

"Are you in love with her?"

"Possibly. No, not really. Not in the dramatic sense. But in a way I . . . hell, I don't know. Don't push me. *Don't push me.*"

DeLaroza scowled. He was on dangerous ground and he knew it. Now was not the time to start pulling the strings. And yet, the issue was crucial to him. "Am I to believe that you would risk something like this for a piece of ass?" he said.

Hotchins glowered at him, his face red, anger boiling in his eyes. "What was that?" he demanded.

DeLaroza shook his head violently and waved his hand in the air. "I am sorry," he said quickly. "That was a foolish remark. Forgive it."

They sat without speaking and the minutes crept by.
Finally DeLaroza said, "We will drop it for now. I did
not mean to cause harsh words. I was speaking as one
friend to another. Just promise me that you will consider it. Think about it. Will you do that?" It annoyed
him to patronize Hotchins, but he sensed two egos
keening the air like dueling swords.

"Sure," Hotchins said, "I'll think about it."

More silence.

Hotchins felt boxed in, but the furies began to settle
down inside him. Perhaps DeLaroza was right. And yet
he had never known anyone like her. Her sexuality had
given him a new vigor, a vitality that he had missed for
years. It was not a motivation; it was fuel for the motivation. And yet if giving her up was part of the key to
winning . . .

"Let us get back to the money," DeLaroza said. "We
have . . . commitments from individual contributors
for almost a million dollars. I can call them in today. In
the meantime I can make the funds available through
my own accounts. Immediately if necessary. Oh, don't
worry, it will be done properly. Nothing would ever appear as a loan."

Hotchins held up a hand. "I trust you, Victor. I am
sure it will be done in a way that's above . . ." He
started to say "suspicion" but quickly changed it to "re-
proach." He sank back in the seat. His shoulders
drooped and he sighed. "I'm sorry too," he said. He
held out his hand and they shook.

"There will be many anxious times," DeLaroza said.
"I sometimes forget that we are both emotional men."

"It's forgotten," Hotchins said. "Look. I've got to get
back. It's hard for me to get away at all these days, even
for a few minutes. They want an itinerary when I go to
the bathroom."

"Get used to it," DeLaroza said. "Your private days are about over."

"I'll be in touch," Hotchins said. "Thanks."

He left the car and DeLaroza settled back. The smile vanished from his face. He sat deep in thought for several minutes. *Yes, his private days are over,* he thought, *and so are mine.* Thirty years of living in shadows and now, in a few short days, the recognition he had needed for so long would be his. He had built an empire and was about to create a king and now, finally, he would have what he deserved—applause. An ovation! The plan to emerge from his self-imposed cell of secrecy had started forming in his mind when he met Hotchins. It had taken sixteen years to gestate. Sixteen years. And now the blood hammered in his temples. Four more days.

He pressed the button, lowering the window between the front and back seats of the car. Chiang, his chauffeur-bodyguard, handed him a cassette. Another addition to the *Gwai-lo* file. It was time to discuss matters with Kershman.

Gerald Kershman was sprawled face down on the bed, his hands and feet bound to the corners by velvet cords. Sweat stung his eyes and he gulped for air as the strips of leather bit into his already tortured flesh. He turned his face into the silk sheets that muffled his cries of pain. The naked young man standing over him with the cat o' nine tails was hard and lithe; his blond hair tumbled in sweaty ringlets over his forehead.

Finally Kershman turned his face toward the youth. "Enough," he gasped.

The blond, who was in his late teens, lowered the whip and stood over him. Kershman took several deep breaths and shivered involuntarily and then relaxed. "Untie me," he said.

The young man freed him, and Kershman, his back and rump slashed with red welts, struggled from the bed soiled with his own semen and grimaced with pain as he sat on the edge. He was a small, fat man with thick, contemptuous lips and froglike eyes. Black hair curled obscenely on his shoulders and back. He reached out to the night table near the bed with chubby, trembling fingers, feeling for his thick glasses and putting them on with some effort.

"Okay I get dressed now?" the youth asked.

Kershman stared at his naked body for a few more moments and nodded. He wiped the sweat from his face with a towel and watched as the young hustler slipped on a pair of red bikini briefs and arranged himself. "You really love it, dontcha?" he said. "I never seen nobody eat up a beatin' like that before."

"Shut up," Kershman groaned. He got up and walked toward the bathroom, a silk bathrobe trailing from one hand.

"Hey," the blond said, "how about my bread?"

"You're not through yet," said Kershman. "Come in here."

He lay face down on a massage table in the opulent bathroom and pointed to several bottles of ointment and balm in a tray attached to the table. The boy spread them on carefully, chattering aimlessly as he did. Kershman turned his face away from the youth. Tears edged down the side of his nose. They were tears of humiliation, not pain. The blond completed his task and Kershman eased himself off the table.

"All right," he said, "you can leave now."

"The bread, the bread," the hustler said, snapping his fingers at Kershman. The small man looked at him and hate filled his eyes. His lip curled viciously.

"You snap your fingers at me one more time," he said, "and I'll have them broken, one at a time."

"Hey," the blond said. He stepped back, balling up his fists.

"Your bread," Kershman said wearily, "is on the dresser."

The younger man went into the bedroom and emptied the contents of a brown manila envelope, eagerly counting the bills. His eyes lit up. "Jeez, thanks," he said, "ya want me to come back again tonight?"

"I don't want to see you again," Kershman said. "You show your face around this building again and you'll regret it."

The hustler looked at him for a moment and then grinned. "Wotsa matter, doll, was I too rough on you?"

Kershman stood in the bathroom doorway, regarding him through thick glasses that distorted his already bulging eyes, his mouth still trembling from the combination of pain and ecstasy. He said, "If it makes you feel any better, you were magnificent. I happen to prefer one-nighters."

"Sure, honey, that's cool. Different strokes for different folks, right?" He pulled on his leather jacket and left.

Kershman struggled into his clothes and left his apartment, taking a private elevator down one flight to the eighteenth floor of the Mirror Towers, where the giant computer awaited him. There were only three entrances into the sprawling computer complex which consumed most of the eighteenth floor. One was by private elevator from Kershman's apartment, the second a private elevator between DeLaroza's office and the console room. The third was by the exterior elevator, which had to be programmed to stop as it descended from the top two floors. Special keys activated the computers and the elevators.

Only three other people worked in the computer complex, none of whom really understood its complexities or the maze of interlocking information it contained. They were simply technicians.

It was a little after 2:30 when Kershman's elevator opened and he entered the main console room, the nerve center of the complex. A young woman wearing a white uniform was stringing a spool of tape on one of the computer banks.

"Anything unusual?" Kershman asked.

"Not really," she answered brightly. "We have to complete the annual audit on WCG and L today. I'm running the totals now."

"Fine," Kershman said and went into his private office. The audit on West Coast Gas and Light Company, when complete, would require Kershman's final personal touch, since DeLaroza planned to have its directors apply for a rate increase.

It was a measure of Kershman's financial genius and tenacity that while still an undergraduate at the University of Pennsylvania's Wharton School of Business he had once appeared at the office of the president of Ticanco, one of the world's largest conglomerates, and asked for an appointment. Although he was told it would be impossible, Kershman had appeared at the office every morning at precisely 8:30 and remained there until five in the afternoon. After twenty-six consecutive working days, he had exhausted the executive's resistance and was finally ushered into his office.

"You have two minutes," the man said sternly. "If you can't state your business by then you're wasting your time as well as mine."

"Oh, I can do it in one sentence," Kershman replied confidently. "I can show you an absolutely foolproof method that will save you eight million, three hundred thousand dollars in corporate income taxes this year. Are you interested?"

The actual saving was a little under seven million dollars, but it had earned Kershman, an orphan from the slums of East Saint Louis, his tuition and a generous living allowance for the remainder of an educational odyssey that included two more years at Wharton, three years at Harvard, where he earned a doctorate in corporate finance, and a stint at Georgetown Law School, where he received his degree in international law. After completing his studies with distinction at all three universities, Kershman had refused a generous offer from Ticanco, to go to work instead for the Internal Revenue Service where during the next three years he designed an infinite variety of schemes for beating the income tax laws. By the time he was thirty-three Kershman was earning six figures a year as a consultant for several corporations.

To Kershman the world became a giant financial chess board and he took Machiavellian delight in developing methods for circumventing the international trade agreements and treaties which were its rules. In 1968 Kershman had proposed to one of his clients that within a few years the Arab nations would use their control of oil to dominate prices all over the world. Kershman, a Jew, had negotiated a dangerous and volatile deal with two Arab nations which, in exchange for enough guns and ammunition to supply their armies, would provide to the company Kershman represented crude oil at a low fixed price for fifteen years. The arms were delivered by boat to Turkey and from there were shipped overland by caravan to the Mideast. The oil was sold to a refinery in Jakarta, shipped to a refinery in Yokohama, and resold as surplus to the Y and D Oil Company in Philadelphia. By 1975 Y and D had grown into one of the largest U.S. gasoline companies, with its own coast-to-coast chain of filling stations. It constantly undersold all competitors by two or three cents a gallon.

Y and D was owned by Victor DeLaroza. He was amazed by Kershman's ability, as well as by the alacrity with which a Jew had dealt with Arabs. In the seven years that had followed the oil deal Kershman had become the financial architect of DeLaroza's tentacled empire, carefully constructing a maze of contracts, stock transfers, holding companies, and silent corporations throughout the world which concealed the ownership of more than three hundred corporations, controlled the prices of three major industries, and had on its payrolls (including several heads of state) more than a hundred thousand people. Only Kershman and the electronic brain on the eighteenth floor understood the complicated corporate polygamy he had created, although two men were being groomed to succeed him if the need should arise.

In exchange DeLaroza had insured Kershman's loyalty by providing him with an opulent cocoon, an outrageous lifestyle which Kershman could never have achieved personally—a salary of two hundred thousand dollars a year, stock equity in several key corporations, an executive jet, homes in Tokyo, London and on Crete. To satisfy Kershman's gluttonous appetite for gourmet food, there were open accounts in the world's greatest restaurants and a personal chef from the Cordon Bleu who created exotic dishes in Kershman's own kitchen when he was not traveling. And there were bonuses, each one unique, among them an awesome pornography collection that included five priceless volumes stolen from the personal collection of King Farouk by the same thief who had stolen a Picasso from the Musée de l'Art Moderne, a Rembrandt from the National Gallery in Washington, and three Van Goghs from the private collection of a Greek shipping magnate.

Finally, to protect Kershman from the danger of scandal-making indiscretions, a onetime film actor named Tod Donegan, whose sexual deviations had destroyed a promising film career, had been hired as Kershman's Judas Goat, to cruise the gay haunts and deliver to the financial wizard young lambs for his sexual slaughter and—although he secretly despised the less than attractive Kershman—provide the service himself when Kershman so desired.

The protective shell provided by DeLaroza had done its job. Kershman had become a pathologically private man, terrified by normal social situations. He had no close friends and seemed irresistibly drawn to the sordid side of life. His need to occasionally escape the cocoon was fulfilled by playing fantasy roles. He cultivated bizarre relationships, subtly exploiting them in order to bolster a veneer of superiority that covered a battered and confused self-image. One was an alcoholic veterinarian who worked for the humane society. Kershman frequently visited him on those days set aside for the extermination of unwanted animals. Kershman often achieved orgasms watching the puppies and kittens in the final spasms of death. Another was a self-defeated police detective to whom Kershman represented himself as a journalist for several foreign news agencies so he could accompany the policeman on assignments or buy him lunch and listen to the gruesome details of some particularly shocking police case.

Kershman had just poured a cup of tea when the red light near his phone began blinking. It meant that DeLaroza wanted him. He picked up the receiver and punched 0. DeLaroza answered immediately.

"Can you come up here right away, Dr. Kershman?" he said softly.

"Of course," Kershman answered. He went into the console room and unlocked the private elevator to De-

Laroza's office. He punched out an intricate code in a hidden keyboard and the car rose two stories.

DeLaroza was seated behind his desk pondering over an open briefcase.

He nodded and handed Kershman the cassette from the meeting with Hotchins. "Add this to *Gwai-lo*," he said.

"Right away."

"Are you totally current with the laws regarding political contributions?" DeLaroza asked.

"Of course, sir. The full disclosure laws . . ."

"I don't care for a review," DeLaroza said, "just make sure that everything we do with the *Gwai-lo* file from now on will stand the most rigid investigation."

"I've always been extremely careful on that file," Kershman answered.

"I want to move five million dollars into the campaign account. We'll start with a million. I'd like it in today if that's possible. The rest of the money will be made available to you during the next ten days or so in cash from my personal accounts." He shoved the briefcase across the desk. "Here is the first million. Any problems?"

"No, sir. I would suggest we make them all personal contributions. Keep them low, no more than fifty thousand per individual, range from thirty to fifty I would say. We can backdate the contributions and arrange for Jefferson Trust to loan this million, using the pledges as security. That way it will not appear as if all the contributions were made in a short period of time. I'll rearrange the accounts and—"

"Doctor."

"—we can reimburse with bonuses spread out over—"

"Dr. Kershman?"

Kershman, who had been momentarily entranced by his evaluation of the ploy, stopped. "Yes?"

"I'm not interested in how. I assume you know exactly how to handle that. Just keep me informed on the progress. I would like to know which of our people we are going to use, so I can brief them personally."

"Right."

"I think that should do it," DeLaroza said.

"May I ask, sir," Kershman said, "are we going to move on the final phase of the *Gwai-lo* project?"

"Yes. The cassette is self-explanatory. I may add some personal notes to the file later today."

"Well," Kershman said, his thick lips rolling back in a fat smile, "may I say I am delighted?"

"It's been a long time, hasn't it?" DeLaroza said.

"Yes sir. I was hoping it would be this election."

DeLaroza smiled and leaned back in his chair. Not even Kershman knew that he had been planning this move for more than sixteen years. He felt a sudden surge of excitement. His fingertips tingled.

"He's ready," DeLaroza said. "He'll never be readier."

6

"Jesus," Friscoe bellowed as he swept debris into one corner of his desk, shoving into a single disordered pile case reports, file folders, bits of paper, a half-eaten Swiss cheese on rye and a cardboard container of coffee with what looked like penicillin floating on top. "I wish to hell we could get the goddamn cleanup committee down here. What we got here is the makings of a bubonic plague."

He was stringing a reel of tape on the Sony which now sat on the cleared space on his desk.

"What we got, Sharky, is about two hours of phone taps here, spread over about three, four weeks. It's all legal—Judge Alvers gave us the flag. Now before we get into this good I want you to listen to this take just so's you'll get an idea of the range of this little operation. We got each take tagged on front, so you'll know who, what, and where. The rest, it speaks for itself."

He turned on the switch and adjusted the volume. The tape hissed for a moment and then Livingston's voice came on.

LIVINGSTON: This is tape PC-1, a recording of a telephone conversation between the subject, Tiffany Paris, made from the phone in her apartment, Suite 4-A, the Courtyard Apartments, 3381 Peachtree Street, Northwest, November 22, 1975, one ten P.M., and two male callers, the first identified as Neil, n.l.n., and the second Freddie, n.l.n., also referred to as Freaky Freddie.

Click.

TIFFANY: Hello?

NEIL: What's happening?

TIFFANY: I'm dead. That joker last night belongs in the zoo.

NEIL: Yeah, well, his money's as green as anybody else's. Guess who I've got on the phone?

TIFFANY: I'm too tired for guessing games, Neil.

NEIL: Freddie.

TIFFANY: Freaky Freddie?

NEIL: Freaky Freddie.

TIFFANY: Don't tell me. What's on his mind?

NEIL: Now what the hell you think's on his mind?

TIFFANY: Oh not now. I'm just not ready for him. I haven't even had a bath. . . .

NEIL: Hey, you know the score. When he's ready, he's ready, and right now he's ready.

TIFFANY: I've got to get my head on straight. Tell him . . . have him call back in twenty minutes.

NEIL: Now! Twenty minutes, he'll beat off and save the money.

TIFFANY: Christ, Neil—

NEIL: I said it's now, baby. Now straighten your head up and let's get it on.

TIFFANY: (Groans) Okay, five minutes, stall him for five.

NEIL: I'll give you three.

Click.

LIVINGSTON: Tape PC-2, same subjects, one-thirteen P.M.

Click.

TIFFANY: Hello.

NEIL: You ready?

TIFFANY: I guess. This won't win any prizes.

NEIL: I'm looking at a bill-and-a-half, not any Academy Awards. I'm patching you in now.

Click.

FREDDIE: H-h-h-hello?

TIFFANY: (Very softly) Hello Freddie.

FREDDIE: I, uh, h-h-how you b-b-been?

TIFFANY: Just fine, and you?

FREDDIE: Okay.

TIFFANY: Freddie, guess who I've got here with me?

FREDDIE: (Excited) I d-d-don't know. I g-g-give up.

TIFFANY: My photographer friend.

FREDDIE: Y-y-you mean the one w-w-with . . .

TIFFANY: The redhead, Freddie, with the big tits.

FREDDIE: Oh y-y-yeah.

TIFFANY: She's shooting for *Penthouse* this time.

FREDDIE: *P-P-Penthouse?*

TIFFANY: She looks really wild today. She's wearing a silver, uh, lamé jumpsuit.

FREDDIE: W-w-with z-z-zippers?

TIFFANY: All the way down the front. Why don't you just relax Freddie? Lay back and relax and let it happen, baby. You have some music on?

FREDDIE: B-B-Berlioz.

TIFFANY: Perfect.

FREDDIE: Are the z-z-zippers p-p-pulled down?

TIFFANY: Give me time, honey.
The zipper goes all the way down the
front.
And . . .
she's zipping it down,
now . . .
real slowly,
down . . .
down . . .
It's spreading open, Freddie. I can
just see.
Oh, wow, I can see the edge . . .
of her nipples.
The suit zips aaaall the way down
and under, you know?
When it's open, Freddie,
you can see it all.

FREDDIE: W-w-what else?

TIFFANY: You know what I'm wearing, Freddie?
She brought it. It's black,
silk, very thin silk,
with beige lace
across my tits . . .
and on the bottom, too. Just under my
hair.
And you know what's under it, Freddie?

FREDDIE: W-w-what?

TIFFANY: A white garter belt
and white stockings.
Sheer white stockings.
Her zipper's pulled down
below her stomach . . .
I can just see . . .

                I can see the edge of her hair,
                bright red,
                curling over the slit in the zipper . . .

FREDDIE: The p-p-pop-p-poppers, d-d-don't for-
                get . . .

TIFFANY: Oh, wait until I tell you about that.
                She has this, this special little inhaler.
                It has two little tubes,
                one for each nostril.
                She's breaking the poppers,
                putting them in the tubes . . .
                and . . . she's
                waving it . . .
                waving it under my nose.
                Oh! Oh, my God, Freddie . . .
                I'm tingling . . .
                tingling all over. Even my skin is ting-
                ling . . .
                and my tits are hard . . .
                hard like you, Freddie.
                My pussy
                feels like it's going to . . .

FREDDIE: C-c-cunt . . . say *c-c-cunt,* I love it
                w-w-when . . .

TIFFANY: My cunt
                is burning up.
                It's throbbing . . .
                It feels like it's . . . it's
                vibrating
                and getting wet.
                I'm getting ready and
                she's beginning to shoot,
                she's straddling me.
                Can you hear it, Freddie, the camera?
Sound of camera discharging.

FREDDIE: Oh yeah . . . I hear it . . .

TIFFANY: She's making me
spread my legs. And she's
kneeling
in between them . . .
leaning over.
Her knee is so close
I can feel the heat of her body. I . . .
I'm going to just
move down a little . . .
maybe just, touch it against her . . .
But she's moving away, her knee
is moving away.
I can't stand . . .
Oh Freddie, she's pulling down one of
the straps
on the . . .
the . . .
oh, oh . . . on the negligee, sliding the
lace
over my nipples.
Back and forth.
Jesus, I'm hard.
It feels . . .
I feel . . .
like I have a volcano between my
legs . . .
shivering
ready to explode,
with hot lava.
She's got the negligee down.
My tits are free.
They're so hard and pointing up at her.
And now she's
taking my hand . . .

putting my fingers in her mouth,
sucking them
She's leaning over . . . her tits . . .
are rubbing mine.
God.
Oh, God, Freddie,
she's taking my fingers, putting them on
our tits
making me squeeze them,
together,
and putting my other hand,
moving it down,
down,
Freddie . . . I'm touching it. All warm
and wet,
swollen,
swelling up.
Oh, yeah, she's doing me . . .
with her hand on mine.
I can't tell who's doing . . .
doing what to who.
She's zipping the jumpsuit down . . .
It's taking her forever.
Um . . . okay . . . I can see it,
I can see the top
of her cunt.
She's slipping out of it, taking it off.
Jesus.
She's moving up on me.
Her cunt . . .
Oh, God, Freddie, her cunt is just . . .
just kind of brushing my tits.
And it's so soft . . .
sooo soft,
like feathers, Freddie,

and my tit is wet from her.
I want to come Freddie . . .

FREDDIE: Not y-y-yet, *no!*

TIFFANY: She's sitting down on me.
My nipple is . . .
God, it's inside her.
She's moving,
back and forth
and my
tit
is fucking her, Freddie . . .
Oh yeah,
oh yeah,
I'm so hard, Freddie,
my clit is standing up . . . like your cock.
Are you hard, Freddie, good and hard?

FREDDIE: Y-y-yes . . .

TIFFANY: She's rolling over on her side.
Taking my hand,
putting my fingers inside me,
moving them . . .
in and out . . .
in
and out . . .
and she has my other hand
on her cunt.
I'm stroking her
and she's moving
back and forth
faster
faster
and I'm moving my hand in and out of me with her.
She's rubbing me

she's right on it and rubbing . . .
everybody's together, moving together.
Jesus, Freddie, she's getting off,
she's moving real fast and
her mouth,
her mouth is wide open.
She's
going
to come, and so . . .
so . . .
so . . .
Freddie, I can't wait. Don't make me
wait. She's coming, Freddie.
She's coming.

FREDDIE: Oh yeah,
oh yeah,
oh yeah . . .

TIFFANY: Here it comes, Freddie,
here it comes, Freddie.
Ohhh, Freddie,
ohhh, Freddie.
Ohhh,
ohhh,
Freddie . . .
Freddie . . .
Freddie . . . Freddie, Freddie Freddie,
Freddie . . .
Oh, oh, oh, oh, oh, *Oh,Oh,Oh*
AHHH!

Freddie cried out with her, a pinched, tight squeal,
caught in the constrictions of his throat, and ending in
a whimpering sigh.

Pause.

The tape was quiet except for the sounds of their
labored breathing and an occasional sigh.

TIFFANY: Jesus, that was good.
           It was *really* good. How about you
           Freddie? How was it for you?

Pause.

TIFFANY: Freddie?

More heavy breathing.

FREDDIE: (Groans) Oh, God.

TIFFANY: Tell me about it, Freddie. I could get off
           again, you know that, if you just tell me
           how it was.

Still no answer.

TIFFANY: Freddie?

FREDDIE: Uhhh . . .

TIFFANY: You know what I'd like? I'd like you to
           be here right now. Deep inside me. Make
           me feel like a woman again. Can you do
           that?
           Can you get me off, Freddie?

FREDDIE: I w-w-want to t-t-try . . .

TIFFANY: Great. Because it's building again,
           Freddie. All for you.

Friscoe switched the tape recorder off. "Well, enough
of that," he said, "the rest is X-rated."

Sharky sat in stony silence, staring at the machine.
He was repulsed, yet strangely turned on by the intensity of the woman's performance and by the eroticism of
the phone conversation. He was embarrassed, but he
shielded his feelings.

"If that Freddie has any problems, that's pretty good
therapy," Arch Livingston said. "Look at Sharky, he's
struck speechless. Bet you never heard anything like
that before, did you, speedy?"

Sharky shook his head.

Friscoe was laughing. "Little dirty trick there,
Sharky," he said. "That one there, that's an odd-ball

situation. Tell you the truth, I'd like to get a look at old
Freaky Freddie. He's the kind, sounds like he gives
freaks a bad name. It's what we call an ear job. A
hunnerd-and-a-half ear job. Normally, see, what happens this Neil—he's the pimp, okay?—he lines up the
johns, makes the deal, then calls the girl. It's strictly a
one-way street, from the john to old pimpo deluxo to
the hooker. She never calls Neil or the john. I don't
even think she knows his phone number. And neither
do we yet. Anyway, it's a very cautious set-up. Probably
the neatest phone-and-fuck operation I've ever run
into."

Friscoe ran the tape forward; its garbled squeal filled
the room. He stopped several times, seeking a particular
take.

"How, uh, did you get on to this?" Sharky said finally.

Livingston smiled. "Believe it or not, a snitch."

"One of the johns?"

Friscoe shook his head. "Naw, don't I wish? You
think any of these bimbos gonna say anything, put their
balls in the wringer? Shit, no. It was this old campaigner
we call Mabel the Monster, been street trickin' must be
ten years now. Her heels are so round she has to hang
on to the lamppost keep from fallin' over backwards.
What happened, back there late in November we had
some kind of religious convention in town. Shit, on Saturday night we had about a thousand Jesus freaks runnin' all over town screamin' and hollerin' like a grizzly
bear with his nuts caught in the door jamb. So, about
seven o'clock the goddamn switchboard lights up like
it's the Fourth of fuckin' July and then The Bat calls in,
and the chief, and finally the commissioner himself. It
seems the whole Peachtree hooker line turned out in
force. Musta been, we counted thirty-two pros working
the two blocks between the Regal Hotel and the Tow-

ers. So we go over, drop the hammer on about twenty of 'em, and poor old Mabel turns up in the lineup. Usually, see, she's quiet as a lamb. She's been nailed so much she oughta be payin' rent down at the pound. Only this night, Jesus, we had a fuckin' maniac on our hands. So Papa there, he takes her in the backroom, waltzes her around a bit, and turns out she's pissed, see? She says we're pickin' on the low-renters and turning a deaf eye on the high-rolling ladies. For a while Papa can't get anything specific outa her and then he offers to let her walk, she gives him something we can hang our hat on, and she comes up with a name and address. Bingo, we got Tiffany.

"We figure, the last three weeks or so, we got—how many, Arch?—ninety-one phone calls on tape, eighty percent is jobs. She's turnin' four tricks a week at five and six bills a pop and you gotta figure it's at least a hundred g's a year, tax free. Still, *still* misdemeanor, but, you know, *big* misdemeanor. Worth workin' on. Then three days ago, we turn up this take I'm gettin' ready to play for you. Now it's a new ballgame because we got what looks like a shakedown. A fat one. And that's felony extortion, baby." Friscoe smiled and licked his lips.

"Also," Livingston said, "we got a joker popping up in the deck."

"We'll come to that in a minute," Friscoe said.

"Wouldn't the IRS love to get a piece of this action?" Sharky said.

Livingston cringed. "Wouldn't they though? And fuck it up for everybody else, as usual."

"All those assholes are interested in is their own chunk of the kiwash," Friscoe said. "They don't give a diddly shit about anybody or anything but their own shitass little backyard. They're as much help as a broken leg."

"Maybe we could lean on Tiffany, get to Neil. He knows everything that's happening," Sharky said.

"You're jumping the gun," said Friscoe. "Just listen to this here take. There's a lot happening. We move too soon now and we could blow the whole machine right down the fuckin' toilet, believe me. Just hook an ear on this."

He turned on the recorder.

LIVINGSTON: This is tape PC-74, tape recording of a telephone conversation between the subject, Tiffany Paris, Suite 4-A, the Courtyard Apartments, 3381 Peachtree Street, Northwest, December 15, 1975, three thirty-two P.M., and a male caller identified as Neil, n.l.n.

Click.

TIFFANY: Hello?

NEIL: It's me.

TIFFANY: Oh, thank God, I was afraid it was—

NEIL: Hey, calm down, calm down.

TIFFANY: He came by here, no call, no nothing, just showed up at the door. Anybody could have been here. My mother—

NEIL: I said calm down. It's taken care of. It won't happen again.

TIFFANY: But it never happened before . . . it was like that . . . terrible little man following me that ti—

NEIL: Bag it, Tif.

Friscoe turned the machine off for a moment. "That bit there. We think what happened, some john probably took it on himself to bypass Neil, call in person. Blew her mind, see."

"What's that about somebody tailing her? Was that one of your people?" Sharky asked.

"No. We haven't figured that one out yet. Anyway,

moving along here we get to the meat." He switched the machine back on.

NEIL: Listen to me. I talked to him, eye to eye, read him the facts of life. It won't happen again, believe me.

TIFFANY: It really upset me. The man that was following me that time, the one in the leather jacket, I know he was cop and—

NEIL: He was not a cop. He was some shitass little conman looking for a buck. Besides, he vanished, right? When's the last time you saw him?

TIFFANY: He was following Domino, too, Neil. She told me—

NEIL: Shit!

TIFFANY: I still think Norman sent him. He was so angry and he made those threats.

NEIL: Norman did *not* send him. And Domino's forgotten all about it. Norman's back in Texas, playing with his oil fields. Drop it. Now, I mean it.

"Here we go," Friscoe said, "now listen close."

TIFFANY: He told me, he was going to do something to my face. You try forgetting something like that.

NEIL: Tiffany, the son of a bitch was a pussycat. Those fat shmucks have to show the hair on their chest, make a little noise. You know, they think they got balls as big as the Ritz. One look at the stills and he coughed up his fifty grand and rolled over like a pet dog and that was that. The other guy, maybe he wanted a free piece, who knows?

TIFFANY: Domino told me she thought he was following her too—

NEIL: Domino forgot it, goddammit! She's cool and you better . . . Jesus. That was back in October. You gonna carry that around the rest of your life?

"Who's Domino?" Sharky asked.

"She's the joker Livingston was talkin' about," Friscoe said. "All along we figured it was this Neil and Tiffany, period. Now we know he's got another one in his stable. Listen . . ."

TIFFANY: Anyway, I think it's too soon to try it again.

NEIL: You let me decide that.

TIFFANY: Can't Domino do this one?

NEIL: Keep Domino out of this. What Domino and I do is none of your business. She ever bang your ear about what's happening with her? Hell, no, she doesn't.

TIFFANY: How come I get the dirty deals?

NEIL: (Pauses) Let me ask you, since when is twenty-five g's a dirty deal? It's passed. And this time we're going for bigger stuff, maybe a hundred big ones, Tif. You want to sneeze off your half of a hundred grand?

Silence.

NEIL: Now are you set up for tonight? I don't want you getting ants in your pants around Domino, got that straight? These two tonight, they're worth a bloody fortune. Diamond merchants from Amsterdam. They're throwing out fifteen hundred for the night. I don't want you doing a sad-ass on me. They may be back and that's big money for everybody.

TIFFANY: I'll be fine.

NEIL: Good. They'll pick you two up about eight-thirty in a limousine. Have a good time.

TIFFANY: Thanks.

NEIL: Later.

Friscoe switched the recorder off.

"Okay, there it is," he said. "The way we put it together, this Neil and the Tiffany broad took some Texas oil millionaire named Norman for fifty grand. They had pictures, who the hell knows what else? But they stuck it to him and now it sounds like they're getting ready for another round, only this time they're sniffin' after a hundred g's. Christ, that's just plain greedy."

"You got any idea who?" Sharky asked.

"Not the foggiest. But whoever it is, the way I see it, we let it start to come together, then we step in and maybe we can bust the whole lot."

"Who's this Domino?" Sharky asked.

"Another lady in the stable. All the while we figure it for a twosome, now all of a sudden up pops the devil and we got another one in the act."

"You think maybe she's got a scam working too?" Sharky said.

"Why not? It seems to be the season for it."

"Then let's go after her too," Sharky said. "Do we have a line on her."

"Yeah. Livingston and Papa dutched them the night they went out with the boys from Holland," said Friscoe, "then followed Domino home."

"We should all live that good," Livingston said. "A Caddy limo the size of a 747 picks them up. They hit Nikolai's Roof for dinner, dancing afterward at Krazz. The bill for the four of them must have been five hundred bucks."

Sharky whistled. "Maybe we're in the wrong business," he said and grinned. "I wonder if she'd give me about ten dollars worth?"

"Yeah," Papa said, "for ten bucks she'll goose ya."

"On your pay you can't even afford to smell it," said Friscoe.

"Maybe she'll take a dollar down and a dollar a week," Sharky joked.

"Look," Friscoe said, "I agree we need to go after the Domino broad too. I already got the office from Alvers. After I played that performance between Tiffany and Freaky Freddie, he was ready to give me permission to bug her church pew."

Sharky's mind was humming. He had survived on the street for eighteen months with instinct and little else.

Now every nerve ending was telling him that this Domino would provide a key, although he was not sure why. Perhaps because it had taken almost four weeks for her name to pop up. It seemed to him she was being well shielded and there had to be a reason.

"What we need," he said half to himself, "is a first class wireman. Somebody who can do it right. The apartment. The phone. The whole shooting match."

"Yeah, well, that's tough shit," said Friscoe. "All we got is what's down here in the dump. One lousy tape recorder and maybe a little help from the phone company to tap into her phone."

"I want the whole place," Sharky said.

"Good luck," Livingston said.

"I got just the guy for the job," Sharky went on. "He'll love it. It'll be a challenge."

"Who is this genius?" Friscoe asked.

"The Nosh," Sharky said.

"Who the fuck is The Nosh?"

"Larry Abrams. He's got everything we need. Voice-activated recorders. Mikes the size of your fingernail. FM preamps for the pickup. Let me tell you, The Nosh could plant a bug in a hummingbird's ass."

"So where do we find this wonder boy?" Friscoe asked.

"Right here in the House. He's in OC."

Friscoe rolled his eyes. He shook his head. "Forget it," he said forlornly, "Organized Crime is D'Agastino's outfit. That cheap guinea wouldn't loan us the dog shit on his shoes."

"The hell with D'Agastino," Sharky said. "The Nosh and I go back long before either of us was on the force. I can sneak him out long enough to get it done."

Friscoe thought about it for a few moments, then shrugged. "Look, it's your machine, see. We all figure, maybe you can bring something into it we can't. We've all been . . . you just get jaded after a while. You wanna do some dog-robbing here in the House it's okay with me. If the shit hits the fan, well . . . we'll all duck."

Sharky was thinking about The Nosh. Little Larry, fiddling around in the workshop in his garage, inventing gadgets that only he would ever use. He chuckled thinking about it.

"I tell you what we're gonna do. We're gonna be all over this Domino. Before we're through we'll know what she's *thinking*. Because The Nosh and I, we're going to put more wire in her place than an AT and T substation."

7

Sharky guided the gray Dodge Charger down through a squalid warehouse district known as the Pits and parked in front of a bleak, washed-out two-story brick building. He switched off the engine.

Livingston, sitting beside him in the front seat, slid down and lit a plastic-tipped cigar. "Welcome to Creepsville," he growled.

From the outside the building looked deserted. Weeds pushed through cracks in the sidewalk, water stains streaked its sides, a sign, ravaged by time and weather and barely readable, announced: For sale or lease. B. Siegel and Sons. The building had no windows, although here and there along its grimy face large squares of new brick indicated where several had been sealed up. Midway in the building was its only opening, a scarred, grim, ugly door with a single window covered

with steel mesh. It was electrically operated and everyone entered and left the building through this single for-
bidding portal.

"Looks like something you'd see in Russia. The *bad*
part of Russia," Livingston said.

The building housed the Organized Crime Division,
known as the OC, which was run by a pompous, taci-
turn political opportunist, Captain D'Agastino. Inside, a
maze of computers, readouts, photo lines, and electronic gadgetry connected the building, like a giant umbilicus, to the FBI.

"D'Agastino runs this place like the fuckin' CIA,"
Livingston said. "He doesn't do zilch for us out on the
street, him and that bunch of elitist shits."

"Bunch of assholes, you ask me," Papa volunteered
from the back seat.

They fell silent. Livingston stared up at the sky thick
with black, swarming clouds and blew a smoke ring
which wobbled through the air like a flat tire and fell
apart against the windshield.

"Gonna rain like a son of a bitch," he said.

More silence.

Sharky stared straight ahead, toying aimlessly with
the steering wheel.

"Thing is," Livingston said, "I don't trust any of
those turkeys in there."

Silence.

"Do you trust any of them, Papa?" he asked.

"Shit," Papa said with disgust.

Sharky picked lint from his suede pullover.

Livingston finally looked over at him.

"And this Abrams, he's a buddy of yours, hunh?"

Sharky nodded. "Yeah."

"Well, uh, how come you're so thick with somebody
in the goddamn OC?"

There it was, the big question. Sharky had felt it

coming. They were testing him. And why not? He was
the new kid on the block and already he was captain of
the ball club and bringing in his own pitcher.

Livingston blew another imperfect smoke ring,
watched it fall apart. "I heard that bastard D'Agastino
won't even consider you for the OC unless you'd turn in
your own mother. You hear that, Papa?"

"Anything you heard, I heard worse. I heard you
gotta pass the bad breath test just to get in the door."

Sharky started to burn, but he held his temper in
check.

"What've you heard there, Sharky?" Livingston said.

"Not much."

"Not much, hunh." More silence. Finally: "Wanna
tell us about this Abrams?"

Sharky did not answer immediately. What could he
tell them? That he and The Nosh, which is what he had
called Abrams since they were kids, were born across
the street from each other, grew up together, fought together, had even broken the law together? Should he
tell them about Red Ingles or the night the transmission
fell out? Shit. In high school Sharky and The Nosh had
befriended a grizzled, solitary alcoholic named Red Ingles who lived up the street from them. Ingles had a
singular talent; he souped up cars. Boy, did he soup up
cars. Ingles souped up cars the way a piano tuner
coaxed perfect pitch from the strings of an old baby
grand. The chromium touch, Sharky called it. Ingles
worked in his backyard, a backyard cluttered with battered old wrecks that looked as if they might fall apart
if you slammed the door too hard.

But under those tarnished, dented hoods, engines
gleamed with stainless-steel carburetors, chromium
headers, and glistening valve lifters. Ingles usually
worked on two cars at a time, interchanging parts and
tuning one against the other until the engines hummed

in perfect harmony. Then he gave The Nosh and Sharky five dollars apiece and told them to "take those Jessies and blow them mills out good." And he would settle back with his jar of still whiskey while they drove out to the river, poised fender to fender on hidden dirt roads, motors straining underfoot, and then took off, the engines whining and shivering in their mounts, speedometers inching up to 150 and 160 as they skimmed over the dirt, skittering at the very edge of disaster with that reckless and wonderful sense of indestructability reserved for the young.

They never asked what Red did with the cars. They didn't have to. At night they sneaked down to his place and lay under the shrubs, watching him negotiate with heavy-set men in galluses and sweaty felt hats, passing the fruit jar back and forth as they argued and cursed and ranted. Finally Red would smile and slam his hand down on the fender of the car in question and the good old boys would count out the price. In the morning the cars were gone. Sharky was certain that Red Ingles was the sole supplier of transportation for every moonshiner in North Georgia.

Then Ingles had made them an offer. He needed transmissions, tough transmissions. He would pay them seventy dollars for every working Corvette transmission they delivered to him. The Nosh was delighted. "I can drop a Vette transmission in fifteen minutes flat," he confided to Sharky and they went into business. They put roller skate wheels on a piece of plywood and once a week they borrowed the rumpled pickup Sharky's old man used at the hardware store and they cruised the dark streets, looking for prospects. When they found one, The Nosh rolled up under the car and dropped the transmission while Sharky sat behind the wheel of the pickup, ready to sound the horn in case of trouble. They were the toast of Grady High. The Nosh, barely five feet tall, became a ladies' man while Sharky, already a cocksman of some renown, became the Beau Brummel of Ponce de Leon Avenue. Then one night the owner of a brand new Stingray appeared suddenly and unexpectedly while The Nosh was toiling under his car. It was too late to blow the horn. The owner flicked a speck of dust off the trunk, kicked a tire, climbed in, revved up, and took off with his tires chewing up the pavment.

But no Nosh. He was caught under the Vette, his jacket hung up on the transmission, and he went right with the car, rocketing along on his plywood platform. When he finally tore himself loose, the platform flew out from under the Vette, sparks showering from the tortured roller skate wheels. It screamed down the street, hit a curb, and splintered, the wheels soaring off into the night while The Nosh was launched end over end into a fishpond.

Sharky ran to his side. A dazed, soggy Nosh staggered from the pool. And at that moment, with an anguished clatter, the transmission fell out of the Corvette. They ran to the pickup and took off down the street while the teary-eyed Corvette owner ran after them, hands waving wildly overhead.

"I don't ever want to take a ride like that again," The Nosh said.

"Right," said Sharky.

"Besides, I feel sorry for that guy."

"Me too."

"There's got to be an easier way to make a buck."

"Yeah."

And they quit.

So how come I'm so thick with The Nosh? Sharky thought. It was basic. They had grown up together, exchanged bloody noses and embarrassed apologies, got laid together, and had joined the cops together. Their roots went deeper than blood or family.

"I'll tell you," Sharky said, "we been asshole buddies almost since the day we were born. And I don't give a damn if he's in the OC, the PDQ, or the screw-you, it's okay with me."

Livingston puffed on his cigar. Papa cleared his throat but said nothing. Finally Livingston nodded. "Well, it ain't much detail, but it's sure clear as hell."

After a moment, Papa said, "Where did he get that crazy monicker?"

"It's Yiddish. Means to nibble, eat between meals. The Nosh is one hell of a nibbler. He can also fix plumbing, do carpentry, fix radios, cameras. Shit, he can do just about anything. And he just might be the best wireman that ever came down the pike."

Between puffs Livingston said, "Does he walk on water?"

Sharky laughed. "Probably. One of his ancestors did."

"Well, I just got to wonder, okay? I got to wonder how in hell he ever got tied in with that mother-humping piece of camelshit, D'Agastino."

"Like I said, he's the best wireman in the country. Maybe D'Agastino needed him."

"I don't care if he can bug running water. If he ain't white, Christian, six-feet tall, and don't wear pin-stripe suits and look like a goddamn stockbroker, he's in the wrong outfit."

Sharky pointed toward the door of the OC. "Does that look like a six-foot stockbroker to you?" he asked.

Larry Abrams, The Nosh, came out of the building, a short, boxy little man, a hair over five feet tall and almost as wide, wearing faded jeans, a blue work shirt, a suede jacket, and carrying a black tool box almost as big as he was. His thick black hair was longer than regulations permitted; he was wearing glasses a quarter-inch thick and his crepe-soled hiking boots were as muddy as they were ugly. The Nosh was grinning; he usually was.

Livingston looked shocked. *"He's* in the OC!"

"Jesus," Papa said, "there ain't much to him is there?"

Livingston watched the little man approach the car. "Amazing," he said, "everything in the world that fuckin' D'Agastino hates. He's Jewish, he's too short, his hair's too long, he's overweight, his shoes are dirty, he's smiling, he's dressed like a janitor, and he looks human."

The Nosh leaned against the door of the car. "Hey, Shark, what's up?"

"Any problems with D'Agastino?"

"Nah. I told him I had to go over and do a trick for the FBIs. That's the magic word in the fortress there. You say *FBI,* everybody wets their pants."

"Hop in."

The Nosh crawled into the back seat and Sharky introduced him around.

"Where we headed?" The Nosh asked.

"Moneyville. Lancaster Towers," Sharky said.

The Nosh whistled through his teeth. "Who we after?"

"A very pretty lady," Livingston said.

"Aww," The Nosh said, "I hate to pick on pretty ladies."

Livingston turned sideways in his seat so he could look at Abrams as he talked. "Me too, but this lady happens to be a very high class hooker whose pimp just shook fifty g's out of a Texas oilman. We think she may be involved in a new scam and this time the stakes may be even higher. What we'd like is to wire up her place like a Christmas package and see what we can turn up."

"What kind of set-up?"

"Nobody's been inside yet. You know the Lancaster Towers?" said Livingston.

"I've driven by it, never been inside."

"Okay, what we got is twin towers, twelve stories each, an east tower and a west tower. They're connected at the third floor by a terrace that runs between them. Swimming pool, bar, that sort of thing. The parking garage is below ground-level, three stories, with a gate that's activated by one of those plastic coded cards. Visitor parking on ground level. Both buildings have security guards. She's in 10-A, facing the east wing. We been checking her number for the past hour or so and her machine answers."

The Nosh nodded. "She could be up there doing a number."

"We considered the possibility," Sharky said.

The Nosh said, "We can give the door a rattle. If she answers, we tell her we're checking the TV cable, something like that."

"Sounds good," Livingston said. "We also have the security guards. I'd like to keep this in the family, but I don't see any way to get past them without showing our hand."

The Nosh smiled and opened his tool chest. It was meticulously arranged. Wire, diodes, phonejacks, screws, nuts and bolts of all sizes, miniature amplifiers, microphones, and tape recorders, all were neatly fitted into the case. A tray on top contained tools of all kinds and, arranged neatly in one corner, two Baby Ruth bars, a box of Good n' Plenty and a coconut Twinkie. The Nosh opened a drawer and took out a bundle of business cards. Leafing through them, he stopped and smiled. "Here we go," he said. "We're from the elevator inspection department. That's city. Suppose we, uh, suppose we're doing a stress check on the elevators. We'll be in and out for the next couple days."

"What's a stress check?" Papa asked.

"Hell, I don't know," The Nosh said, "but it sounds good."

They all laughed.

Papa stared at the candy bars. "I got a weight problem," he said. "You got a weight problem?"

"I can put on a couple pounds driving past a deli," The Nosh said.

"I gain weight readin' recipes," Papa said.

"Wanna split a Baby Ruth?"

"Love it."

He cut one of the candy bars in two and gave Papa the larger half. Livingston turned back to Sharky. "It's love at first sight," he said. "They'll be engaged before the weekend's over."

"Here it comes," Sharky said as raindrops began pummeling the windshield.

"You mind I ask you a personal question?" Livingston said to The Nosh.

"Shoot."

"How the hell you ever get in the fuckin' OC?"

The Nosh giggled. "It was because of the Feds," he said. "I was workin' radio maintenance down in Central and one day this FBI named Weir shows up and he's lookin' for somebody can really do a number on an automobile, so they loaned me to him. What it was—you remember that Mafia guy, Degallante, retired down here about a year ago?"

"Sure," Livingston said, "he got deported."

"Well, not exactly. That's what the Feds are puttin' out. What really happened, the FBIs figure Degallante is not really retired. He's down here maybe to get his foot in the door and they wanted to pin something on him, only they were striking out all over the place. So they decide maybe if they bugged his car he might, y'know, be doin' business there and they could get something on him. A big black Lincoln limo. I hung around the Lincoln place until they brought the car in for service and I wired it front to back. The first tape we pulled, you wouldn't believe it," and he began to giggle. "What it was, the old bastard had his son-in-law giving him head in the back seat."

There was a moment of stunned silence before everybody laughed.

"No shit, there he was cruising down the interstate and his daughter's husband is blowing him. Well, Weir takes the tape out to Degallante's place on West Wesley Road and they're all sitting around the living room finessing each other out and Degallante is telling them how he's not connected anymore and he's retired and they can get lost and then Weir turns on the tape recorder. Thirty seconds and the old man throws up all over the floor and Weir tells him what they're gonna do, they're gonna give copies to *The New York Times, Time* magazine and *Playboy*. A month later he was back in Sicily and the whole family was with him and that's the way it really happened."

"So how did you get in the OC?" Papa said.

"Weir told D'Agastino and D'Agastino drafted me. I got a workshop in the basement. He never sees me, I don't see him. We're both very happy about the arrangement."

Sharky turned into Lindburgh Drive and headed toward Peachtree Street. The two white buildings loomed through the rain like stark, windowed tombstones.

"How much time we gonna need?" Sharky asked The Nosh.

"Not long. We give the place a quick wash, decide where we want the buttons, then plant 'em. I want to see the roof first, maybe set up a listening post up there.

I'd say fifteen, maybe twenty minutes and we'll be out."

"You're on," Sharky said.

"Papa and I can recognize her," Livingston said. "How about I stay in the car so I can spot her when she comes in? Papa can ride the elevator, slow her down if he has to."

"That's the play, then," Sharky said.

They parked the car. Sharky, Papa, and The Nosh entered the building. The security guard, a large white-haired man with a wasted body lost in an oversized uniform and a seamed face, was sitting in a small office reading *The National Enquirer*. The Nosh laid the card on the desk in front of him.

"I'm Friedman, city inspection department. We're doing a stress check on your elevators," he said. "We'll be in and out of the place here for the next couple of days."

The guard looked at the card and reached for the telephone. "I better check the main office," he said.

"You didn't get the letter?" The Nosh said quickly.

"I didn't get no letter," the guard said, his hand resting on the phone.

"Well, your main office got the letter. We already checked with them."

"Hell," the old man said. "I sit here on my duster all day, nobody tells me shit."

"Ain't it the truth. We're always the last ones to know, right?"

The guard relaxed. He had found company for his tarnished ego. "Sure is the way. The workin' man is always the last one to know anything. Well, I go on Social Security in six months. After that they can all dip their wick in the mashed potatoes for all I care. You need any help?"

"Is the door open onto the roof?"

"Yep."

"Then we're in business. Tell you what, we'll leave Johnson here in the elevators. That way, if we have to shut down for a minute or two he can calm down the residents."

"I appreciate that. I get enough crap as it is. People ain't happy if they ain't bitchin' about something."

"Keep the card so the night man'll know we're here, okay? Don't want anybody takin a shot at us." The Nosh winked at him.

"Gun ain't loaded anyway."

They got on the elevator.

"There's a guy got the wrong end of the chicken all his life," Papa said. He looked at The Nosh. "You coulda been a pretty good conman."

"He *is* a pretty good conman," Sharky said.

They got off at twelve. Papa said, "Keep in touch," as the elevator doors hushed shut. Sharky and The Nosh went up to the roof, surveying it through a hard, slanting rain. "Over there," said the Nosh, "that concrete blockhouse." They ran through the rain to the concrete shed in the middle of the roof and entered it. It was a single room, fairly warm and spotless. Fluorescent tubes flickered overhead, shedding uncertain light on a row of humming motors. On the wall facing the motors was a bank of power and water meters.

"Perfect," The Nosh said.

"What are we doin' up here?" Sharky asked.

"What we're gonna do, we're gonna set us up a listening post in here, okay? The mark is only two floors down so we can use wireless mikes." He opened the tool chest and took out an object no larger than a button which was attached by a single wire to a rectangular box about the size of a disposable cigarette lighter. A pin protruded from the back of the button. It looked like a thumbtack.

"This is the mike," The Nosh said, "and the little box

is the amplifier. We preset the amplifier to a specific
frequency and it can be picked up by this miniature FM
tuner." The tuner lay in the flat of his hand. "Then I
plug this cassette deck into the tuner. It's voice-
activated. When anybody down there talks, the tuner
picks it up, the recorder turns on automatically, and it's
all on tape." The cassette deck was also miniaturized.
"I made it myself," The Nosh said. "Real simple. Only
one circuit."

"You could put the whole works in your pocket,"
Sharky marveled.

"Each mike has its own tuner and recorder. If she
walks from room to room talking, one recorder cuts in
when the other one cuts off. We'll plant the mikes in
each room." He pointed to a button on the tape decks.
"This is a monitor button. Push it down and you can
listen continuously. I also have a set of earphones I'll
leave up here which will help with the monitoring."

"Amazing," Sharky said. "Will it pick up anything
else?"

"Yeah, stereo, radio, like that. Not walking or normal room noises. But don't worry. Later on, see, we can
go in with a dip filter and erase the background noise.
What we do, we dip in there and set the filter for the
voice frequency, then—"

"Nosh?"

"Yeah?"

"You're telling me more than I want to know."

"Right."

He took out three tuners and recorders and fitted
them together and placed them in one corner of the
room behind the motors. "One more thing," he told
Sharky. "I got you a dozen or so cassettes and they're
clearly marked so you don't put 'em in backwards. The
tape's good for ninety minutes a side. There's a beep-

er on each tape which sounds off thirty-seconds before the end."

"Right."

"Okay, let's go down and see what we got on ten."

Sharky removed a walkie-talkie from a case attached to his belt. "This is Zebra One, we're leaving topside."

They found 10-A next to the elevators. Sharky rang the bell. Nothing. He rang it again and they waited. Still nothing. He knocked sharply on the door.

"Okay," The Nosh said, "let's do it."

He took a case from the tool chest and opened it. It contained a set of stainless steel needles varying in length from one to six inches. He studied the lock carefully, then selected one of the needles and, holding it between his thumb and forefinger, eased it into the keyhole, twisting it slowly as he did. It caught for an instant and The Nosh gave it a quarter-turn, felt it slip farther until it caught again. Another quarter-turn and the tumblers clicked. He smiled, stood up, and opened the door.

They moved in quickly and quietly, closing the door behind them, waiting, listening. There was not a sound. "Okay," Sharky said, "check it out." They went swiftly through the apartment, peering into each room. Empty. They returned to the small entrance hall by the front door and studied the layout. The living room was directly in front of them. On either side of it was a bedroom and bath. The dining room was immediately to their left and the kitchen was adjacent to it. A balcony connected the living room and the master bedroom to the right.

Sharky curled his tongue against his teeth and whistled softly.

"I'll give her one thing," he said. "She's got class."

The living room was done in beige and cream with pale mauve walls. A large Olympus beige-on-cream sofa faced them. It was several feet in front of the french doors, which opened onto the balcony, and half the width of the room. Two brown and beige striped Savoy chairs faced each other on each side of the sofa. A Porto Bello coffee table in antique white sat in front of the sofa and between the chairs. The vicuna rug was gray. There were plants all over the room, beside the french doors, in the corners and hanging from the ceiling, tall nephrolepis ferns, bottle palms, begonias, columnea, and spider plants. The stereo sat in a lowboy against one wall with the speakers in the ceiling.

The dining room had mirrored walls and a large smoked glass table with chromium and silk chairs.

"Shit, the furniture in here cost more than my house," The Nosh said.

"You take that bedroom and I'll check out the master," Sharky said. "We may run out of time."

The bed was king-sized and covered with a llama blanket. The wall behind it and the ceiling were mirrored. The rest of the furniture was white wicker with pale green cushions. An enormous Norfolk pine filled one corner of the room and several hanging baskets dominated the corner facing it. Sharky checked the drawers in the night tables. One contained a small bottle of pills, a vial of white powder, a silver cigarette case, and three vibrators of various sizes, one of which was shaped like an egg. Sharky tasted the powder, opened the cigarette case, smelled one of the cigarettes, and examined the pills.

"Hey Shark, c'mere," The Nosh called from the other room.

He put the pills back in the drawer and closed it. The other room contained a massage table over which was a light bar with four sunlamps aimed at the table. The two windows were stained glass. A pair of lovebirds cooed and kissed each other in a tall wicker cage that hung among the flowering baskets that dominated the room. A small marble-topped table covered with vials of oils and body creams sat beside the massage table. In one corner there were perhaps a dozen multicolored pillows of all sizes arranged on the floor and against the wall. Tropical fish peered bug-eyed from an enormous gurgling aquarium against the other wall. The fish stared at them, then darted soundlessly through dancing seaweed.

"It's Disney World, Sea World, and Jungle World, all wrapped up in one," The Nosh said with delight. "I could let the kids loose in here for hours."

"The table in there by the bed has some first-rate machine-rolled Colombian grass, Quaaludes, poppers, and some coke that must've cost a bill-and-a-half on the street."

"You ever get the feeling we're in the wrong business?" The Nosh said.

"Only when I'm awake," said Sharky. "Let's get it on."

"The plants are perfect," The Nosh said. He took one of the button-mikes and slipped the pin into the stem of a broadleafed calathea plant in a corner of the room. The mike faced the massage table. He ran the wire down along the stem of the plant, securing it with a roll of green tape. Then he pushed the aerial down into the soft earth and brushed loose dirt over it. He opened one drawer of the tool chest and took a small tube of green paint from among many multicolored vials and dabbed the mike until it blended into the plant. He stood up and smiled.

"That's it. This room is fixed."

"What if she waters the plants?" Sharky asked. "Won't it hurt that equipment?"

"Nope. All the stuff is coated with silicone. It's waterproof. Let's hit the living room."

He stood in the center of the room and snapped his fingers several times, checking the ambient sound. "Not bad," he said, "not bad at all. All the furniture, plants, that shit, deadens the room. We won't get too much bounce. But we gotta keep away from those speakers in the ceiling." This time he chose a ficus tree and jabbed the mike into the trunk, close to the dirt. He dabbed it with brown paint, whistling softly to himself as he buried the amplifier. Sharky stood on the balcony, trying to look down at the parking lot, but he could barely see it.

"Hey, Shark," The Nosh said, "you remember the time I bugged the teachers' lounge at Grady and we caught old man Dettman screwin' the phys ed teacher?"

"Are you kidding? That's how I passed geometry."

"I was just thinkin' how at the time we thought they were such degenerates. She was a real hunk, Shark. A real hunk." He smoothed dirt over the amplifier. "Lookin' back, I can't say I blame old Dettman."

"Maybe we should've worked out a trade-out with her. Who ever uses geometry anyway?"

"What was her name?"

"Old Torpedo Tits."

"No, her real name?"

"Jesus, I don't remember."

There was no way to see into the parking lot. He went back into the living room. "Old Torpedo Tits," The Nosh said, heading into the master bedroom.

Down below, a blue Mercedes 450SL drifted into the complex and stopped in front of the east tower. Sharky's walkie-talkie came to life.

"Zebra One, this is Zebra Three," Livingston said. "You got company."

"Okay Nosh, she's back," Sharky said. He pressed the button on his box. "Zebra Two, this is Zebra Three. We need a little time."

"You got it," Papa said.

A porter came out of the building, running through the rain, and held the door for her. She got out, a long silk-sheathed leg preceding her. She stood an inch taller than the porter as she slipped him a dollar.

"She's heading for the lobby," Livingston said. The Nosh was on his knees, dabbing paint on the mike. "I'm wrapping it up," he said.

Sharky started to leave the room, then went back to the night table. He opened the drawer, took one of the joints from the cigarette case, and dropped it in his pocket.

"Let's hustle, brother." The Nosh was checking out his case.

"I'm missing a paintbrush," he said. "It's gotta be right around these plants somewhere."

"Shit," Sharky said.

Papa had seen the blue Mercedes pull up in front of the apartment, watched as she got out carrying a large Courrèges bag, tipped the porter, and then walked through the rain. He pressed several buttons on one elevator and sent it up, then waited in the other one. She entered the building, smiling at the security guard, walking with her chin slightly raised, looking straight ahead with azure eyes that glittered with life. She was taller than he remembered and very straight and as she approached the elevator she looked straight at Papa, but her gaze seemed to go through him, past him, off someplace beyond him. Papa was suddenly embarrassed, not from tension, but because she was probably the most stunning creature he had ever seen.

Jesus, he thought, *no wonder she gets six bills a pop.*

She stopped, hesitating a moment at the elevator that was already going up. "Going up," Papa said. "We're just checking this one out."

"Thank you."

A voice like down feathers.

She stood beside him.

The back of Papa's neck got very warm. "What floor?"

"Ten, please."

He pressed the button and the doors closed. The elevator started up. Papa shifted slightly so his body shielded the control buttons and, reaching out very cautiously, he pressed the stop button. The elevator glided to a halt.

"Oh, no!" she breathed.

Papa pressed the button on his walkie-talkie.

"Say, uh, up there, uh, this here's Johnson. I got a passenger, uh, and, uh, like the power just cut off."

"Is something wrong?" Delicately.

"Nah," Papa said, "they just shut us off there for a second. Don't you worry none, little lady." His walkie-talkie came alive. It was Sharky's voice.

"Uh, yeah, sorry about that, Johnson, we, uh, just had to, uh, reset the flatistan up here. Uh, it's okay now, uh, you can crank it up again."

Papa pushed the ten button and the elevator started up again.

"Sorry about that," Papa said.

She smiled at him, looking directly into his eyes.

"It's perfectly all right."

Hardly more than a whisper. Papa felt a thrill like he had not felt for many years.

"Nice weather," he stammered for lack of something better to say.

She laughed. "Yes. I love the rain."

Beautiful, Papa thought, *nice weather all right. There's a typhoon outside.*

The elevator slowed to a stop and the doors slid open. Sharky and The Nosh were standing there. Domino looked first at The Nosh and then at Sharky. She stared at him for a fraction of a second and then her lips parted very slightly in a smile.

"Hello," she said as she walked past him.

Sharky was immobilized, nailed to the floor, stunned as though he had been clubbed. It was more than her elegance, her beauty, something else. A softness he had not expected, a vulnerability he sensed, in her eyes and the softness of her voice. The Nosh had to pull on his sleeve to get him into the elevator. Her scent was still there. He watched her until the doors closed.

"Okay," The Nosh said, "we're in business. We go back on the roof, check everything out, and then maybe we swing by Taco Bell, grab a quick burrito supreme."

Papa smiled. "You got my vote."

But Sharky did not hear either of them. He was like a statue, staring at the closed door. In just a few seconds Domino had claimed a new victim.

8

DeLaroza was hunched down in the rear of the power launch. A forgotten Havana twirled unlit between his fingers. He stared straight ahead, a man hypnotized by his own thoughts, as the boat moved toward the northern end of the lake.

Suddenly his concentration was jarred by a speedboat which charged from a nearby inlet, skipping like a stone across the choppy surface of the lake. He watched through cold eyes as the boat arced wide around them and sped south, its engine buzzing like an angry bee, the driver perched on his haunches at the stern.

By the time the surly north wind had whipped the speedboat's wake into frothy whitecaps, DeLaroza was deep in thought again, repeating over and over a single word:

"*Gowmanah . . . gowmanah . . . gowmanah . . .*"

It was a form of Shinto meditation he had learned in Japan. In a few seconds the intrusion was forgotten. He was entranced, his mind cleansed.

Once his concentration was purged, he dealt with the problem at hand as he dealt with all problems. His method had been developed thirty years before in Brazil, where he had spent five years and a fortune becoming Victor DeLaroza and developing a personality that fit the man he created. These had been the difficult years, the dangerous years just after the war, when his constant companions had been paranoia and fear. It was the Jews he feared most, for they could have become the unwitting instrument of a cruel and ironic joke. The Nazis had come to Brazil, seeking anonymity, trying to rebuild their failed dream. And behind them came the Jewish commandos, cold, efficient, zealously checking every record, perusing all newcomers, methodically rooting out war criminals. And always there was the gnawing fear that they might tumble onto him by accident. He was a man wary of every footfall, suspicious of all strangers. The fear of surprise was a worm in his gut. To avoid surprises, he learned to predict them before they happened. His reflexes became as swift and deadly. He lied when necessary, bribed when expedient, arranged murder when he had to, a ruthless survivalist, as he moved on to Hong Kong, where he *was* Victor DeLaroza, the international businessman who destroyed competitors, sucked up companies, and built his empire.

His method was always the same. First, cleanse the mind of all emotional or personal considerations—they weakened logic; second, feed the facts into the mental computer; third, consider all alternatives, options, dangers. Once this was done, logic released the solution from his brain.

Sitting in the rear of the launch, he considered the

facts. He was safe, safer than he had been for thirty years. They had lured Corrigon to Atlanta and eliminated him, and with him the last danger of recognition. His partner was about to leave the country but DeLaroza no longer felt he needed him. In Yokohama friends in the Yakuza were waiting to take care of that problem. Hotchins was no longer the dark-horse candidate. With Lowenthal and his people on the team Hotchins would become a serious contender and eventually the favorite.

Now only Domino posed a threat. No, more than a threat, she was dangerous. She could connect DeLaroza to Hotchins and possibly Corrigon to DeLaroza. Unwittingly she could tie the noose that would hang them all.

Those were the facts. The logic? Hotchins did not love the girl; he was obsessed by her sensuality. But he had made his decision clear that morning and although he had promised to consider giving her up, DeLaroza knew *all* the hungers that go with power. Like all self-made men, Hotchins was fiercely protective of his independence. In the end he would deal with the Domino situation emotionally and DeLaroza knew he could press the issue no further.

For he also knew Hotchins's passion to become president.

The conclusion was obvious.

His mind made up, DeLaroza leaned forward, cupping his hands against the chill breeze, and lit the cigar.

"Chiang," he called to his bodyguard and the Chinese turned to him. In addition to his powerful build Chiang had a scar running from his hairline down the right side of his face, across his eye to his jaw. The eye dropped from the old wound, half-closed, and the pupil had turned almost white. It added another dimension to his imposing size. "We must put the cover over the seats back here," DeLaroza said in Chinese. "It is too cold for open riding."

Chiang nodded and DeLaroza knew it would be done before the day ended. DeLaroza had saved Chiang from a prison in Macao almost ten years before. Now no task was too menial or too demanding: Chiang had devoted his life to DeLaroza.

Twenty miles north of the marina the lake narrowed and the current became stronger. A mile or so ahead there was a steady rumble as the river emptied into the lake. It was a desolate area and rarely traveled. The launch slowed, swung easily around a tree-scarred peninsula. A cove emerged in front of them and at its far end, partially obscured by tall pines, the curious geometry of a Chinese junk appeared. Its polished stern rose high above the water, sloping gently toward the bow. Its tall masts were partially obscured by spidery burnt-orange sails which were furled tightly against them. The cabin was slightly astern, its roof bordered by a frieze of temple dogs and dragons that curled around the cornice.

Chiang guided the launch expertly alongside a small pontoon dock that was lashed to the side of the junk and quickly tied it down. Then he helped DeLaroza out of the launch. The big man slowly mounted the jacob's ladder to the deck and stood for a few moments admiring his treasure. The deck and cabin glistened with teak oil that had been hand-rubbed into every crevice and pore. The paint, although old, was perfectly preserved. He called her *Psalm-Lo,* The Three Devils, after the legend of the dragons.

DeLaroza looked at Chiang and pointed below decks. *"Hai,"* Chiang answered.

DeLaroza knew that the three Orientals who manned the junk despised the *Gwai-lo,* the foreign devil, who was living on board, although they would never say anything to DeLaroza. They had been his servants, his

bodyguards, his soldiers, for many years. Each was a
master of karate; each was an expert at Tai Chi, the
Way of the Peaceful Warrior; each had a deadly profi-
ciency with the dagger and the *yinza,* a small steel disc
the size of a silver dollar with twelve barbs around its
perimeter which when scaled with the flick of a powerful wrist could pierce the skull and drive deep into the
brain. And each of them religiously followed the ancient
rituals of his ancestors. To them the *gwai-lo* was a cow-
ard who killed without honor.

DeLaroza went below. The cabin was divided into
three sections. Below the foredecks each member of the
crew had his own quarters and behind them, toward the
stern, was the galley. To the rear, under the lofty stern,
were two bedrooms, one decorated in modern decor,
the other with antiques smuggled out of Kowloon to
avoid the new laws that prohibited the removal of historic artifacts from the crown colony. The living room
was a museum: teak and rosewood chests with sculptured gold handles and hinges; sofas and chairs covered
with thin-striped silk from the finest shops on Pearl
Street; hand-painted mandarin screens dating from the
dynasty of the boy emperor Ping, eight hundred years
ago; delicate Royal Doulton porcelain figures, jade statues, and Lalique crystal.

Against one wall was a mahogany cabinet with glass
doors and inside, displayed against purple velvet, were
several ancient weapons: a jewel-encrusted samurai
sword; an awkward blunderbuss with an ornate buttplate and a curious swirling hammer; several daggers,
their worn blood gutters hinting of dark deeds from the
clouded past.

DeLaroza stood quietly in the darkened room looking for—who was he now? His partner had had so many
names through the years that DeLaroza sometimes had
difficulty remembering who he was from day to day

Howard? Yes, Howard Burns, that's what he again called himself.

At least I have been consistent in my own alias, DeLaroza thought.

The junk moved gently in the water. The screens muffled the sounds of the lake, the water slapping against the hull, the dock nudging the side, timbers groaning underfoot. But the cabin was still.

And yet DeLaroza knew he was there, could sense that deadly presence and smell the odor of death that seemed to exude from his partner's every pore.

"Howard?" he said, peering into the dark corners of the cabin.

There was no answer. But there was a stirring, a shifting of shadows, and then he saw the eyes, gleaming, alert, cold, the eyes of a snake. Burns moved into the light filtering through the portholes and DeLaroza sensed that he was in the presence of a man verging on madness. His gaunt face reflected a lifetime of killing. His thin, veined fingers were taut. A muscle in his jaw jerked with the beat of his pulse. He had a stubble of gray beard and the nostrils in his hawklike nose twitched, like a predator sniffing out his prey.

In one hand he held a .22 caliber Woodsman, its long, slender barrel encased in the ugly silencer.

Burns said nothing. He moved slowly into the center of the cabin, his eyes darting feverishly.

He stepped closer to DeLaroza and held the gun an inch from his heart, his eyes afire with rage.

"Bang," he shouted and an icy hand squeezed DeLaroza's heart. "You're an inch from being dead," he said. "Next time don't keep me hangin' like that. I ain't heard shit from you in almost a week."

DeLaroza stared down at the gun. "Don't make jokes," he whispered.

"You think I'm joking?" He waved the pistol around,

backed into the shadows. "You think I'm *joking?* Stuck out here with these goddamn slant-eyed creeps of yours. They don't ever talk. Move around like mice. Half the time I can't hear them, don't know where the hell they are. I got the willies. They're all the time doin' this weird slow-motion shit, moving around on one leg, like a bunch of faggot ballet dancers. The TV ain't worth a shit. All I get on this fuckin' radio is static . . ."

He lashed out suddenly, smashing the pistol into the loudspeaker of the radio, which flew off into the corner and crashed in the shadows. An instant later the hatch opened and Chiang stood above them, glaring down, his fingers stiff at his side. Burns aimed the pistol at the Chinese.

"Get outa here. Tell that gook to get lost or—"

DeLaroza held a hand toward Burns and turned quickly to Chiang. *"Jaaw hoy! Jaaw hoy,"* he said quickly and the Chinese disappeared. He turned to Burns. "Easy."

"Don't tell me easy," Burns roared. His face flushed, his eyes danced from corner to corner, back to DeLaroza, over to the hatch door. "They're pushin' me around the bend, them gook monkeys of yours."

"When they move like that, what you call slow motion, they are practicing Tai Chi, the Way of the Peaceful Warrior it is called."

Burns wiggled the gun under his nose. "They come around me, fuck with me, I'll make peaceful warriors outa them."

"To attack them is like attacking water. When you strike them, it is like striking air. They cannot be hurt and they cannot be stopped when they are committed. They can kill with one finger. And they have been ordered to protect you at all costs."

"I protect myself. Me and Betsy here is all the protection I need. The bullets are soaked in garlic, know what that means? It's poison inside you. You die screaming for your mother."

A shiver rippled through DeLaroza.

"Please. Everything is good. Believe me, I've been very busy, very busy. I do not want to use the mobile radio; it could be dangerous. From now on I'll come every other day . . ."

"From now on! How the hell long? . . ." Burns's shoulders slumped. He dropped the gun with a clatter on a polished rosewood chest and rubbed the knuckles of one hand furiously into the top of his close-cropped hair. "It was only gonna be a month, gettin' this show on the road. Christ, I been here what, eight weeks? Nine? Don't fuck me over, you got it? *Don't fuck me over*."

"Nobody is fucking you over, Howard. It takes time to get passports, visas, make the proper arrangements. Your wife is safe, we moved her to Canada, then across to the coast, and then on over to Yokohama. Nobody knows. Even the FBI lost her. It was done perfectly, as promised."

"Yeah, well, it ain't perfect with me. Twice you ask me to do a job for you, twice in what?—the thirty years I've known you? Both times I come through." He snapped his fingers. "Just like that. Quick, right? Clean, right? Everything down to a tee. Now you got this thing to do for me, it's a month of Sundays already."

He paced the room on the balls of his feet, tense and alert, like a prizefighter stalking his opponent. His nerves were stretched out like violin strings. DeLaroza could almost hear them keening.

"This ain't my turf, okay. I don't even know where the hell I am, out here, some fuckin' lake, eighty miles from nowhere. Nothin' to do all day but listen to those fuckin' monkeys doin' that slow-motion shit. It's a . . . I'll tell you what, it's a goddamn bad dream come true is what it is. Get me outa here. Get me outa here, Victor."

Madness burned in Burns's eyes. There was hate there, and fear. DeLaroza could see it. He was a different man from the cool killer in Hong Kong.

"You and this nut idea, wantin' to put your fuckin' mug in every paper in the world. Lemme tell ya, pal, I didn't mind doin' that job for you in Hong Kong, I could understan', see, how you could go a little off the wall when you seen that Colonel from Italy. But suckin' Corrigon in, plantin' that seed in his brain, and bringin' him down here, right in your own fuckin' back*yard,* that was crazy. Suppose he told somebody else, hunh? Suppose he wrote it down somewheres to cover himself? You ever think of that?"

"There was no reason for him to do that. You think he *knew* we were setting him up?" DeLaroza said.

"After thirty years, a guy gets prison wise, learns a lot. I'm just sayin' we coulda left it alone. We didn't have to wiggle the finger, get him down here and kayo him just so's you could come outa the closet after all these years. Shit, you got the fuckin' tenderloin, you gotta have it all?"

"You do not understand what it was like, all those years, all I have done, and no recognition for any of it."

"I unnerstan' this, pal, all that what you done you're so proud of? It started with the rip-off. I don't care if you made fifty billion, see, you couldna done it without the four mil we took off Uncle Sam. Any way you slice it, you and me we're both thieves. And a gonif's a gonif. A genius gonif, maybe, but a gonif all the same. You ain't changin' that by puttin' your fuckin' picture in the papers."

"There is no way for you to comprehend what it has been like for me. All these years, hiding my face, letting others take the credit, give the interviews . . ."

"Hey, I been in a closet myself there, seven years now. Don't tell me what it's like, livin' with your face to the wall. All I'm sayin' is that pushin' over Corrigon, that wasn't necessary. I done it, okay?, but that wasn't part of our deal, see, that was a personal gift, me to you, got that?"

"Howard, for thirty years I have lived in fear of the day Corrigon got out of prison. Wondering whether I might turn around in an airport one day and find myself face to face with him."

"He wouldna recognized ya, not after all that time."

"I never would have been sure. And if he had recognized me, you would have suffered too."

"Yeah, yeah, yeah, yeah, ya made the point. Okay. Look, whaddya want from me, anyways? Ya think it was easy, phonyin' up my own death a *second* time? My old lady still ain't made sense outa the whole thing. Point is, it's done, okay? Corrigon is caput. Now I want outa here!"

"Very soon, now, I promise you."

A thin line of sweat formed at the edge of Burns's brow. It began to inch down his forehead. He wiped it with the back of his hand.

DeLaroza walked cautiously to the chest and picked up the gun by the barrel. Burns turned as fast as a hummingbird, took two steps, reached out, and grabbed the pistol, twisting it sharply in toward DeLaroza's body and snapping it out of his hand.

"Don't touch my piece. You got that? That clear? Nobody touches my piece."

"Of course, of course."

Burns slid the gun back under his arm.

"I was just, uh, you see this chest is six hundred years old—"

Burns cut him off. "Fuck the chest. I don't give a shit, Moses stored the tablets in it. When am I movin', gettin' outa this fuckin' scow? Away from them Chinks?"

"A few more days."

"Shit!"

"Just a few more days, Howard."

"Too long!"

"It's the passport, Howard. It's going to be clean, no strings. You will never again have problems. This is all being done right for you."

Burns leaned against the wall and breathed hard through his nose. He wiped his mouth with his hand, pinched his nose several times.

"Too old for this kinda shit, anyhow," he said.

"I know, I know."

Burns looked up at him and said quickly. "It don't mean I lost my touch. I mean, don't go blowin' smoke rings up your ass, you think I ain't what I used to be."

"I didn't say anything about that, Howard."

"I like things to happen quick. No bullshit, see? I'm on the run. You don't get that, do you there, Victor?"

"Of course."

No, he didn't understand. Victor had it made, all the aces. But him, he had spent years developing one cover, losing it, and now he was starting again dodging from rock to rock like a fox with the hounds snapping at his heels. DeLaroza had offered a chance, a chance to get out for good. But the closer it got, the more terrified he became. His insides were burning, his guts grinding with turmoil.

Burns sighed and leaned against the bulkhead, breathing deeply through his mouth. Tears gathered in the corners of his eyes.

"Easy, my friend. I promise you, you're almost out."

"Yeah, yeah, I hope so. Hope so."

"Have you, uh . . . you aren't taking . . . pills?"

Burns's eyes jumped back and glared at DeLaroza.

"So what. What if I did? Yeah, I had a little shot there, took a red, one stinkin' red to get started this morning. Any of your business?"

"Of course not, I—"

"You're big time there, ain't you, Victor? Get all that nookie, that's your reds, Vic, hunh? Right? I pop a red, get a little shot, you get your ashes hauled. Same dif, same dif."

He rubbed a wrist with the palm of his hand, then shook the hand as though it might have fallen asleep.

"Feelin' better," he said. "I just got the willies, okay? I'm tellin' you, Victor." He lowered his voice, stepping so close to DeLaroza the garlic on his breath almost brought tears to the big man's eyes. "It's them fuckin' gooks is what it is. Could you, maybe tell 'em to knock off that slow-motion shit while I'm here? It's makin' me whacko. I'm off the wall, see?"

"I'll have a talk with them. It is a discipline, Howard. A thing they must do each day. But I will tell them to do it in the forward cabins, not in front of you if it upsets you."

"It upsets me, okay. Upsets the shit outa me."

DeLaroza nodded.

"Y'see, I ain't used to this. Cooped up here and all. Not used to it at all. Goddamn, I'd give anything for, y'know, a day at the track. Watch the ponies, lose a few bucks, win a few bucks. Maybe catch the Jets, watchin' Namath throw that ball. See what I mean, I gotta have some action, not sit here, listenin' to the fuckin' water grow."

DeLaroza moved away from him, sat down in a chair on the opposite side of the cabin and lit his cigar, which had gone out. *Now was the time*, he thought, but he had to handle the situation carefully. Perhaps it was too volatile. Perhaps Burns was too hyper.

"You mind?" Burns said.

"I beg your pardon?"

"The cigar, do ya mind? It smells like a fuckin' cow-turd burnin', Victor. Jesus, it's close enough in here."

"I'm sorry."

"Yeah, okay. It's I don't like boats, see? All I need is to get seasick. Puke my guts out, that's all I need."

"It's just a lake."

"I don't like *boats!*" His voice rose again, near hysteria.

"I understand, I understand."

"Jesus, I don't like to be this way, y'know." Burns shook his head. "I like everything easy, no hassle. Slick ice. I'm sorry, okay?"

"Of course. I was thinking . . ." He paused, trying to word the proposition just right.

"Yeah?"

"We have a situation. Something has come up. If you, uh, felt up to it. It could, uh, you could stay busy for a day or two. No. No, it's not a good idea. Forget it."

"Forget what? You ain't told me anything to forget."

"A bad idea."

"You wanna tell me about it? Let me decide?"

"It's the girl."

"What girl?"

"I told you about the girl. Domino."

"The one you and Hotchins share. That one?"

"It is not exactly like that. He knows nothing about the woman and me."

Burns laughed hard. He sat down next to DeLaroza and slapped his knee several times. "That's rich, that is. You and him fuckin' the same broad and he's not in on it. I'll tell you somethin', Victor. You got some kind of funny balls, you do."

"The problem is not funny."

"It is to me. You ever hear of Angel Carillo? Big don

in Philly, maybe *the* big don in Philly. No? Well, you
don't read much, because Angel makes the headlines
now and then. He had an arm, name of Donny Duf-
field, Irish punk but a good arm. Very quick. He did a
hit, it was no planning. He'd just go out, do it, go have a
beer. Anyways, Donny introduces Angel to this broad
which Donny has been punchin' since high school. A
real looker. And Angel gets a thing for her, starts takin'
her out, buyin' her shit, clothes, jewelry, the old wham
bam. Sets her up in this cushy apartment. And all the
time Donny is giving her the old squirtaroo on the side.
I mean Angel is maybe gettin' it once, twice a week;
Donny, he's over there dippin' in morning, noon, and
night. You know those goddamn micks, got a hard-on
thirty-six hours a day. So Angel finds out about it and
he muscles Donny down to the old ice house there and
he says to him, 'Whaddya mean, you're fuckin' my girl?'
And Donny says, 'Whaddya mean, "your girl"? I was
fuckin' her long before you.' And Angel says, 'Yeah,
but she's my girl now.' And he takes out the old stiletto
and whacko, clean as a whistle, he takes off Donny's
cock and balls. 'Okay,' Angel says when he's through,
'you want her, you got her.' And like that he gives her
back to Donny, who has to piss through a hole in his
belly. Funny, hunh? What a sense of humor." Burns
leaned back in his chair and laughed again.

DeLaroza rubbed gooseflesh from his arm. "I really
don't see the analogy," he said.

"You don't make the connection, hunh?"

"I seriously doubt that Donald Hotchins would cas-
trate anyone."

"Ah, what ya mean, you take me literally there. No, I
ain't sayin' he'd do it in so many words. But what's the
dif between him and Angelo Carillo? They both of them
are heavy hitters there, Victor. You don't take from
them. Angel, he does his own cuttin'. Hotchins gets it

done for him. Maybe in a different way, see. But the
end result, that's the same. Like they say, don't fuck
with Matt Dillon, he's got the biggest gun. I was you,
I'd back off."

"That is not the problem. I cannot tell him about her.
That she is a prostitute, I mean. After all, I introduced
them. There is too much at stake here."

"So let him dump on her. Lemme tell you something,
partner. You better stay outa the picture. You better be
the man that wasn't there, you know what I mean?"

"I just give advice."

"And money," Burns said viciously.

"Yes, money. This man is going to be the next president."

"I don't get you, Victor. What's in all this for you?
Takin' these chances. You were afraid Corrigon would
make you, somebody else could too. All this so you can
call the White House when you get the urge? Big deal."

"It is what I want. What do you want? To walk free,
yes? To put the past behind you. I have done that already. We have played a different kind of game, you
and I."

"I played the only game I knew. The spots, there,
they come on the leopard."

"Well, you will get what you want, finally."

"I'm still busy cleanin' up, Victor. I'll never walk free
again. The onus was on me before I ever met you. It
started when I was a kid. You think they ever let you
off the hook? Shit, the only way you get out, they take
you away feet first, throw roses in your face. All they
gotta do, somebody sees my face one time and every
pistol in the fuckin' country's after me. You think them
years in Nebraska was easy, livin' like a goddamn shirt
salesman? All I want is to be covered until I get lost
again, see what I mean? Go someplace, sit in the sun,
get freckles. I'm fifty-six, I ain't got all that much time

left. But I wanna use what I got. I want the rest of it to
be good, see? It ain't gonna be easy now, keeping the
Feds *and* the Family from tumblin' on to me. Thing is,
what's all these millions you parlayed for us gonna do
for me, I can't enjoy it, right?"

DeLaroza toyed with the cigar.

"There's something else about all this," he said.

"Oh, yeah? How's that?"

"She knows something. She saw you with Corrigon
that night. She was leaving my place."

"She saw me hit Corrigon?"

"No. After. Putting him in the car."

"But she saw me?"

"I do not think, honestly, that she can recognize
you."

"Ho ho. Bullshit there." Burns's eyes narrowed. His
breath hissed through clenched teeth. "She saw me. She
saw me."

"It was dark. It could have been—"

"She saw me." Burns stood up and paced the cabin.
He rubbed his wrist again and then snapped his hand.
"Okay, so they turn up Corrigon. Sooner or later they'll
probably turn him up, know what I mean? Maybe even
figure out who he is. Then they put his picture in the
paper. She recognizes *him*, see. She leads them to the
scene. Your front door. And then she starts doin' the
mug books. Maybe she didn't see me, but then maybe
she saw enough there, to make me from the pictures."
He turned and stood over DeLaroza. "See what I
mean? She could put me together with Corrigon at your
front door and there goes the fuckin' ballgame. You got
that picture there?"

DeLaroza nodded.

"I was, uh, I didn't want to worry you," DeLaroza
said.

"Oh, you didn't, hunh? Gonna let me sit around, wait till the building falls in on me?"

"It is both of us."

"I did the hit. Just like in Hong Kong that time. It was *me!*" Burns bellowed. "I'm the one they'll come squat on. You may go down the toilet there, Victor, but I get the gas pipe."

"Well," DeLaroza said and let the sentence hang.

"We got a saying in the rackets. The rope only has one noose. You know what I mean, Victor? I only got one neck. How many times you think they can stretch it? How come you wait so long to gimme this piece of news?"

"I just found out."

"When?"

"At noon."

"Jesus. I don't believe you. I don't fuckin' believe you. Here we got this broad can hang us both higher than the church steeple, you're still gettin' a little. You just finished tellin' me you don't know how to handle this here with Hotchins, you're dippin' the wienie. Jesus Christ!"

"It was not like that. I talked to her. Told her to step out of Hotchins's life. She is a threat to his future."

"Well, I'll bet she lapped that up with a fork all right."

"No, you are right. She did not lap it up with a fork."

"What do ya need, a picture book? They'll get ya every time. Ask Adam. Ask John the Baptist. Ask Samson. Ask 'em all, man. She's got a meal ticket. He goes to Washington, she goes along for the ride. Besides, that ain't the question here. You know what the question here is, Victor. Can she put it on us? Can she finger me for chilling Corrigon? And if the answer is maybe, that means the answer is yes."

DeLaroza said nothing. He wanted desperately to

light his cigar. Outside, the first deep rumble of thunder rolled across the sky.

"Listen to that. It's gonna rain like a son of a bitch," Burns said. He fell quiet. The juices were beginning to run. He felt the first nibble of excitement, the first surge of lust. His palms tingled. He licked his lips.

DeLaroza went up the steps and opened the hatch door leading to the cabin, watching the storm clouds race angrily across the sky. He lit the cigar, letting the hard, cold wind carry the smoke out across the lake.

"You know where she lives?" Burns asked.

"Yes. In fact, I, uh, I am going there tonight."

Burns shook his head. "Unreal," he said.

"It is something special. A goodbye. I have known this woman for a long time," he said. Then, after a pause: "Too long, maybe."

Burns smiled but there was no mirth in the grin. Then he said, "Not *too* long. *So* long. Get what I mean?"

DeLaroza turned and looked back at him. "What do you mean?" he said.

"What do you mean, what do I mean? You know what I mean. Don't act dumb, because I know you ain't dumb."

A sudden flash of lightning jarred DeLaroza. A second later it cracked like a whip snapping in the trees nearby. Burns seemed to draw strength from it. His eyes lost their coldness and began to beam with exhilaration.

"You're gonna be right there," Burns said. "So you can case out the situation for me. You're in the catbird seat there, Victor, because we ain't got a lot of time. Now do you know what I mean?"

DeLaroza did not answer. His lower lip began to tremble. He was thinking about tonight, about making love to her. Burns was totally calm, the killing machine, lubricating itself with visceral oil.

"You did good, Victor," he said.

"I don't understand."

"Sure you do. You didn't come out here to feed me all that bullshit about my passport, that crap. You came out here to put the edge on the knife. Right?"

DeLaroza fell quiet again. He stared down at the cigar.

"I ain't pissed about it, Victor. In fact, I gotta hand it to you. In your own sweet way you're just like me. You'd kill your own mother for a two-point safety. You worked it out nice. It's one and one makes two, just that simple. You're here because the chippie has to take a hit and I'm the one's gotta do the job. Ain't that right, Victor?"

DeLaroza stared at the floor. Finally he nodded very slowly.

"Lemme hear you say it there, partner."

DeLaroza continued to stare at the floor.

"Lemme hear you say it," Burns said flatly. "Say it out loud."

DeLaroza remained quiet.

"Say it."

DeLaroza started to speak. His lips moved, but the words died in his mouth. He coughed, trying to clear his throat.

"Say it!"

The voice was hoarse and seemed far away. "Kill her," DeLaroza said.

Burns grinned. "See how easy it is when you try."

9

The ant was as big as an elephant. It crawled across the ceiling and Sharky watched it, wondering what it was doing on the roof of a twelve-story building and why it even wanted to be there at all.

Sit and wait. Boredom. The curse of the stakeout.

At least Livingston had provided him with what Arch called his stakeout kit—an army cot, blanket, hot plate, and several packets of instant soup and coffee. It helped. They had also left a car on the street below near the exit of the apartment parking deck in case he had to tail her.

But he had nothing to read. After all the stakeouts Sharky should have remembered something to read. And he would be there until Papa relieved him at eight A.M.

He lay on the cot with the blanket under his head

and the earphones on and watched the ant scurry across
the ceiling and start down the wall. The recorder for
Domino's living room whirred quietly on the floor near
the cot. The radio was on. Led Zeppelin boomed in his
ears.

She was moving around, singing to herself, the recorders for the bedroom and massage room cutting on and
off as she went from one to the other. She was in the
master bedroom when she made the phone call.

"Hello, is Mister Moundt there, please? . . . Hi, it's
Domino . . . Fine, and you? . . . Oh, you do? Wonderful. I was afraid it wouldn't get in. . . . Thank you,
that's so sweet. It's for tonight. I hope it wasn't too
much trouble. . . . Wonderful, I'll be by in a few minutes. Bye."

Good. He could pick up a paperback or some magazines. He pulled on his suede pullover, smoothed back
his hair, and walked down to the ninth floor, making
sure the elevator he took did not stop at ten. He did not
want to end up in the same elevator with her. He
walked through the cold drizzle to the stakeout car, a
blue Chevy, got in and waited. A few minutes later the
gate swung open and the blue Mercedes pulled out.

He followed her down Peachtree Street, staying several car lengths behind her. When she turned into the
lot at Moundt's he drove past, u-turned, and ambled
back, giving her time to enter the store.

Moundt's was a gourmet supermarket, possibly the
best in the city. It had two entrances, the main door on
Peachtree Street and another through the side that led
past a snack bar. He got a cup of coffee, stood in the
doorway, watching her as he sipped it. She was in the
rear of the store, talking to Moundt, a tall, gray-haired,
amiable man who seemed to know her well. He gave
her two cans which she put in her shopping cart.

Supposing she makes you? Sharky thought. *Remembers you from the elevator?*

He went to the fruit department, got some white seedless grapes and half a dozen hard apples, then cruised the store, staying two or three rows away and well behind her. He reached the paperback rack and, keeping his back to her, looked for a book. He selected a thick novel by Irwin Shaw, then turned cautiously, and looked back over his shoulder.

She was gone.

He moved toward the checkout counter, peering over the tops of the aisles. As he reached the end of the aisle she stood up. She had stooped down to get some crackers and now, suddenly, they were face to face, an aisle apart.

He left the basket, went back up the aisle, aimlessly searching the counters as though he had forgotten something. She was facing the other way when he came back and he pushed his cart hurriedly to the checkout counter.

An elderly lady got there at the same time. He smiled, reluctantly, and motioned her in front of him.

Goddamn, she must have fifty dollars worth of stuff in that cart.

He watched her put the items on the checkout counter. It took forever. Sharky waited. Then he casually turned sideways and looked back over his shoulder toward the store.

Domino was standing there, right behind him, three feet away.

Well, shit!

She smiled at him, blue eyes crinkling at the corners. *His nose is broken. How interesting.* "We seem to be following each other," she said pleasantly.

Do something, stupid, don't just stare at her. He smiled back. "Looks like it, doesn't it?" he said.

"You live in the neighborhood?"

"No," he said, then realized it was a stupid answer and added quickly, "I like to shop here."

"Me too. It's my absolute favorite." *I'd like to reach up and just touch him, there between the eyes.* "Are you going to be working in the building for long?"

"Well, uh, I, uh, yes, a couple of days." *Neat, Sharky. Why don't you give her an itinerary? Show her your shield. Take out the old pistol and spin it on your finger, do a couple of John Waynes for her. Back out of the conversation. You're blowing it. Putting it all in your mouth. Foot, socks, shoe, the works.*

And she thought, *He's interesting. Trim and hard, almost skinny. Faded green eyes, very warm. And that flat place across the bridge of his nose. He'd be pretty if it were not for that.*

He was staring into her shopping cart.

"Shark's fin soup?" he said with surprise.

"Have you ever tried it?" *I'm glad he's not pretty. Good God, what are you doing? Getting off on his broken nose!*

"I'll be honest with you," he said, "I never heard of shark's fin soup."

His eyes wandered. She was wearing a tee-shirt with *ice cream* written across the chest in dribbling letters, as if it were melting, and tight Italian jeans that hugged her ass and a fur jacket that looked like it would have cost him a year's salary. There was no doubt about it— she was something special.

"It's quite a delicacy," she said, "Mister Moundt ord—"

She stopped, aware that he was not listening, that he was looking, no he was *lost* in looking at her. And she liked it. It seemed open and honest and it felt good to her and she looked him over again, admiring the way he held himself, loose, like an athlete, and confident.

She looked back at his eyes and a moment later he looked up and knew he had been caught.

He's blushing! I haven't seen anyone blush since college. She turned it on, staring hard into his eyes. The lady at the checkout counter was almost through. *Do something. He'll be gone in a minute or two.* "I think you should try it," she said.

"Try what?"

"Shark's fin soup."

She's making a pass, Sharky. "Well, I, uh, yeah . . . you know, one of . . ."

"I mean today."

"Today."

"Um hum, today. About six o'clock."

"Six o'clock today?"

"I'm making it for a friend. I'll be finished cooking it by about six o'clock."

She bored in with the blue eyes and he just stared at her, half-smiling.

"10-A," she said.

"10-A."

"10-A, six o'clock."

"Right. 10-A, six o'clock."

What the fuck!

She smiled. "Splendid."

He sat on the edge of the cot and nibbled grapes and tried to read, but his eyes kept wandering to the tape recorder. Finally it clicked and he slipped the earphones over his ears and shoved the monitor button, heard her close the door, followed her footsteps into the kitchen, listened to the rattling of paper bags, the refrigerator door opening and closing, pots slamming about, heard her singing to herself, filling in forgotten lyrics by humming:

She went into the living room and he could hear her shuffling through record albums. She put one on and the softness of a guitar took the edge off the hollowness of the room. A moment later Joni Mitchell's plaintive voice came on singing the plaintive lyrics to "Harry's House."

Sharky's mind wandered back to a high school picnic and a girl in a bright yellow bikini that barely covered her swelling breasts and she had turned out to be, what was her name? Mary Lou? Mary Jane? Mary-something-or-other, who had suddenly grown up, and remembering her, he made up aimless lyrics to nothing song:

"Baby did I lust for you,
Da da da da da da da,
And everybody else did too,
Dadadada da da da . . ."

He heard the sound of water running in the bathtub and he forgot the yellow bikini bathing suit and Mary-something-or-other and thought about Domino taking off the tee-shirt with the melting ice cream, envisioned her slipping off the tight Italian jeans, pictured her in his mind, naked, and he closed his eyes.

She poured bath oil in the tub, turned, and looked at herself in the full-length mirror and, singing along with Joni Mitchell, slowly stripped off the shirt, let it fall away from her shoulders, turned sideways, and studied her breasts, was pleased that they were still firm, curving up and away from her body, reached up under them and traced the curve with her fingertips, sliding her fingers out to the nipples, and squeezed them gently, watching them grow hard at her touch. She unbuttoned the jeans, pulled them over her hips, let them fall to the floor. Her panties had pulled down too, and she looked at her hair curling up over the top of them and ran her hand across the flat surface of her stomach, let her little finger slip down under the band, enjoyed the softness, and finally edged them down and stepped out of them, running her hands down the insides of her thighs, letting her thumbs ripple across the thick black down.

The beat of the music began to change to the blues and she hummed as Joni Mitchell sang:

"The more I'm with you, pretty baby,
The more I feel my love increase,
I'm building all my dreams around you
Our happiness will never cease."

She tested the water with a toe, slipped down into its oily warmth, let it envelop her, and lay back with her eyes closed, caressing her legs, her thighs. Her thumb found her belly button, lingered at its edge while the rest of her fingers slid down between her legs and she slowly pinched thumb and fingers together, lightly, slowly, and she thought about the elevator man, about his trim, hard body, the rugged face, the shattered nose.

"We'll find a house and garden somewhere
Along a country road a piece,
A little cottage on the outskirts
Where we can really find release,
'Cause nothing's any good without you.
Baby, you're my centerpiece."

And while Domino prepared herself for Victor, thoughts of the elevator man kept intruding. Intruding. Intruding . . .

She opened the door on the first ring and stood facing Sharky, her chin slightly raised, an arrogant, almost impish look on her face, her thick black hair, not quite dry yet, hanging damply about her ears. She wore no makeup. She didn't need it and she knew she didn't. She was wearing a scarlet floor-length kimono, silk, trimmed in brilliant yellow and split up both sides almost to the hip. There was nothing under it, nothing but her; he could tell by the way it stayed with her, molded to her breasts, her hips, her flat stomach. Her eyes sparkled mischievously. The sweet odor of marijuana drifted past Sharky.

She smiled and said, "Well, I just lost a bet with myself."

"How come?"

"I bet you wouldn't come."

"I can always go back."

She stepped back, swung the door wide and leaned against it, cocking her head to one side. "No," she said, "no, I don't think so."

He went past her, into the familiar living room, looked around, and feigned surprise. "Very elegant," he said, nodding his head.

She closed the door and came very close to him, staring up at his face for several seconds, then said, "Thank you."

She had set a place for him on the smoked-glass table. A linen placemat with delicate silverware, Wedgwood china and a tall, fragile wine glass. "If you'd like to wash up, you can go in there," she said, pointing to the bathroom. The door to the massage room was closed. He went into the bathroom and washed his hands. Patches of mist lingered in the corners of the mirror and the room was warm with the memory of her bath and smelled vaguely of bath oil.

When he returned, she was pouring white wine into

two glasses. She motioned for him to sit down. Soup steamed in the bowl.

There was a record playing, a soft ballad sung almost off-key by a Frenchman.

"That's a very pretty song," he said. "I don't think I've ever heard it before."

"It's called 'The Dreams In Your Soul.' It's my favorite song. That's Claude DuLac. He's very popular in France but it's hard to find his albums over here. Americans don't appreciate romantic singers anymore, do you think?"

"No, I agree with you."

I'm glad you like it.

"I'm . . ."

"Yes?"

"Nothing."

You're getting pushy. Don't rush it.

He swirled a pat of butter into yellow patterns on the surface of the soup. She raised her wine glass toward him.

"Bon appétit," she said.

"Thanks."

The glasses pinged as they touched. She leaned forward on her elbows, holding her wine glass between her fingertips, and stared at him again, the blue eyes digging deep.

"I have to ask you something," she said, very quietly, almost confidentially.

Jesus, does she know? Does she suspect? "Fire away," he said.

"How did you get that?" she asked, pointing toward his nose.

"What?"

She reached out and ran her middle finger very delicately down between his eyes, lingering for a moment where his nose flattened out between them. "That," she said.

"Oh, that."

"Um hum," she said, adding, "If it's something unromantic, like you got it caught in an elevator door or something, lie to me."

"The first thing they teach you in elevator school is not to get your nose caught in the door."

She laughed and the laugh became a smile and stayed on her lips.

"Well, when I was in high school there was this bully named Johnny Trowbridge and he hit me with a brick."

She paused and then laughed again. "Really?"

"Really."

"And what did you do?"

"He was about, uh, three feet taller than me, so I went to the Y and I took boxing lessons for six months and then I beat the living bejesus out of him."

She was laughing hard now and she shook her head. "Did you really?" she said. "Did you really do that?"

"I really did it. Acceptable?"

"Oh, yes. Oh, absolutely. If it's a lie, don't change it."

It was a lie, although a bully named Johnny Trowbridge had hit him with a brick and he had taken boxing lessons and a year later he'd kicked the shit out of Johnny Trowbridge. But his nose had been broken in an alley behind the bus station when he was a rookie cop. A drunk had scaled the lid of a garbage can straight into his face with uncanny accuracy.

She sighed. "I'm so glad we got that settled."

"What?"

"The business about your nose."

"Does my nose bother you?"

She shook her head very slowly, staring at it. "No. It gives you character."

"Thanks."

"Eat your soup before it gets cold."

Upstairs on the roof the tapes were whirring, recording their conversation. He could envision the rest of the machine listening to it in Friscoe's Inferno. He knew what The Nosh would think. But how about Friscoe? Livingston? Papa? And The Bat! The Bat would have a coronary. He would sit in his office and his face would turn red, then blue, and he would clutch his heart and make a face like a fish out of water, and he would fall dead on the floor. *I may have to erase this tape.*

He raised the spoon to his lips, sipped the soup. It was unreal. Fantastic. Soup wasn't the right word for it. It was nectar. He held it in his mouth a moment, savoring it, before he swallowed.

"Well?" she asked.

"It's . . . incredible."

"Incredible good or incredible bad?"

"Good? Hell, it's . . . historic."

"Historic"! What a wonderful choice of words.

"Of course I'm not an expert. Is your friend Chinese?"

"No, but he lived in the Orient for years."

Is he the mark? Is the dinner tonight part of the set-up? Sharky decided not to push it. "Do you pick up strays in the supermarket very often?" he asked.

"Only in Moundt's. I would never pick up a stray in just *any* market."

He laughed.

"Actually I felt kind of sorry for you. You looked so forlorn, wandering around, trying to decide what to buy. I can usually spot a bachelor in the market. They can never decide between what they want and what they need. In the end it's a disaster."

She leaned forward and stroked the broken place on his nose again. He felt chills. It was like school days again. He was reacting like a kid. But he liked it. *You can keep your finger there for the rest of the night*, he thought. *You have fingers like butterfly wings.*

"You know something," she said. "I don't know your name."

"That's right, you don't."

"What is it?"

"Sharky."

"Sharky what? Or is it what Sharky?"

"Just Sharky. How about you?"

He reached out and ran his finger down between her eyes, felt the tip of her nose.

"D-D-Domino." *My God did I stutter?*

"Domino?"

"Um hum, just Domino. Like just Sharky."

He smiled and nodded and took his hand away and she wanted him to leave it there. "That's fair enough," he said.

It went on that way. Small talk and jokes. And occasionally they touched, no—brushed, as if by accident. They flirted with subjects, never getting too personal, keeping it light.

"Did you ever play football?" she asked. "You look like you played football."

"I thought about it in college, but I wasn't good enough."

"Where did you go to college?"

"Georgia."

"What did you study?"

"Geology."

"Geology?" she said, surprised.

"Sure, geology."

"Why geology?"

"I like rocks," he said.

"Okay, so why aren't you a geologist?"

"Well, it was like, uh, there wasn't a lot happening in geology when I finished."

"You spent all that time and then just . . . forgot it?"

"It made my father happy. He took out an insurance policy when I was born, and when I graduated from high school, he handed me the check. It was a dream of his, that the kid should go to college. So he deserved it."

You're a nice man, Sharky, she thought. *Naïve, maybe, but what's wrong with that?* "That's a generous thought," she said.

"Look, I like my old man. He was always good to me. It was something I could do back, make him happy. What the hell."

"I liked my old man, too," she said, without thinking, then wondered whether she should have brought it up.

"What was he like?"

She could make up a story. She was used to that. Something glamorous, something they wanted to hear. She didn't.

"He was a mining engineer. Well, actually he was a roustabout, you know. He loved brawling and whoring and drinking with the boys. Mister Macho, that was old Charlie. The word was invented for him. Itchy Britches, mom called him. We went wherever the action was. I grew up in one temporary town after another. They were always either too muddy or too dusty. Mom still says the saddest thing about losing Dad was that he died so ingloriously. He really would have liked to go out in a blaze of glory like Humphrey Bogart in some old movie. Instead, he died in a miserable little town called Backaway in Utah. He came home one afternoon, got a beer and the paper, sat down in his favorite chair, and died."

She seemed weighed down by the memory. Sadness

crossed her face, very briefly, like shadows on a cloudy day, then it passed.

"Well," Sharky said, "I'm sure he would have been proud of you. It looks like you're doing pretty well."

She closed the subject quickly.

"I'm independently wealthy," she said, smiling. "A rich aunt."

Sharky laughed and raised his glass.

"Okay, here's to rich aunts."

She sat with her chin in her hand and stared at him again, then shook her head. "I just, uh, I don't believe it. I mean, a geologist working as an elevator man?"

"I'm not an elevator man. I'm an engineer. An elevator man is an old guy with spots on his uniform who never stops in the right place. You know, he's always too high or too low."

She was laughing. "Yes," she said. "You always have to step up or step down."

"Besides," Sharky said, "I once knew a dentist who quit and became a mechanic."

"A mechanic?"

"You know, in a garage. It's what he got off on."

"And you get off on elevators?"

"Well, you know, I'm not going to do this for the rest of my life. It keeps me off the street."

She felt warm toward him. Secure, comfortable. And she wanted him, wanted his arms around her, stretched out on the floor listening to DuLac, free and easy, just letting it happen. It was something that had been missing from her life for a long time. She had given up on it. *It's a silly notion*, she thought. *A nowhere notion*. But it was a nice feeling.

And Sharky felt the same way. *I want you*, he thought. *Here. Now*. But he let it pass. Even a one-time shot wouldn't work. No future. In a week he might be putting her in the slams. And yet, he didn't want to leave it.

"Tell you what," he said, "I'll come back again before I leave, okay? Maybe I'll be lucky, catch you on a day when you're having a whale stew or barracuda steak."

This time she didn't smile.

"How about just plain steak?" she said. "I can handle that."

"Any time," he said.

"Then come back," she said and touched his cheek.

And Sharky realized that for a few minutes he had forgotten why he was there because he wanted to come back.

10

Chiang drove the black Cadillac Seville up into the plaza and circled it slowly, observing the entrance to the apartment and the location of the security guard, then he turned back into Peachtree Street, went half a block to a side street, and parked. He sat immobile, staring straight ahead, awaiting his instructions.

DeLaroza looked at his watch. Seven forty-five. Three hours, he figured. Domino could perform a miracle in three hours.

DeLaroza's mind was still in a turmoil. The day had been eventful, exhausting. But now his thoughts were on Domino. *I want you to think about it all day long,* she had said, *it will be much sweeter that way.* And he had. Images of her had flashed continually through his mind, images of other times, when he had introduced her to a world reserved for the gods and the very rich.

Burns was right. He was concupiscent, a man driven
by lust as others are driven by fame.

Now it would end. But not before tonight.

They walked back to the apartment and DeLaroza
stood in the shadows while Chiang entered, standing in
front of the night guard, his bulk concealing the front
door as he haltingly tried to explain that he was lost. The
guard, confused by his broken English, concentrated on
every word while DeLaroza slipped into the building
and trotted to the stairwell. He did not want to risk
being seen on the elevator. He walked up to the tenth
floor, preparing himself for her pleasures as he climbed
the steps, cleansing his mind.

Gowmanah

remembering her in Paris, flaunting her sensuality
until even the fag couturier was bewitched by her

gowmanah

remembering her at Quo Vadis, where even the arrogant waiters stopped and looked when she made her entrance

gowmanah

remembering her in the bathhouse in Tokyo and
the four geishas, flocking around her, bathing her, caressing her breasts while he sat forgotten in an adjoining
tub

gowmanah . . .

The pressures of time slipped away. DeLaroza was
prepared for whatever Domino had to offer.

She too had prepared herself for his arrival. It was to
be her game, her rules tonight. She answered his first
ring and DeLaroza stepped back in awe when she
opened the door.

Her eyes were sketched into delicate almonds by the
subtlest of eye-liners. A dust of shadow accentuated her
high cheekbones. Her black hair was pulled to one side
and pinned behind her ear by an azalea blossom. Her

form-fitting gown of white gauze was split almost to the hip on each side and trimmed in gold. She wore no shoes, no jewelry.

The scent of flowers surrounded her. Behind her the room shimmered in the glow of candles, revealing freshly cut daffodils and the coffee table bearing wine and other delights. A recording whispered Chinese love songs She stepped back into the cool, dim fragrance and he could see her body through the thin cotton. Her skin seemed to glow in the dark, to provide its own radiation. The chocolate points of her breasts held the gauze at bay and he could see the thick black triangle of hair where her trim legs joined.

She put her hands together and bowed her head.

"Welcome, Cheen Ping," she said, "to the lair of the Third Dragon."

———————————

Sharky listened, heard the doorbell ring, heard her open the door but her remarks were lost among the tinkling bells and the Oriental music on the stereo. What was that? Something about dragons? There was movement, a rustling as though she perhaps had removed his coat.

"Dor jeh." A deep voice. Mature. But what was he saying?

"There will be only three courses to dinner," she said and her voice was soft. Melodic. Almost . . . subservient? "And before each you must satisfy your innermost desires so that you may enjoy the meal to its fullest."

God *damn!* Sharky lit a cigar, held it between his teeth, and pressed the earphones so he could hear better. Was this the same woman he had followed to Moundt's? Who had joked with him about being an ele-

vator man? Served him soup and wine and seemed hypnotized by his broken nose?

"Only two courses, Ho Lan Ling. I am afraid three
might be more than enough."

He heard her laugh. *Well, shit,* Sharky said half
aloud, *they're off and running in Peking!*

She led DeLaroza to one of the Savoy chairs, stood
behind him, began massaging his temples. Her touch
was so light he hardly felt it. She pressed her thumbs in
the middle of his forehead, held the first three fingers of
each hand just inside the depression of his temples, and
began rotating them in circles, widening the circle until
her fingers moved over his eyelids. He sat with his
hands resting on the arms of the chair. Her fingertips
relaxed him. His head grew light under her touch. He
eased into the chair. The music filled his head.

She poured him a glass of dry white wine and offered
him a white pill on a satin pincushion. He washed the pill
down with the wine, watched her do the same. She
opened a long, shallow antique box, removed a pipe
from it. Its porcelain stem was eight inches long and the
rosewood bowl was well worn and scorched black. Then
she took a piece of what appeared to be black putty and
rolled it between her thumb and forefinger into a perfect ball. The Quaalude began to work on him, he felt
his organs being stroked as though her hands were inside him. The room was a warm, protected place for
him. She knelt beside him, humming in harmony with
the music, put the ball in the bowl of the pipe, and held
a match to it. As it glowed red, she offered him the pipe
and he took it, drawing deeply, feeling the smoke burn
his throat and lungs. He took it deep, holding it in until
he thought his chest would burst. She turned the stem to
her own mouth, drew deeply herself, closing her eyes,

letting her head fall back. Then she offered the pipe
back to him.

The first rush of opium engulfed him.

His body began to vibrate. He seemed to be sinking
into the pillows.

The music engulfed him.

His skin was caressed by invisible feathers. His groin
began to swell.

Domino lay back in a bed of pillows she had arranged
at the foot of the chair, the Quaalude and opium etch-
ing her desire, defining her prurience. She felt another
presence outside of herself, like a second skin, shimmering, protecting her and caressing her. The dress slipped
down between her legs, rested against her hair and she
felt its weight along her vulva. Her thighs began to
tighten and relax. Tighten and relax.

The chimed music filled her head, flowed down
through her throat and filled her chest. Her nipples
grew until she thought they would pierce the gauze that
enslaved them. The music began to flow again, down
through her stomach, deep inside, and finally into her
vagina. Her body spasmed, very lightly, and again. She
stared at DeLaroza through eyes already fogged with
passion. Her mouth was open. She was beginning to
breathe in a long pattern, inhaling to the count of seven,
holding to the count of seven, exhaling to the count of
seven. It enhanced the music inside her. She put her
hands on her stomach, searched lazily, lightly, for her
navel, found it and brushed her fingertips around and
into it. She looked at DeLaroza and the swelling between his legs excited her even more. She crossed her
chest with her hands and began moving them up her
sides, exploring her armpits while the palm of her hands
grazed her nipples. She rose to meet the hands but they
were elusive, rising as she rose. Her nipples swelled to
meet them finally—the touch. The thrill shot through

her, like electricity, firing sparks into her breasts, her
stomach, her neck, into her vagina, her rectum. She caressed her neck, slid her fingers under the gauze dress,
savored the roundness and then felt the dimpled ridges
of her nipples. She held them gently between her fingers, began to squeeze them. DeLaroza now was breathing with her, his erection straining against his zipper.

She took one hand from under the dress and moved it
down between her breasts to her stomach, slid it over her
thigh, reached the bottom of the skirt, and pulled it up,
slowly. Her hand disappeared under the skirt, slipped
along her thigh, brushed over her hair and moved back
down.

She began to rock up and down to the rhythm of her
breathing, rising up to meet her hand as it grazed her
thick patch. She let her hand slip between her legs, her
finger probing, closed her eyes, stretched her head
back, and gasped, then began rocking and breathing
faster and faster and faster. . . .

Sharky listened to the sounds. First her singsong
humming, then the breathing. He tried to picture the
man. Deep voice. Probably large, not fat, but large. The
voice was mature. A man in his forties, possibly early
fifties. And there was a trace of accent or perhaps the
lack of an accent. An Americanized foreigner. German?

Then he envisioned Domino. Naked.

The Big Man was touching her, kissing her, possibly
going down on her. The Big Man's hands caressed her,
stroked her tits. He was touching her now, his hand
stroking the dark fur between her legs. Now she rolled
him over and got up on her knees and straddled him
and he was hard and he reached out for her.

Only it wasn't the Big Man anymore, it was Sharky,
reaching out for her, touching her.

He pulled the earphones off and dropped them on the bed. His pulses were jumping in his wrists. He wiped sweat off his forehead with a corner of the blanket. He felt guilty, embarrassed, humiliated. And then he began to question his feelings. Guilty? Of what, getting a hard-on listening to a beautiful woman screwing another guy? Hell, who wouldn't? Embarrassed: For whom, by whom? There was nobody else there but him. And why should he be humiliated? They were not even aware he was listening; they certainly were not trying to humiliate him. He lit another cigar. And thought again about Domino.

As Domino began rocking faster, she began chanting, at first very faintly.

"Hai . . . hai . . . hai . . . hai . . ."

She felt her lips swell and open, her fingers slide down across her trigger, felt it harden and grow under her touch, just as DeLaroza was growing. Her finger slid inside her, was entrapped by the moist muscles which tightened around it, held it, then released it. She rocked faster, increasing the tempo of her cries.

"Hai . . . hai . . . hai . . ."

DeLaroza gripped the arms of the chair until his knuckles were swollen white. His pulse thundered in his temples and the muscle under his testicles jerked in spasms.

He was hypnotized by her fingers, grazing, brushing, their whispered touch urging her lips up through the forest of her sex. Her cries urged blood up into his swollen penis. He slid down in the chair. His legs stiffened.

She was rocking in a frenzy, her redolent must torturing his nose, her hair weaving frantic patterns across her face as her head jerked back and forth.

"Hai . . . hai . . . hai . . . haihaihaihai*haihai*.
H-h-h-aaaaiii."

She stiffened, her head thrust back among the pillows. Her body jolted in the spasms of orgasm. DeLaroza was on the edge of madness. He too began to spasm and as he did, she rose slowly, tantalizingly to her knees before him, shuddered, zipped down his pants, freeing him, and, with a tiny animal cry, let her face fall across his lap. Her mouth enveloped him, her tongue brushed him, the moist membranes of her mouth closed on him, and an instant later he too exploded.

———————

The meal was prepared by the chef of the finest Szechuan restaurant in the city, who arrived at precisely nine o'clock, assisted by two busboys, and moved silently into the kitchen, where he set up and awaited her command. Domino sat at the head of the table. She was no longer the servant, now she ruled like an empress, clapping her hands once at the beginning of each course and twice when they were finished, the busboys appearing and disappearing as silently as time passing. DeLaroza sat at the opposite end of the table, eating slowly, savoring every bite, smiling, and nodding approval after each course. They ate in silence, in the manner of Chinese royalty, devoting their full attention to the food.

It was spectacular. The courses were small, to prevent overeating. And while Domino had prepared only one course, the shark's fin soup, she had planned the entire meal, selecting the most succulent dishes from the menu of the Princess Garden restaurant in Hong Kong. It was truly a meal fit for an emperor: *t'ang-t'su-au-pien,* a salad whose main ingredients were fresh lotus roots, sesame seed oil, and soy sauce; *chow fan,* a mound of rice concealing bits of egg, shrimp, ham, peas, and onions, all deep-fried in peanut oil; *hsai-tan,* a side dish of deep-friend bamboo shoots and water chestnuts served over noodles; and Peking duck, basted in salad oil and roasted until the skin crackled, then served as three different courses. First, the skin was presented, dipped in thick soybean paste, sprinkled with onions, and wrapped in Chinese pancakes. Next the bones were offered, boiled into a gravy with cabbage and mushrooms and served with the *chow fan.* Finally, the meat itself, juicy, spicy, hot, and sliced into thin strips. The dessert—sliced bananas dipped in batter and deep-fried, then immersed in ice water that froze the outer crust into a glaze while the bananas remained steaming hot—was the perfect conclusion.

When the meal was over and the chef and his assistants had departed as silently as they had come, she served absinthe, smuggled in from Ecuador, and they smoked a joint of pure Colombian grass the color of cinnamon. It warmed and mellowed them, stirring the libido again. They stared dreamily across the table at each other. Not a word had passed between them for more than two hours.

Finally she left the table and went back to the massage room. DeLaroza lit a cigar, leaned back in his chair, fully content, awaiting whatever surprises she would offer next.

His thoughts began to wander. To Hotchins. To the campaign.

To Burns.

The thought of Burns chilled him and he closed his eyes, summoning his mantra to purge the devils from his mind.

Gowmanah

thinking about her, lying before him among the pillows . . .

Gowmanah

stroking herself, turning herself on, performing for him . . .

Gowmanah

visualizing her undressing, revealing her immaculate body . . .

Gowmanah

and it was simple. Once again, Eros commanded his mind.

He heard her clap her hands and, turning, saw her silhouetted against a dozen or more candles, her body oiled and glowing. He obeyed her command and went to her. Feather fingers stripped him, eased him down among the pillows on the floor, spread warm oil over his body, massaging him from head to foot, subtly caressing his genitals, stroking him, her tongue teasing him to fullness. She knelt over him, resting on her knees, her spiderweb plume brushing against him, her moisture preparing him. He began to throb and she shifted, rolling to her side beside him and reaching to the small table beside her, picked up a mirror, and placed it on her stomach.

She had prepared four long rows of cocaine on the mirror, carefully chopped and arranged in narrow files, each one about five inches long. Beside the rows were a short piece of glass straw perhaps four inches long and a spoon of pure Andean gold brought from Cuzco, the capital of the Inca empire, in southern Peru, its handle delicately hand-carved in a sculpture of Virgo, the Inca goddess of coca, the minutely detailed headdress containing the tiny bowl of the spoon itself.

He turned and lay between her legs, her tuft against his chest, took the straw and, holding one nostril shut, moved the straw up one row of coke, inhaling sharply. He snorted deeply through the other nostril. The coke hit him in a rush. His groin surged. The tartness of the drug burned his throat. He slid the mirror toward her, slipped down, buried his head between her legs.

She laid the mirror beside her, turned slightly, snorted the second row, let it sizzle through her body, felt it charge up deep into her sinuses. She lay back down, shuddering as the cocaine surged through her senses, touching every organ with life.

DeLaroza rose up on his elbows, retrieved the mirror, and, using the straw as a pusher, filled the spoon with the powder. She bent her legs slightly at the knees. Venus rose toward him, lips apart and moist, inviting him, enticing him. He held the spoon between her legs, lowered it until it almost touched her. Her ringlets rose toward his hand and parted and he lowered the spoon, touched her vivid heart-shaped opening, tapped his finger against the side of the spoon, watched the minute crystals sprinkle as he moved the spoon along her waiting lips.

Her eyes were closed. She began to shudder.

He moved the mirror, slid up between her legs, rose up above her, overpowered by her lust. She was his erotic master, orchestrating his orgasm. He felt godlike. He was Priapus, son of Dionysius and Aphrodite, who fornicated for eternity without losing his erection, and he roared with desire as he surged against her.

The cocaine felt like ice, first numbing her membranes, then suddenly setting them afire. She cried out, feeling him against her, rising up to meet him, her senses screaming for satisfaction.

"Ohhh . . . my God!"

Sharky lay on the cot smoking a Schimmelpenninck, staring up at the smoke hanging near the ceiling like strands of cotton candy, his thoughts jumping to Domino, envisioning her. He dropped the cigar on the floor and put the earphones back on, heard her peculiar breathing pattern starting again.

Seven in, hold seven, seven out.

And he joined her, closing his eyes, letting his own fantasies take control.

He was lying among the pillows in the massage room. She was standing over him, her long legs dominating him.

Thick black swansdown inviting him as she stared down . . .

Stared down between her breasts, smiling . . .

He reached up, touching the soft skin behind her knees, stroked it, then pressed lightly.

She lowered toward him, an agonizing vision in slow motion.

Seven in, hold seven, seven out.

She stretched out over him, not quite touching him. Her nipples brushed his, her lips hovered over his, her thick tuft teased his shaft. Their lips brushed together, tongues searching, touching, melding into one.

He kissed her neck, her throat, the bulge of her breasts, her nipples, and felt her settle against him, moving against him, like a wave washing over him.

He could wait no longer. He reached down, lifted her by the hips, and together they stared down between their bodies, moving, touching, and moving apart until neither of them could stand the agony any longer and as he poised her over him and they both looked down at what was waiting and he reached between them, brushed his hand across her silken mound, she moaned, "Ohhh . . . my God!" as he rose up and felt her against him. Open and waiting, she sucked him inside. . . .

DeLaroza rose high above her and then plunged down, the power, grasping, taking, and she felt him inside her, only her eyes were closed and now her fantasy took over and it was not DeLaroza entering her, it was Sharky, for now she no longer wanted the lust of power, she wanted to get and to give, to join him, not be his for the taking. She felt his hard, muscular stomach, his lean chest, his neck, taut and straining, his arms with their pinion fingers stroking, gentling, hardening her, and his mouth against hers, lightly at first, then crushing against hers.

Her breathing pattern shortened.

Five in, five hold, five out.

She counted faster as her breathing quickened. He was breathing with her, thrusting with her.

Two, two, two.

Two, two, two.

two, two . . . two, two . . . two, two . . .

One, one.

One

One!

"Ahhh!"

She cried out again and again. Her body stiffened. Volcanoes sputtered, rumbled, spat fire, and erupted inside her. Hot lava engulfed her, warmed her, flooded through her head, her throat, her chest, her stomach. Her vagina burst and words tumbled from her lips that made no sense, a disconnected alien vocabulary surging from her throat.

DeLaroza popped the amyl nitrite tube and passed it back and forth between them, felt her instant response, the renewed assault on her senses. She was an errant star, lost in space, as it hit again and again and again. The mountain below his testicles swelled and slammed between his legs and he too convulsed and erupted. . . .

In his post on the roof Sharky heard them, felt the same urgent rush, the same mountain between his legs, the same volcanoes blowing apart, the same fervid explosion in his groin and, crying out, he came.

DeLaroza lay beside Domino for only a few minutes, then got up, showered, and dressed. When he returned to the room she was still lying on the table, although she had covered herself with a robe. He was anxious to leave. With his orgasm DeLaroza had closed the book on Domino.

He leaned over the table and she looked at him with smoky eyes, smiling. "Magnificent," he said. "You exceeded your promise. I shall never forget tonight. When next we meet, it will be as old friends. The past is erased."

"Thank you," she said softly, "for everything. For showing me the world and its treasures. You have been a dear friend. *Joy geen.*"

"Goodbye to you," he said and kissed her, knowing it was the last time he would ever see her. Then he closed the door. In his mind Domino was already dead.

She lay alone for several minutes before the tears came and then she cried softly to herself, not so much because she would miss him, but because it was an ending and endings always saddened her.

Sharky did not hear them. He had pulled off the earphones and dropped them beside him on the cot. The last twenty-four hours had burned him out. He had killed a man, been chewed out royally by The Bat, been transferred to Friscoe's Inferno, assigned to this machine, bugged an apartment, and had not only been attracted to a suspect but joined her vicariously while she made love to another man.

Great, Sharky. You aren't even hitting the slow pitches.

His nerves were stretched to the breaking point. Everything seemed amplified. The buzzing fluorescent tubes overhead, the humming motors, the wind whistling at the crack in the door, all agitated his skin. He scratched his arms and neck.

I'm cracking up, he thought. *Standing in the doorway of the rubber room.*

He remembered the joint he had lifted from the drawer earlier in the day. He put on his jacket and went out into the icy air. Leaning against the wall of the utility room, he lit up and took two deep hits, holding the smoke in his lungs as long as he could before exhaling. The high came quickly, soothing his tattered nerves. He closed his eyes, let the cold wind wipe his face.

He thought more about Domino, surprised that he felt no ill feeling toward her, that he did not condemn her open sensuality, her need to embrace pleasure, and he understood why. He had the same needs, the same desires, and for the first time in his life he accepted them without guilt.

He wanted Domino. Period.

"So what?" he said aloud and then chuckled.

He appraised the situation. She had done nothing illegal tonight. No money had changed hands. There wasn't even any *talk* of money. Hell, there was hardly any talk at all. She had entertained a friend and how she entertained him was her business.

Unless, of course, the man below was the mark and tonight was part of the set-up. If so, the tapes would prove she knew him. Intimately. They would provide the connection.

He would have to identify the mark. He could call in Livingston, have him follow the guest when he left her apartment. But that would take time. So he would do it himself.

He returned to the dim interior of his listening post. The tape recorder to the master bedroom was spinning. *Jesus*, he thought, *they're not going at it again!*

He held one of the phones to his ear. There were *two* women speaking now.

He put the earphones on, pressed them to his ears, concentrating on the voices. One was talking, the other was singing. And the shower was going.

Of course, the television was on. Virginia Gunn, Channel Five, was giving the weather report. The shower stopped. He heard her come into the bedroom, heard the click of a remote unit, and the television went off.

Silence.

The recorder stopped.

The mark was gone. He had left while Sharky was out on the roof.

"Shit!"

He went back out on the roof, knowing it was too late. He looked over the parapet, down at the parking lot, but there was no activity. He went to the other side of the roof and stared down into darkness. The wind rattled the treetops below him. Overhead the storm clouds moved silently away and the cold stars mocked him.

He went back to his solitary room, dropped wearily on the cot, then stretched out, and before he could decide on his next step, Sharky fell into a deep, dreamless sleep.

11

Sharky was still asleep when Papa arrived to relieve him at 7:48 the next morning. He jerked awake when he heard the door open. Reaching under the blanket he had used for a pillow and grabbing his 9 mm automatic, he flipped the blanket off and sat up quickly.

Papa stopped short, appraised the situation through bored eyes and smiled.

"Easy there, Roy," he said, "it's only Gabby Hayes."

Sharky sagged, letting his gun hand drop between his legs.

"I musta died," he said.

"Why not? Tough day," Papa said.

"I was jumping outa my skin last night."

"Any action?"

Sharky put his gun under his arm. "Lots of action, very little dialogue. Nothing we're interested in."

"Who was the trick?"

Sharky looked up at him and an embarrassed grin played on his lips.

"You're not gonna believe this," he said.

"Fell asleep," Papa said. "Missed him."

"How the hell did you know that?"

"Done it myself," Papa said smiling. "Fifteen years. I fucked up every way you can fuck up. Arch, too. Friscoe. Nobody hits a thousand. You got the tapes."

"Shit, if there's twenty words on the goddamn tapes I'll eat them."

"Answer me something, okay, Sharky?"

"Sure."

"Why we staked out? We got the tapes, why not check 'em, you know, every three, four hours, see what's doin'?"

"I figure if they go after the mark and somebody's here, on top of it, we can maybe nail them while it's happening. We're four hours late, we could come in on our ass."

Papa nodded. "Okay, I buy it. Go home."

"Yeah. I feel like I was born in these clothes."

Sharky reached down to retrieve the used tapes. Then he noticed that the fresh tapes in the machines to her bedroom and the living room had advanced.

"Well, I'll be damned," he said. "I slept through something here."

He rewound them and listened. The machine to her bedroom had been activated by the television set, *The Today Show*. She was moving around in the background, opening and closing the closet doors, obviously getting dressed. The tape ended abruptly when she turned off the television. The radio had activated the machine for the living room. Once again he heard her in the background. A disc jockey's fast patter was interrupted by music and traffic reports. Then:

"Okay, all you pillow pounders, it's Doctor Dawn here on Z-93 and it's a c-o-o-o-old Friday morning out there. Seven twenty-nine and here's one to get you on your feet. ELP, Emerson, Lake, and Palmer and—"

The radio cut off. The tape went dead, then cut back on. She was opening the door, leaving the apartment. It closed and the latch clicked. The tape ended.

"I'll be a son of a bitch," Sharky said.

"Early starter," Papa said.

"I don't believe it. She got out on us."

"She'll be back."

"Yeah, but we should be on top of her right now. For all we know, she could be—"

"Go home. Forget it for a while. See ya at six."

"Okay," Sharky said. He wiped the sleep out of his eyes and stuffed the tapes in his pocket. "There's some fruit in the bag there, also a book to read."

"Got my own," Papa said, taking a worn copy of *The Guinness Book of World Records* out of his coat pocket.

"You read that on stakeout?" Sharky said.

"Easy to put down, if I gotta move," Papa said.

"You got a point there," Sharky said, walking to the door.

"Hey, Sharky?" Papa said.

"Yeah?"

"Car keys?"

Sharky tossed them to him. "Maybe at six o'clock I'll be back with the living," he said and left.

He flagged down a passing patrol car and had them drop him off at Moundt's, thinking she might be doing some early morning shopping. The place was deserted. He had a cup of coffee and called The Nosh.

"I got some weird tapes for you, pal," he said.

"X-rated?" The Nosh asked sleepily.

"You better believe it."

"Where are you?"

"Moundt's, on Peachtree. I got to get home, get a shower, and change clothes. I don't have a car."

"Can you give me thirty minutes? I need to walk through the shower myself."

"I'll be here. Listen, on the front end of one of these tapes there may be something I can use, a name maybe. But there's heavy interference from the record player."

"Don't sweat it," The Nosh said. "We'll lift the music out."

"Beautiful," Sharky said. "See you when you get here. Take your time."

It was almost dark and the damp, cold wind hinted of more rain. A man walked leisurely past the exit gate from the parking deck of the Lancaster Towers. He was wearing dark glasses and a long blue overcoat, his dark, close-cropped hair hidden under a plain cap, an undistinguished-looking man taking an early evening walk.

A vintage Buick pulled up to a post near the exit gate and the driver slipped a plastic card in a slot in the post. The exit gate swung open and the Buick pulled out. The gate remained open for twenty seconds and then swung shut. The pedestrian was inside when it closed, standing in the shadows near the wall. He took off the dark glasses, studied the interior of the garage. It was empty. Burns smiled to himself. That was the most dangerous part of it, getting in without being seen.

He walked briskly to the east tower elevators and pressed the up button, holding a handkerchief over his nose and mouth, prepared to fake a sneeze if someone was in the elevator. His right hand extended down through the vent in the right-hand pocket of the raincoat. He held a .22 Woodsman, pointing at the floor.

The elevator doors opened. It was empty. He stepped in and pushed the button for the twelfth floor. He was lucky. It went straight up without stopping.

He got out, looking up and down the hallway. Empty. He moved swiftly to 12-C and rang the bell. Nobody answered. He picked the lock, stepped into the apartment, and closed the door quietly behind him. He listened, the ugly silenced snout of the .22 poking between the buttons of his coat. He heard only the sound of his own breathing, nothing else. The apartment was dark and smelled musty. He moved rapidly from room to room, checking closets, even looking under the beds. He relaxed. It was empty. He holstered the .22.

He felt a sudden urge to relieve himself and swore under his breath. Age and tension conspired against his kidneys. He went to one of the bathrooms and urinated.

He returned to the living room and took a pair of surgical gloves from his pocket, pulled them on. He pulled an easy chair over to the large picture window facing the west tower. He propped open two slats of the venetian blinds with two wooden matches, making a small peephole about six inches long and two inches high, and leaned forward and peered through it. He had a perfect view of Domino's apartment, two floors below in the opposite tower.

He took off the raincoat and spread it out on the floor beside him. The coat had three special pockets sewn in the lining. From one he drew the twin-barreled carriage of a twelve-gauge shotgun, from the other its well-worn stock. He snapped them together, cocked both hammers, slipped his finger inside the trigger guard and barely touched the two triggers. The hammers clicked a fraction of a second apart. He slid the rubber buttplate back and removed two shells from a special pocket. He popped the shotgun open, loaded both barrels and snapped it shut.

From the third pocket he took a small pair of opera glasses and a device that looked like two long tubes soldered together. He slipped them over the end of the short-barreled shotgun and tightened them in place with a thumbscrew. He laid the shotgun on top of the coat.

He put the opera glasses on the windowsill and took a small plastic bag from his shirt pocket and laid it beside them. It contained two red pills. He went to the kitchen, got a glass of water, brought it back, and put it beside the pills. The excitement was starting. He scanned Domino's windows with the opera glasses. It was dark. He smiled. Plenty of time. He put the glasses back on the sill, and leaning forward with his elbows on his knees, he waited.

———————

In his post on the roof Sharky too waited. He had returned at 5:30, clean, refreshed, wearing jeans, a turtleneck, a leather jacket, and sneakers.

"Not back yet," Papa reported, smacked him on the back and left. He settled down with his book, aware that he was rereading passages several times and concentrating more on the tape recorders than his book. He finally put it aside. He had been thinking about Domino all day. He had been thinking a *lot* about Domino.

He could go down there when she came home and lay it all out for her, give her a chance to cooperate in exchange for immunity.

And she would probably tell him to get stuffed.

Or blow it out his ass.

Or maybe tell him she didn't know shit. And just maybe she didn't. In which case she could blow the whistle on them to Neil and flush the whole machine.

The thing was, at that moment, Domino was clean. They had absolutely nothing on her but an association with a man they knew was a shakedown pimp.

Forget it, Sharky.

The machine in the bedroom suddenly turned on and he grabbed the earphones. It was the phone ringing. After the third ring her recording machine came on.

"Hi, this is Domino. I'll be away from the phone for a little while. Please leave your name, a short message, and your phone number, and I'll get back to you as soon as possible. Wait for the beep tone before you start. Goodbye and have a pleasant day."

A second later the beep sounded, followed by:

"Hi, it's Pete. Look, I'm running a little late. No problem. I'll call you back in fifteen, twenty minutes. So long."

Pete? A new name for the catalogue. Perhaps the big man from last night. *No,* he thought. *Different voice. Maybe it's her trick for tonight. In which case, since it's almost ten to eight, she's cutting it a little thin.*

The machine in the living room turned on. She was coming in the door. She closed it, turned on the radio, and went into the bedroom. He heard the bed groan under her weight, heard Maria Muldaur's voice:

". . . 'til the eve-nin' ends,
'til the eve-nin' ends . . .
. . . Mid-night At The Oasis,
Send your camel to bed. . . ."

The phone rang again. She caught it on the second ring. *Eager Pete,* he thought. But he was wrong.

"Hello . . . hello . . . ?" A pause, then an exasperated, "Hel*lo?*" She slammed down the phone. Sharky lay on the cot, waiting for her trick to arrive.

———————

Burns cradled the phone gently and smiled, the mirthless, ugly grin of anticipation. He shook one of the reds out of the plastic bag and washed it down with water. He put his raincoat on, put the glass back in the kitchen, swung the chair back to its original position. He sat down with the shotgun between his knees, waiting for the speed to start.

It surged through his blood and his heart began pounding. His scrotum pulsated. He closed his eyes, taking the ride up, letting the red carry him along until his nerve endings were keening with excitement.

He was ready, his senses sharpened, his guts buzzing with anticipation.

He stood up and put his hand through the pocket vent and took the shotgun, aiming it at the floor. He buttoned the coat and started toward the door and stopped.

Jesus!

The fuckin' matches.

He went back, took the two matchsticks down, and straightened the venetian blinds.

I'm gettin' too old for this, he thought. *Well, this is the last one. Just don't get careless now.* He hated the thought of giving it up. It was like having his last piece of ass, knowing it was all over. The speed raced along his nerves, like fire burning along a fuse. He shook his shoulders, closed his eyes, and let his head fall back for a moment. He was getting hard and he sighed with ecstasy.

Oh, yeah. Jesus.

Was he ready.

He took the stairs to the third floor, walked across the connecting terrace. The wind rattled the plastic pool cover and he jumped, the shotgun coming up. His eyes burned fiercely, then he relaxed and kept moving. He entered the stairwell of west tower and listened.

Nobody. Just the wind, moaning through the shaft. He climbed the stairs, thinking about what was coming, reached the tenth floor, and cracked the door. The hall was empty.

He closed the door and ticked the steps off in his mind. He cocked the shotgun. Unbuttoned the bottom buttons of the raincoat. Double checked the location. Apartment 10-A was between the door and the elevators. On the right.

Perfect. Twenty, maybe twenty-five feet, no more.

He took several deep breaths. His pulse battered at his temples.

Four apartments on the floor. The one across from her, 10-D, was being repainted for a new tenant. No one was home in either of the other apartments at the corners of the hall, he had called both numbers. He was lucky tonight. Tonight was definitely his lucky night.

He went through the door and walked to the elevators, pushed the down button and waited. One of the elevators arrived. He stepped in, pushed all the buttons between ten and the ground, and stepped back out. The doors closed. He pushed the down button again. The other elevator arrived and he repeated the maneuver.

He held his thumb across both hammers of the shotgun to make sure it did not discharge accidentally and walked to the door of 10-A.

He rang the bell and then swung the barrels of the shotgun up through the opening of the raincoat.

They were playing a golden oldie, "Long Time Comin'" by Crosby, Stills, Nash, and Young when the doorbell rang.

"Coming," she said. There was gaiety in the voice. She sounded happy. Was it part of the act?

Sharky heard her take the chain off the door, turn the latch.

The two muffled shots came almost as she opened the door.

Thumk thumk.

Almost together and no louder than a fist hitting a refrigerator door.

There was a cry, not loud, like an animal whimpering.

A sound like gravel hitting the wall.

Something fell, heavy, on the floor.

He heard the door close.

Shotgun. A silenced shotgun.

He forgot the earphones. They ripped from his head as he bounded for the door. He had his automatic in hand before he reached the stairwell. He bulled into the stairshaft without precaution. Below him, several floors down, someone was running, taking the steps two or three at a time.

"Hold it!" he yelled. "Police, hold it!"

He followed the sound, taking the steps six at a time and hanging onto the railing to keep from falling. Several flights below him he saw a shadow flee across the wall. He kept going. A door opened and slammed shut.

What floor? What fucking floor?

He reached four, flattened himself against the wall, pulled the door open, and held it open with his foot as he swung around and leaped into the hall.

Empty.

He went to three, swung the door open and went through head first and low, almost on his knees, the 9 mm held in front of him in both hands. He was outside on the terrace and he jumped quickly into the shadows, letting his eyes grow accustomed to the darkness.

He listened. The wind flapped the plastic pool cover. He started moving through the shadows toward the door on the other side of the pool. His reflexes were ready, but his mind was jumping back and forth. *What had happened on the tenth floor. Was she all right? What the hell was going on?*

He remembered his walkie-talkie. As he ran to the east tower he pulled it out of the case on his belt.

"Central, this is urgent. Contact Livingston, Papadopolis, and Abrams and tell them Zebra Three needs them at base immediately."

The walkie-talkie crackled. "Ten-four."

He reached the other door, pulled it open and waited a second, listening, before he went through.

Nothing.

He waited and listened.

Nothing.

He went back on the terrace, checked it quickly, and then returned to the west tower. Both elevators were on the bottom floor. He went up the stairs. His mouth was dry and he was gasping for air when he reached ten. His heart felt as though it was jumping out of his skin. The hallway was empty. He went to 10-A and rang the bell, then pounded on the door. He stepped back and smashed his foot into the door an inch or two from the knob.

The door opened halfway and hit something.

He went in and slammed it shut with his elbow.

The first thing he saw was a scorched pattern of tiny holes near the ceiling. Blood was splattered around the holes. The second pattern had chewed a piece out of the corner of the entrance hall where it led into the living room.

A small marble-topped table lay on its side, a vase of freshly cut flowers spilled out on the floor.

She lay beside the table. Her face was gone. Part of her shoulder was blown away. The right side of her head had been destroyed. She was a soggy, limp bundle, lying partly against the wall in front of the door, blood pumping from her head, her neck, her shoulder. A splash of blood on the wall dripped down to the body. Her hands lay awkwardly in her lap.

Sharky clenched his teeth, felt bile sour in his throat, and swallowed hard and cried out through his clenched teeth.

"No. Goddammit, no!

"No.

"*No!*

"*Go-o-od damn it . . . no!*"

BOOK TWO

12

It was another country, another world, a place ripped from the past and sown with the fantasies of a mastermind.

The gardens, a tiny paradise stitched with walkways and encompassing almost three acres, stunned the eye with color. Purple, yellow, and fuchsia azaleas were in full bloom, surrounded by hundreds of small pink and red camellia blossoms. Beds of iris, their praying flowers streaked with lavender and pastel blue, lined the pathways and grottoes, and small lotus trees and lush green moss covered the cliffsides and stream-fed alcoves.

Only a chest-high fence which prohibited pedestrians from straying off the path tainted the landscaped beauty. There was good reason for the fence. At the far end of the garden, hidden from the bountiful and lush sprays of color by a sixty-foot-high cliff, was an arroyo, a tortured place that split the cliff in half. It was foreboding, a stark and shocking sight compared to the beauty of the gardens. There were no flowers here. Steam rose from between the rocks. A chill breeze blew down through its crevices.

Halfway up the cliffside, almost hidden by red clay banks, boulders, and scattered foliage, was a dank and ominous cave.

Within its depths yellow eyes glittered evilly, accompanied by a sibilant warning, an intermittent hissing that sounded like air rushing from a giant punctured tire. The creature lurking in the cavern was more sensed than seen. But its presence feathered the nerves.

One heard the other creature before seeing it, a half-growl, half-cry that drove icicles through the heart. A moment later it appeared, moving cautiously around the edge of the cliff, a towering myth, at once terrifying and majestic, like some primordial sauropod. It was a dragon, a golden dragon, each scale of its lutescent skin gleaming as it reared back on its hindlegs, stretching a full forty feet from its fiery mouth to the tip of its slashing, spiny tail. Green eyes flashed under hooded lids. Five ebony claws curled out from each padded foot. As it opened its fanged jaws a stream of fire roared from its mouth and roiled upward.

The dragon moved like a cat on the prowl, sensuously, slowly, sensing its prey nearby.

The yellow eyes inside the cave followed the dragon's every move. It began to hiss again, a dangerous sound that reverberated off the cavern walls.

Then it moved. Slowly it slithered from its hiding place and emerged, an enormous two-headed snake, its sinuous muscles sheathed in blood-red skin, the nostrils flat and piglike in its ugly snouts, its forked tongues flicking from two moist mouths as it slid up through the rocks seeking a vantage place high in the grim landscape.

It moved with chilling grace toward its adversary, eyeing the dragon through glistening black beads.

It began to coil, its thirty-foot body curling into a tight spiral. Then it struck, the vicious twin heads streaking from between the rocks, swooping down, its mouth yawning malevolently, then snapping shut, the fangs sinking deep into the neck of the dragon.

The dragon screamed in outrage and pain, twisted its head, and spat an inferno that engulfed the hissing serpent. The viper's body surged forward, wrapping itself around the neck of the dragon while one of its two heads snapped back and struck again. The dragon's shriek joined the hissing of the serpent. The two unearthly creatures were locked in a nightmare embrace.

High above them, from a soundproof booth overlooking the primeval battle, his face shimmering in the red glow of the flames below, DeLaroza looked like a vision from hell. The eerie reflection sutured his features with fleeting scars. His eyes flashed with joy and he clapped his hands together. He was, in that instant, an incarnation of the devil.

"Incredible, absolutely incredible!" he cried out. "Nikos, you have outdone yourself."

Seated beside him in front of a large electronic controlboard, the creator of the scene smiled. His name was Nikos Arcurius, a wiry little man, trim yet powerfully built, his biceps hard and veined, his black hair frosted white at the sideburns, his brown eyes twinkling with the rush of achievement.

The dragon and the snake, coiling, hissing, spitting fire, fought on.

"Enough," DeLaroza said. "Save the climax until Monday night."

Arcurius leaned over the controlboard and pressed buttons, twirled dials, and the two mammoth creatures slipped apart. The snake retreated back to its cave and the dragon, like a regal legend come to life, stalked back to its hiding place among the rocks.

"It is a masterpiece," DeLaroza said with awe. He laid his hand on the shoulder of his collaborator. Arcurius leaned back in his chair and surveyed the atrium and then nodded. It was true; it was a masterpiece.

Arcurius was Greek. Abandoned by his parents, he had grown up a street thief and pickpocket. When he was thirteen his quick hands had earned him a two-year sentence in Da Krivotros, a dismal island prison known as The Boxes because of the rows of solitary cells where even the slightest infraction of prison rules resulted in weeks in squalid isolation.

Thrown in with hardened criminals, Arcurius had earned their respect by putting his nimble fingers to a new use, carving puppets in the prison shop. He earned cigarette money and other favors from the prisoners by putting on Sunday shows in the visitors' compound for the wives and children of other prisoners. He was back on the street by the time he was sixteen, first joining a traveling circus, then trying to make a living as a puppeteer in Athens, but by the time he was twenty he was on the run again, fleeing from one country to the next, always with the law snapping at his ankles.

The salvation of Nikos Arcurius came when he signed on as a crewman on a steamer going from Marseille to New York to escape the local gendarmes. In New York his fortunes finally changed. Starting as an apprentice, he moved up quickly to become one of Broadway's most innovative set designers and while still in his twenties Arcurius was lured to Hollywood. There, on the vast sound stages of the big studios, his imagination flourished.

And it was there that he had met a visitor from Hong Kong. Victor DeLaroza was drawn to him not only by his enormous talent but by the candor with which he spoke of his early life.

"These fingers," he once told DeLaroza, wiggling all ten in the air, "belong to the second best pickpocket in Athens. The best one was never caught."

DeLaroza quickly realized that Arcurius's real genius lay not only in design but in production as well. He put Arcurius to work developing a new concept for toys and together they had revolutionized the industry. The Greek had an uncanny ability for breathing life into De-Laroza's wildest fantasies, designing and building toys of remarkable realism. Small transistor cards hidden inside dolls whose skin felt almost real caused eyes to blink, mouths to open and close, and activated tape loops through which the lifelike creations spoke simple sentences. His animals were marvels of innovative miniaturization. One, a small horse, performed four different gaits, its ingenious insides set in motion simply by the snap of a finger.

DeLaroza's exhaustive marketing skills had turned Arcurius into a household word and his creations, called Arcurions, into the most popular toys in the world, several of them so remarkable that even though mass-produced, they had already become collector's items.

Then DeLaroza had conceived an idea so exciting, so challenging, that he and Arcurius had devoted five years to designing it, another four to building it, and spent more than ten million dollars on the project.

Now, the result of their combined genius sprawled below them. It was to be the instrument by which De-Laroza would emerge from his self-imposed world of secrecy.

Now, with Corrigon out of the way—and tonight,

Domino—DeLaroza felt secure at last. Publicity releases would now begin revealing his contributions for the first time. Now he felt he could face cameras for the first time, unafraid.

Now he himself would introduce the world to his grandest accomplishment.

Pachinko!

The most outrageous, the most breathtaking, the most stunning madness of all.

Pachinko!

The ultimate playground.

In the heart of the glass tower DeLaroza had gutted six floors and replaced them with a towering atrium that began five stories above the ground. It was encircled by a narrow, eight-foot balcony from which spectators could view *Pachinko!* as if they were standing on a precipice looking down on it. Behind them the city of Atlanta could be seen, sprawling out behind floor-to-ceiling windows.

The panorama was staggering. Within the great space, nearly the size of four football fields, DeLaroza and Arcurius had recreated their own version of Hong Kong. A bustling, vibrant, ebullient amusement park and bazaar, as startling as it was ambitious, had been built in the middle of a skyscraper.

The journey to *Pachinko!* began on the first floor where an imported Chinese arch led to four bullet-shaped glass elevators that traveled up the exterior of the building. The arch was guarded on either side by two ten-foot temple dogs, their red tongues curling humorously beneath gleaming, dangerous eyes. A blazing Art Deco sign over the arch announced *Pachinko!* always with the exclamation point. A booth in front of the gate converted American dollars into reproductions of Hong Kong dollars, the medium of exchange for special attractions in the complex. One elevator lifted spec-

tators who simply wanted to observe the spectacle to the
special balcony where, for another dollar, they could
watch the revelers below. Four other elevators opened
on the eleventh floor, the entrance to *Pachinko!*, where
two ancient stone posts imported from Macao stood on
either side of a long, rambling stairway that led to the
main floor, six stories below. The stairway was a replica
of Hong Kong's bustling Ladder Street, a narrow con-
fined alley teeming with shops, cubbyholes and snack-
food stalls, and intersected by several other avenues.

DeLaroza surveyed his version of the city. Looking
down on the exciting maze below him, he envisioned it
crowded with tourists and sightseers, entertained by
strolling magicians and acrobats while a traveling
Chinese band provided the background music. It was a
splendid bazaar, with banners floating over more than
thirty shops where everything was sold, outrageously
expensive antiques, cheap souvenirs, suits custom-made
by Kowloon tailors, Oriental rugs, postcards, imitation
Buddhas, cameras, the finest jade. Food stalls offered
snacks of sizzling ribs and Peking chicken. Cats strolled
the steps.

On the main floor the Greek had created a shallow
lake with a small version of the Tai Tak floating restaurant in one corner, its cuisine presided over by Wan
Shu, one of Hong Kong's finest chefs, its garish decks
reached by small sampans which carried diners from the
main promenade, a winding path where theaters offered
karate, judo, and weaponry exhibitions, excerpts from
Chinese opera, and puppet shows for the children.
There were three night clubs and two other fine restaurants, a recreation of the Man Mo Temple, known as the
Place of a Thousand Buddhas, a sixty-foot model of the
Shinto Pagoda, an opium den, and a sampan ride
through a tortuous series of tunnels under Ladder Street
where like-real Arcurions played out some of the most

dramatic moments from the turbulent history of Hong Kong. The main street terminated at one end at the gardens with its abundance of rare flowers and beautiful young Chinese guides, who would escort visitors through the enchanting maze, explaining the icons of Chinese mythology found in its grottoes and pavilions. As they ended the tour the guides recounted the legend of Kowloon, the Ninth Dragon, and his battle with T'un Hai, the two-headed snake of the Underworld. Throughout, DeLaroza had insisted on historical, mythological, and architectural integrity.

The grand opening, now only three days away, would attract all three major television networks, radio, magazine, and newspaper reporters from all over the world, leading politicians and British and Chinese dignitaries, all to be flown in on special junkets. Photographs and visitors had been barred from the amusement complex until opening night, for DeLaroza knew that the reaction would be much more excited if an aura of mystery were created about *Pachinko!* So it had remained an enigma, a giant surprise package to be unwrapped the following Monday night.

What better time for Donald Hotchins to make his announcement?

Julius Lowenthal stood a few feet from DeLaroza, his eyes saucers of amazement as he stared down through the glass front of the soundproof control booth at *Pachinko!* DeLaroza turned to him, towering over the weary Washington lawyer.

"Well, sir," DeLaroza said, "what do you think of our toy, eh?"

"Toy?" Lowenthal said incredulously.

DeLaroza chuckled. "Perhaps I should say 'playground.' Until tonight no outsider has seen it. I have forbidden photographs and all but the most general description."

Lowenthal shrugged his shoulders in an almost helpless gesture. "I, uh . . . I've lost my tongue," he said. "I'm speechless."

"You do not approve?"

"Oh, my God, of course. It's monumental. A monumental undertaking."

DeLaroza took him lightly by the elbow and led him out of the booth and along the balcony toward Ladder Street.

"I'm flattered that you let me take a look," Lowenthal said.

"The least I could do," DeLaroza said. "Once again I must apologize for Donald's absence. It is an old and personal political commitment. He will be back tomorrow and you two can get back to business."

"I've been around politics long enough to understand these things," Lowenthal said.

"Good. Besides, this will give us a chance to know each other a little better, yes?"

"Of course."

But Lowenthal doubted it. He had been close to many rich and powerful men during his career but had never really known any of them well, for they were guarded people. Secrecy went with power and money— it was a thing he had learned early on. But he had to admit that DeLaroza was perhaps the most shielded of all. There was nothing but the skimpiest of dossiers on DeLaroza. No pictures, no stories. Lowenthal knew that he had come to America sixteen years before and had become a naturalized citizen four years ago. He had managed Hotchins's campaign finances almost from the beginning and done it impeccably. There was little else available. His holdings and personal worth were unknown, his companies privately held. If this was to be

an opportunity for anyone to get to know anyone, it was
DeLaroza who would find out about Lowenthal and
Lowenthal knew it.

Oh, well, he thought, *what's to know about me?* He
had no secrets at all.

"You're taking quite a gamble," he said as they approached the long, winding steps of the Ladder Street
bazaar.

"I suppose so," DeLaroza said.

"And if the public doesn't bite?"

DeLaroza paused a moment, then said, "I never consider failure. There is a Chinese proverb—The fish that
fears it will be eaten becomes dinner for the shark."

Lowenthal smiled. "And you don't fear the shark?"

DeLaroza looked at him and smiled faintly. "No," he
said, "I do not fear the shark."

They turned into Ladder Street and started the long
walk down to the main floor, DeLaroza stopping occasionally to chat with shopkeepers. Along the way, they
passed two jugglers tossing fire sticks back and forth as
though they were playing catch.

"What's the story behind the dragon and the snake?"
Lowenthal asked.

"Ah, my favorite legend, although I must say there
are many Oriental myths which stir the imagination.
The guides in the garden explain it quite poetically. My
chef has prepared for us a potpourri of the menu, a
preview of its delights. I will have one of the young ladies tell you the story while we eat."

At the foot of Ladder Street, an elderly Caucasian
gentleman with soft, gentle features and snow-white hair
sat on a wall playing the violin. He nodded to DeLaroza
as the two men passed him.

"That is Mr. Reynolds," DeLaroza said. "He has
journeyed all over China with a traveling band, played
first chair in the Vienna Symphony, played ragtime mu-

sic with the greats in New Orleans, and he once taught
at the Boston Conservatory. I have known him for
many, many years and I have no idea how old he is. He
is not interested in age. For him, every day is a new
experience. He is the leader of our Chinese band."

"Where did you find him?"

"He found me," DeLaroza said cryptically and ended
that part of the conversation. "The restaurant is over
there. On the other side of the pond. It is a replica of
Tai Tak, the finest restaurant in all Hong Kong—at
least *my* favorite. But first let me show you one more
thing. I think this may excite your imagination more
than all the rest of this."

They walked up a curving pathway to the end, near
the outside wall of the building. Lowenthal saw the
looming figure before they reached it, seven feet tall, his
eyes gleaming slits, his mustaches plunging down to his
chest, his fingernails curved like talons.

"Meet Man Chu, the war lord," DeLaroza said
proudly. The giant turned its head and glared down at
the two men. For an instant Lowenthal almost held out
his hand to shake its menacing fist.

"It's almost real," Lowenthal breathed in wonder-
ment.

"The definitive Arcurion," DeLaroza said. "Nikos
does not make toys or robots; he makes people and
creatures. Sometimes I find myself talking to them as
though they were alive."

"What is this?" Lowenthal asked.

"The *pièce de résistance*. A thrill ride like no other
in creation. This is where the park gets its name. Pachinko."

The robot stood in front of a hollow stainless-steel
ball large enough to seat two people. The door in the
front of the ball opened toward the floor.

"Step inside," DeLaroza said. Lowenthal got into the

ball and settled into the soft leather seat. DeLaroza closed the door. The top half was open so that the rider had a clear view out of the round car.

"Now imagine Man Chu, here, firing this ball into that tunnel in front of you. You drop down a chute to the floor below, which is an enormous pinball field. Bumpers, lights, tunnels, mirrors. The car rolls freely on ball bearings, it never turns upside down and the speed is electronically controlled by an operator who sits in the middle of the pachinko board. Once it leaves the chute here, it is on its own. Only the speed is controlled, so it does not fly out of control. Otherwise it bounces from bumper to bumper up to thirty miles an hour at times before it drops through another chute and arrives on the first floor . . . where your attendant hands you your car keys."

Above the entrance tunnel was a large replica of the pachinko board itself, an electronic grid on which a blip followed the course of the ball, lighting up the bumpers and registering the score on a digital counter.

DeLaroza helped Lowenthal from the ball. "Now come along," he said.

He led the way from the entrance to the ride, along a narrow alley and through a fire door. A flight of steps led down to a second door, which opened onto the field itself. Its walls were mirrored. Strobe lights flashed intermittently and the bumpers gleamed gaudily. It was the bumpers that intrigued Lowenthal, for they were like a vast field of strange statues, each in the shape of a Chinese deity.

DeLaroza strode out on the board, and was immediately dwarfed by the jazzy hardware of the giant pinball machine. He pointed first to this bumper, then that, talking continually.

"This is Shou-Lsing, the god of long life. I call him the laughing god. That one, the serene one, is Lu-Hsing, the god of salaries. Over there, that fat one? Who else but the god of wealth, Ts'ai-Shen? And this lady here, this is Kuan-Yin, goddess of mercy and compassion. Forty-two bumpers in all, enough to satisfy even the most masochistic thrill-seeker. The ball makes one complete revolution of the board here at thirty miles an hour before it rolls through that chute up there. The box in the center is the control-board. One man can control three balls. On opening night, of course, we will shoot them through one at a time."

He turned and looked at Lowenthal. It was indeed a fitting climax for *Pachinko!*

"Well," DeLaroza said grandly, "now what do you think?"

Lowenthal held his hands out at his sides, palms up. "What can I say? It is the definitive fantasy. Congratulations."

Obviously pleased, DeLaroza led him back to the main floor of the park.

"And now," he said, "we shall enjoy the *crème de la crème*. Wan Shu is waiting. Now that we have excited your emotions, we shall do the same for your palate."

13

Barney Friscoe stormed through the lobby of the Lancaster Towers West with Papa trotting at his side. The security guard watched them enter and came out of his office with his eyebrows arched into question marks.

Papa managed a lame smile. "Superintendent," he said, pointing to Friscoe, whose face looked like a volcano about to erupt.

"Everything hunky-dory up there?" the guard said, with a touch of panic in his voice.

"Fine, fine," Papa said, "nothin' to worry about. Routine." They got into the elevator. The guard watched the door shut and finally shrugged and returned to his television set.

"What's this 'superintendent' shit?" Friscoe snapped.

"A cover. He thinks we're workin' on the elevators," Papa said.

"The elevators? Jesus H. Christ, Papa, this better be important, that's all I got to say, pullin' me outa the symphony, right in the middle of Prokofiev. And *Lieutenant Kije* at that! My oldest kid made third chair tonight, you understand that? It's important."

Papa said nothing.

"A fantastic program, we got Brahms, we got Schubert, and we got Prokofiev! And there I am, third row center." Friscoe, who was wearing a tuxedo, pulled his velvet tie loose and opened the top button of his shirt as the elevator stopped.

"To the right, first door on the right," Papa said.

Friscoe stomped down the hall, muttering to himself. "This better be good. This better be fingerfuckin*lickin'* good."

Friscoe hammered on the door to 10-A.

"Who is it?" Livingston asked from inside.

"It's Little Red Riding Hood, for Chrissakes, who do you think it is? Open the goddamn door."

The chain rattled and Livingston swung the door partially open. Friscoe charged through it without looking to the right or left. He came face to face with Sharky and The Nosh. Friscoe stood in front of them, his hands on his hips and his tie dangling like black crepe paper from his open collar.

"Awright," Friscoe bawled, "what the fuck's so urgent you jokers get me outa the symphony right on the dime, when in ten more minutes I could've sneaked out between numbers and nobody woulda been the wiser? I had to crawl over half of Atlanta society to—"

Livingston was tapping him on the shoulder and at the same moment Sharky pointed back toward the door. Friscoe spun around.

"What the hell do you—" he said, and stopped in mid-sentence.

He saw the bloody pattern near the ceiling, the splash

of blood on the wall where the force of the shot had thrown her, the streaks down to the crumpled body below.

A gaunt spider of a man was leaning over her, examining the body.

"Terrible for the blood pressure, Barney, blowing up like that," the gaunt man said quietly.

"Holy shit!" Friscoe said, half under his breath. He took a few steps toward the corpse and stopped. His face contorted. He swallowed hard, shuddered, looked at Livingston, back at Sharky, and then at the corpse again.

"What the fuck . . . who is it? What happened here?"

Sharky started to speak but his voice cracked and he stopped to clear his throat. Livingston finally spoke up. "It's the Domino woman," he said. The words cut deep into Sharky's gut when he heard them said aloud.

"Domino!" Friscoe said.

"Yeah."

Friscoe's eyes widened. "So what happened?"

The gaunt man, his hands encased in blood-covered plastic surgeon's gloves, looked up at him. "Somebody aced the lady," he said in a voice that sounded tired.

"I ain't blind," Friscoe bellowed. "What I wanna know is, what happened?"

"What happened, Sharky's on the roof monitoring the bugs," Livingston said. "She got away from us this morning and was out most of the day. About seven forty there was a call from somebody named Pete saying he would be late and would call back. She came in at seven forty-four. Two minutes later another call. Whoever it was hung up. At seven fifty-eight the doorbell rang, she opened the door and"—he nodded toward the corpse. "Couple more things. She was packing her suitcase when she got hit. It's in there on the bed. Then

about fifteen minutes after . . . it happened . . .
there was another call. We let the machine answer it. It
was this Pete again. I picked it up, but he hung up as
soon as he heard my voice."

The gaunt man stripped off his gloves, put a hand on
his knee, and stood up. And up. And up. He was a
shade over six-foot-six, thin as a stalk of wheat, his
clothes hanging from bony shoulders like rags on a scare-
crow. His complexion was the color of oatmeal, his
hair—what there was of it—the color of sugared cinnamon. The bones in his long, angular face strained
against wafer-thin skin. His long needle fingers seemed
as brittle as the limbs of a dead bush. Art Harris, one of
the city's better reporters, had once profiled him thus:
"Max Grimm, the Fulton County coroner, is a cadaver-
ous stalk of twigs who looks worse than many of his
subjects . . ." The description provided Grimm with
his nickname, Twigs. At sixty-seven he had been coroner for forty-one years and had managed to stave off
compulsory retirement at sixty-five with the excuse that
he was suffering some vague terminal disorder and
wanted to work as long as possible at the job he had
held for almost two-thirds of his life. Nobody believed
him, but that was immaterial. He was too good to retire
anyway.

His partner in crime was George Barret, head of the
forensics lab. Together, they were the Mutt and Jeff of
Pathology, the Tweedledee and Tweedledum of crime
lab and morgue. Barret stood barely five-five,
outweighed Grimm by at least twenty pounds, wore
rimless bifocals, and parted his strawberry-colored hair
down the middle like a turn-of-the-century snake-oil
peddler. He was an arch-Baptist who neither smoked,
swore, nor drank and was constantly offended by
Grimm's penchant for Napoleon brandy, which the coroner nipped constantly from a Maalox bottle. Barret

entered the scene from one of the bedrooms carrying an ancient black snap-satchel which his late father, a country doctor, had willed him. Inside were crammed all the mysterious vials, chemicals, and tools of the forensic trade.

In his soft Southern voice he said, in a single sentence virtually uninhibited by punctuation: "Nothing here, I got all the pictures and measurements I need, oh, hi, Barney, I think we can assume from the tape and what we can—or more correctly, what we can't—find that the killer never ventured beyond the door there."

Friscoe was a man fighting frustration, pearls of sweat twinkling on his forehead. "Well, where's everybody else?" he asked.

"What do you mean?" Livingston replied.

"I mean where the hell is everybody else? Where's Homicide? I see the ME there. I see Forensics. Where is everybody else? Here it is an hour and five minutes since it happened and there ain't a Homicide in sight yet."

"Nobody called Homicide," Livingston said.

Frisco's eyes went blank. "Nobody called Homicide?"

"Nobody called Homicide."

"Well, uh, is there a reason nobody called Homicide? I mean have all communications between this here apartment house and the main station busted down or what?"

Sharky was staring at the floor. He had said nothing since Friscoe arrived. He was still having trouble putting together an intelligible sentence. The one thing Friscoe would not understand, would not accept, was Sharky's personal feeling and Sharky knew it would be difficult, if not impossible, to put his personal anger aside. He had to be cautious and it was that necessity that kept him from saying anything. Friscoe finally turned to Livingston. "Arch?"

"Sure," Livingston said and then suddenly words seemed to die in his mouth, too. It was Papa who finally broke the awkward, stammering cadence of the conversation. "We wanna do it," he said simply.

"We wanna do what?" Friscoe said.

"We wanna handle this one."

"What are you talkin' about?"

"He means we want to run with it, Barney," Livingston said. "We know more about—"

"Wait a minute! Wait a fuckin' minute," Friscoe said, and his voice wavered. He held up a finger. "You all understand, right, that the golden rule, I mean rule number *one* of the holy scriptures according to The Bat, is that in the event of any sudden or unexplainable or suspicious death, *any* death of that nature, Homicide gets notified first. Before anybody even goes to the fuckin' *bath*room, the Homicides are brought in. That's gospel, boys."

"Listen a minute," Livingston implored.

"No! I don't believe my ears. Maybe the robust second chorus of *Lieutenant Kije* has temporarily damaged the old ears here, because if what I'm hearing is what I *think* I'm hearing, you're all off the wall. You're all dangerous if that's what's comin' off here. You're as dangerous as a goddamn cross-eyed barber if you're thinking what I think you're thinking." Friscoe's face had turned red with anger.

"Look, don't take it personal, for Chrissakes," Livingston said.

"Well I am takin' it personal. How about that? I'm takin' all this bullshit personal. And that's what it is— bullshit."

"Look," Livingston said, "we're all a little, uh, freaked right now."

"Oh, I can tell that, yessiree. You're all around the bend, if you ask me. You—you're Abrams, that right?"

The Nosh nodded.

"And you go along with this?"

The Nosh nodded again.

"Shit, you're all nuttier than a team of one-legged tap dancers, you wanna know what I think. That's if anybody's interested in what I think."

The Nosh smiled.

"It ain't funny there, Abrams," Friscoe roared. "You got yourself one hell of a pile of trouble. What you think's gonna happen when D'Agastino hears about this? You think I'm going up? Hah! D'Agastino's gonna break eardrums in Afghanistan. That fuckin' wop can outscream Billy Graham."

"Will you just listen for a min—" Livingston started to say.

Friscoe cut him off. "Crazy," the lieutenant said, "craz-eeee." He put his hands over his ears.

Livingston looked at Sharky and shrugged. "What'd I tell you?" he said.

"What'd I tell who?" Friscoe said, still holding his hands over his ears.

"I told him you'd think we were nuts."

"You are nuts. Absogoddamnlutely nuts. The lot of you. N-u-t-s."

"I thought at least you'd . . ." Livingston started, and then let the sentence dangle.

"Thought what? Thought what?" Friscoe said, his voice beginning to rise again.

"I thought you'd hear us out."

"What is this here you're layin' off on me, Arch? What's with this heartbreak hotel shit? Jesus, right now, this here very minute you are all up to your ass in alligators. And for Christ's sake, so am I. I ain't even involved in this and I'm in trouble. The Bat's gonna have ass, man. Ten fat cheeks nailed to his fuckin' wall. And you, too, Twigs. You and George there. You know the procedure."

"I work for the county," Twigs said quietly. "Captain Jaspers can go suck a duck egg."

"That's real cute," Friscoe said. "How about you, George?"

"He owes me," Livingston said. "I just called in my green stamps."

"Jaspers won't bother me," Barret said. "I can remember when he was pounding a beat. He had difficulty tying his shoes in those days."

"He still does," Twigs said. "Besides, until you arrived, Barney, Arch was the senior officer on the scene. All I am required to do is make a preliminary study of the corpse on the scene prior to performing an autopsy. The officer in charge gets the results. In this case, I believe Sergeant Livingston was the ranking man on the scene."

Barret smiled. "I follow the same procedure. Livingston will get my report. If he handles it improperly, it's his problem, not mine."

Friscoe sat down on the couch. "Cheez," he said. He sat for several seconds shaking his head slowly. Finally: "Okay, okay. Everybody here's gone a little ape. I can understand that. I'll work it out. I'll take on The Bat and get it straightened out."

"Barney, all we want is the weekend. Sixty hours. What the hell's that? Until Monday-morning roll call," Livingston said.

"It's nuts, that's what it is," Friscoe said. "Look, I said I'd get it straightened out. But right now we got to get some Homicides up here and fast."

Ironically, it was Papa who exploded. Papa—who rarely said anything and when he did could reduce the Constitution *and* the Bill of Rights to a single syllable,

Papa who rarely showed any emotion—exploding like a wounded bull.

"Fuck 'em!" he roared, jolting the anguished Friscoe. "Fuck 'em all. Fuck The Bat, fuck Homicide, fuck that goddamn psalm-singin' moron of a DA. Fuck 'em all. Arch and me have been stuck down in that stinkin' garbage pail at Vice for six years. You been there longer, Friscoe. Everybody in the House thinks all we're good for is puttin' the arm on hookers and perverts and wipin' dogshit off our shoes. We ain't a bunch of morons, y'know. Between you, me, and Arch there we got about fifty years in. This here's our caper. We turned it up. I'm the one waltzed that goddamn Mabel around interrogation until my arches fell and that's what started it all, got us into this here spot in the first place, or maybe you forgot that. Now you know what we're gonna get outa all this? More shit, that's what. The rest of the force is gonna come down on us with their wisecracks and insults. It don't make no never mind that Sharky was up there on the roof doin' his job proper. Don't make no never mind that we turned this whole thing up and followed through. Hell, no! All we're gonna hear is that we had a man on the roof when that lady there got her brains handed to her. Well, I'll tell you what—I'm tired of bein' the asshole of the whole police department. Fuck 'em all, Barney. I say we go after this son of a bitch ourselves and when we get him we hang his goddamn balls on Jaspers's wall. I'm tired of bein' shit on." Papa pulled open the french doors and stormed out on the balcony, his face as pink as a salamander.

Friscoe was flabbergasted. "I don't understand what's happening to everybody. I've known Papa for ten years. Worked with him for six. That's more in one breath than he's said the whole rest of the time I've known him. What the hell's the fuss? What we got is a hooker suspected of complicity in a felony who got totaled. Big fuckin' deal. It ain't the first time somebody put the zap on a goddamn prostitute."

"She was a nice lady," The Nosh said.

"*A nice lady?*" Friscoe said.

Sharky had been sitting on the couch without a word. Now he had to say something. But what? How could he possibly explain that he had met Domino and the strange circumstances of the meeting. Or that he had sensed a vulnerability that had drawn him to her. Or that because he had felt an attraction to her this senseless violence that had snuffed out Domino's life seemed somehow directed at him, too.

"Don't you understand," he said finally. "I feel responsible. Whether I am or not, I *feel* responsible."

Friscoe stared at Sharky and his anger began to subside. "Okay, I do understand that. Thing is, nobody here's responsible. You were doin' exactly what you were supposed to be doin'. Look here, did you—did *any*body —have any idea she was gonna get shoved over?"

No answer.

"Anybody at all?"

Still no answer.

"Of course not. Nobody's responsible for nothin'. Nobody knew it was comin' down, right? Now I can understand Doc Twigs here goin' a little off the wall. You gotta be a little weird, goin' around sniffin' that goddamn formaldehyde all the time. But not the rest of you. See, no matter what we did, if we wrapped this one up before breakfast, we'd all end up one through five on The Bat's shit list. When he finds out, that's it. And he's gonna find out, make no mistake about that. Anybody wanna argue that point? No, there ain't no argument there. And even, see, even if Jaspers falls deaf, dumb, and blind in the next thirty seconds, we still got one J. Philip Riley to contend with. I'm sure you will all recall that Lieutenant Riley heads up Homicide, but what maybe you don't know is that when God handed out brains this same J. Philip Riley was on the front of the line. And also what maybe you don't know is that J. Philip Riley has got a temper that when *he* blows, The Bat and D'Agastino're both gonna sound like a pair of sopranos in the Sunday school choir. I mean, Riley ain't gonna take too lightly to the fact that a bunch of stand-up comics from Vice just hi-de-ho stepped in and took over one of his homicide cases. That's for openers. For closers I would like to point out that this same J. Philip Riley happens to be a friend of mind and a damn good cop and I ain't inclined at this minute to stick my dick in the meat grinder just because Sharky here feels re-*spons*ible."

"That was quite a little speech, Barney," Barret said in his quiet, funereal voice. "All they want is the week-end. I happen to know that Jaspers is in Chicago ad-dressing the NAPO convention. He won't even be back until Monday night."

"That's fuckin' immaterial," Friscoe snapped.

"I don't think so," Twigs said.

Friscoe whirled away from him as if he had the plague. "Just keep your dime out of it, Twigs," he snapped.

"Why? What you're saying merely points up the fact that Sharky and Livingston, Papa out there on the porch, are right. It doesn't make any difference what you do now, The Bat and Riley are both going to be on the warpath. What've you got to lose?"

"I don't go for breakin' procedure—that's one thing I don't go for. That's suicide!"

"Yeah, Barney," Livingston said, "the reason you've been in Vice for almost seven years is because you're so big on procedure. Shit, we haven't followed *procedure* since I been in the squad."

"This is interdepartmental," Friscoe said.

Sharky stood up and began pacing around the room. The shock was wearing off and in its place was anger, a welling fury deep inside him. "Maybe you like it down there in Friscoe's Inferno," he said, and his voice was brittle. "Maybe you been lying with the dogs so long you like the fleas."

"Who the hell do you think you are, say a shit thing like that to me?" Friscoe said, his face turning blood red.

"I'm just thinking about that spiel I got when I checked in yesterday," said Sharky. "Was that all bullshit? About how you and Arch and Papa were down there because you didn't suck ass. Didn't play by the book. A bunch of hardheads. I'll tell you what, Lieutenant, you gave me this machine and Arch and Papa and The Nosh there are along for the ride. Now you want to hand it over to Riley? Shit, maybe you were right. Maybe I should walk. Maybe I should walk right now, right out that door, and go after the son of a bitch myself."

"You do and I'll bring you down myself. I don't go for headhunting. That's cheap shit and you know it."

"Look, every minute we sit around here arguin', the son of a bitch is moving farther away," said Livingston. "Why not give Twigs and George a chance to tell us what they've picked up? Five, ten minutes more. Like you say, we're up to our asses in alligators anyway."

Friscoe's shoulders sagged. Defeated, he waved his hand at Twigs. "Go ahead, for Chrissake."

Twigs smiled. "Don't worry about Riley. He's got seven stiffs down there in the icebox and two of them are John Does. He'll probably be grateful for any help he can get at this point."

"That's a laugh," Friscoe said. "Riley ain't happy unless his caseload looks like the casualty report from World War Two."

"May we go ahead?" Barret asked.

"Sure, why not?" said Friscoe. "Before this is over we're all gonna be directing traffic on the outskirts of Boise, Idaho, anyhow."

"What do you remember from ballistics training?" Barret asked.

"You must be kidding," Friscoe said. "I been in Vice so long, I can remember when they busted Socrates for pinchin' little boys on the ass. Keep it basic."

"All right. First, the obvious. The weapon was a shotgun, twelve-gauge, judging from the number of pellets in the shot, and I think we both agree that it was sawed-off. Why? Because the shot leaves the barrel at a muzzle velocity of about eleven hundred feet per second. Up to about three feet the shot is contained; the effect is like a single rifle bullet. After that, the pellets begin to spread. If you want the shot to spread faster, the best way to accomplish your purpose is to saw the barrel off. The effect of a sawed-off scattergun is the same at about three feet as the pattern of a normal shotgun at about eight or ten yards. Now, let's take a look at the scene a minute. Mr. Grimm?"

"Yes, Mr. Barret."

The gaunt man took a pencil from his inside pocket and drew the point along his hairline at the forehead. "Singed hair along the frontal lobe here. In fact the hair was burned in places. Also some scorched bits of skin embedded in the wall with the pellets that didn't hit her. The heat from a shotgun blast dissipates very rapidly. So I would say the weapon was three to four feet from the victim's face when it was fired.

"Judging from the destruction, the pattern was already wide, seven to eight inches in diameter. Where it hit the wall there it has already spread to ten inches. That's the kind of dispersal we would normally expect at eight or ten yards. So I would say the gun was fired from the vicinity of the door and that it was sawed off pretty close, maybe eight or nine inches from the firing pin as opposed to a normal barrel length of thirty or thirty-two inches. Mr. Barret?"

"Thank you, Mr. Grimm. As for the weapon," Barret said, "if you listen to Sharky's tape recording you will notice that the two shots came almost simultaneously; in fact they overlap slightly. They are too close together for the weapon to be an automatic or a pump or lever action. So what we got is a sawed-off double-barrel twelve-gauge shotgun and one that was very effectively silenced."

"A *lupara?*" Livingston asked, and there was surprise in his voice.

"What's a *lupara?*" Sharky said.

"It's Sicilian for a shotgun of this kind. The classic Mafia execution weapon," Barret said. "Certainly a possibility."

"You sayin' this is a Mafia hit?" Friscoe said.

"I'm saying it's a similar kind of weapon. And I'm also saying that this was no amateur at work. No amateur would have a weapon like that. Certainly not one that was silenced. Besides, this was very well planned."

"There's another thing," Twigs said. He knelt and picked up one of the pellets from a plastic bag with a pair of tweezers and held it under Friscoe's nose.

"Smell anything?"

"Yeah," Friscoe said, "gunpowder."

"Anything else?"

Friscoe closed his eyes and sniffed. His forehead wrinkled up. "What is that—garlic?"

"Exactly," Twigs said.

"Don't tell me," Friscoe said, "the shotgun had spaghetti for dinner."

Barret smiled. "Perhaps. It is another Mafia trademark. The *caporegimi*, the Mafia lieutenants, sometimes soaked their bullets in garlic. It infected the wound and also made the wound more painful. It was a tactic used mostly for revenge or official executions. But never in a shotgun. It's quite strange."

"You're not saying this is some kind of official Mafia hit?" Friscoe said.

"I tend to doubt it."

"What then?"

"Maybe it's part of his m.o.," Sharky said.

"That's more like it," Barret said. "A habit. Or perhaps even a trademark."

"So he could be an old-time *caporegime*," Livingston said.

Barret nodded.

"What the hell good is that?" Friscoe said. "So you've narrowed the field down to a coupla thousand ace hitmen spread out all over the country. Big deal."

"Profiles, dear Barney, profiles," Twigs said. "A few more details. The projectile was upward. You can tell from the way the shots hit the wall. The victim measures approximately 178 centimeters, that's about five-ten. Assuming from the other physical evidence that the killer was standing in the doorway, we can draw an imaginary line from the center of the pattern through the victim's head to a point where the killer was standing. We can assume he did not shoot from the hip. If he had, the second shot probably would have hit him in his own chin. So he either fired with the piece under his armpit or against his shoulder. From all this we can make a pretty good guess at the killer's height. Mr. Barret?"

Barret had drawn a diagram on a sheet of paper and

was punching the keys of a small pocket calculator. "Five-nine tops. More likely five-seven or eight. Also from the position of the two shots, I would say you're looking for an over-under double-barrel rather than a side-by-side."

"Pretty common, right?" Friscoe said.

"Yes," said Barret, "I wouldn't waste my time trying to trace the gun. The significant thing is that it adds to his m.o."

"The more you talk, the more I think we better get Riley and company up here fast," Friscoe said. "Let Homicide and the OC worry about it—it's their problem."

"If D'Agastino gets involved you can forget it," The Nosh said. "Before it's over, he and Riley will be killing each other. That D'Agastino actually keeps evidence to himself so the OC can get the glory."

"That's okay. I'll put Riley against him any day. You ain't seen nothin' till you've seen that crazy Irishman mad."

"Barney, Phil Riley got his job because he deserved it. D'Agastino is a politician. In your experience, which gets preference in the official hierarchy, politics—or talent? Riley's going to spend weeks wading through the red tape and then he'll be lucky if the case stays in his department." Twigs took out his Maalox bottle and celebrated his analysis with a swig of brandy.

"Let's add up what we know about the shooter, shall we?" Barret said. "I think we're looking for an old-timer, someone with definite habits. Extremely cautious, a careful planner, experienced enough to be sure of himself. I'd say he goes back a ways. The young ones avoid habits. They vary their methods constantly to avoid detection. The older ones are too set in their ways. They follow traditions. They're scared to make changes. They stick with what they know works. So I'd say an old-timer definitely. Late forties, early fifties at least, maybe older. Five-seven to five-nine. Quite possibly a contact killer, someone who likes to work close to the victim, perhaps even psychopathic in that sense. Mafia and possibly an executioner fairly high in the Mafia hierarchy, because of the garlic thing. The use of garlic these days, I would think, is part of his ritual, something associated with luck or tradition."

"Thank you, Mr. Barret," Twigs said.

"Thank *you*, Mr. Grimm," Barret said.

Papa broke into the conversation from the balcony. "You know what I think?"

"God knows," Friscoe said.

"The fink was watchin' the apartment. Had to've been. Wouldn't stand in the stairwell all day waitin' for her to come home. Wouldn't be out in the open—too easy to spot. Phone call was probably to make sure she was home. Had to be where he could see lights come on. He was watchin'. From over there someplace." He gestured toward the east tower.

They all looked toward the other building, at the irregular boxes of light shining through apartment windows. Sharky felt a sudden chill. Goose pimples rippled along his arm and he rubbed them away as surreptitiously as he could. Perhaps the killer had been there, all day, watching as Sharky listened from his perch on the roof. Anger began replacing the sorrow he felt for Domino, worms nudging his instinct for revenge, urging it into motion. He remembered the previous day when they were planting the mikes in the apartment and Domino had returned. He said, "Papa's right. He had to be watching. It happened too fast to be luck or coincidence. And you can't see this apartment from the street. Yesterday Arch had to warn The Nosh and me when we were up here. We couldn't see her when she came home."

"You can't see it too good from the swimming terrace, either," Papa said. "Which leaves the north side of the building, and that's all residential, a lot of trees and backyards . . ."

"And over there," Papa said.

They all stood on the balcony, looking across at the east tower.

"He could be sitting over there watching us right now," said Twigs.

"You kiddin'?" Friscoe said, "He's halfway to Detroit by now."

"Makes sense, y'know," Barret agreed. "Perhaps an empty apartment?"

"Too chancy," Friscoe said. "He's sittin' in there, somebody comes in for a look-see, a prospective tenant, you know. Bingo, he's made. Too smart for that."

"How about somebody who's out of town?" Sharky suggested.

"Sounds like a lot of crap shootin' to me," Friscoe said.

"No," Twigs said, "it's deduction. And that's what's going to break this one no matter who handles it. You, D'Agastino, Riley, or whoever."

"There's not enough physical evidence at this point. I agree," Barret said.

"I think," said Sharky, "it's time to have a chat with the security man."

"Look," Friscoe said, "if we *are* gonna do this we can't even tell the press she's dead. We can't even notify her next of *kin*. What the fuck are you going to tell the security man?"

Sharky smiled for the first time since Domino had been killed. "I'm goin' to con him," he said. "How do you think I stayed alive on the street for eighteen months?"

The security guard was in his office watching an old Randolph Scott movie on television when Sharky appeared at the doorway. He smiled and said, "Hi."

The guard nodded back. "Everything copesetic up there?" he said.

"Yeah, sure," Sharky said. He lit a small cigar. "Old Randy was tough, wasn't he?"

The security guard said, "Don't make 'em like that anymore," without taking his eyes off the screen.

Sharky blew smoke toward the ceiling and decided it was time for a long shot. "How long were you a cop?" he asked.

The guard looked up, surprised, "How'd you know?" he said.

Sharky took out his wallet and flipped it open, baring his shield.

"I'll be a son of a bitch," the guard said. "You know somethin'? I had a feelin' all along that story about the elevators was a lot of crap." He leaned toward Sharky and said very softly, "What in hell's goin' on, anyway?"

"We need to trust you," Sharky said. "What I'm going to tell you is very confidential."

"Hey, I was nineteen years on the College Park force. I'd still be there only I piled up a blue-and-white chasing some goddamn teenagers and almost lost a leg. Had to retire early."

"That's tough," Sharky said. "What's your name?"

"Jerry. Jerry Sanford."

"This stays between us, right?"

"Tellin' Jerry Sanford is like talkin' to a grave."

"Okay. The boys up there with me, we're all a special team from burglary. For three weeks now we've had a cat burglar working the high rent apartments and condos along Peachtree. He's very good, driving us up the wall. He always knows exactly what he's after, who to hit, and who not to hit. He knows when people are out of town. He can pop a double-lock LaGard box easier than opening a can of beans. So far he's been two feet ahead of us all the way. We figure he's got to take this place sooner or later."

"We got good security," Sanford said.

"He's hit just as tough."

"Yeah?"

"Believe me, this guy is first rate. He's into tricks we never heard of."

"No shit. What'd you say your name was again?"

"Sharky."

"Tell you, Sharky, Raymond Security is tough."

"Here's the thing. We figure he does a real number before he hits. Checks out the residents. Maybe even has a method for scoring financial statements. He usually hits apartments or condominiums where the tenants are out of town for a while. Business, maybe, or traveling. He might even call ahead, ask questions about the tenants. But very clever."

"We don't tell nobody nothin' about our occupants."

"He's clever, like I said. Maybe passes himself off as a delivery man. A salesman, like that."

"No solicitations in the building."

"Maybe a door-to-door thing?"

"Nobody gets by this desk without we check who they're going to see and get an okay from the occupant."

"How long are you on? What's your shift?"

"I'm on two to ten right now. The graveyard man takes over from ten to six in the A.M. Then the early man does six to two. We revolve the shift every six weeks. I been on the evening trick for a month."

"How about the other men?"

"First rate, everybody. I'm telling you, Raymond Security is the best."

"And there hasn't been anyone around? No phone-calls?"

"No, sir."

"Nobody suspicious hanging around?"

"If there was, you'd be the first to know. We've had a couple of people looking at apartments, asking about vacancies. The place stays a hundred percent full. We got four on the waiting list now. The two empties are bein' renovated. They're both leased already."

"Which ones would they be?"

"Let's see, there's 10-B west and 4-C east."

"10-B west?"

"Yeah. They're puttin' in the carpeting now. It goes to an elderly lady. A widow. Very well fixed. The other one goes to a young couple. He's a doctor."

"Anything temporarily vacant? You know, people away on vacation, anything like that?"

"Sure. But we got the list. Let's see. There's the Cliffords, 9-C east. They're in Florida for the holidays. Go down every year. He's retired. And then there's Mrs. Jackowitz. She's in Hawaii with her daughter. They take a trip every year this time. The daughter's a travel agent. Mr. Jackowitz passed on about two years ago."

"Where's her apartment?"

"That would be 12-C in the east tower."

"That would face?"

"West. A and B are on the east side of the building. C and D on the west. Four apartments to the floor."

"So the Jackowitz apartment is on the twelfth floor of the east tower facing the west tower?"

"Right."

"And the Cliffords?"

"9-C, east."

"Both apartments face the other tower, right?"

"Right."

"And nobody soliciting, no calls, nothing like that?" The guard shook his head.

"Okay, Jerry, thanks. We'll be in and out for a couple of more days."

"You want to stake out one of the empties, it's okay with me. I got a passkey."

"Thanks, we may just take you up on that." Sharky started out of the office and brushed against a tall corn plant in the corner, its leaves turning brown at the tips. "You're overwatering your plants," he said to Sanford. "You can always tell when the leaves turn at the ends like that."

"I got the original brown thumb. I already killed one of the Jackowitz plants and two more in here."

"You go in the Jackowitz apartment?"

"Yeah, I water the plants for her. I hate to do it, too. I don't have the feel for it, know what I mean?"

"Yeah. When's the last time you were in there?"

"Jackowitz? Lessee, it was Sunday. I water them on Sundays."

"Thanks. We'll keep in touch."

Sharky started to leave and Sanford suddenly snapped his fingers. "Hey, I just thought of something. There was a call. I just thought about it when you started talkin' about those plants. It was . . . uh . . . day before yesterday. He was with some plant store. I'll think of it here in a minute."

"What did he want?"

"It was a new service. Plantland, that's the name of the place. Right up the street. What they do, they water and fertilize plants for people."

"Did you tell him anything?"

Sanford chewed on his lower lip for a moment. "What I did—see, I hate takin' care of the plants, like I said. I told him to send them some literature."

"Who. Send who?"

"Everybody in the place. I was afraid, you know, I'd forget if he sent the stuff to me."

"Did you tell him the Cliffords and Jackowitz were away?"

"Uh, well, I told him I was having trouble, y'know. I thought maybe he could gimme a tip or two."

"Did you tell him they were out of town?"

"I didn't say anything *specific*. I told him they were potentials, see. Send the stuff direct to them but that it may be a little while before they get back."

"You gave him the names and addresses?"

"Yeah, four or five different people who travel a lot, not just them."

"But did you mention specifically that the Cliffords and Jackowitz women are out of town now?"

"Just so he'd know it might be a while before they got back to him."

"I see."

"I fucked up, right?"

"Maybe not."

"I'll call them right now, check it out."

"No," Sharky said quickly. "I wouldn't do that. If it is a possibility you'd just warn them, right?"

"Oh, yeah. I didn't think of that."

"Let us handle it."

"Sure, sure."

"I'll keep this between us."

"Hey, Sharky, that's damn white of you. I appreciate it."

"Any time, Jerry. Any time."

Forty minutes in the Cliffords' apartment yielded nothing but bruised knees. Barret was a fanatic. He checked everything. Under the beds, in the commode, behind pots and pans in the cabinets, the disposal, the windowsills, under chairs and couches.

Forty minutes later he said, "Forget it," and they headed to the Jackowitz apartment on twelve. Barret told Sharky and The Nosh to stand back until he vacuumed the carpeting around the door and dusted the doorknob. He carefully swept the small camel's-hair brush on the brass handle, smoothing out the black powder.

He looked up and grinned.

"What d'ya know," he said. "Clean as a new dime."

"So?" The Nosh said.

"So how many people do you know polish off the doorknob when they enter or leave their place?"

Sharky stepped close to Barret. "You through here?" he asked.

"Yep."

"Then why don't you step over there out of the way and let Nosh and me take the door, just in case."

"Why, indeed," Barret said and walked ten feet down the hall. The Nosh knelt down and popped the lock with less trouble than it would have taken to open a can of soup. Sharky took out his automatic and, holding his arm close to his side and bent at the elbow, pointed the gun toward the ceiling and slipped the safety catch off. The Nosh took out a snub-nose .38 and leaned back against the wall on the opposite side of the doorway, the pistol nestled in two hands.

"Here we go," Sharky whispered and The Nosh nodded. He twisted the doorknob slowly and then pushed the door open, jumped inside and fell flat against the wall in the dark room. An instant later The Nosh came through and kicked the door shut behind him. They waited for a few seconds, listening to each other breathe. "Scares the shit outa me, doin' that," The Nosh said finally.

Sharky clicked on the light. The apartment was empty. They let Barret in. Barret slipped on plastic surgeon's gloves and went to work. Slowly and methodically he moved through the apartment. The doorknob inside was also devoid of fingerprints. He spot vacuumed the rug, marking each bag of dirt and grit with a small diagram of the room showing the exact location of the sample. He got down on his hands and knees with a flashlight and perused the carpeting. Then he told Sharky to turn off the lights.

"Kneel down here beside me," he said. The finger of light skipped across the piling of the carpet. Barret moved it slowly back and forth. "See anything?" he asked.

"You mean the marks there on the floor?"

"Um hmm."

There were four deep grooves in the rug. Then Barret saw something else twinkling in the rays of the flashlight under the chair. He took tweezers and picked it up. It was a small red oblong pill.

"Look familiar?" Barret said.

"Looks like a red devil to me," Sharky said.

"Could be, could be. Or some kind of angina medication. Perhaps the woman who lives here dropped it." He plopped it in a baggie, then turned his attention back to the chair.

"Somebody swung this chair around in front of the window," Barret said. "And see here, on the windowsill, those circles. Still damp. It looks like somebody put a glass of water down here." He looked at it under his magnifying glass. Along the edges of the water ring was a slight red discoloration.

"When's the last time anybody was in here?" Barret asked.

"Last Sunday," Sharky said.

"Hmmm."

Barret went over the living room in minute detail, then the kitchen and bedroom.

"Okay," he said finally, "here's what we got. Somebody moved the chair. Somebody dropped a pill on the floor. That could've happened a week ago, yesterday, or last month. But the water rings on the windowsill—that was recent. No more than a few hours. Still damp. Also there's water in the sink in the kitchen and one of the glasses is damp. I'd say three or four hours on the outside, or both the glass and the sink'd be dry by now. That red discoloration on the sill could have come from that pill we found on the floor. I took a scraping. The lab'll confirm that. No prints in the apartment, no *recent* prints in the apartment. Everything's latent. Okay, we can expect that. There's also a trace of oil on the carpet in front of the window. Smells like machine oil but I'll check that out. It could have been from a gun if somebody laid one there on the floor. The phone is clean. Some old prints and smudges. My guess is somebody wearing gloves picked up the phone. It's operating, by the way." Barret went to the window and parted the venetian blinds with two fingers. "Direct view of the other apartment from here."

He stopped and for several moments he stared into space, saying nothing. Then he said, "I think he was in here. Somebody was, and within the last few hours." He nodded to himself, still staring.

"I have one more idea," he said.

He took his brush and vial of black powder and went first to the guest bathroom and kneeling down, dusted the handle on the toilet. It was clean. He went to the other bathroom and repeated the procedure.

The loops and whorls seemed far away at first.

Then as Barret dusted them they seemed to jump out at him.

"Well, I'll be a son of a gun," Barret said with a grin. "Bingo! We got ourselves a fresh print." He looked up at Sharky and The Nosh and winked. "Keep that in mind," he said. "Nobody likes to wear gloves when they take a leak."

14

From a table near the railing of the Tai Tak Restaurant Lowenthal watched as a beautiful young Chinese woman dressed in a red silk mandarin dress jumped lightly from the sampan and came up the walkway to the deck of the floating restaurant. She was a tiny flower of a girl, barely five feet tall with an almost perfect body and an ebony ponytail that cascaded over one shoulder.

Wan Shu, the chef of the restaurant, motioned her to the table. He was almost a parody of the stereotyped Chinese, a fat man, Buddhalike, with thin mustaches that drooped down over the corners of his mouth and a perpetual smile on his lips.

"Is Heida," he said as she joined Lowenthal and De-Laroza, "from Wanchai section. Three weeks here. Okay?"

"A splendid choice, *p'eng-yu,*" DeLaroza said.

Wan Shu beamed. "You drink before dinner?"

DeLaroza nodded and turned to Lowenthal. "What would you like?"

"Would Scotch be irreverent in present company?"

"Hardly. You forget, Hong Kong is a crown colony. There is probably more Scotch consumed there than anything else. Ice?"

Lowenthal nodded and DeLaroza gave the order to Wan Shu in Chinese. He rushed away, snapping his fingers and issuing commands to waiters.

"Where do you live in Wanchai?" DeLaroza asked Heida.

"On Jaffe Road near O'Brien. I live with my brother who sews for Jau Pun in Kowloon."

DeLaroza nodded. "I know him well. One of the finest of all tailors in the city. He has made many suits for me. How old are you?"

"I am nineteen," she said in a high, melodic voice. "I have gone to the university for one year. I study history. I hope to work for one year here and save my money so I may finish."

"What're you going to do with the history?" Lowenthal asked.

"I hope to be a school teacher, perhaps in the British settlement at Tseun Wan."

"Very ambitious," DeLaroza said. "I assume you know the legend of Kowloon and T'un Hai well, then?"

"*Hai.* My father told me the story many times before he died. It was a special thing between us."

"Mister Lowenthal here does not know the story. Would you honor us?"

"Of course, *nin.* It is *my* honor."

"Would you like something to drink first?"

"*Um, dor jeh.* I have had too many Coca-Colas already. I will be fat like T'sai-Shen if I am not careful."

"Who is T'sai-Shen?" Lowenthal asked.

"The god of wealth and happiness. He is so-o-o big," she said, holding her arms in front of her in a large circle.

"I doubt that," Lowenthal said with a smile.

"Should I begin then?"

"Please," DeLaroza said.

She stood bowing, pressing her hands together in an attitude of prayer, and then began reciting the myth in her bell-like voice, acting it out in pantomime, moving slowly in place, each gesture a ballet of grace. Lowenthal could not take his eyes off her.

"In the land of my father the most wondrous and ancient of all creatures is the dragon, for the dragon represents both earth and water.

"The dragon has the power of the rains, he puts color in the cheeks of the flowers. He brings the bountiful rice crop.

"But if the dragon is offended by the misdeeds and dishonor of the emperors, he becomes angry. The rains do not come. It is a time when the earth is like the wrinkled face of the prophet. The crops die in the ground, the rivers become like dusty pathways. The harvest is a time of sorrow and weeping.

"And so, once a year the ministers and lords of the empire honor Chiang-Yuan, the Dragon of the Ten Toes, and it is a great celebration which is called the Feast of the Dragon Door and they adorn the dishes from which they eat, the robes they wear, even their thrones, with the countenance of Chiang-Yuan.

"In the time of Fu Hsi, who was by legend the first of all the great emperors of China, a dragon horse arose from the Yellow River and presented himself to the emperor. He was sent by Yu-huang-shang-ti, the August Emperor of Jade, and god of all gods, to serve Fu Hsi and give to him the wisdom of the gods. On the back of the dragon horse was a mystical chart from which all of the written language of China was taken. And in the time of Fu Hsi there was peace in the land and it was a time of plenty.

"And so, from that time on, the Dragon of the Ten Toes has been the imperial symbol of all emperors.

"His enemy was T'un Hai, the two-headed blood snake of the dark world, for it was believed that the snake tore the souls of the dead to pieces and scattered them to the sea. Only Chiang-Yuan could save them and lead them to everlasting peace in the kingdom of the Jade Emperor.

"And so it was in the time of the boy emperor Ping, eight hundred years ago. The young king loved Chiang-Yuan and believed that when an emperor died his soul lived on in the body of the dragon. And he believed also that in the eight mountain peaks surrounding Hong Kong there lived eight dragons, each with the soul of one of Ping's ancestors. His prime minister told Ping that there would be another dragon when Ping died and it would live in the high mountain on the western side of the island of Hong Kong and it would be called Kow-Loon, which means 'ninth dragon,' and Ping's soul would live in its great body and would protect the harbor and the souls of the dead from T'un Hai.

"When Ping passed on, the dragon Kow-Loon appeared on the western peak and its soul was the soul of Ping and Kow-Loon went forth on the island in search of T'un Hai and in the place now known as Tiger Balm Gardens he found the snake of lost souls in a cave. T'un Hai came from the cave and attacked Kow-Loon and they fought for twenty-three days and nights until the earth was scorched from Kow-Loon's fiery breath and the earth was scarred from their battle and the hills fell into the sea. The earth trembled. A great earthquake shook the island and the people escaped to the sea in their sampans and waited until the battle was over and T'un Hai slid into the sea and was never seen again.

"And since that time Kow-Loon has protected Hong Kong and many people still live on sampans so they will be safe if T'un Hai ever returns and there is another great battle and the earth trembles again."

Heida closed her eyes and bowed her head. The story was over.

"Thank you," she said.

Lowenthal sat back and stared at the young lady, entranced by the story and by her visual interpretation. "No," he said, "it is I who thank you. I'm very touched by your story. You tell it with great passion."

"It is only because my father told it to me with passion, for he believed the story, just as he believed that when he died he would ride on the back of the dragon horse to the place where the August Supreme Emperor of Jade resides."

"And do you believe the story?" Lowenthal asked.

A smile touched her lips. *"Hai.* Of course. I believe it because it is a legend that sings with truth." She reached inside her blouse and took out a thin gold chain with a gold pendant hanging from it. On the pendant in bas relief was the tiny figure of a dragon, grinning ferociously, his head crouching between his five-toed feet. "It is always around my neck," she said, "even when I sleep. It protects me from T'un Hai."

DeLaroza thanked her and she bowed and was gone.

"I must say, you make all of this very real," Lowenthal said. "I wonder why it is that Easterners have much more interesting and dramatic gods than we Westerners."

"You Westerners," DeLaroza said with a smile. "I am a Buddhist. But enough of that. Let us talk about

the campaign. Needless to say, I am delighted you have joined us."

"So far you seem to be doing just fine without me."

"So far we have played in our own territory."

Wan Shu arrived with the first of many dishes, what appeared to be tiny chicken wings covered with a clear sauce. "This looks delicious," Lowenthal said. "What is it?"

"Well, it is hardly what we would call *chia-ch'ang-pien-fan*—everyday food—in China. You eat the whole thing, the bones and all. Just chew it well. They are sparrow wings."

Lowenthal paused in mid-bite and there was a moment when he seemed to be wondering whether to go on or not.

"Please, do not stop," DeLaroza said. "Heida mentioned the Feast of the Dragon Door. What Wan Shu is preparing is a meal based on that feast. There will be some rare delicacies, such as these sparrow wings. Also quail, elephant trunk, sturgeon intestines, bear paw, and deer tail, along with more traditional fare. The meal for two hundred guests will cost one hundred thousand dollars."

"That's five hundred dollars a meal!"

"Exactly. The banquet originated during the time of the Emperor Tsi Tzu of the Sung Dynasty, about seven hundred years ago. It usually went on for days. I have eliminated some of the more exotic dishes. Peacock tongues, monkey brains, gorilla lips."

"Gorilla lips?"

"A truly rare delicacy in China. But I don't want to discourage any of the guests."

"Elephant trunk and deer tails may take care of that."

DeLaroza leaned forward and winked. "We won't tell them until *after* they've eaten."

The sparrow wings actually were quite delicious and Lowenthal finished them with relish. He sat back and said, "Tell me, what took you from Brazil to Hong Kong?"

"I see you have been checking up on me."

Lowenthal shrugged. "There's not much to check up on, actually."

"I have always avoided publicity. A quirk of mine."

"Modesty hardly becomes you," Lowenthal said, motioning to the spectacle of *Pachinko!*

"I am about to change my image."

He chuckled and then the chuckle became a hearty laugh.

"Fate dictated the move to Hong Kong," he said. "I was on holiday in the Orient and visited the plant of a gentleman named Loo who manufactured radios, which also happened to be my business. Mr. Loo was in trouble. His company was undercapitalized and a British concern was about to buy him out. But the British were stupid. They would have engulfed him, eaten him up. Loo's strength was his ability to produce components cheaply. His weakness was assembly and marketing. So I formed a partnership with him. He produced the parts; I assembled and sold them. We were highly competitive and the merger was quite successful. Had I bought Loo out, as the British proposed to do, I would have lost his expertise. A man always works better for himself than for others."

"And how did you get into the toy business?"

"Fate again. This time an accident of nature. Loo had a side venture, producing toys for the tourist trade, cheap little items. Our electronics plant was seriously damaged in the 1961 typhoon, but the toy company was hardly touched. While we were undergoing repairs I decided to concentrate on toys. Before long it was—how do you put it?"

"The tail wagging the dog?"

"Yes. The Chinese might express it more poetically, but the Americans are more to the point. It was soon after that I met Nikos Arcurius. Now the tail wags many dogs."

"Where does Hotchins come into the scenario?"

"I decided to move to the United States. This is the marketplace. Also the place to assemble and sell products. My company was the first to make that move. At the time Donald was in the state—Congress?"

"Legislature," said Lowenthal.

"Right. He was about to run for governor. He sponsored a law that made it advantageous for us to come to his state. We became friends and I offered my business knowledge to the campaign."

"You are really quite savvy to American politics for a . . ." He hesitated, letting the sentence hang.

"Foreigner?" DeLaroza said. "The word does not offend me, although I am now an American citizen. I have studied politics all my life. It is not a hobby, it is an avocation. Not only American. British, French, Chinese, German."

"And what attracted you to Hotchins?"

DeLaroza considered the question for a few moments. "Aristotle once wrote that law is reason without passion. Hotch is a man of law and a man of passion. I found the combination irresistible. He is also quite honest. In fact blunt at times."

"Pretty good answer."

"And how would you answer the question?"

Lowenthal toyed with his wine glass, making small circles on the table top. "A lot of things. He's a winner. I guess that must be number one. We need a winner badly. He's a self-made man. A lawyer and a businessman. And he's tough. Anybody who can survive four years in a Korean prison camp with his foot blown off is tough. So far he doesn't seem to owe anybody. Somebody once said, 'Capitalism gives all of us a great opportunity if we seize it with both hands and hang on to it.' I think the man on the street wants to believe that again."

"An interesting comment. Who said that?"

"Al Capone," Lowenthal said and they both laughed.

"There are some things I want to make sure of," Lowenthal went on.

"Anything."

"Is he clean, Victor? I mean is he *really* clean?"

A vision of Domino flashed before DeLaroza and then it vanished. A danger he hoped no longer existed.

"Is anybody *that* clean, Mr. Lowenthal? Richelieu told one of his bishops once, 'Give me six sentences written by the most innocent man and I will find something in them to hang him.' I assure you, Donald can withstand any scrutiny."

"Excellent. Will his wife make a good campaigner?"

DeLaroza nodded. "And a find First Lady."

Lowenthal nodded, but there was still doubt in his expression.

"What else?" DeLaroza asked.

"I am concerned about opening the campaign this soon. I know that you have very carefully designed his strategy, but it is contradictory to the normal campaign strategy, coming out this soon. For one thing the cost will be staggering to keep a bandwagon rolling that long."

"Cost is not a factor. We can afford it."

"Also it makes him a public target for that much longer."

DeLaroza's eyebrows rose. "At this point he is virtually an unknown quantity. We are not selling a dark horse, we are selling an un*known* horse. That is why we plan to open the campaign here, Monday night. We

have some political supporters already on hand. We
have tremendous press exposure. Hotch must have a
chance to become not only a household word but a face
to go with it."

"I agree with that. But to go on the campaign trail
for ten months? It's scary."

"Just think. Monday he makes his announcement.
Tuesday you make yours. Wednesday he will be in Dallas for the opening of the new Merchandise Mart
there."

Lowenthal smiled. "It'll knock Fitz on his Irish
blueblood ass."

"And send the competition into a panic. Who will
throw down the gauntlet first? Which one will try to
follow his lead? The old-timers cannot afford the public
exposure for too long. They have already made their
views known. They will become boring and die of attri-
tion."

"There's still Fitzgerald."

"We have some surprises for him, too. How do you
think this Fitzgerald will react when he discovers we do
not need his money?"

"He won't believe us."

"Good. When he finds out it will be too late." DeLaroza leaned forward and lowered his voice. "The planning is done already. It is totally computerized.
Every state, every county, every city, demographically
charted. Voting histories recorded. Voting records of
party leaders recorded. Complete dossiers on prospective competitors. We can tell you how much it will cost
to have a barbecue in Topeka, Kansas, next year.
Availability of assembly halls. Key political dates. Everything you need to know, available with a press of the
finger."

Lowenthal was impressed. "Well . . ." he started
and then stopped.

"And now about you, sir. The Chinese have a proverb—'The beginning of wisdom is calling a thing by its right name.' "

"In other words, let's be blunt?"

"Yes, let us be blunt."

Here it comes, thought Lowenthal. *Now it's his turn.*

"What do you want out of all this?" DeLaroza said.

I'll outlast him, Lowenthal thought, *with word games*.

"I'm an idealist," Lowenthal said. "Idealists never want anything for themselves."

"Hmm. I have always thought that an effective idealist is one who gets what he wants in such a way that the public thinks he is doing them a favor by taking it."

Lowenthal laughed. He held up his glass to DeLaroza. "Good shot."

"We were going to be blunt."

All right, Lowenthal said to himself, *what the hell*.

"I want to be attorney general."

DeLaroza settled back in his chair and slapped his hands together. "Well, sir, that is what I call the beginning of wisdom. And what is the problem?"

"I don't think there is any. I'd make one hell of an attorney general."

"No question about it. And as I see it, no competition. So, will you think about our plan to announce here on Monday? Sleep on it. We can talk in the morning, over breakfast. Donald should be back late tomorrow afternoon, hopefully with Senator Thurston's endorsement, and I am sure it will be the first thing he will want to know."

Lowenthal nodded and lifted his glass again. "To sleeping on it," he said with a smile.

"No, sir. To victory."

On the sixteenth floor of the Mirror Towers, DeLaroza's holding company, Internaco, maintained a guest apartment, a handsomely decorated suite, its silk-draped windows overlooking the city. There were two keys to the suite. One was given to the guest, the other was kept by the guard. After sending Lowenthal back to his hotel in his private limousine, DeLaroza took an elevator to the apartment. He stood outside the door listening for several moments and then very quietly slipped the guard's key into the lock and opened the door.

Howard Burns, standing in front of the windows, staring out through a cold haze that circled the city in the wind, was captivated by the city lights, which looked like hazy shards in a kaleidoscope. He heard the key enter the lock and the door open. He whirled, crouching as he did. The wine glass clattered off into a corner and the .22 Woodsman appeared in its place, like a coin in a magician's sleight-of-hand trick.

"It's me!" DeLaroza screamed, falling back against the doorjamb.

Burns stared at him with a flash of white hate, his hands trembling, his trigger finger twitching in the steel guard. He stood that way for a very long time and then slowly bent his elbow and pointed the weapon at the ceiling. The hand was shaking.

"That's how close you came," he said nodding to his hand. "Walk in on me like that, from behind, no knock, no nothin'. Whatsa matter, you *crazy?*"

"I thought you'd be asleep. I thought after . . ."

"Asleep? Who you shittin', asleep? I'm high. I'm up there somewhere. I blew a chippie's head off an hour or two ago. Whadya mean, sleep?"

"I am sorry, I, uh, I don't know . . ."

"No, that's right. Somebody always does it for you. No powder burns on your lily whites, is there? Shit, lookit that, I spilled my fuckin' drink. *You don't walk in behind somebody!*"

"All right, all right."

Burns went to the wet bar and poured himself another glass of Bertolucci red wine and plunked an ice cube in it. "I seen that circus downstairs. I sneaked a look on the way up here," he said.

DeLaroza stepped into the room and closed the door behind him. He wiped sweat from his forehead with the back of his hand.

"You oughta be sweatin', a dumbass play like that," Burns said. "Thirty years you stay clean, then all of a sudden you're gonna walk right out there on the trap door and spring the trap yourself. Whaddya want, me to tie the noose around your neck?"

"It's safe now. I have been working for this moment since 1945. The dangers have all been removed."

"Bullshit."

"Listen to me, Howard—"

"*Bull*shit. I scratch the colonel in Hong Kong, Corrigon shows up. I scratch Corrigon, there's the dame. Now she's outa the way, who's next, hunh? Who's gonna pop outa the box next? You think somewhere there ain't *some*body's gonna look at that face of yours and start thinkin' and then start rememberin'? Lemme tell ya, partner, I been livin' like that for seven years. A new name, new business, new place. Had to give up everything and live in Nebraska. Neb*raska* for Chrissakes. Shit, they don't even get all the fuckin' television stations in Nebraska. Took me two years to find a bookie. And with all that, see, with the Feds practically feedin' me with a spoon, I was waitin' every time I turned around to see somebody from the old life."

"It is thirty years for me," DeLaroza said, "not nine. Nobody will recognize me. I do not even look like the same man."

"I'd spot you in a minute, kiddo. That phony accent, red beard, all that fat, that wouldn't throw me." Burns sipped on his wine, then added, "You bring it down, I go down with it, know what I mean?"

"There is no way to put us together."

"Oh no? How about those Chinks on the boat? The gook that picked me up tonight? How about the guard downstairs when we come in?"

"They have no idea who you are."

"Well, they ain't blind, are they? One picture, pow! I'm made. They'll dump me, don't make no difference if I'm in Yokohama, Singapore, or the fuckin' South Pole, I'm a gone gosling."

"Look, what you did with your life, I cannot do anything about that. I did something else. What you were is your business, what I am is mine."

Burns turned his back to DeLaroza and stared out the window again. He said, "This Domino, the one I burned, she was a hooker, you said."

"A very high class hooker."

"She have a pimp?"

"Well, I suppose you could call . . ."

"She had a pimp, right? And he didn't know about this Hotchins, this pimp didn't?"

"No. Nobody knew."

"But he knows about you, right? He knows you knew her and he can tie you two together. All it takes is your name, they'll be knockin' at the door."

"He will not do that. He will put them on to many others before that."

"Shi-i-t. I gotta laugh." He looked over his shoulder at DeLaroza. "I been in the rackets all my life. Had a couple dozen buttons on my payroll at the time. Know what a button is, DeLaroza? A shooter. Very loyal people. But if the need comes up that one of them has to go quiet, there's only one way."

"We can't keep killing."

"Hah, that's my line. One goes, then another, then another. It don't stop. You take out the pimp, it'll be somebody else. Whyn't you leave it alone, keep yourself in the background? You got it made. All the power. All the money. The heavy friends. You're gonna blow it. You're gonna get us both killed."

"You are getting melodramatic, my friend. That's ridiculous."

"No, it's experience. Which you ain't got and that's what scares me shitless."

"You are safe, Howard, believe me."

"You listen to me, see, because I been around a long time. I know how this system works. You gotta hit the pimp. Your people, well, okay, I can't go whackin' off half the population of China. But the pimp goes. You don't like it, that's too bad. I cover my own ass."

"You can do it again, this soon?" DeLaroza said and there was a look of shocked disbelief on his face.

Burns smiled. He poured another glass of wine, plopped in another ice cube. "You think it's real tough, don'tcha? That's funny." He closed his eyes, remembering the way the room looked and her, her head haloed by the lamp, the perfect target. "I forgot how good it was," he said. DeLaroza's arms went numb. Burns kept talking. "Up close like that, I was Dominic Scardi again, not some name I don't even know. You get your balls off thinking about all the people you control, all the money, all that power. Well so do I, baby. I get off too because I got power, right here in this hand, in this fuckin' *finger* I got it. I hold the vote. Yes, they live. No, they go down. You think that ain't power? When you see it in their eyes? You know what, partner? I had to change my underwear when I got back here. That's right. I shot off in my drawers. I always do. You take a little pill, it makes it even better. Works in two ways. It keeps you on top, see, keyed up, y'know. But it also makes coming that much better."

He reached in his pocket for the other red devil. His fingers searched the corners of his pocket. It was gone. But where? He had had them both in the apartment. He tried to think back, remember where he had seen it last.

"Is something wrong?" DeLaroza asked. "Did something go bad tonight?"

"Go bad. Did it ever go bad with me?"

"No, I can honestly say no to that."

"You there, you're a little off your feed. Kinda sends you up when it happens, don't it?"

"No."

"Who ya shittin', Victor? You ain't cut for the real messy stuff. Anyways it's my thing, right? You make the money, I clean the cat box."

DeLaroza turned toward the door. "I guess I better get back downstairs."

"Don'tcha wanna hear about it?"

"Not really."

"Boom, boom, just like that. The first shot took her straight on. Gorgeous. She saw it a second before she got it. The second one caught her as she was going down. Three feet, four feet—"

God, I hate him, DeLaroza thought. He was a pariah, a killing machine, enshrouded by death, and the carrion smell of his flesh filled the room.

"—quick and easy. I don't torture people there, Vic. It ain't my style. But the second before I squeezed it off, that's when it felt best. Waitin' just for that fraction of a second when they're between heaven and hell. You think that ain't power?"

DeLaroza said, "Yes, I suppose so."

Burns's lip curled back revealing his yellowing teeth. Suddenly there was hate burning in his eyes, too. "Ya know somethin', Vic old boy? I was thinkin', on the way back over here with that Chink friend of yours. All these years I been hearin' about what a hot shit you are. Big brain. You been pullin' the strings, playin' the big cheese all over the world. You had me believin' all that shit, y'know. But if it wasn't for me, you wouldn't be nothin'. Just another dumb yokel kissin' ass someplace to get a five dollar raise. And when your eyes turned white, when you needed somebody pull the ol' trigger, you hadda come cryin' to me. When the tit was in the wringer, who did the dirty work? Me. And don't you forget it."

"I never—"

"Don't say nothin', pal. Just put it in your scrapbook. Oh yeah, only one other thing, buddy-boy. There was a cop in the place."

"A cop?"

"Take it easy. Don't panic. He was on the premises somewhere. I don't know exactly where. He was on top of me, just like that. I can't figure it out exactly. The shots, you couldn't hear twenty feet away. But he come into that stairwell three, four floors above me, like a bat outa hell."

"Are you sure it wasn't the security guard?"

"Maybe, but that ain't what he said. He said *police*. 'Stop, police!' That's the words he used. And he wasn't wearing no uniform. I still can't figure it out. Anyways he was yellin' and runnin', and I kept on rollin', out on the terrace there. I was reloaded already when the motherfucker came out. He was ten feet from me once. A young guy in a suede jacket carrying some kind of 9 mm piece. All he hadda do was turn around once there, and pow, right in the gut. He was in a hurry though. I walked away from it clean. Nobody saw nothin', nobody heard nothin', just this fuckin' pig."

Worms crawled deep in DeLaroza's gut. Burns was

paranoid and it crept over him, suffocating him like a blanket.

"*Pachinko!* opens Monday night. Tuesday you go to Vancouver on my JetStar. That night you're on your way to Yokohama. Do not worry about the pimp. I'll take care of that."

"Did you take care of that bet for me?"

"Ten thousand on Dallas."

"How about the spread?"

"Seven points."

"Good. So, the wine's beginning to get to me. Don't catch your asshole on the doorknob, okay?"

"Yes," DeLaroza said, and after he had left the apartment he leaned against the wall and closed his eyes, breathing like a man who had just run a very long way.

15

It was the hour of the ravens and Sharky's Machine prepared to invade the heart of darkness, seeking among the bookies, gamblers, pushers, strongarms, prostitutes, conmen, muggers, and killers, those who could be cajoled or threatened into revealing the secrets of the night people.

Time. Time was against them. The hour was right, but the clock was their enemy. For though Friscoe had joined them (at first reluctantly, then after the discovery of the fingerprints, enthusiastically) they all knew the chase would end with Monday morning roll call. He would not be pushed farther than that.

"Remember," a wise old cop told them, "never trust a snitch. They're lepers. Give a squealer a piece of confidential info, he'll try to sell it to your partner twenty minutes later. You got to catch 'em with their hands full, get 'em on the hook, or needing help, then you can maybe trust 'em—for at least thirty seconds."

The wise old cop was Friscoe, who operated on the theory that no matter how experienced his men were, no matter how much they knew, it never hurt to repeat good advice.

The plan was devised in Domino's apartment: Work fast, dig up what you can, bring in any scraps you get, rendezvous at the Majestic Grill at seven in the morning to begin putting the pieces together.

"Just don't waste time," Friscoe said. "If you got a lead and it starts to crap out, get off it, move to something else. What we ain't got, we ain't got time, see, to beat on any dead dogs. Let's see what a night's digging turns up. We ain't got anybody on base by morning, I say we flush it."

Barret and Grimm headed to their respective laboratories. By ten P.M. Twigs had gathered up the remains of the victim in a body bag and moved it by freight elevator and his own station wagon to the morgue, where he eagerly went to work, prying into its vital organs.

Barret, alone in his lab working under a single lamp, pored over the scraps of physical evidence, beginning with the little red pill.

The Nosh returned to the OC, there to wire the two fingerprints from the top and underside of the commode handle to the FBI in Washington and to begin filtering out whatever voices existed on Sharky's tapes.

Friscoe hastily drafted a vice cop named Johnny Cooper and went in search of Tiffany Paris, hoping to begin an interrogation which might lift the veil of the mysterious Domino.

The apartment was sealed. Sharky would return later to check it out. For now, he would go with Livingston looking for information. The time was right.

Papa, who preferred to work alone, quietly went hunting.

As did Sharky and Livingston, cruising the night haunts, searching out the weak among the vipers.

———————————

Disco music thundered at Papa as he entered Nefertiti, the city's most hallowed night spot—at least for that week. Two leads had already gone down the toilet. Now he was looking for Leo Winter, a good old boy with an easy grin whose casual charm had dazzled more than one jury. There was only one problem—Papa had nothing in his pocket. Right now Leo was clean. It would have to be a bluff and Papa was not the best poker player in the world.

The maitre d', sartorially splendid in a cocoa-colored tuxedo, stood at the inner entrance to the club, dwarfed by a tall image of the Egyptian queen that stared enigmatically down at the lobby through gleaming emerald eyes. He eyed Papa skeptically, starting at the black tie-up shoes, the rumpled suit, the faded blue shirt, and the outrageous tie which did not go with anything else he had on. His patronizing smile never went beyond his lips.

"Sorry, sir, full up in there," he said. "Could be thirty, forty minutes before there's any room in the bar. You might like to try a little place up the street—"

"I got a reservation," Papa said and flashed his shield.

The maitre d' looked distressed. "Is there going to be trouble?"

"I don't know. Are you expecting some?" Papa said and went into the club.

The interior was outrageous. The decor was Egyptian with music surging from enormous amplifiers hidden in two mummy cases at each end of the large room. Brass

palm trees shimmered before its onslaught, hieroglyph-
ics decorated the sconces, and the announcer worked
the controlboard with the frenzy of a concert pianist, his
booth nestled between the paws of an enormous sphinx
that dominated one end of the room. Spotlights roved
the club, while the dance floor, illuminated from below,
seemed to pulsate with the beat of the music.

The place was jammed but Leo Winter was easy to
spot. He was on the dance floor, moving casually with
the beat, dancing with a blonde whose gothic chest,
wrapped in see-through cotton, jogged in rhythm with
the music.

Winter, a triangle of a man with bullish shoulders,
hardly any waist, and large hands, was dressed in a yellow leisure suit, brocaded at the collar and open to the
waist, a gold chain with a charm the size of a manhole
cover bouncing around his neck. As one record segued
into another Winter and the woman returned to their
table beside the dance floor. His eyes made an alert
sweep of the room, passed Papa, then flicked back and
lingered on him for a moment. The big cop jerked his
head toward the door, turned, and went outside.

He stood near his car in the parking lot, outside the
perimeter of light around the flamboyant entrance, with
his hands stuffed in his pockets, protecting them against
the frigid night wind that had chased away the rain.
Winter emerged a few minutes later and joined him, the
wind rippling through tight curls on his head. He held
his jacket closed with one hand.

"Hi, Cowboy," he said to Papa.

"How's it going, Leo?" Papa said.

"Right now I'm freezing my ass off. This gonna take
long?"

"Depends on you."

"Uh oh. I got some trouble I don't know about?"

Papa shook his head. "Information."

Leo's attitude changed. His body tightened and seemed to grow an inch. He stood with one shoulder toward Papa, staring into the dark parking lot.

Papa said, "I'm gonna tell you something and you're gonna forget it as soon as I tell you. Then I'm gonna ask you something. Then we'll go from there."

Leo continued to look into the darkness.

"First off, you know a fancy pros calls herself Domino?"

Leo thought about the question, then said, "Is this a freebie or can we do a little trading?"

"Leo, I got this big problem. I'm runnin' outa time and I ain't even got started good yet. Can we talk about Domino or not?"

Leo rubbed his shoulder with his free hand then shrugged. "I've seen her here and there."

"You know her pimp?"

"You mean, do I know him or are we asshole buddies?"

"I mean, do you know him? That's what I mean."

"I know him. We're not thick."

"I got Neil. I need the rest of the name and an address."

Leo looked down at his foot, tapping his toe gently against the car tire. "This Neil, is he in trouble?"

"Maybe."

"Bad trouble?"

"If he's in trouble, it's bad trouble."

"You're a regular encyclopedia of facts there, Papa."

"If you ain't wrap-around pals, what's the difference?"

"Yeah, I suppose there's something to that. Okay, his name's Dantzler. He lives out on Peachtree in The Courtyard."

The name struck a bell. Papa's mind dug back as he kept talking.

"The apartments?"

"Dantzler lives in a condo."

"How about Tiffany? What do you know about her?"

"You're really fishin', ain't you, Papa. From here I'd say you don't know shit for sure."

"If I did, would I be here?"

"You got a point."

"So?"

"So, Tiffany's Dantzler's old lady. She lives in the apartment complex out there, but mostly she uses her pad for tricks. Whenever Dantzler snaps his fingers, she's up at his place with her legs spread."

Now Papa remembered why Dantzler's address had ticked off his memory bank. It was the same complex as Tiffany's. "You mean this Dantzler pimps for his own girlfriend?"

"You got it. Real sweetheart, right?"

"Okay, gimme the package on this shmuck."

"Dantzler's a scam artist. Rich kid. His old man took a bath in real estate about ten years ago, got in the shower, and emptied his brains out with a .45. All Dantzler had goin' for him was a shaky pedigree and a smooth mouth. A pretty boy, y'know? He played off his country club connections and worked some fast deals but he got in trouble with the state over some pyramid scheme he had goin' and he dropped outa sight for awhile. When he came back up, he has this Tiffany in tow, and she's a real piece, not just your everyday low-class honey, know what I mean?"

"And he was pimping for her?"

"More than that. Dantzler's living with her and pimping too, and she's turning three, four-hundred a night tricks with his uptown friends and the fat-wallet out-of-towners. But she doesn't quite have it, okay? Then a couple of years ago Dantzler pops Domino outa the closet. She was like a super version of Tiffany. More of everything and a class act, to boot. At first she was kind of shy and Tiffany got the soreass, but then this Domino sprouts wings, man, a real angel, and she kinda has a soft spot for Tiffany, so they end up tighter than a fat couple in a single bed. Domino won't have anything to do with any of the other street people—didn't want to and didn't. But all of a sudden you see her everywhere, dressed like she come off a magazine cover. Let me tell ya, Papa—this lady, when she walks in a room even the clock stops tellin' time. A very selective lady and smart as a kick in the ass. The way it comes to me, she doesn't like the trade, she packs it in and goes home. Left more than one big spender with his thumb in his ear."

"But Dantzler was pimping for her?"

"Sure. He's got the connections. He's got the ins."

"And Domino is independent?"

"You know it. A no-shit lady. Even starts shaping up Tiffany. In fact, the way I get it, Tiffany's got another old man on the side and this Domino covers for her all the time. I mean, shit, man, how long could anybody put up with that little mama's boy?"

"But Domino gives Dantzler a hard time, right?"

"Hey, c'mon Papa, between the two chicks Dantzler must be knockin' down fifteen, sixteen a week after the split and no tax. Does that sound like hard times to you?" He paused for a minute, then said, "I thought you were gonna give me something I got to forget."

"Okay, here it is. Somebody put this Domino on ice about four hours ago."

"Hunh!"

"Right in the doorway of her apartment. And from my end of the street it wasn't no amateur hit."

Leo looked hard at Papa and a scowl crossed his face. "Are you tellin' me there was paper out on her? You tellin' me that?"

"I'm tellin' you somebody staked out her apartment

for several hours and then punched her out with a sawed-off shotgun. Does that sound like amateur night to you?"

Leo whistled softly through his teeth, then shook his head. "Bad news."

"If this goes any further there, Leo, I'll be back out and step all over those pretty Mary Janes of yours."

"Did I tell you it stops with me? Did I tell you that or not?"

"Just so it's clear."

"You put me in a funny kinda box, Papa."

"How's that?"

"Let's just say this was a local contract, okay? And it wasn't run past me first. Then I would be very unhappy with some people. Like if a local shooter took this on, I would want to know it's comin' down. And if there was any hotshot freelancers around, I would know that, too. Now I'm not saying I'd have anything to do with that kind of action, okay. What I'm saying is, there are courtesies and out of courtesy it would come to me and I would say no, or maybe I would say it ain't any of my business."

"What you're saying is the shooter is an out-of-towner."

"What I'm saying is if the shooter *isn't* an out-of-towner, it's going to hit the fan. I mean there's going to be a shit storm that'll make Hurricane Alice look like somebody sneezed."

"Could you gimme a guess why it happened?"

"Papa, I never got closer than ten feet to the lady. Couple of months ago I came up a heavy winner in a poker game and Dantzler lost his ass. I took his marker for five bills. I offered to trade it out for a night with Domino and *she* nixed it, not him. Maybe, you know, she thumbed her nose at the wrong guy."

"You hear anything about Dantzler and Tiffany juicing some tourist recently?"

Leo began to laugh. "Jesus, you sure want a lot for your nickel, don't ya?"

"Leo, how long we known each other?"

"Too long."

"Did I ever stand short on you?"

"No, I can't say that."

"So when I tell you time is short, I mean time is short. We do my problem, then we do yours. Now tell me about this shakedown."

"A few weeks ago Dantzler shows up with a new Ferrari. And he buys up my marker and generally settles up around town. So I ask him, 'What did you do, hit a bank or something?' And what he says is this: 'Tiffany and me found ourselves a turkey in a ten-gallon hat.' So I says, 'Was Domino in on it?' And he says, 'Don't I wish! If I could get Domino in on it I could retire.' The figure I heard was fifty g's. The way he was throwin' money around, I believe it."

"So Domino was *not* in on it."

"I don't know how to say it, but she was a very classy lady. I don't think she'd get her hands dirty in that kind of action."

"Shit, she's . . . she was a hooker, Leo."

"You asked me, I'm tellin' you. If I was making book on this question, I would give odds she didn't know a thing about it, and if she did, she would have given Dantzler the long goodbye."

"Could she maybe have found out about it and given Dantzler some trouble?"

"I see where you're goin' with this. Let me tell you, this Dantzler's got balls the size of a blackhead. Phony paper, pyramids, pimping, that's his style. He don't have the guts to step on an ant—or ask anybody else to. Anyway, even if he had it in mind, you know, he would have known to run it past me and I would have kicked his ass all the way to Alabama for even thinking about it. No, you can scratch Dantzler. He might be able to tell you why he thinks it was done, but he didn't have a thing to do with it. That's my opinion."

"So I end up exactly nowhere."

"No, you end up with a travelin' hit man on your hands. If you want to come down on Dantzler, it's going to have to be for something else."

Papa nodded. "Okay. I want you to do this for me. I want you to listen around and if you hear anything, *any*thing about this gambit, you give it to me. And if you hear anybody outside the Vice Squad askin' questions about Domino or Dantzler or any of that crowd, you get on the horn to me."

"You want me to let you know if I get pneumonia from standing out here?"

"You wanna run around half naked that's your problem."

"Okay, but I got another problem."

"I'm listening."

"I got married a couple of weeks ago. Maybe you heard."

"You got a problem all right but there ain't anything I can do about it."

Leo laughed again. "It ain't her, it's her brother. He got dumped for running a red light and they turned up two lids of reefer in the car. It was strictly for personal use. The kid doesn't push dope."

"Two ounces for personal use?"

"So he smokes a lot, what do I know? He's twenty. You know how it is when you're twenty. You don't do anything in moderation."

"You need to have a heart-to-heart with the kid."

"I already did. What it is, they hit him with felony possession."

"Anything over an ounce, the law says you're pushing."

"Look, the kid's okay. Anyway, I only been married a month, I'd like to give the old lady a little delayed wedding present, know what I mean?"

"This the kid's first time out?"

"He got caught in a little bust here about a year ago. A bunch of kids were selling tax-free cigarettes they brought in from North Carolina. They must have cleared all of twenty bucks."

"Careless son of a bitch, isn't he?"

"He's not real bright."

"Okay. I got a pal just off the Narcs. I'll talk to him."

"Whatever you can do."

"I can maybe work it out for a suspended sentence. He'll have to do about six months probation or so, cough up a couple of yards for the fine."

"That's okay. Maybe a little probation'll straighten him out. I can handle the fine."

"Okay, Leo, we got a deal. Just keep in touch. Keep your ear close to the ground for the next forty-eight hours or so."

"That's cool."

"And forget you heard anything about Domino from me or anybody else."

Leo's eyebrows rose. "Who's Domino?"

———

A harsh chilling wind had replaced the rain, turning dirt in the gutters into dervishes as Livingston cruised down the dark streets. Beside him, Sharky stared silently through the windshield, his mind assaulted by nightmare demons—the what ifs and maybes, all the ways he might have prevented Domino's death. In the brief time he had seen her, talked to her, listened to her make love to another man, in those few hours she had touched a place deep inside him nobody had ever touched before. He knew it was crazy. But it was a reality he could not escape and the reality tortured him.

"Okay," Livingston said after several minutes of silence, "what the hell's eatin' you?"

The question shook Sharky back to the present.

"All of it," he said. "The whole thing."

"Got to kick that monkey, m'friend."

"Yeah."

They drove another block without words.

"I got this, this, uh, lump in my gut, like a bad meal layin' down there," Sharky said. "Like maybe I'm missing something."

"Hunch, hunh?"

"Maybe. Yeah, could be that."

"Really got to you, didn't she?" Livingston said. "Got to thinkin' about it, right? Wonderin' what a five-hundred-dollar piece was like."

Sharky felt himself bristling. *It wasn't like that,* he felt like saying, but then he began thinking about it, remembering how he had felt, listening to her making love the night before. He felt cold and he huddled deeper into his suede pullover.

"Yeah," he said finally, "she really got to me."

"I been in Vice a long time, Shark. Too long. Seen lots of fancy tricksters come and go. I done my share of wondering, too. All of us have. I mean, if you *didn't* think about it, it wouldn't be natural."

"It's more than that."

"What? You talkin' about duty, that kinda shit? Listen here, you're a cop, you ain't God. You make mistakes just like everybody else. Only trouble is, in our business a man can take an extra cup of coffee, fall asleep at the wrong moment, make a bad guess, it ends up disaster for somebody. You learn to live with it or get out. You're gonna make a fuckin' mistake now and then, you can't afford to, but you're gonna make 'em anyway. Couple of years ago a friend of mine named Tibbets lost a material witness. They had this cat under protective custody in a house off Highland Avenue and it all started comin' down on this guy, y'know, he got the shivers. So one night he goes to the can and hangs himself in the shower. Tibbets is twenty feet away watchin' a ball game. He never got over it, started in drinkin', two months later he blew his brains out. So what did that prove? We had already lost a witness. The court case went down the toilet. Then we lost a good cop and for what? We all human, baby. You start thinkin' otherwise, you're in deep trouble."

"Keep reminding me of that, will you?"

"Okay. For now just put it aside. She's dead, man. That boat's sailed. What we need to be doin' right now is figure out where we goin', not where we been. Now would you like to hear a thought?"

"Anything at all."

"These Mafiosi are usually big gamblers. It goes with the territory, y'know. Comes to me that maybe this shooter's found himself some local action. There ain't that many bookies around and if he's a heavy player, maybe we can get a line on him."

"Terrific. Only trouble is, I wouldn't know where to place a fifty-cent bet on anything right now."

"Well, I know a few bookmakers. What I'm gonna do, I'm gonna quietly check with Whit Ramsey on the Gaming Squad, see if any new bookies are operatin'. Maybe we can shake somethin' outa their pockets."

"Let's get it on then," Sharky said. "Pull over to that phone booth. You can touch base with Whit, I'll call Barret and see if he's turned up anything at the lab."

"That's cool."

It took Sharky a minute or two to get the night operator and another minute to get George Barret on the phone.

"Sharky, I haven't got much, but I just thought you'd like to know you were right about that little red pill. It's a red devil all right. Seventy percent speed, thirty percent nitroglycerine."

Sharky whistled through his teeth. "Jesus, that's pure dynamite!"

"I'd certainly agree with you. Blow a normal man straight through the roof. Whoever's using these is flirting with a coronary."

"Anything else, George?"

"Well, they'd be highly addictive, if that helps. I'd say two or three a day at least."

"Just a shit kicker, right? No medicinal value?"

"I miss the point."

"Well, it wouldn't be the kind of thing maybe he'd have a prescription for?"

"Not unless the doctor that prescribed them is a homicidal maniac. No, this is not the kind of thing you would find on the medicine shelf. It's narcotics, period."

"George, you're a winner. Got anything else?"

"Really, sir. I've just gotten started."

"Talk to you later."

He got back in the car. A moment later Livingston joined him.

"Got anything?" Livingston asked.

"Yeah. You ever heard of red devils?"

"Some kind of upper, right?"

"Upper is right. You could launch a rocket with one of them. Our shooter was probably using. And if he was, Barret says he's more than likely addicted."

"You're gonna have a hell of a time trackin' down

every pusher in town that might be peddlin' this shit, ain't you?"

"Maybe not. I haven't seen any red devils on the street in a year or two. Too expensive. They go down for about five bucks a pop."

"Jesus, you can do smack for that kind of money."

"Different kind of high. Point is, maybe they were specially ordered. That would narrow the field a bit. How about you?"

"I got three names. M'man Ramsey says if these three juicers ain't bookin' him and he's a big player, then he's using a phone contact somewhere else. And I know one of these guys. We grew up together. I can always finger him, so I figure we try to run down the other two first, save old Zipper until last."

"Zipper?"

"Got a scar down his back at least a foot long. I grew up in a rough neighborhood."

"Okay, but first let me try one more call."

Ben Colter had worked his way through Georgia State University playing "Melancholy Baby," "One for the Road," and other such classics for raucous salesmen and aging divorcees in a red-and-black vinyl lounge called Mona's Piano Bar. It was a job he had learned to hate passionately while staring out across the elongated piano six nights a week at faces he later said had only two expressions, drunk and desperate. The day he received his diploma he swore he would never again play the piano, not even in the solitude of his own home. The world had heard his last rendition of "My Way."

Retirement from the keyboard, however, was not in the cards for Ben. After serving six months as a rookie on the APD and two years and three months as a patrolman, Colter was promoted to third grade detective and assigned to Captain Vernon Oglesby in Narcotics. Oglesby was a competent officer, but he had a flaw. He was intrigued by intrigue. Because he loved the drama of subterfuge, Oglesby had more men on the street undercover than he had on straight duty. Any excuse at all and Oglesby would put another man out with phony I.D.'s and some new and flamboyant cover.

Colter was made to order for Oglesby. His presence on the Narcs summoned forth one of the captain's most outrageous ideas. Colter's past had caught up with him. He would form a trio and the Captain would arrange for the group to play at the Arboretum, one of the city's more popular uptown bars, there to get the inside on the dope traffic among the better-heeled swinging singles.

Within four weeks, an appalled Colter found himself the leader of the Red Colter Trio, the other two members being a hastily drafted teenage drummer who thought he was Buddy Rich and a guitar player who, as one of the patrons once observed, probably could make better music picking cotton than guitar.

Nevertheless the trio was modestly successful and Ben Colter, to his joy, discovered a marvelous fringe benefit: flesh. The ladies were young, liberated, and among the best looking in town. Hardly a night passed that the latent groupie instincts of some female patron were not vested in Colter's corner. They always had a little Colombian weed and occasionally a snort of coke to share. Ben properly excused his transgressions as part of the job and one night he had experienced his first amyl nitrite popper, later likening the resulting orgasm to a combination of the Mount Vesuvius eruption and the San Francisco earthquake.

Almost as a side benefit of the job Colter became an expert on the latest hip talk, the ultimate styles, the fashionable drugs—pot, Quaaludes, coke, poppers—

anything that stimulated bedtime organs, heightening the allure and dulling the uneasiness of the one-night stand. He also was compiling an impressive list of the uptown pushers, those who made their contacts at the crowded Arboretum Bar and delivered their dream cigarettes and nose candy in the seats of the Mercedes, Corvettes, and baby Cadillacs that nightly filled the parking lot.

On this particular Friday night Colter was feeling very lucky indeed. A young woman in a black skintight jumpsuit zipped down the front almost to her navel and bulging with incredible natural endowments was sitting just below the bandstand where for an hour or so she had been staring at Colter without even blinking her eyes.

Colter was stirred. He was also encouraged by her escort, a thirtyish loudmouth who obviously thought he was still in a fraternity. His size indicated that he had probably played either guard or tackle, although what had once been muscle had long since congealed into blubber. For an hour he had been extolling the virtues of the Auburn University War Eagles while quaffing down one bottle of Bud after another, swallowing the contents in a single long, horrifying gulp until eventually the beer took its toll. The War Eagle rose, his face the color of a bishop's vestments, and headed unsteadily toward the men's room.

Now is the time to strike, thought Colter, and abruptly ended his version of "Take the A Train" while his two partners floundered hopelessly in mid-chord. As Colter hit the floor a waiter handed him a note.

"Guy says it's urgent," the waiter said.

The note said: "Sharky. P-929-1423."

The *P* was a simple code for phonebooth. The call was indeed urgent.

Colter smiled at the jumpsuit zipper and winked, then hurried across the room to the public phones.

Sharky answered on the first ring.

"Sharky?" Ben said.

"Yeah. That you, Ben?"

"Yeah, man. How ya doin'?"

"I've had better days."

"I heard what The Bat did to you for icing High Ball Mary. That dumb shit. For what it's worth, Shark, I think we lost the best street man we had."

"Thanks, Ben. How's it with you?"

Ben wasn't listening. The girl in the jumpsuit was leaning over, saying something to one of the other girls at the table.

She's comin' over here, thought Colter. *I know she's comin' over here. I gotta get off the phone.*

"Uh, what did ya say, buddy? It's loud as hell in this place."

"I said, how ya doin?"

"Oh, yeah, man. It's a drag, y'know, a real drag."

She was getting up, looking his way. A bead of sweat popped out between Colter's eyes.

"Ben, I need some help."

"Okay, name it."

Here she comes.

"When's the last time you saw any red devils on the street?"

"Red devils," Colter repeated and then looked frantically around for fear someone had heard him. "Red devils," he said, lowering his voice. "Shit, nobody buys red devils anymore. Who's gonna lay out five bucks a pop, when you can get good uppers for two bits?"

She had caught the wind and was in full sail, coming straight at him, her course irreversible. He had to get off the phone. The sweat was now dribbling down the side of his nose.

"What I need, Ben, is a line on a pusher, somebody out in your territory who maybe scored very big in red devils in the last two, three weeks."

"Two or three weeks," Colter repeated, watching the jumpsuit slink closer.

A customer reached out and took her by the arm. But she looked down, said something terminal, and he dropped his hand.

"Red devils, hunh?" Ben said. "Lemme see, that could be, you know, three or four shovers I know of. Gimme an hour, I'll see if I can pin it down without blowing my cover."

"Thanks. Should I call you?"

"Use the squad room drop. Give 'em a number at . . . eleven o'clock. I'll call in and get it."

"That's cool, Ben. And thanks."

"Any time, buddy. Later."

He hung up. She was three feet away, staring up at him with eyes that looked like they had dust in them.

"Lining up your dance card for the rest of the night?" she said. The voice was perfect.

"I just broke all my plans until after the holidays," Colter said.

"Aren't I the lucky one?"

War Eagle came out of the men's room with tears in his eyes, wiping his tie with a paper towel. A blast of heat and noise hit him like a tidal wave. His cheeks bulged and he turned and fled back through the door.

"I bet you're gonna need a ride home tonight," Colter said.

"Nope," she said, "he is."

"I'll call a cab."

———————————

The Nosh leaned intently over the controls of his electronic magic set, a carefully organized series of tape recorders, filters, rerecorders, and other electronic hardware that looked like a small radio station. He was in his glory, punching buttons, twisting dials, hunched under padded earphones as he worked to lift the voices from one of Sharky's tapes.

He looked up suddenly, startled by the appearance in the doorway of Sergeant Anderson. The Nosh felt sorry for Anderson, a man beaten down by life, his hair an ugly tangle of gray, his shoulders sagging under the weight of an unhappy marriage. Anderson seemed always to be around, offering help where it wasn't needed and advice where it wasn't wanted. The squad room was his home. He remained there, night after night, until he was too tired to stay awake or until he ran out of excuses to avoid going home.

The Nosh pulled off the earphones.

"Give you a hand?" Anderson said.

"Nah. Thanks anyway."

"Coffee or something?"

"Thanks anyway, Sarge."

"What you up to, anyway?"

"Just giving Vice a hand. A little wiretap operation."

The tape was still running and a cacophony of sound emerged from the loudspeaker. A combination of soft music and cries of passion.

"What in God's name is that?" Anderson asked.

The Nosh giggled. "Sounds like a Chinese orgy," he said.

"Well, I'll be around a while longer if you need anything."

"Tell you what, Jerry. I got a fingerprint report coming in on the telex from the Bureau. If you hear the bell ring, gimme a call, will ya?"

"Glad to," Anderson said and smiled, grateful for something to do. "But they won't come in with anything before morning, will they?"

"I tagged *urgent* on it and I got a flash back. They're gonna pull the package for me tonight, if there's anything to pull."

"Okay," Anderson said. His curiosity was aroused, but before he could pursue the subject further, The Nosh said, "If you should run out of the house for anything, you might swing by Grady morgue. Twigs has a tape over there for me."

The coroner had called a few minutes earlier to report that he had completed the autopsy on Domino. But, he had added, there was little in the post mortem that would help the Machine.

"I'll just go on over now," Anderson said. "I need a little air." And he left.

The Nosh slipped the earphones back on and was immediately lost in his electronic fantasy world. *Somewhere in that Chinese orgy,* he thought, *there's a word or two, something, that'll make sense to somebody.* All he had to do was lift them out, get rid of the background noise. Eagerly he returned to his dials.

———————————

Sharky was stamping his feet in a phonebooth near the Peacetree-Battle shopping center when the phone rang. He lunged for it.

"That you, Sharky?" Ben Colter asked.

"Right."

"I got lucky."

"Good! Give it to me."

"There's a pusher named Gerald Lofton, a regular in the place. I got enough shit on this guy to bury him. But I can't move on him yet. There's a lot more where that came from. Anyway, right after you called, Lofton came in and we had a drink together and I moved the subject around to speed. I mentioned a friend of mine in Chicago told me something about red devils and was he hip to them and Lofton's eyes lit up like a church steeple and he tells me red devils are dynamite but expensive. Then he tells me a friend of his just moved—are you leaning on something?"

"I'm leaning on something."

"Fifty pills. At ten bucks a jolt!"

"Ten bucks!"

"I say this buyer must work for the mint and Lofton tells me he don't know who the big score was, but during the conversation he dropped the name of the connection."

"And . . ."

"The pusher's a first-class asshole who uses the name Shoes."

"Shoes? Like on your feet?"

"Right. Shoes. Anyway this Shoes, you gotta watch him. What he does, he plays the redneck joints out near Inman Park on payday. Does some heavy over-the-counter trade in pills and even some nickel bags."

"The red-devil buy was made in Inman Park?"

"No. He also has some select clientele out this way."

"What's he look like?"

"Hell, you won't have any trouble there. Tall, all bones. Has long white hair, almost like a high yellow, only he's white. Dresses like a cowboy. Also he never holds. He usually pays a teenager or some wino to carry the shit for him. He makes the deal, goes out in an alley, puts the stuff in a paper bag, and then the customer picks it up from the decoy. By that time Shoes is half a block away."

"Neat."

"Tonight's a good night to dump him. It's payday."

"Good."

"What's comin' down, anyway? I thought you got dumped off the dope squad?"

"I did. This is something else. In fact you can do me a favor and forget we even talked."

"That's cool. One more thing about this Shoes. He was dropped twice in New York state, both felonies. The last time he did a nickel-dime and went thirty-three months before parole. He'd put his own mother on ice to stay out of the slams. But Oglesby doesn't want him busted right now. He's hoping the son of a bitch'll lead us upstairs."

"Thanks, Ben."

"Anytime, Shark. Everybody on the squad owes you one. You took a bad rap. Anyone of us woulda done the same thing in your boots. I guess we're all just glad it wasn't us The Bat dumped on."

"See you in the lineup, Ben."

Sharky returned to the car.

"We scored," he said to Livingston. "You know a pusher does the country-music scene name of Shoes?"

"Nope."

"Tall. Beanpole. Mulatto-white hair. Dresses like a rodeo rider."

"Sounds like we could make him in the dark."

"He just dumped fifty red devils on somebody at ten bucks a hit."

"Holy shit!"

"Yeah."

"Well, you wanna take him first or visit my friend Zipper?"

Livingston had struck out on the first two bookies. He was obviously losing faith in his hunch. Sharky decided he deserved to run his string out first.

"Let's do your guy first. Mine'll be around till they turn the streetlights off."

"You got it."

He turned the red light on and went down Peachtree

Street to Spring and then into the middle of the city
with his foot on the floor. Sharky casually hooked up
his safety belt as they screamed in and out of traffic
past the Omni complex, a cluster of tall buildings that
included a hotel and a sports arena. Livingston turned
into the city viaduct and went down to Hunter Street
where he turned again. Six blocks later he pulled up to
the curb. A block ahead of them was a low, squat building joined like a Siamese twin to a three-story indoor
parking garage. A sign flashed on and off over the
building, announcing that it was the Lucky Strike Bowling Alley.

"We'll hoof it from here," Livingston said. They got
out of the car and locked it. The street was filled with
festive black men in fur coats and Borsalino hats with
laughing ladies on their arms. Sharky and Livingston
walked toward the bowling alley.

"Let's do this my way, okay?" Livingston said. "I
grew up here. It's my turf. I know every crack in the
sidewalk."

"Whatever you say."

"Here's the set-up. A long mall with the bowling alley at the end. Twelve alleys all together. When you go
in, there's a lunch counter on your right and a concession stand on your left. The motherfucker running the
concession stand owns the place, but you'd never know
it. He's uglier than a cross-eyed kangaroo and twice as
mean. What I need is for you to get his attention long
enough for me to come in behind him and freeze him.
He's got buttons under the counter. If he gets nervous,
he'll blow the whole play on us. Go down in there,
okay? Walk along the alleys until you're right in front of
the fuckin' concession stand, then walk straight back to
it and lose some time there. Buy a candy bar, anything.
If he gets nervous, put him on ice. Stick that 9 mm of
yours right up his nose, otherwise he won't think you're

serious. When I make my play, gimme some room and do exactly as I say, okay?"

"I got it."

"Good. Let's give it a try and see what happens."

Sharky went down the mall and stopped behind the chairs of the middle alley. A tall teenage black gave him a dirty look, then went back to his game. Sharky moved slowly along the alleys, aware of the concession stand to his left but not looking directly at it. When he was in front of the stand, he turned and strolled straight back to it.

The man behind the counter was the size of a warehouse with arms like two sides of beef. Thick lips were wrapped around the short end of a cigar which had gone out hours before. An earring glittered in one ear. He wore a tweed cap pulled down over his forehead and a black tee-shirt with a black-power fist emblazoned in the middle of it.

He eyed Sharky as though he were a cockroach walking across the counter.

"Alley's full," he said as Sharky leaned on the countertop.

"Got any Good 'N' Plenty?" Sharky said. Behind the man with the earring, Livingston entered a side door and moved quietly toward the concession stand.

The black man leaned on the opposite side of the glass countertop. His eyes were not as bored as he wanted them to seem. One arm dropped to his side, dangling near a drawer under the candy shelf.

"Nope. Try the drugstore for that fancy shit."

Livingston reached the other side of the counter. "Easy, Cherry," he said. The owner's face went blank, then he smiled, a gold tooth twinkling in the front of his mouth.

"Yes, suh," he said without turning around. "How they hangin', Sergeant?"

"Hangin' full, babe. What's happenin'?"

"Not a thing, not a thing. Just hangin' around, right?"

"Right. That's my friend Sharky. Say hello."

Cherry kept on smiling. "Hello, brother," he said.

Livingston walked to the side of the counter and lifted a hinged section of the countertop and stepped inside. He ran a nimble hand down one side of Cherry's body and up the other, extracting a stubby .25 caliber pistol.

"I got a permit for that, Sergeant."

"I'm sure you do." Livingston opened the drawer and ran his hand along the top of the space. He smiled. Cherry smiled.

"Now how we gonna do this, Cherry?" Livingston said. "You gonna keep that drawer closed and stay over there while I go upstairs, or am I gonna take this whole fuckin' counter apart?"

"Don't do that, Sergeant."

"Then it's cool, dig?"

"Gotcha," Cherry said and moved away from the drawer with his hands resting on top of the counter.

"Just stay right there. Sharky and I are gonna go over there by the Coke machine and have a chat."

They went to the Coke machine and Livingston dropped in two quarters. He gave one of the soft drinks to Sharky.

"See the door over there, about halfway down the first alley?"

Sharky looked over at the door. A red exit sign glowed over it.

"Okay."

"I'm goin' through that door. You stay here and make sure Cherry don't break the rules. If he gets fancy, bust him up alongside the head and make it good. He's got a head as hard as his bowling balls."

"Got it."

"Anybody gives you any shit, show them some bronze. Then wait for me."

Sharky nodded. He went back to the concession stand and watched Arch Livingston walk to the red exit door, his hands loose at his sides, striding on the balls of his feet like a prizefighter.

Sharky smiled at Cherry. "Just you and me, pal," he said and Cherry said, "Right, brother. You and me."

Livingston disappeared through the door.

Livingston stepped cautiously through the exit door into what was the second floor of the parking garage. The entrance was one deck below on a side street. A noisy car elevator dominated the core of the building, surrounded by numbered parking places. Most of them were full. From somewhere close by, Stevie Wonder's plaintive voice lamented the sorrows of "Livin' for the City."

Livingston moved slowly along the rows of cars, holding his .38 down at his side. The music grew louder. He stopped behind a pale green Lincoln. A black man wearing a floppy white hat and a silver gray full-length suede coat sat in the front seat with the door open, beating his knees in time with the music, a .32 Special lying on the dashboard a few inches from his hands.

Livingston moved around the car until he was directly behind the gunman. It was then he recognized him as a young tough named Elroy Flowers. "Keep your hands on your knees and—"

He never finished. Flowers moved unexpectedly and with the agility of a greyhound, swinging both legs out of the door as he reached for his pistol. It was a mistake. Livingston slammed the car door, smashing Flow-

ers's ankles between the door and the jamb, and swung
his pistol in a wide overhead arc down on top of Flowers's
head. The felt hat deadened the blow but not enough.
The half-conscious gunman grunted, reaching out
blindly with one hand and knocking the pistol to the
floor of the car.

Livingston grabbed a handful of Flowers's shirt and
coat, swung him out of the car, spun him around, and
slammed him against the hood. He put the flat of his
hand against Flowers's head and shoved him hard into
the window of the Lincoln.

The window cracked and Flowers's eyes went blank.
He sighed and dropped straight to the floor. Livingston
dragged him by his shirt front across the floor and into
the car elevator, dropping him face down on the metal
floor. He pushed the up button and then jumped off the
elevator and ran across the parking deck to the fire
steps, taking them two at a time as he raced to the
third floor.

The elevator shuddered, groaned, and started rising.
On the third floor another black man was leaning
against the fender of a cream-colored Rolls Royce. He
was bigger, more dangerous, than Flowers, a blockhouse of a man in a dark blue suit. He was reading a
racing form which he tucked under his arm as the elevator started up. He walked casually toward it. Behind
him Livingston stepped through the third-floor door
and leaned against the back of a parked car, holding his
.38 in both hands and aiming it at the center of the big
man's back.

The big man peered down into the slowly rising elevator and saw Flowers lying on the floor.

"Hunh?" he said. His hand slipped under his coat,
reaching for his armpit.

"Don't do nothin stupid, nigger," Livingston yelled. "I
got soft-nose loads in this piece."

The big man turned toward him but kept his hand inside his jacket.

"Bring it out slow and easy, motherfucker. You do anything sudden, I put a hole in your belly big enough to park that Rolls in."

The big man continued to stare. His hand stayed inside the coat. Doubt troubled his eyes as he calculated the odds.

"Don't get fancy, man. I'm the heat and I don't miss."

The rear window of the Rolls glided silently down and a voice that was part silk and part granite said, "Okay, Steamboat, cool it. I'll talk to the man."

The back door of the Rolls swung open. The man called Steamboat uncoiled and withdrew an empty hand.

Livingston peered over the .38 into the interior of the Rolls. It was a study in gaudy opulence. The seats were unholstered in mauve velvet with gold buttons. The floor was covered in ankle-deep white shag carpeting. Built into the back of the front seat were two white telephones, a bar and an icemaker. A bottle of Taittinger champagne sat on the bar shelf.

The man who sat in the corner arrogantly sipping champagne matched the decor. He was shorter than Livingston and looked younger, but he was beginning to show the signs of good living. His afro flared out, encircling his head like a halo, and his mustache was full and trimmed just below the corners of his mouth. He was wearing a dark-blue pigskin jacket, rust-colored gabardine pants, and a flowered shirt open at the neck, the collar flowing out over the lapels of the jacket almost to his shoulders. Gold chains gleamed at his throat, diamonds twinkled on his fingers, a gold Rolex watch glittered from under one cuff. His mirror-shined shoes were light tan with three-inch hardwood heels. A white

handkerchief flopped casually from his breast pocket.
He stared at Livingston through gold-framed tinted
glasses, then looked down at the .38 that was pointed at
his chest.

"You mind, nigger?" he said, nodding toward the
gun.

Livingston appraised the back seat, lowered his gun,
and laughed.

"Shit," he said, "I could get you ten to twenty for
what you done to this poor Rolls."

"Get on in, goddammit. All my fuckin' heat's runnin'
outa here."

Livingston got in and pulled the car door shut.

"Been a long time, Zipper."

"Ain't that the truth. Last time I saw you, you was
wearin' a fuckin' monkey suit, sittin' in the front seat of
a goddamn patrol car. Bi-i-ig shit."

"Last time I saw you," Livingston said, "you were in
Fulton Superior Court apologizin' for boosting car radios."

"That long ago, hunh? Shit, time do fly. You mind
tellin' me what the fuck all this Wild West shit's about,
comin' in here, bustin' up my people, wavin' all that
iron around? No need for that shit. You here to bust my
ass?"

"This is a social call."

"Shit. What d'ya do when you come on business, kill
somebody?"

"Flowers went for his piece, man. You think I'm
gonna stand around, let some dumb nigger blow my ass
off?"

"He is a dumb fuckin' nigger, no question about that.
Good help's hard to come by these days." He looked
through the car window. Steamboat was standing by the
front of the car, watching. "Now Steamboat's a whole

nother case, baby. You fuck with Steamboat, you better have your plot paid for."

"Used to fight, didn't he?"

"Light-heavy. Mean son-bitch. Cat's never been knocked out. Too slow was his fuckin' problem. He was instant death when he was in-fighting but the fast boys would lay out there, cut him to pieces at arm's length. You just let that motherfucker get in one good shot, though. Shit, they'd think they was run over by a goddamn freight train. What you want, nigger?"

"Told ya, man. It's a social call."

"Un hunh. How long you knowed about this here travelin' bookie parlor of mine?"

"About three years."

"Aww, don't shit me, nigger. We grew up on the same fuckin' street, man, remember?"

"Look here, brother, long as you keep your operation clean, I ain't interested in bringin' anything down on you. You ain't connected. You strictly cash and carry, don't take no markers, so nobody gets their head stove in, any of that shit. I ain't in any rush to turn you up to some white dude on the Gamin' Squad just so's he can make some goddamn points. I'd rather know what you doin', Zipper, have some motherfuckin' stranger come in here bustin' nigger ass all over town, you dig?"

Zipper thought it over, then smiled.

"How about a little wine there, for old time's sake?"

"Thanks anyway, man. It gives me heartburn."

"Heartburn! Man, that shit's fifty dollars a bottle. Ain't no fuckin' heartburn in this shit."

"I'll still pass. I got a partner downstairs starin' down Cherry. I got to get back before they get bored, start hurtin' ass."

"Okay, so get it on. What the fuck you doin' here?"

"I need some information."

Zipper sat up as though he had been slapped. At first he seemed surprised, then surprise turned to anger.

"Shee-it."

"Listen here, motherfucker . . ."

"Sheee-IT, man. What you handin' this nigger? Come in here, think you can . . . god*damn,* hey, Zipper ain't no fuckin' stoolie. Zipper don't rub ass with the heat. Man, you forgot where you came from."

"You ain't changed a bit, sucker. Still put your fuckin' mouth up front of your brains."

"Well, you changed, motherfucker. Shit, give a nigger a piece of goddamn tin and a peashooter, motherfucker thinks he's Father fuckin' *De*vine."

One of the phones rang and Zipper snatched it off the hook. "Closed for lunch," he snapped. "Call back in ten minutes." He slammed the phone back.

"Look, I ain't interested in your goddamn bookmaking, I told you that. I got a problem and I think maybe you can help me with it. Now, the dude I'm lookin' for is white."

"Shit," Zipper said, "I don't do no business with honkies. Ain't you heard? They's a lotta fuckin' rich niggers in Atlanta now."

Livingston looked at the floor. "You tellin' me you don't do business with whitey, I'm tellin' you I'm talkin' to one lyin' nigger. You takin' layoff bets from half the highpocket white bookmakers in town, Zipper, and I know it."

"Layoff bets? Man, that's different. I don't see none of them turkeys. M'bagman picks up the takes, brings me the bread and the slip. Then he takes back what we lose. All I do, I count the money and put down the bets. I don't know any of them motherfuckers personal."

Zipper poured another glass of champagne, huffing while he poured.

Livingston looked around the back seat, stared out

the window, finally lit a cigar. He said, "We gonna talk
or are you gonna get that fuckin' hard head of yours
dragged downtown and let a couple of white cats play
good guy-bad guy with your ass?"

"I told you my position. Zipper don't hand out no
shit to the fuzz. I don't care we was street brothers fifteen years ago."

"I ain't here 'cause we ran together," Livingston said.
"I'm here 'cause you got information I need. And I
don't have time to fuck around."

Zipper looked at Livingston with contempt. "Know
somethin'?" he said. "You was one bad motherfucker.
Nobody shit with you on the street, man. You bust ass.
Now look at you. Two dollar fuckin' suit, wash 'n' wear
shoes, honkie goddamn haircut. And you want me to
turn fuckin' stoolie. I ain't believin' you, now."

"Listen here, Zipper, and listen good. I ain't interested in your goddamn players. We're talking about
murder."

Zipper looked startled.

"That's right," Livingston said. "Murder. Now you
keep your fuckin' yap shut until I finish. Cat I'm after is
white. He's an outfit hitman, can you dig that? Last
night this son-bitch burned a very nice lady. He's a
fuckin' lady-killer. And you givin' me all this shit about
protectin' his ass?"

Zipper said nothing. He stared into his champagne
glass.

"This motherfucker woulda come into town a couple
weeks ago. If he is a gamblin' man, he'd be a *big* gamblin' man. Sports, ponies, any national shit. Now you
don't know anything about such a cat, okay. But if you
do, Zipper, I got to know about it, 'cause man, we
talkin' about rough trade here."

"How come you so fuckin' sure this dude gambles?"

"I'm not. It's a hunch. But right now it's all I got."

The car was quiet. Zipper cleared his throat. Then the phone rang again.

"Go ahead and talk," Livingston said, "I know you're a bookie. What the shit you so shy about?"

Zipper yanked the phone off the hook. "Hello . . . yeah, this Zipper. What it is? . . . It's Dallas and seven . . . Well, that's tough shit, turkey. That's the fuckin' spread and ain't nothin I can do about it. . . . Listen here, motherfucker, I don't make the odds. You don't like it, put your fuckin' money back in your god-damn shoe. Now, you want some action or don't you? . . . Well, fuck you too, nigger." He slammed down the phone.

Silence again.

Finally Zipper said, "Only one possibility. Only one possibility. Cat can't be your man. Can't be."

"Who says?"

"I say. He makes book in a fag bar out Cheshire Bridge Road."

"A fag bar?"

"That's right. This tough-nuts shooter you talkin' about queer?"

"Who is he?"

"Shit, I told ya, nigger, I don't have no truck with any of those fuckers personally. This joint, it's called, uh . . . this stays with us, that right?"

"C'mon, Zipper."

"This joint is called, uh, the Matador. Got this pansy-lookin' bullfighter on the sign out front."

"I know the place."

" 'Bout five weeks ago my bookie friend out there, you know—he does nickel and dime shit out there, nothin' big, mostly local games—anyways, he calls me, says, do I want to take a layoff on the Oakland and Miami game? Fucker took the spread for five grand and lost his ass. Next week he's back again. Motherfucker doubles up, lays out ten grand on some NFL game and a basketball game, and splits. Been goin' like that ever since. Five, ten g's a clip. Right now I'm into him for about five thou."

"When's the last time he bet?"

"Yesterday."

"Yesterday?"

"You heard right, yesterday. He bettin' on the play-off. Took Dallas and the points over Minnesota. Ten big ones."

"Zipper, I got to know who this player is."

"No fuckin' way."

"Just the name, man."

"No motherfuckin' *way*. Shit, I told ya. I don't even know who it is. The bookie deals with the score and I deal with the bookie."

"Okay, who's the bookie then?"

"C'mon, goddammit. You lean on him, he's gonna know I done it to him."

"I'll cover your ass. Don't you worry about that. I ain't interested in the fuckin' bookie. I want his mark."

"You *got* to cover my ass, Livingston. Tell you somethin'. You come down on this little motherfucker, he gonna die on the spot."

"I'll do it right, man. Who is it?"

"The bartender. Name's Arnold."

Livingston sighed. "Jesus," he said, "that was worse than pickin' cotton with your goddamn feet."

"Just don't fuck me over on this, hear? And don't come back with any more of this snitch shit either. I done made my contribution for life."

Livingston started to get out of the car. "Shit, motherfucker," he said, "my eyes couldn't stand any more of this pussywagon."

Zipper's eyes flared. "Pussywagon. *Pussy*wagon! Shit, you fuckin' no-class nigger, this car cost fifty grand. Fifty fuckin' thousand goddamn dollars. Ain't no goddamn Detroit pussywagon. Shit, I don't even scratch my balls when I'm in this machine. You hear me, Livingston?"

But the policeman was gone, down through the fire door toward the bowling alley below.

"Pussywagon, my ass," Zipper growled, then he leaned out the door. "Steamboat!"

"Yeah, boss."

"Take that fuckin' dumbass to the Gradys and get his head stitched up and then fire his ass."

At four A.M., Friscoe quit for the night. He drove home, grumbling to himself, angry because he had turned up nothing at all in six hours of hard work. His back ached and his eyes burned as he entered the house, passing up his customary raid on the refrigerator and going straight to the bedroom. He went into the bathroom and closed the door before turning on the light so as not to awaken Sylvia, splashed cold water on his face, and sat on the commode to take off his shoes. He sighed with relief as he dropped them on the floor, then went back to the bedroom and sat on the edge of the bed, bone weary and almost too tired to get undressed.

His wife rolled over and said sleepily, "Barney?"

"No, it's Robert Redford," he said wearily.

"Oh, how nice."

"If he was as tired as I am, you could forget it."

"What time is it?"

"Past four. I'm dead. My feet feel like I just ran the Boston Marathon."

"You would've been proud of Eddie, Barney. He did just fine."

"Jeeze, I completely forgot. Did you explain? Did it

embarrass him I had to leave like that, right in the middle of Prokofiev?"

"He understood. Nobody saw from the stage; they were very busy."

The lieutenant pulled and tugged at his clothes until they lay in a pile at his feet, then he fell back on the bed in his undershorts.

"Jesus, Syl, there's got to be an easier way to make a living."

"Uh huh."

"It never ends. You clean up one, there's two more in its place."

She rose on one elbow and rubbed his temple with two fingers.

"You been saying that since the day we got married," she said.

But Friscoe did not hear her. His breathing had already settled into a steady drone. Sylvia got up and pulled the covers over him and went into the bathroom.

A moment later the phone rang.

Before she could get back to it, Friscoe, from years of experience, reached out and answered it without opening his eyes.

"Barney?"

"Umm."

"Is that you, Friscoe?"

"Uh . . . yeah."

"It's Max Grimm. You awake?"

"Almost . . . uh, you finish the autopsy?"

"Oh, on the girl? Abrams got that hours ago. I've got something else you ought to know about. Are you listening?"

"Yeah, yeah."

"You remember, I told you Riley had a couple of John Does down here in the icehouse?"

"Right."

"Well, I just finished the post mortem on one of them."

"Christ, what the hell time is it?"

"Who knows? I been going so long I can't stop now. Anyway, this p.m. I just finished? They found the corpse out in the city dump yesterday afternoon. A real messy thing. Face blown off, both hands are missing."

"Hands missing?"

"Yeah, cut off at the wrist. No clothes, no I.D., nothing."

"Twigs, I got one too many bodies on my hands already."

"Listen to me. Like I say, his face was blown off, nothing left, no way to idenitfy him, okay?"

"Um hmm."

"But that isn't what killed him. He was drilled through the right eye. A single .22 caliber long rifle-bullet, with the end dumdummed. It flattened out and laid up against the back of the skull on the inside."

"So?"

"So the bullet was soaked in garlic."

And at almost the same moment that Twigs was telling Friscoe about the stiff in the ice house with the .22 caliber garlic-soaked bullet in its head, Anderson brought the telex message to Larry Abrams, who was sitting half asleep at his table, staring at the tape he had been studying for hours.

The teletype message woke him up.

"Here's that FBI report you were lookin' for," Anderson said. "Looks like a dead end."

"What do you mean?" The Nosh said.

"Read it."

The bureau had made a positive I.D. on the two prints. They belonged to a fifty-nine-year-old white

male from Lincoln, Nebraska named Howard Burns.
But The Nosh did not read any further. His eyes
jumped to the bottom line of the report and he stared in
disbelief.

According to the FBI report, Howard Burns had
been incinerated in an automobile accident on the outskirts of Omaha two months earlier.

16

The sleek white Grebe cabin cruiser rolled gently on a quiet sea, protected by a womb of warm fog that had drifted in from the Gulf Stream just after midnight, a fog so thick that it now obscured the crow's nest over the cabin. Hotchins slipped on a pair of faded corduroys and a yellow slicker and went out on the afterdeck where he sat quietly massaging the calf of his imperfect leg. Occasionally, when tension and weariness weighed on him, he could almost feel the missing foot cramping up on him, the pain spreading slowly up to his knee, the artificial foot becoming a dead weight. It was a discomfort he endured alone, never mentioning it to others.

He had anchored in a cove on the inland side of the island, an unnamed hump of sand and sea grass he remembered from the early days when he worked the shallows off the Georgia and South Carolina coasts with his father. He rarely thought about those days anymore. Time had eased all that, erasing memories of the harsh work and bitter loneliness that were the realities of a shrimper's life. Now he regarded the sea with affection, a friend providing tiny islands along the coast from Brunswick to Charleston that had become his private hideaways.

He sat in the stern, rubbing the leg, drawing strength from the artificial foot, which had become a constant reminder of the humiliation of defeat, of the common weakness he saw in all people who failed, who dreamed too small, and would not pay the price for even their little dreams. His utter contempt for those who simply endured had started in Korea. There were prices to be paid and the greater the prize, the higher the price.

In the prison camp, where he lay nursing his shattered foot for almost a year before it was amputated, Hotchins had learned about survival. He needed a goal, something more than just day-by-day groveling to stay alive. His goal, his single driving obsession to be president of the United States, was born in morphine-crazed hallucinations, but it became his goal for living. He invented methods for keeping his mind alert. He tried to think like a president, act like a president, adopt the attitude of a president.

When he was released from the hospital into the prison population, he was shocked at what he found—a motley, demoralized, filthy group who reflected their senior officer, a colonel named Sacks who was a weak and disheartened shell, tormented by fear and sickness and destroyed by his own nightmares. Hotchins watched as Sacks encouraged the weak to submit to the North Koreans, to collaborate, sign confessions, to do anything to stay alive. He hated Sacks, not because he was weak, but because he had created an atmosphere that eventually would enervate Hotchins himself.

If Hotchins were to survive, he had to destroy Sacks.
His became a constant and subtle voice hammering at
the colonel's conscience, eroding the last vestige of
Sacks's self-respect. It was an insidious and ruthless
campaign, so carefully carried out that when Sacks
eventually hanged himself, he did not realize he had
been driven to the act by the man who assumed his position of command.

For the next two years Hotchins ruled the camp,
hand-picking a small coterie of the toughest men left
and establishing his own harsh rules and regulations. He
restored military discipline to the prison, demanded that
the men practice personal hygiene, that they exercise to
keep their morale up. Twice he secretly ordered the execution of men on the verge of confessing to war
crimes. He was both a frightening martinet and an in-
spiration to his fellow prisoners. They survived because
he needed them to, and in the end he endured his humiliation with dignity and walked out of the camp a
hero.

When he did, he was convinced that he would someday be president, regardless of the price. It was a passion which DeLaroza had eased to life, nurtured, encouraged, and fed. And now it was happening. Nothing
could stop it. In Hotchins's mind, it was destiny.

He sat in the fog, preparing himself for the tough ten
months ahead, for the exhausting personal toll he knew
the campaign would exact, contemplating the price he
would have to pay.

He had already paid dearly by ending his affair with
Domino. DeLaroza had been right, she represented a
constant danger and a foolish one. Besides, she had
served her purpose. Domino had awakened new pas-
sions in Hotchins, arousing a latent need that had been
smothered by ambition. She had fired his carnal desires
with her incredible sensuality and given him a new vi-

tality. Losing her was just the first of many personal sacrifices he knew he would have to make.

The decision to give her up had come quickly once he faced it. Hotchins had trained himself to make fast decisions. He simply programmed the pluses and minuses into his brain, a trick he had learned from Victor. Emotion had nothing to do with it.

It was done. Time to move on.

He started thinking about his own political machine. The nucleus was there, although he recognized that in its strength there was danger. DeLaroza, Roan, Lowenthal, each a shrewd and powerful strategist but each with his own needs to fulfill. It would not be easy, balancing their egos. keeping the machine oiled and moving.

He did not hear her open the hatchway behind him.

"Composing your acceptance speech?" she said.

He turned, startled by her voice, ignoring the remark or perhaps not hearing it. Instead he was staring at her as she stood in the hatchway, huddled in a green jacket which she held shut with both hands, her magical features framed by tousled black hair, her green eyes still filled with sleep, her long, perfect legs bare below the jacket.

"God you're something," he said. "You are really something."

She laughed. "Changing your mind?"

His face grew grew somber again and he turned away from her, staring back into the fog when he shook his head.

"You're making it sad," she said. "It doesn't have to be sad. There are still a couple of very good hours left before the sun comes up."

Without thinking he began stroking his leg. She came out and stood near him, putting her head gently on the back of his neck and moving her fingers lightly in his hair.

"Want me to do that for you?"

"No. It's nothing."

"Did you hear what I said? It doesn't have to be sad. That's for the songwriters."

"It got to me a little, seeing you there. A little nudge, that's all. What is it the French say? 'To say goodbye is to die a little.' "

She sighed. "You're going to get emotional on me. I can tell."

"Well, my mother always said I was emotional. 'Donald,' she'd say, 'don't be so dramatic.' "

She sat down beside him and nestled against him. He put his arm around her.

"Well, don't go getting dramatic on me. Save that for the taxpayers."

Hotchins laughed. "You've noticed that too, hunh?"

"Come on. When that voice begins to tremble and those eyes fire up, I just have to marvel at you." Then, a moment later: "You're going to win, Hotch. You're a straight-line guy and people like that."

"What do you mean, 'straight-line guy'? That sounds stuffy."

"Not at all. It's one of your . . . charms. You get right to it, no fussing around. Now most men would have brought me out here, wined me, had a little dinner catered in a pretty picnic basket, made love to me all night, then made their little farewell speech two minutes before we docked. You gave it to me before we even got out of the harbor. And I like that about you. The only problem is, you've been acting like a little boy who did something wrong ever since."

"Well I—"

"It's not guilt. Guilt is not one of your problems."

"I guess I figured, when you close the door it isn't fair to climb back in the window."

"How about me? How about the way I feel?"

He drew her closer to him, his fingers searching the jacket, feeling her nakedness under it. He remembered a time in Virginia, one of the first times she stirred feelings in him he thought he had lost forever. His hand moved around her and up until he felt the curve of her breast and she turned slightly so it rested against his palm.

Out beyond the cove a foghorn sounded, its mournful tune going sour at the end of the bleat.

"That's old Jerry Stillman's tugboat," Hotchins said. "That foghorn's had a frog in its throat since I was a kid."

"You know what, Hotch? I knew you were going to be a good lay the first time I ever saw you."

"Oh?"

The remark startled him. Her uninhibited observations always caught him off-guard. He laughed and said, "You mean, you thought about bedding me down the first thing? Right in the middle of a cocktail party?"

She thought about that night. She had seen his picture in the newspaper, seen him on television, and had wondered about him the way any woman wonders about a man of prominence. It was Victor who had introduced them.

"Want to meet the next president?" he had asked her.

"Of what?"

"The United States."

Now who could turn down an invitation like that? Of course she wanted to meet him. There had been a fund-raising dinner to save the historic old Fox Theater, with a private cocktail party beforehand.

"He is a lonely man," DeLaroza had told her casually.

"Does it show?"

"Only to those who know him. The public sees only what he wants it to see."

"Bad marriage?"

"Typical. He married a small-town girl when he was quite young. She has not kept up. She is uncomfortable in the political arena."

"Suicide," she had said. "She better get used to it."

"Too late."

She had been overwhelmed by his personal charm, a charisma that television never adequately captured. He was commanding, charming, friendly but formal, and she had watched him from across the room. Several times she had caught him staring back at her.

Thinking back on it, she knew now that it had been more than just Hotch. She had known commanding, charming, friendly, and formal men before, but never one who was going to run for president. It had been a challenge, no question about it. Yes, there had definitely been a challenge there.

What had Victor said? 'You are attracted by power.' *No,* she thought, *not really.* She had known from the beginning that the benefits of power would be denied to her. From the beginning she had been a closet mistress. Nothing would ever have changed that. And there had been affection. But love? No, that was the delusion.

And so she too was relieved that it was over.

"Hey," he said, snapping her back to the present.

"Hey yourself."

"I said, did you really think about bedding me down right there in the middle of that cocktail party?"

"Didn't you?"

"Didn't I what?"

"Think about laying me the first thing?"

"Uh no, but—"

"But you would now?"

"I've got prior knowledge now."

"Hotch, if you met me in a restaurant right now, for the first time, what is the first thing that would go through your mind?"

"You win."

"Thank you. Now you understand. I looked across the room at you and I said to myself, 'He's going to be great in bed.'"

"Why did you think that?"

"I saw your hunger. Not for me, not for any other woman in the room. But you were hungry. And a powerful, hungry man is a powerfully good lay."

He turned and looked down at her. The jacket had fallen open and he could see her breasts swelling against the cloth.

"Did I disappoint you?"

"Of course not. It was fun, like waking up a sleeping tiger. Oh, you were a little shy at first, but . . ."

She smiled and let the sentence drift away in the fog, then after a few moments she said, "You've been a very good lover."

More silence. She moved again, this time against him, and he could feel the heat from her body through the jacket.

"How long have we been lovers?" he said.

"Seven months this Thursday."

"Have you been marking the calendar?"

"I never forget good things. It's a lesson I learned from my dad. If you don't expect anything from the world, everything you get is a surprise. And that makes the really good things that much better."

"He must've been a very wise man."

"Nope, he never kept a promise in his life. But . . . he made some beauties, so he also taught me the value of dreaming."

"That's a very generous way of putting it. What was he like?"

"I don't want to talk about it."

"You know, we've known each other for seven months and I don't know a damn thing about your life away from me? I don't even know your real name."

"You don't like Domino?"

"Well, it always struck me as a bit melodramatic."

"Intriguing. I like *intriguing*. It's a much better word."

"Okay, intriguing."

"Good. And that's the way we'll keep it."

"I, uh, I feel . . ."

She sensed the awkwardness in his voice and held a finger to his lips.

"Shh," she said. And then: "I want to make love to you. Right now. Because it's something we both enjoy and because I find you most appealing out here like this and because I'm horny as hell."

She made a sound in her throat and moved a hand up his leg, sliding her fingers down the inside of his thigh. He turned toward her and kissed her and she reached up between their mouths with two fingers and squeezed his lips very lightly between them, and his mouth opened and their tongues touched, flirted with each other, and she moved against him, very lightly, so he could feel the fullness of her. She slid one leg up over his lap, drew her mouth away from his, and laid her head against his chest. Then she took the zipper of his jacket between her teeth and very slowly moved her head down, unzipping it almost to the waist. Then, raising her head, she kissed him again and this time both their jackets were open and as they kissed she moved her breasts lightly against him and he felt her hard nipples caressing his chest.

He was totally captivated by her, the thought of having her was dizzying to him. He felt her hand touch him and felt himself responding. He reached up, stroked her face and throat, gradually widening the circle his hand was making until it brushed her nipple. And then he knew she was already starting the buildup and at that moment Hotchins realized fully what his obsession to become president had cost him.

17

The Majestic Grill was an obscure and unrecognized landmark that had endured on the same streetcorner since 1934, oblivious to the changes that had occurred around it. The shoe repair shop beside it had become a magazine store which had become a head shop which had become a natural food store which was now a pinball parlor; the theater up the street had declined from first runs to double features to porn; and if the Majestic was a monument to early Thirties style, the hotel across the street was a six-story monument to Early Nothing architecture. It had been boarded up for years. But the Majestic never changed. It had resisted time and transition, catering to a clientele that defied demography or caste. A bum nursing a cup of coffee received the same curt service as a college president.

Inside, bacon and sausage sizzled on ancient grills,

the odors spicing the heady aroma of roasting coffee.
The decor was nondescript, a well-worn combination of
stainless steel, formica, pale green walls, and dark green
vinyl seats. A dining room had been added to the rear
of the diner years before and there Papa sat, at a corner
table, mesmerized by the menu from which he was
about to order a breakfast big enough to delight an entire Marine brigade. Sharky and Livingston joined him
and a few minutes later Friscoe arrived, an apparition
in scruffy corduroys, a peaked deepsea fishing cap, and
a scarred jacket that predated antiquity.

He appraised the ragtag bunch, their eyes charcoaled
from lack of sleep, their cheeks scraggly from not shav-
ing, their bodies sagging under the weight of a sleepless
night.

"Jesus," he said, "you all look like you just got
sprung from Auschwitz."

"And thank you, Cinderella," Livingston said.

"So where's Abrams? He ain't gonna be one of those
late guys, is he?"

"On his way," Sharky said. "He got hung up on a
phone call."

A gargantuan waitress with arms like a wrestler's
hovered over the table. "Are we ready here?" she said.
It was more a demand than a question.

"We'll have coffee all the way around while we're de-
ciding," Sharky said and she padded off toward the coffee urn on slippered feet.

Friscoe leaned back in his chair and looked at the
other three detectives. "I'll tell you what. I hope to shit
you guys did better than me. I musta put in five hours
trying to get a line on this Neil and what do I get out of
it? Sore feet and a fuckin' goose egg, that's what."

Papa took a tattered notebook from his pocket and
licking a thumb, flicked it open. "His name's Dantzler,"
he announced. "With a *t*."

"What'sat?" Friscoe said.

"Dantzler with a *t*. D-a-n-t-z-l-e-r. He lives in a condo in The Courtyard, which, if you'll remember, is also where Tiffany lives. That's because she's Dantzler's girlfriend. She uses her apartment mainly for tricks. She also has another boyfriend on the sly and she occasionally shacks up at Domino's place. Dantzler's a rich kid gone sour. His game's pimping and scam. He's outa town, be back a week from tomorrow."

Friscoe stared at Papa with a hint of indignation. "Sounds like a pornographic soap opera," he said. "Where'd you come up with all that shit?"

"A snitch."

"You got all that from one fuckin' snitch?"

"Had a little help from the security guard at The Courtyard."

"Maybe I just should have stood in bed," Friscoe said, feeling suddenly inadequate.

"Sometimes you get lucky," Papa said.

"Well, sometimes wasn't last night for me," Friscoe said. "Is there anything else?"

"Dantzler's sporting a new Ferrari, braggin' on the street how he took some cowboy to the cleaners. Domino is out. Didn't know about it."

"And just how did you find that out?" Friscoe said.

"Snitch."

"Shit, who is this fuckin' stoolie?" Friscoe said. "Maybe we oughta put him on the goddamn payroll."

"One more thing," said Papa. "Dantzler hasn't got the guts to kill anybody or get it done. Rule him out. Ditto Tiffany."

"Same snitch?" Sharky said.

Papa nodded.

"You sure he's reliable, Papa?" Friscoe said.

"Yes. When this guy talks, it's bankable."

"So that retires Dantzler, Tiffany, *and* the mark in Texas as possibles," Livingston said.

Friscoe shook his head. "Too bad. They would have been the easiest shot we had."

At that point The Nosh arrived, alert, ebullient, and smiling. Friscoe glared at him sourly. "You look like you just come back from a week at the beach," he said.

"I think I'm on to something," The Nosh said.

"Okay, everybody gets their turn. Papa there just made himself an A-plus. Now it's Sharky's turn at bat."

Sharky quickly described the deal on red devils made by Shoes and the layoff bets made by Arnold, the bartender at the Matador. Before he was through, the waitress returned with the coffee and demanded their orders while The Nosh complained bitterly that they might at least have selected a place that had bagels on the menu.

"This here's a diner, not a deli," Friscoe said.

When the waitress had gone again, Sharky said, "We didn't make Shoes. He never showed up on the street last night. But both these leads tell Arch and me that the shooter's still in town."

"Could be coincidence, Shark," The Nosh said.

"If it was just one or the other, I'd agree," said Livingston. "But here we got information from two completely different sources and it dovetails."

"Yeah," Friscoe said, "I never been big on coincidence myself. It's like circumstantial evidence. Where there's smoke there's fire."

"Arch and I are going to move on Shoes tonight," Sharky said. "But we need somebody to get on this Arnold, find out who the big bettor is."

"Can you maybe get a line on this Shoes before tonight, hit him in his nest?" Friscoe asked.

"It's pushy. If we move too hard on him we could blow Ben's cover," Sharky said.

"Okay, I'll worry about Arnold, there, see what I can

come up with," Friscoe said. "We just don't have *time*. We got nothing but maybes and probablies, and what we need, we ain't got. We ain't got a face, we ain't got a name, we ain't got a motive, we ain't got *shit*."

"Is it my turn yet?" The Nosh asked.

"Jeez, you're like some kid in grammar school thinks he's got all the answers," Friscoe said.

"Go ahead, Nosh," Sharky said. "Let's hear it."

"Okay, I got a positive make on the prints."

Friscoe almost swallowed his coffee cup. Sharky, Livingston, and Papa froze in mid-bite, like sculptured figures.

"You know who the killer is?" Sharky said.

The Nosh nolded. "Howard Burns. Male Causasian, age 59, owned a short-haul trucking outfit in Lincoln, Nebraska."

"A *trucking* company?" Friscoe said. "This Mafia button owns a trucking company?"

"What do you mean, owned?" Sharky said.

The Nosh smiled. "According to the Bureau, Howard Burns was killed in an automobile accident on October twentieth."

Again silence, broken finally by Friscoe. "That ain't possible."

"That's right. It sure ain't," The Nosh said. "I checked it out again with George Barret. He says the prints are fresh, no question about it."

"What kind of accident?" Sharky asked.

"A single-vehicle wreck on the outskirts of Omaha. Car went off the road, hit a tree, and exploded. Burns's wife made the identification using dental charts."

"Uh oh," Friscoe said, and a smile began spreading across his face.

"Neat," Livingston said.

"Now that *ain't* a coincidence," Papa said.

"And think about the date," Livingston said.

"Yeah about two weeks before he surfaced here looking for red devils and a healthy bookmaker," Sharky said.

"There's more," The Nosh said.

"I shoulda stood in bed," said Friscoe.

"Look at this Bureau telex on Burns. Notice anything funny?" The Nosh asked.

They all looked it over, reading the lines, the background information on the questionably deceased Howard Burns. Born in Newark, raised in Philadelphia, worked as truck driver and then in the navy yard there during World War II, returned to trucking after the war, left Philadelphia in 1960, worked at various trucking jobs until 1968 when he purchased the Interstate Van Lines in Lincoln. It was sketchy, but a resume nevertheless.

"What do you see here that's strange?" Sharky asked The Nosh.

"Well, he's got no criminal record. So why the package?"

They reread the telex.

"He's right," Friscoe said. "Why would they have his prints on file?"

Sharky tapped on his coffee cup with a spoon, lightly, a rhythmic tattoo that accompanied his thoughts.

"It's a cover," said Friscoe. "It fits. It's hand in glove. It makes sense. It's the *only* way it makes sense. This shooter has a Mafia pedigree. We figure he had to be a *capo*, right? An old-line hitman. So what's he doin' running a truck company?"

"A cover," The Nosh said.

"Damn right," said Friscoe. "This shooter, whoever the fuck he is, he did a turn for the Feds and they fixed him up. He musta been in hot with the mob so the Feds give him Howard Burns and a whole biography to go with it."

"And then something happened and he had to drop out again, only this time he did it so even the Feds thought he was gone for good," Sharky said.

"And showed up here," Livingston said, "not two weeks later."

"Okay," Friscoe said, "now I got a little something. What I got is dessert, buckos. Something that makes it all go down, so it ain't so hard to swallow. You remember Twigs tellin' us Riley had a coupla John Does to keep him busy down in the ice house?"

They nodded.

"Well one of these John Does was dug outa the city dump yesterday. And it wasn't no accidental John Doe. What I mean is somebody went to a lotta trouble to make him into a John Doe, like blowing up his face with a shotgun and removing both his hands."

"Jesus!" Papa said.

"Yeah, ain't it a pretty picture? What makes it . . . the reason, see, why we're maybe interested in that what really put this stiff on ice was a .22 bullet that was soaked in garlic."

He leaned back, satisfied at having brought something to the party at last.

"And," he added, "the illustrious Mr. Grimm says this stiff got kayoed around the end of October sometime."

More silence, then a babble, everyone talking at once. Sharky held up a hand. "Hold on, hold on. Shit, we sound like a bad church choir here. Let's add it up, see what we got. Barney, sum it up for us."

"Okay, we got a Mafia shooter goes underground with the help of the Feds. On October twentieth subject the same wraps a tree around his car and goes up in smoke. His wife I.D.'s him with dental plates and plants him. Ten days later this Burns or whoever pops outa the toaster in Atlanta and puts the freeze on victim number two, fixes up the stiff so it can't be identified and plants him in the city dump."

"How come Victim Two?" Sharky said.

Friscoe shrugged. *"Somebody* burned up in the car on the outskirts of Omaha."

Sharky whistled between his teeth. "I missed that one."

"Okay. So then six, seven weeks more pass by and this same Howard-Whoever-the-Fuck-He-Is-Burns comes outa the woodwork again and dumps Domino. The question is, why? Why? That may be the toughest donkey of all to pin a tail on."

"Why don't we just take it to the Bureau? Tell them this Burns dummied up his own death, came here, and wasted two people already," Sharky said.

Friscoe shook his head. "I veto that one. For a lotta reasons. First place the Feds don't really give a shit about our problems unless there's something in it for them. Right now this is a local problem, so they don't stand to make any brownie points by bustin' their ass tryin' to help us. Also, if this son of a bitch *was* in the Feds' alias program, it'll take an act of fuckin' Congress to get anything out of them. All they'll do, is come in here hot-shittin' around and the next thing you know, Riley, D'Agastino, the fucking Bat, *every*body in the goddamn world'll be in on it. We took it this far, let's take it all the way. What the hell, we got our nuts in the door jamb anyway."

Sharky had been toying with an idea. Now he threw it out to the machine. "This is a long shot, okay. I know that going in. But just supposing this shooter was in the service in World War Two. He's the right age for it. His prints could be in the inactive file."

"Wouldn't the bureau have cleaned that package, too?" Livingston asked.

"Why?" said Sharky. "They didn't need to. The Bureau created Howard Burns. But, when I was in military intelligence there was a couple of times when we turned up an I.D. in the old files. The FBI doesn't have it *all*."

"I say we try everything," Papa said. "You never know when something's gonna work."

"And you got the kalibash to get in there, right Sharky?" Friscoe said.

"I've got a couple of good pals out at Fort McPherson in the intelligence unit there. What've we got to lose?"

Friscoe rubbed his hands together. His weariness was temporarily replaced by a surge of adrenaline. He had expected a few bunts, but the four of them had actually hit a couple of long balls.

"Okay," he said, "tuck this in the back of your minds while you're out there. This John Doe, here's what Twigs gave me on him. And remember, Riley's workin' on him, too. And Riley ain't gonna stop until he knows chapter and verse on him. Anyways, John Doe was five-ten, a hundred and fifty-five to sixty-five pounds, black hair going gray, in his late fifties. A very hard guy in good physical condition. Has two old scars down here, just under his ribs, one in front, one in back. Twigs says it's an old gunshot wound, could go back thirty years."

Sharky said, "Same age as the shooter."

"Just about," said Friscoe. "Also he was suffering from some respiratory ailment. Bad lungs caused by inhalation of hemp."

"Hemp?" Livingston said. "You mean rope?"

"I mean hemp, which is what rope is made out of."

"He worked in a hemp mill?" Sharky said.

"Yeah. And the most common place to find a jute mill is in prison. So we could be looking for an old con here."

"We could check the county and federal probation

officers. Maybe if this guy was paroled he had to register here."

"I already got it on my list," Friscoe said. He dunked the last of a doughnut in his coffee, swished it around, and finished it noisily. "Well, kid," he said to Sharky, "it's your fuckin' machine. You call the shots."

"Okay, Arch, and I'll see what we can turn up at Fort Mac. Papa, maybe you could try to come at this Shoes from another angle, collar him without blowing the whistle on Colter. Nosh, you stick with the tapes and see what else you can dig up on this Burns. All of us keep this John Doe in mind. Maybe there's some talk out on the street about him."

"And I'll take a shot at the local probation officers, see what that turns up," Friscoe said. Then he smiled for the first time since entering the Majestic.

"What the hell," he said. "We got forty-eight hours left. It ain't forever, but it ain't Monday morning yet, either."

18

It took them thirty minutes to drive out to Fort McPherson, a tidy but sprawling army oasis within the city limits that was headquarters for the Third Army. Sergeant Jerome Weinstock was waiting for them in front of the spotless headquarters building, a tall, florid man in starched khaki whose appearance had changed from the cherubic innocence Sharky remembered to an authoritative scowl. He had put on twenty pounds and lost a lot of hair in the eight years since Sharky had served with him in Army Intelligence.

"You like playing cops and robbers, Sharky?" Weinstock asked as he led the way into the headquarters building and down a long, stark hallway to the military intelligence offices.

"It has its moments," Sharky said. "What's with the

scowl, Jerry? I remember you as sweet, smiling Jerry
Weinstock, the pride of Jersey City."

"I made top kick," Weinstock growled. "It's part of
the act. Only time I smile anymore is when I'm alone in
the latrine." He looked at Sharky and winked, then
said, "So what's your problem? I don't see you for eight
years and then you call me in a panic at the crack of
dawn on a Saturday."

Sharky handed him a lift of the two fingerprints. "I
need to match these prints to a face. They'd be inactive,
probably dating back to World War Two."

"You're playing a hunch, aren't you, Sharky? That's
what it is. Shit, you haven't changed a damn bit. And it
can't wait till Monday, hunh? Got to be right now, before the bugler's even got his socks on."

"By Monday I'm dead."

"Always the same story. Eager beaver." Weinstock
looked at Livingston. "This one'll drive you apeshit. He
never stops, he's either coming or going all the time."

"So I'm learnin'," Livingston said.

A nervous young recruit was waiting in the telex
room, looking like he had dressed in his sleep. Weinstock handed him the two prints. "Send this to DX 10,
attention Sergeant Skidmore. And come get us down in
the coffee room when you get a response."

"Yes, sir," the youth said. "Should I send it urgent?"

"Willoughby, I seriously doubt that anybody in his
right mind is using the twix before nine o'clock on Saturday morning. Just send it off. Skidmore's waiting at
Fort Dix for it."

"Yes, sir."

Weinstock turned and marched out of the room followed by the two detectives.

"Skidmore? Is that old Jocko Skidmore?" Sharky
said.

"The same," Weinstock said. "Had to get him outa

bed, too. I'll tell you something, Shark. If he didn't remember you—and like you—we'd've been shit outa
luck. Know what he said? He said, 'That silly son of a
bitch never did do anything at a civilized time of day.'
To which I say, amen."

"I'll drink to that," Livingston said. "I haven't been
to bed since I met Sharky."

They drank coffee and made small talk about the old
days, sitting in the coffee room in the basement for almost forty-five minutes before Willoughby appeared at
the door.

"It's comin' in now, Sergeant," he said.

Sharky bolted from his chair and took the steps two
at a time, his heart racing in anticipation. This had to
work. He needed more than just Shoes and Arnold the
bartender, much more, to keep his machine rolling, to
keep its adrenaline pumping. As he entered the room
and saw the teletype message a shimmer of disappoint-
ment rippled through his chest. The report was short,
no more than a few lines. Livingston rushed in behind
him as he tore the sheet from the machine and read the
peculiar print argot of the military:

POS ID, 2 PRINTS, ANGELO DOMINIC SCARDI. B SIRA-
CUSA, SICILY, 1916. EMGRTD US, 1935. VOLTRD
CVL LSN SICILY INV, JUNE, 1943. CIV ADV GELA-
PACHINO-CALTAGIRONE, JULY, 43–MARCH 44.
TRNSFD FIRENZE, ITALY, JNT MI/OSS OPSTITCH
(TSEC), MARCH, 44–OCT 44. RET US OCT SERV
TERM OCT 21, 44. SKID.

"Not too much," Weinstock said.

But Livingston was staring at the first line, his eyes
bright with excitement. There it was. The name.

Angelo Dominic Scardi.

And what a name it was.

"Shit, all we need's right here on this first line," he said. "Angelo Scardi. Does that ring your bell, Sharky?"

"No. Should it?"

"Angel the Undertaker," Livingston said. "This guy was a top button for Genovese, Luciano, Costello, all the biggies. When Valachi spilled his guts to the Senate, Scardi's name popped up all over the place. Then a couple of years later who should turn up doin' the same number Valachi did for the Feds? Angelo Scardi."

"What happened to him?" Sharky said.

"He died of cancer about six months after testifying."

"How convenient," Sharky said. "And would you like to make a little bet that Howard Burns turned up in Nebraska just about that time?"

"No bet. It fits, man. It fits like a glove." He turned his attention back to the report. "How the hell can anybody read the rest of this shit?"

Weinstock took the sheet from him. "Here," he said, "Let me translate for you. It says this Scardi was born in Siracusa, Sicily, in 1916. Came to the U.S. in 1935. In June, 1943, he volunteered as civilian liaison advisor to the Sicilian invasion forces and then worked with the Army in the Gela-Pachino-Caltagirone sector until March 1944. He was transferred to Firenze, Italy, and attached to a joint Military Intelligence–OSS operation—something called Opstitch—until he returned to the States in October '44. Service was terminated the same month."

"What the hell was he doing over there?" Sharky said.

"Beats the hell outa me," Weinstock said. "That's the year I was born."

"Arch?"

"All I remember is that he was a number one hitman for the Cosa Nostra and he blew the whistle on them."

"But it fits, damn it, it fits!" Sharky said.

"What's so important about this guy if he's been dead for seven or eight years?" Weinstock asked.

"Jerry, when this is all over, I'll come out and we'll spend a night at the noncom club on me and I'll tell you the whole story. How about this Opstitch, what would that be?"

"That translates Operation Stitch. With the OSS involved it was probably some cloak and dagger number. TSEC means it's classified secret."

"You mean it's still classified after thirty years?"

"Could have been a royal fuck-up of some kind. Nobody in the army wants to admit a screw-up, so they just keep the lid on. Or maybe they just never got around to declassifying it. You know the goddamn army."

"Who cares?" Livingston said. "We got the name, that's what's important."

"It could relate, Arch. How could we find out about this, Jerry?"

"Forget it. You got to go through the Adjutant General in Washington and probably the CIA to bust it out. That could be a lifetime project."

"Somebody must remember something about it," Sharky said.

"We're pushing for time, Shark," Livingston reminded him.

"I know, but as long as we're here, why not check it out?"

"He's havin' another hunch attack, if you ask me," Weinstock said.

"C'mon, Jerry, this is headquarters for the whole Third Army. Think! There's probably a dozen guys on this base could help us."

"See," Weinstock said, "a goddamn bulldog. He gets something by the ass and he won't let it go."

Weinstock stroked his chin for a few moments.

"Well, your best bet, I guess, is General Bourke. Hardy W. Bourke himself. He was in Italy during the war. If he don't know, maybe he knows where you can find out."

"Can you call him, ask if he'll see us?"

"When, right now?"

Sharky patted him on the cheek. "Jerry, we're fighting the clock. You're a goddamn prince."

Weinstock leered back at him. "No, you're the goddamn prince, Sharky, 'cause this little operation here, this morning is gonna cost you one gallon of Chivas Regal."

Sharky nodded. "Do it."

Weinstock grinned. "Don't have to call him. You'll find him out on the golf course." He looked at his watch. "I would guess he'll be somewhere around the third hole by now. And good luck. I hope he doesn't hit you with his mashie niblick."

———————————

General Hardy W. Bourke was built like a footlocker standing on end and had the face of an angry eagle. Sharky was leaning against a tree at the edge of the third tee when he rolled up in his golf cart and stepped out, a tough little man with pure white hair cut an inch long.

Sharky walked across the trim green tee as the boxy little man leaned over and placed his ball.

"Excuse me, sir. Are you General Bourke?"

The general glared at him.

"Yes. What is it?"

Sharky showed him his buzzer. "My name's Sharky. Atlanta PD."

The General looked at the badge, then at Sharky's hair and snorted. "I see," he said. "What's wrong? Has something happened?"

His partner, a tall, thin man whose fatigue cap covered a bald pate stepped up beside Bourke. "Something I can handle, General?" he said.

"It's all right, Jesse. Something to do with the police."

"The police?"

"I'm sorry to interrupt your game like this, sir, but it is important. We're investigating a murder case and—"

"Murder! Good God, sir, one of my men?"

"No, sir. No, not at all. Thing is, it relates to a military operation in Italy during the war and—"

"Ah," Bourke said, obviously relieved. "Well, can't this wait, young man? We should be back at the clubhouse in a few hours. We're backed up here, as you can see." He pointed back to the number two green. A foursome was just putting out.

Bourke stepped up and planted his feet firmly in the grass, addressing the ball as if it were one of his junior officers.

"Time's pressing, sir," Sharky said.

Bourke sighted down his club. "If it's waited for thirty years, it can wait until I tee off," he snapped. His club whipped back and slashed the air. The ball cracked off the tee, soared out about thirty yards, and hooked drastically, plunging into the rough a hundred or so yards away. Bourke turned toward Sharky, staring at him, his face contorted with disgust.

"Did you see that?" he bellowed.

"Sorry, sir, I—"

"Goddamnit to hell!" the general screamed. He stared at his club for a full thirty seconds, his face turning the color of a carrot. Finally he threw it down in disgust.

"All right," he snapped. "You've got two minutes. Get in the cart. You can help me find that goddamn ball. You can walk down there, Jesse."

The cart purred down the fairway.

"All right," Bourke said. "Now, what's this all about?"

"We're interested in a military operation that occurred in December, 1944, near—"

"What kind of operation?" Bourke growled.

"OSS, sir. It was—"

"Young man, I was a command officer assigned to Omar Bradley. I don't remember some goddamn spy operation that occurred thirty years ago. What do you think I am, a military encyclopedia?"

"No sir, but—"

"There were probably a hundred OSS operations during the time I was in Italy. Quite frankly, I was too busy trying to win the war to be bothered with those spooks."

"Yes, sir. Perhaps if I told you—"

"Eureka! There it is. Right beside the fairway. What luck." He pulled up and got out of the cart and looked down the fairway toward the green. "A straight shot to the pin. Look at that. Bloody good shot after all." He looked at Sharky and winked. "Have to take that club over to Ordnance and have the boys take that hook out of it, eh? Heh, heh."

"General, is there *any*body on this base who might remember the incident?"

Bourke looked at him for a few moments more, then turned to the caddy. "Gimme that five iron, caddy," he said. He held out his hand and waited for the caddy to put the club in it. "Martland. Martland's your man. If anybody can help you, it'd be Martland."

"Martland?"

"Colonel Martland. A bird colonel waiting for his star so he can retire. He was in intelligence and he was in Italy during the war. I believe he lives on K Street."

"Thank you, sir. Thank you very much."

"Young fellow?"

"Yes, sir?"

"Colonel Martland has a mind like a razor, particularly about World War Two. In fact, he's a goddamn bore about it. There's one thing. He's a little whacko, if you know what I mean. His wife died about two years ago and he's been somewhat out to lunch ever since."

"Oh."

"He has his moments. I'm not saying he's a goddamn loony bird. He's just, uh . . . a little loose in the attic. What I'm saying, son, is it may take a little patience. So be kind to him, all right?"

"Yes, sir."

"And don't get hit by any goddamn golf balls. I don't want to be sued by the police department."

It was a tidy street with tidy lawns trimmed neatly to the sidewalk and tidy white frame bungalows, each one a replica of the one next to it, each one sitting exactly the same distance back from the road. The only distinction among the houses was the landscaping, an obvious attempt by the officer tenants to bring some individuality to their homes.

A white Cadillac, several years old but in mint condition, sat in the driveway. They waited for several minutes after ringing the bell before the door was opened by a wiry little man, trim and erect, with pure white hair and a white mustache which might have been elegant had it not been trimmed slightly shorter on the right side than on the left. He was dressed in a tight-fitting Army jumpsuit with a white silk scarf at his throat. He was also wearing a baseball cap, tennis shoes, and held a riding crop in one hand.

"Yes?" he said, squinting out through the screen door.

"Colonel Martland?" Sharky said.

"I am Colonel Martland."

"Yes, sir. I'm Detective Sharky and this is Sergeant Livingston."

Martland stared from one to the other. "Yes?"

"From the Atlanta Police Department, sir. Sergeant Weinstock called about us?"

"Oh, yes. Weinstock. Of course. Well, won't you come in?"

He held the door and they entered a house whose walls were barren of paintings or photographs. There was little light inside. He led them into the living room, a room so bleak, so obvious, that Sharky immediately felt burdened by its sadness. Propped against the mantelpiece was an oil painting of a woman in riding clothes with a smoking volcano in the background. That and a chintz sofa were the only furnishings in the room. No tables, no lamps, no chairs, only unopened crates shoved into the corners.

Martland pointed to the sofa and then sat down on the edge of one of the crates, his knees together, the riding crop resting on his thighs as he held it at each end.

"You must forgive the place. I don't entertain much anymore. Not since my wife, Miriam"—and he turned and looked up at the painting and smiled—"went away," he said. "I really must . . . do something. . . ." and then the words died as he stared around the oppressive room. He looked back at Sharky and stared at him.

Sharky said, "Uh, Colonel, if you have a few minutes, we'd like to ask you some questions."

He continued to stare at Sharky and frowned. "Is it something to do with the car? Did somebody hit the car?"

"Oh, no, sir, it hasn't got anything to do with, uh, this

isn't a personal matter. It, uh, we're conducting an investigation."

Martland did not change his expression. He continued to stare at Sharky.

"What it is, sir, we, uh, this relates to some things that happened in Italy during the war."

Martland still did not speak.

"You were in Italy during the war, weren't you, sir?"

"Is that World War Two?"

"Yes, sir, World War Two."

"Oh, yes." And he stopped again, staring past Sharky now, frowning for perhaps a full minute before a smile spread over his face.

"North Africa, Sicily, Italy. 1942 through 1945. Then we were in West Germany for three years and then on to Schofield Barracks. That's in Honolulu, you know. We lived there for ten glorious years, my wife and I." He looked back up at the painting and smiled again. "I believe the years in Hawaii were the best years in our career."

And he stopped and stared again.

"Do you remember during the time in Sicily and Italy, meeting a man named Scardi? Angelo Scardi? He was a civilian who was there in some kind of advisory capacity."

Another frown. Another blank stare. Martland stared past Sharky into a dark corner of the room. A full minute crept painfully by, then suddenly he almost bellowed:

"The American racketeer!" And began laughing. "Dom, that's what he preferred to be called. For Dominic, his middle name. Hah! Haven't thought about that rascal for years. Quite a fellow, you know. Very tough. And courageous, oh, yes, particularly for a civilian. Knew him well. Told some shocking stories about the underworld. He was assigned to an intelligence unit commanded by one of my junior officers. Lieutenant McReady. John Sisson McReady from Virginia. Killed at Cassino. Bloody shame. But then . . ."

He stopped in mid-sentence, as abruptly as he had started, his mind searching back in time for other memories.

"Uh, what did this Scardi do? In Sicily I mean?"

Another minute or two crawled by as Martland stared and frowned, stirring through the mass of time and dates and places. And then, once again, the words came in a rush.

"He was a native of Sicily. Let me see . . . Siracusa, a little town on the southeastern tip of the island. We made a beachhead there during the invasion. Scardi knew the place like the seat of his pants. Every road, every footpath, every stone wall. He went in a month or so before the assault, scouted the entire area, radioed information every night. Set up little pockets of resistance to badger Jerry."

And that was it again. It was as though he were turning a switch in his brain on and off.

"What was, uh, Gela-Pachino-Calta—"

"Caltagirone. Towns in southern Sicily. A little triangle. After Sicily fell, Dom Scardi was the civilian liaison between the military government and the locals. Our objective was territory, gentlemen. Geography, not people. The sooner they returned to self-government the better. That's what Scardi did, helped them get back on their feet. And kept them out of our hair."

He stopped again, but this time as Sharky started to ask another question he cut him off. There was a touch of anger in his voice when he spoke.

"They were going to deport him, the Justice Department, did you know that? Undesirable alien, that's what they said. Well, he acquitted himself admirably. Unless

I'm mistaken he became an American citizen after the war."

Livingston looked at the floor and muttered, "Great!"

Sharky ignored him, pressing on. "Later on, after Sicily, Scardi went to Italy, didn't he?"

Another long pause. More frowns, followed by the customary burst of information.

"He worked with the guerrillas, behind the German lines. They were Communists, of course, been fighting the Germans since the beginning of the war. Totally disorganized. Scardi scouted them out, got them supplies, money, medicine. He had an idea to try and bring them all together so they'd be more effective. A dangerous thing to do. He was a civilian involved in espionage. If the Germans had caught him, bang! Would've been shot, just like that, on the spot. No ceremony." And he stopped and after a few seconds, almost reflectively he repeated the name, "Dominic Scardi," and it lingered in the dreary room like a mention of the plague and Sharky felt the furies building inside him, thought about Domino and a man, humiliated in death, tossed away in a garbage dump without any face or hands. *Dominic Scardi*. How could this possibly be the same man who Martland regarded as a hero?

Finally Sharky said, "Do you remember something called Opstitch?"

Martland reacted immediately, turning and looking straight at Sharky.

"I believe that information is classified, sir," he said.

"Colonel, that was thirty years ago."

"Classified nevertheless."

"Sir, this is important. We're investigating a murder case involving people Scardi knew. Anything you give us could be helpful."

Livingston finally spoke up. "It might prevent innocent people from getting hurt," he said.

"Humph," Martland said and snorted through his nose. He struggled with the question, balancing it. Then he began to nod vigorously.

"Bureaucratic folderol!"

"I beg your pardon, sir?"

"Bureaucratic folderol. Utter nonsense. No reason really for Opstitch to be classified. It was a snafu. That's all, plain and simple, a snafu. Opstitch was Operation Stitch, for 'a stitch in time.' A bit obvious, of course, but then nobody ever accused the army of being subtle. Stitch was Scardi's idea. Brilliant, absolutely brilliant. I'm sure you know very little about the Italian campaign. God knows, few do. The forgotten war. And a bitter one. This was in the autumn of '44. The war in Italy had gone badly. Terrible terrain. Incessant rain. Very costly. Every inch paid for dearly. So, that fall the Americans and Germans were face to face in the Po Valley. A stalemate. Three months it went on like that, neither side giving up a foot.

"Scardi had gone on reconnoiter up in the northern section around Lake di Garda. There were dozens of guerrilla outfits up there. The most effective, according to Scardi, was led by a resistance fighter who called himself La Volte. The Fox. Had a price on his head. Scardi suggested that we provide him with the money and supplies to consolidate all these bands into a single strike force. Hit Jerry from behind while the American and British troops would launch a massive frontal attack at the same time. And it could have worked to break the deadlock. So . . . that was Opstitch."

Martland stopped and smiled, as though he were proud of himself. He ran his tongue between his teeth and his upper lip, smoothed his mustache with his fin-

gers, and looked back at the painting of Miriam Martland.

"Did Scardi pull it off?"

"Oh, no, no, no. No, sir. Scardi got sick. Intestinal
malaria I believe was the diagnosis. That was in October. The mission actually was carried off in December.
Two weeks before Christmas, as I recall. I was in Rome
at the time. A major named Halford took over the as-
signment. Moody fellow. Killed in the Orient some
years ago. He sent a bright young officer named
Younger in several times to make arrangements with La
Volte. It was Younger who actually took the mission in.
But Scardi had nothing to do with it by then. Been back
in the States for two or three months."

"And what happened?"

Martland drummed on his crop with nervous fingers.
His forehead wrinkled and he shook his head in short
jabs several times before answering.

"A disaster. Younger and three men parachuted in.
The next night the air force dropped supplies, weapons,
and four million dollars in gold bullion. The Germans
overran our position, killed Younger and two of his
men. The other one was wounded and hid out in an
Italian village until it was liberated. After the war
Younger and his men were found buried near the lake.
The gold was never recovered."

"How about this other man, the one that got away?
Do you remember his name?"

He stared out the window, almost entranced, and
said, "An Irish name . . . Lonnigan . . . Harrigan
. . . ah, I've got it. Corrigon. That was it, Corrigon."

"You wouldn't have any idea where he is today,
would you, Colonel?" Livingston said.

Martland nodded slowly. "In prison. Federal prison.
Courtmartialed. Accused of murder and grand theft,
tried, and convicted. I was there. Sketchy evidence

really. Mostly circumstantial. Never would have held up in a civil court, y'know. But in courts martial a man is guilty until he proves his innocence."

"And the four million in gold?"

"Yes?" Martland said.

"What happened to it?"

"Oh, God only knows."

"You mean the army just wrote it off?"

"It was wartime. Four million dollars was . . . really nothing at all. I should guess . . . hmmm . . . probably charged off to the operational budget of the OSS, although military intelligence might have had to split it. I was gone before that was all settled."

The room was quiet. Martland seemed to be drifting away from the conversation.

"I have one more question," Livingston said, but Martland did not answer. "Colonel?"

"Ah, yes?"

"How were the other Americans identified after all those months?"

"Dog tags. Personal belongings. No question about it. Ah, and one other thing. A Thompson gun issued to the man Corrigon was found in the grave. It was the most damaging piece of evidence against him."

Sharky said, "Can you think of anything else about Scardi?"

Martland reflected a few moments and said, "Oh, it was exciting, having an American gangster there with us. He was quite a celebrity. Quite a celebrity." Then he fell silent again and this time his gaze became almost glassy.

Sharky stood up. "Well, thank you, sir. You've been a great help."

"I did well, then, eh?"

"Yes, sir. You did well."

Martland turned to the portrait. "Hear that, Miriam.

My memory's just as good as ever. Takes a while now, but it all comes back, my dear. It all comes back."

And he sat on the crate, his shoulders beginning to sag, his gaze fixed on another time, the memories reflecting in his faded eyes, a time of mirror-shined shoes and white gloves, of chin straps and marching orders echoing through the barracks and tattoo in the late afternoon.

They drove for ten minutes without speaking. It was Sharky who finally broke the silence.

"It was like turning on a tape recorder, listening to someone dictating his memoirs. All of a sudden it would just pour out, like rote."

"He's probably told that story a thousand times in the last thirty years, all about the wonderful American gangster."

"Yeah, and probably word for word."

"I feel sorry for the old coot," Livingston said. "The Army's all he's got left and it ignores him, letting him hang around long enough to make general, so he can get a few more bucks in a pension he'll probably never spend. Shit."

"What about Scardi? This Opstitch thing?"

"Anybody thinks Angelo Scardi didn't have a hand in a four-million-dollar ripoff ought to be committed."

"But why wasn't that obvious to the army?"

"You heard what the old boy said. Four million in gold was just a piss in the ocean. All they needed was a fall guy so they could close the book on it, charge it off on some budget. Jesus!"

They drove another block in silence and Livingston said, "Go down Spring and turn into Carnegie Way."

"Where we headed?"

"The public library. Best place I can think of to get a photograph of Scardi."

Sharky waited in the car while Livingston went inside. He was gone for almost half an hour and when he returned was carrying a large manila envelope. He got into the car and took out a photograph and laid it in Sharky's lap.

"There's the face to go with the name," he said.

Sharky stared down at it. It was a copy of a newspaper photo of a man seated at a table surrounded by reporters and photographers, his hands splayed out in a gesture of innocence. But the look was there, in the vapid stiletto face, the hawk nose, the dead eyes, the humorless grin on thin, cruel lips, the slick black hair. It was a face that was easy to hate and Sharky's anger welled up anew, stirring his lust for retribution, an almost perverse passion that overwhelmed him, swelling in his groin, churning in his stomach. At that moment Sharky could easily have killed Scardi with his bare hands.

Livingston took Xerox copies of several clippings from the envelope.

"I ain't gonna bore you with a lot of details," Livingston said, "but I thought you might like to get a taste. This creep's got a pedigree you won't believe. When he was fourteen he had to leave Sicily because he slit a neighbor's throat in some kind of family squabble. He lived in *northern* Italy for five years before he came over here. His uncle was Lupo the Wolf, the son of a bitch who started the Black Hand movement. . . . Came here in '35, arrested the next year for extortion and kidnapping . . . Christ, here's an article says he was suspected of killing over fifty people. You know where he got the nickname The Undertaker? He supposedly invented the double-deck coffin, to get rid of hits."

"And when did he *supposedly* die?"

Livingston checked through the sheaf of Xeroxed clippings. "Here's his obit. February 16, 1968. Cancer."

"And Howard Burns arrived in Lincoln in 1968. How convenient."

"I wonder if the Feds really think they got their money's worth out of him?"

"Anything else in there? How about that . . . heroic war record of his?"

Livingston rummaged through more articles. He stopped at one and said, "Hey, listen to this. According to this story Scardi did his first hit for Lucky Luciano and he screwed it up and Luciano chewed his ass and told him he didn't get close enough to the mark. The next day Scardi gives Luciano a box with the guy's ears in it and says, 'Here, was that close enough?' "

Sharky's grip on the wheel tightened.

"All it says about his war record," said Livingston, "is that he was about to be deported in 1944 as an undesirable alien, but the case was dropped after he, quote, 'performed valuable and courageous services for the invasion forces of Italy.' Unquote. Nothing about guerrilla operations."

"Extortion . . . kidnapping . . . murder . . . and they made a deal with him," Sharky said. "That's the courageous war hero Martland thought was such a sweetheart."

"Makes you wonder what the hell kind of deal they made with him in '68," said Livingston. "He musta come down on half the Mafia."

Sharky thought to himself, *This time there won't be any deals, because this time the government isn't going to get near him, this time we're going to put that son of a bitch out of business permanently—one way or the other.*

And he said aloud, "This time he's ours."

"We gotta get him first," Livingston said.

19

There were only two things in Sergeant Herb Anderson's entire life that he was proud of: a commendation he had won when, while off-duty, he had overpowered an armed robber sticking up a Seven-Eleven Market; the other was his son Tommy, an all-city football player who had already been offered three college scholarships and the season was only over a week.

The rest of his life had been a downhill slide. His other son, Harry, had been a problem since he was a child. The boy had been in and out of private schools all his life and as a result Anderson's wife, Lucy, had gradually turned into a hypertense, morose hypochondriac, a woman who complained constantly of back trouble, headaches, female problems, and lumps in her breast which the doctor somehow could never find.

Anderson himself had changed through the years

from a jovial man, well liked by the other members of the force, to a depressed and involuted misfit, a man harassed by financial problems and a son he both loved and despised, who worked long hours to escape the enervating atmosphere at home. It was his reputation as a tireless workhorse that had earned him a sergeant's stripes.

He was grateful when Priest called him on Saturday morning, his day off, because it gave him an honest excuse to escape the house and enjoy a lunch at the Regency.

The man Anderson knew as Priest was actually Gerald Kershman. It was Kershman who picked the busy bars in the better hotels, which were more popular with transients than with the local trade. He usually arrived fifteen minutes ahead of Anderson, seeking out the most secluded and the darkest corner in the room. Not that anyone would recognize Kershman or particularly remember him; it was his own paranoia at work. It was one of DeLaroza's peculiar quirks, and he had many, that the corporation should always have a strong police contact in every city in which it did business. Kershman, for his own reasons, had been more than willing to oblige. He was called on to provide information from time to time, nothing particularly onerous, and yet Kershman, a man with many complexes, always became nervous when he met with Anderson. He didn't like his hangdog attitude, the inevitable spots on his ties, and mostly the fact that, while Anderson was a fair police officer, he was not too sharp. It was a struggle for Kershman to conceal his contempt and his sense of superiority when he was around Anderson.

Kershman nursed a marguerita until Anderson arrived, a few minutes late and apologizing as usual. He ordered his usual Michelob draft and sat with a forced grin on his face. Kershman avoided asking about Anderson's family, a question that usually resulted in a fifteen-minute monologue that ended like a chapter from a soap opera. Kershman had established himself as a correspondent for a European news syndicate, a perfect cover story for the kind of information he usually sought.

"I'm in a bit of a jam," Kershman said, getting right to it.

"What's the problem?" Anderson asked and his concern annoyed Kershman.

"I heard there was a homicide in one of the fancy apartment houses out on Peachtree last night," Kershman said. "Thing is, there's been nothing reported so far on it. Nothing on TV, the radio, in the newspapers. My problem is I queried our news office about it before really checking it out and they're hot for the story. Now it looks like my tip may have been unreliable."

"Did you check the police reports?"

"Yes. Nothing."

Anderson frowned. Then shook his head as though disagreeing with his own thoughts. "There was this John Doe turned up in the city dump yesterday. Now, that would make a good story for you. No hands. His hands were *cut off*. And he was shot in the face with a shotgun."

Kershman listened intently to Anderson, making mental notes of everything he said. He always was prepared to tell DeLaroza more than he wanted to know rather than less.

"This was definitely a woman," Kershman said.

"I was around until four o'clock this morning. Lot of crazy things going on, but I would have heard if there was a killing in that neighborhood."

"Well, if you check around, discreetly. Perhaps, uh,

there's some reason the police are keeping it under wraps. I would prefer not to create any curiosity. I just thought I might get something from the inside on it."

"I'll go on down after we leave here, snoop around quietly. See if Twigs knows anything. He's the county coroner."

"Remember, I don't want to make any waves. This must be done carefully just in case they are working on something they don't want the press to know about." He paused to sip the marguerita and then asked, "What crazy stuff was going on?"

Anderson chuckled. "Oh, Larry Abrams was screwing around with something half the night. A tape of some kind for the Vice Squad. He's working with a new man over there named Sharky."

"What was on the tape?"

"I don't know. Neither does he. Know what he said? He said it sounded like a Chinese orgy."

Kershman took another sip and kept listening.

"What made me think of it is that I picked up a post mortem tape for Abrams about two A.M. from Grady Hospital. It wasn't the John Doe, because Twigs was complaining that Riley in Homicide was pushing him to do it before he went home."

"I see. Well, if you could just kind of check around. The thing is, I'm pushed for time. If there is something I can chase down, I'd like to know by this evening."

"I'll do my damn best," Anderson said sincerely.

"Was there anything else?"

"Nope. Actually it wasn't a very lively night. Oh, yeah, Abrams pulled a fingerprint report for somebody, too. I took it down to him. Funny thing, he got a positive make on the prints, but the subject's been dead for a couple of months. Some truck driver from Nebraska."

"And who is this Abrams?"

"A wiretap man, been in the OC six months or so.

Nice little guy. Very talented. The Feds even borrow him every once in a while."

"Maybe he was doing this job for the government people," Kershman suggested.

"No, I saw the tape. It had Sharky's name on it."

"And what about this Sharky?"

"I'm surprised you didn't do something on him. He's the narcotics cop who shot the pusher on the bus the other night."

"Oh, yes, of course." Kershman remembered seeing the headline, but he had not paid much attention to the story.

"He was transferred into the Vice Squad because of it," Anderson said. "Now keep that under your derby, okay? It hasn't been released publicly."

"I won't say a word," Kershman said.

20

Sharky had filed a radio message through central for Friscoe to meet him and Livingston at a pizza parlor on Peachtree Street called Franco's. They had been there less than ten minutes when Friscoe arrived, puffing through the door and looking no better or worse than he had at breakfast. Friscoe plopped down in the booth with them and waved the waiter away.

"I got so much coffee in me, I couldn't eat if I wanted to," he said. "So, you got some news?"

Livingston was eating a submarine sandwich. Without looking up he said, "We just wanted to say hello. We thought maybe you missed us."

"Anything new?" Sharky said, concentrating on a piece of pizza that had everything on it but chocolate syrup.

The lieutenant smiled proudly. "Yeah, I made a little

score. I got lucky like Papa. Kenny Bautry, a Fed probation officer, has a guy who fits the description of the stiff in the city dump pretty good. Did *thirty* years plus in the joint at Leavenworth. Got out in October, reported once, and Kenny hasn't seen him since."

Sharky took another bite of pizza. "Name isn't Corrigon, is it?" he said.

"Well shit!" Friscoe said. "I'm gonna get a goddamn complex."

Livingston slid the picture of Scardi across the table in front of Friscoe. "That's who hit Corrigon and Domino."

Friscoe looked at the picture and reared back in surprise.

"That's Angelo Scardi!"

"That's very good, Barney," Livingston said.

Friscoe looked back at the picture with disblief. "Angelo *Scardi?*" he repeated.

Sharky nodded. "There's no question about it, Barney. We got a positive on the prints." Then he leaned across the table and quietly told Friscoe about Scardi, Operation Stitch, and Corrigon. Friscoe listened without comment and then leaned back in the booth, letting it all sink in.

"So, what's your theory?" he asked.

"Arch and I think Scardi rigged the whole operation from the front end and somebody finished the job for him and fingered Corrigon."

"Such as . . ."

Sharky said, "Maybe this La Volte. Look, Scardi lived in that same area from 1930 until 1935. And Scardi was the only person who ever actually *met* La Volte face to face. Martland says Scardi only knew him by his code name, but I think that's bullshit. I think Scardi knew this guy from the old days. I think it was set up from the beginning that La Volte would hit the team when it went in. Scardi put it all together, then conveniently got sick and came back to the U.S. That took him out of the action and put him three thousand miles away when it happened—with a perfect alibi. Then he and La Volte split four mil in gold."

"That's pretty good," Friscoe said. "But what we can't do, we can't get too cocky yet. We got to collar Scardi. But we also got to fill in some blanks here."

"Like what?" Livingston asked.

"Like why did Scardi come here? And why did he off Domino? And what was Corrigon doin' here? This guy gets outa Leavenworth after thirty years, gets on the first bus south, and comes straight to Atlanta. But he wasn't looking for Scardi, because Scardi was still in Nebraska at the time."

"That's right," Sharky said. "Which means Corrigon was after somebody else and that somebody else pulled Scardi in to do the number on Corrigon."

"And you think it was La Volte he was after, right?" Friscoe said.

"What the hell would this Italian guerrilla be doin' in Atlanta?" Livingston asked.

Friscoe shrugged. "It's thirty years ago this other thing happened. Shit, in thirty years you can get born, grow up, go to college, get married, lose your cherry, have a coupla kids, and buy a house. You can do that, this fuckin' guinea could certainly hop a plane to Atlanta."

"Whoever it was," Sharky said, "Scardi can lead us to him."

"That's right," Friscoe said. "But now's the time we gotta handle this here thing with kid gloves. What it comes down to, we gotta nail this Scardi with his hands full and we got to tie him to La Volte or whoever brought him in to glom Corrigon. If we don't, you know what's gonna happen. The goddamn DA ends up with

the case and that's like dropping a diamond in a dirty
diaper. Unless we got an iron-clad case against these
people, Hanson'll fuck it up. He's a legal moron, remember. I mean, shit, we could bribe the fuckin' *jury*
and he could manage to lose the case.

"Look at what we got now," Friscoe continued. "We
can put Scardi in the Jackowitz apartment, but at this
point we can't get him from there to Domino's door
with a shotgun in his hands. And we can't tie him to this
La Volte, or whoever the hell his partner in crime is.
Knowing all this is one thing, proving it is a whole
'nother ballgame."

"So we need to tie Domino to Scardi somehow,"
Sharky said.

"A big somehow," said Livingston.

"Okay, I'm going to take on Domino's apartment,"
Sharky said. "It's been sealed up since the shooting.
Maybe there's something there, an address book, letters,
something that can put us closer to Scardi's accom-
plice."

"Okay. Papa's still trying to run down Shoes. Your
friend Abrams finally went home for a little shuteye.
He'll be back in his workshop there by six. How about
you, Arch?"

Livingston leaned back in the booth and grinned.
"I'm gonna do the best thing possible for this machine
right now," he said. "I'm goin' home and grab a few
hours of z's, because if I don't Sharky's gonna have a
sleepwalker on his hands tonight."

21

DeLaroza was in a black mood and it got worse as he
sat under the subdued lights in his office listening to
Kershman's succinct yet detailed report on what appeared to be several unrelated events at the police station. But the more Kershman talked the more the
worms nibbled at DeLaroza's insides. Bits and pieces
came at him. And as Kershman continued, the pieces
seemed to start fitting together. The rambling report
was beginning to make an uneasy kind of sense to him.
A single thread seemed now to be weaving through the
information.

A sheet of paper lay on the desk in front of him,
covered with doodles, with names and words. As soon
as Kershman finished, DeLaroza dismissed him and
then sat and stared at the sheet, at the Freudian short-
hand dictated by his subconscious.

Who were these two, Sharky and Abrams, and what were they up to? The questions hammered at his brain. He began circling words and phrases on the sheet.

Sharky.

Abrams.

Truck driver.

Nebraska.

Orgy.

Chinese orgy.

Wiretap expert.

Fingerprints.

He made a new list, arranging the words in what he felt was a chronological order. Sharky and Abrams. Wiretap expert. Orgy, Chinese orgy. Fingerprints, truck driver, Nebraska. And he added another: post mortem. And then ahead of the words "truck driver" he added another word. "Dead."

Finally at the bottom of his new list he added still another word, "Corrigon," for that had been the first upsetting news. He had hoped that Corrigon's corpse would elude the police until after Burns was gone. It was an unfortunate stroke, but one which he did not consider serious. There was no way they could possibly connect all this to Corrigon, he thought. He scratched the name off.

The rest of it was serious. He tried to shrug off the feeling of danger that had turned the worms in his stomach to writhing snakes. The dead "truck driver" from Nebraska had to be Burns, there was no question in his mind now that they knew it. Could Burns have made such an amateurish mistake as to leave fingerprints on the scene? And what about this wiretap of the Chinese orgy? He could not erase the memory of Domino that last night from his mind. Was it possible that this Abrams had bugged Domino's apartment before she was killed?

He threw the pencil down. No, these were not unrelated bits and pieces. These two, Abrams and Sharky, were on to something.

His panic slowly turned to rage and then to quiet deliberation. Too many dreams were about to come true for him. Hotchins. *Pachinko!* His own final release from the self-imposed prison in which he had lived for thirty years. He had outwitted governments, the army, the FBI, the CIA, some of the keenest police minds in the world, and now, at this moment, he was threatened by two simple cops. Two cops? Ridiculous!

He sat that way for perhaps half an hour, almost transfixed as he stared at the doodles. A plan was formulating in his mind. It was daring and dangerous but it would work. He considered alternatives and mentally disposed of each one. The more he considered it, the more perfect the plan became. Finally he began to smile. He reached under the desk and pressed a button. A moment later Chiang loomed in the doorway of the office, his scar accentuated by the soft overhead lights, his sightless eye gleaming like a shining coin in the shadows that masked part of his face.

"Get the car," he said. "We must go to the county airport and meet Hotchins."

Chiang nodded and was gone. Ten minutes later DeLaroza climbed into the back seat of the Rolls and they pulled out of the indoor parking lot under the building. DeLaroza lowered the window between the front and back seats and spoke in Chinese to Chiang.

"There is something that must be done," he said. "It must be done quickly but with great caution. The doctor will help you make the arrangements. The foreign devil, Burns, who was on the junk, has become a danger to me. He is insane. He makes threats. And he also makes mistakes. Also there are two policemen who threaten me."

Chiang listened quietly. He asked no questions as DeLaroza outlined his plan. Nothing changed in Chiang's face, not a muscle. It was as if DeLaroza were telling him the time. When he finished, Chiang nodded again.

"Remember," DeLaroza said, "use the shotgun. It must appear like the work of the *Gwai-lo*. When that is done, then we must deal with Burns. Do not underestimate this man. He is sixty years old, but he is still very quick. He will kill without thinking; it is his nature. He trusts nobody and he is very suspicious. That part of it must be done with great skill."

Chiang nodded. The silent Oriental was thinking about Burns, the *Gwai-lo* who killed without honor. The barest hint of a smile touched the corners of his mouth.

DeLaroza settled back. He felt relieved. In his mind, the problem was resolved. Now he faced a bigger one. In fifteen minutes he would pick up Hotchins and tell him that Domino was dead. How he would do that already consumed his thoughts.

22

The JetStar sighed to a comfortable landing and taxied to the hangar where its door swung quietly open and the hydraulic stairway unfolded to the ground. DeLaroza sat in the back of the Rolls, watching as Hotchins came down the stairway and was led to the car by Chiang. He looked good, although he was limping slightly, usually a sign that he was tired or his artificial foot was acting up. But he smiled as he got into the car.

"Well, it is good you are back," DeLaroza said as the Rolls floated onto the highway. "There is much to be done."

"I've accomplished quite a bit already," Hotchins said enthusiastically.

"Ah, the trip was successful, then?"

"More than you think."

"Excellent. And the senator, will he endorse you Monday night?"

Hotchins nodded slowly. "He's his crusty old self, of course. Just as overbearing and patronizing as ever. I spent three hours with him this morning wandering around that damn farm until I thought my foot would fall off, but he's in. The old boy wants a cabinet post."

"Not a great surprise to either of us. What does he want?"

"Agriculture."

DeLaroza considered the point and nodded. "Not an unwise choice, do you think? He is quite popular with the farmers."

"Yeah. And the insurance companies. The food processors. The power companies and gasoline companies. God, he's sold out to every seedy lobbyist in Washington."

"Still, he is respected."

"He's more important to us in the Senate. We need that seniority. But I'll work that out. The important thing is that he'll be there Monday and he'll endorse me."

"Splendid. It is going well, exceptionally well."

"There are still a couple of other congressmen who are playing hard to get. I think we should give them a chance to get on board now or screw them."

"You are feeling heady. I can tell."

"I'm feeling like a winner."

"Well, the trip was a success. Excellent." DeLaroza took out a Havana cigar, but he did not unwrap it. He twirled it in his fingers. He had been waiting sixteen years for this moment, the moment of reckoning. Now at last was the time to test power with power. He enjoyed the moments of anticipation. Hotchins sensed his mood.

"Is something bothering you?" he asked.

"No, not really. Why do you ask?"

"Victor, I've known you intimately for sixteen years. I know when something is bothering you."

DeLaroza smiled. "And here I thought I was so inscrutable."

"You may be to others. Your Chinese friends are certainly inscrutable. But I know you. What is it? Are we having a problem with Lowenthal?"

A problem with Lowenthal, DeLaroza thought. *If we were, who is more capable of handling it than I?* He was somewhat nervous anyway, although he had carefully planned the conversation. But now Hotchins was beginning to annoy him. He was being . . . he was being *smug.* DeLaroza smiled and said quietly, "Not at all. I spent the evening with him and we had coffee this morning. He was nervous about starting the campaign so soon, but I believe he is convinced it is for the best."

"Good," Hotchins patted DeLaroza's leg. "I'm glad you're finally getting directly involved."

Directly involved. There it was again. The man is beginning to treat me as though he is the president.

"I was under the impression I was always directly involved," DeLaroza said, trying to hide his growing anger.

"Oh, of course, of course," Hotchins said. "I just mean you're more open now. You were always so damn cautious about publicity and pictures. It was almost a phobia."

"Phobia?"

"Well, you know what I mean. Anyway, of course you're involved. You've been a close confidant for years."

Confidant. DeLaroza began to laugh out loud. *The audacity of this man.*

"What's so funny?" Hotchins said.

"You are. My God, your smugness goes beyond conceit."

"Smugness. What do you mean, smugness?"

"You are smug, Donald. You think you have done this, gone this far, all by yourself? The one-man show, eh? Why do you think Lowenthal is here? Because I talked to him. Several times. Because I paid his expenses down here. Because I guaranteed that the financing is available. You think he is an amateur? And now that he is here, it is business, not charisma. Politics is business."

"I don't believe you. The first thing we discussed was the cost of the campaign."

"Of course. It is the key to victory. He wants reassurance. Mr. Senator. He cannot afford to ride another loser. And then, after you discussed the business, to whom did you come running? To me. Your *confidant*, Donald? I have pulled your strings for years."

"Nobody pulls my strings," Hotchins said. His eyes burned with fury.

"Oh? And who told you when you were ready for the senate race? You were not sure. I made the decision. And I paid for the campaign. And who decided this would be the right year for the big one. Was it you, Donald? No. I said, this is the right year, this is the year we do it."

"Why don't you just run the race, too?"

"I wish I could. I am a naturalized citizen. It could never be."

"Nobody owns me, Victor. And nobody's going to own me when I get into the White House."

"Without me there will be no White House."

"What is this?" Hotchins said. "Why this sudden attack? What do you want?"

"Recognition. For years I have been the man in the wings, giving away the credit for everything I have achieved. You take the credit here and you take the credit there. I want recognition," he said, and then, louder: "I want recognition."

Hotchins sneered at him. "I should have known. Sixteen years and you've never asked for anything. And now, the worm turns."

"Now the worm *can* turn," DeLaroza said.

"What's that supposed to mean?"

DeLaroza smiled. "It is quite a long story. I do not think now is the time to bore you with it. Besides, there is something else I must tell you. And believe me, it is not a happy task."

"What? What's happened?"

"It concerns Domino."

Hotchins relaxed. He waved his hand toward DeLaroza as if dismissing the discussion before it started. "You can forget Domino. Domino is past history. That problem's been solved."

"I am not sure you understand what I am trying to tell you."

"What the hell are you driving at?"

"Donald, Domino is dead."

Hotchins stared at him intently. He shook his head very slightly.

"She's what?"

"A police friend of mine told me as I was leaving the office. I don't have the detail—"

Hotchins cut him off. He was wild-eyed. "What do you mean she's dead? How did it happen?"

"She was shot."

"Shot?"

"Yes. It happened in her apartment last night. . . ."

He stopped. Gooseflesh rose along his arm. Hotchin's reaction chilled him for a moment. He was laughing. *Laughing.*

"I knew there was a mistake," he said. "You better get a more reliable police friend."

"Believe me," DeLaroza said. "What I am telling you is true."

Hotchins leaned across the seat toward DeLaroza. "It's bullshit, Vic."

"My source is unimpeachable," DeLaroza said sternly.

"No, my friend," Hotchins said, "my source is unimpeachable. My source is me. Domino was with me last night. *All* night."

Now it was DeLaroza who looked stunned. The lines in his forehead deepened. He seemed almost angry.

"Look, she flew down to Savannah yesterday and we spent the night on the boat. It was all very safe. And I told her we had to stop seeing each other. I think she was as relieved about it as I was. So relax. It was a mistake, that's all."

A mistake, DeLaroza thought. *That maniac Burns had made a mistake. Or had he lied?*

"Was someone else staying in her apartment?" DeLaroza asked.

"I have no idea. Why?"

"Because someone was shot in her apartment last night. A terrible mistake had been made."

"Mistake? What kind of mistake?"

"It was Domino who was supposed to die."

"Supposed to . . ." Hotchins stopped. A frightening thought swept past his mind, but he immediately dismissed it. "What do you mean, 'supposed to'?"

DeLaroza's mind was churning. He had to move fast, get to Domino before the police. But first it was time to deal with Hotchins. Now was the time of reckoning. It could wait no longer.

"Did you hear me?" Hotchins said. "What did you mean by that?"

"Donald, maybe it is time we had that talk I referred to a few minutes ago. The one I said would bore you. You may find some of the details a bit unsettling, so prepare yourself."

"What are you talking about?"

"I am talking about Domino. I am talking about the minute planning that went into your career. I am talking about where the money comes from to finance this gamble. And I am talking about why, suddenly, I have decided to go public, as they say. Do you want to hear the story, Donald?"

"Of course," Hotchins said, but there was a nervousness in his tone.

"Just listen to me," DeLaroza said. "Please do not interrupt until I am finished."

Hotchins was somewhat mystified by the coldness in DeLaroza's tone. He shifted in his seat so that he was facing him. "All right, I'm listening."

"When I introduced you to Domino, you were aware that I had known her for several months. When I first met her, she was a charming woman and of course her natural attributes were undeniable. She was like a bud and I nurtured the bud into a blossom of paradise. She was the perfect answer to my problem and my problem was you. You were teetering on the edge of disaster, my friend, consumed by loneliness. Depression hovered over you like a cloud. Domino was the perfect answer. It took several months, of course, to develop her latent treasures, but it was a task that was not without its rewards."

"Damn it, Victor—"

"*Listen to me,*" DeLaroza snapped, his eyes afire. "When you met her she was the ultimate seductress because of *me*. I am the one who saw the incredible potential. And you know why? Because she understands that in order to satisfy others she must first satisfy herself. And she loves power as much as you or I. There was no question from the beginning. The infatuation would be total. She provided you with fire when you needed it most. And of course you took it, took it all. It was a dangerous game because it had to end. Sooner or later she would become a liability. And the liabilities must be destroyed. The danger during the campaign would have been unbearable and—after you become president—impossible. So you see, dear Donald, her death was inevitable."

Hotchins withdrew to his corner of the seat, his expression reflecting the terrifying truth in DeLaroza's words. He could hardly speak and when he did his words came in a hoarse whisper.

"Stop talking about her in the past tense."

"Why not?" DeLaroza said, unwrapping his cigar. "She is past tense to me. I ordered her death."

Hotchins was hollow-eyed. "You . . . arranged her murder?"

"Of course. It was a political necessity. It was a political necessity from the day you met her."

"You planned it all along? You never considered an alternative?"

"I considered all alternatives. Among them the danger of blackmail, or perhaps ghost-written memoirs filled with lurid details. No, there never was an alternative."

"There has to be an alternative to murder."

"Not always."

Hotchins shuddered and looked as if he were going to be sick. He beat on the front seat and yelled at Chiang. "Stop the car I need some air."

"Get hold of yourself," DeLaroza snapped. "And if you are considering a lecture on morality, please spare me. We are survivalists, you and I. We survive at all costs. It is one of the things that attracted me to you."

"I won't be made part of this," Hotchins said. "I would never have sanctioned—"

DeLaroza waved his hand at Hotchins. "Please. It is not just murder we are talking about. Where do you think the fortunes came from to finance your career— all the millions of dollars, all the small contributions, so carefully planned and perfectly legitimate? Everything above scrutiny. You never asked, did you? And we know why. Because you do not want to know the answer, right? Now you see the tip of an iceberg and suddenly you want to see the whole thing. Well, I say, forget it. Think about *your* alternatives."

Hotchins could think of nothing but the horror. Like an insane newsreel, names and faces swept past his eyes. Sacks, the prison camp, the endless political campaigns, and the hollow personal life. And Domino and the energy she had brought to him. Now all the years of planning and dreaming began to crumble in his mind. Was he going to lose it all?

"The alternatives, Donald. It is really quite simple. You will either be the most powerful political figure in the world, or the most despised. Nobody likes a martyr. They are losers. If you should suddenly feel overly honest and decide to reveal all, remember that. In six months no one will care whether you revealed the truth or not. Those who believed in you will feel betrayed. Those who are against you will be delighted. And you? You will be destroyed. What is it going to be, eh?"

Hotchins leaned back and slumped into the seat. He did not answer.

"Let me tell you a quick little story. In 1945, at the height of the war in Italy, an American soldier disguised as an Italian peasant led eight mules loaded with gold bullion through the Brenner Pass in the Alps into Switzerland. The gold was stolen from the army. I spent five years in Switzerland, learning to speak like a Brazilian, manufacturing the identity of Victor DeLaroza. The millions we have spent financing your career? All of it started with stolen government money. It is not just Domino, my friend. It is your entire career. And every dollar of it is recorded, Donald."

The bigger the prize, the higher the price, Hotchins thought to himself. *And now it is time to pay. The moment of reckoning.*

"They'll find out," Hotchins said quietly. "Somebody always finds out."

"No. I have been at this a very long time. I am an expert at deceit."

DeLaroza laughed, devils dancing in his turquoise pupils. The web had been spun with such care, such patience, spreading a strand at a time across so many years that no one could comprehend the maze. It was a work of terrifying ingenuity.

"Everything is well covered, believe me," he said. "The last person who might have recognized me has been eliminated. There is only one danger to the entire plan right now. Domino."

Hotchins said nothing.

"She will realize we tried to kill her. When is she due back?"

Hotchins still said nothing.

"Get hold of yourself, Donald," DeLaroza said with annoyance in his tone. "When is she due back?"

Hotchins looked down slowly at his watch.

"Now. She is on her way back to the apartment right now."

"Then we have no time to lose. It must be done right this time."

"No!"

"You prefer to be destroyed then?"

"She won't say anything."

"Don't you understand? Somebody was killed in her

apartment last night. They will put her under lights. She will break down. They will find out everything. Is that what you want?"

"I . . . don't know."

"I have never known you to be self-destructive before."

"I've never been involved in murder before."

"Ah. Yes, that is true. So, you are the leader. The one-man show who does it all. Tell me, shall I forget about Domino, then?"

Silence.

"I am awaiting your answer, Mr. Senator. Now it is *your* decision."

"I . . . can't. . . ."

"Of course you can. Think about it. The alternatives, Donald, the alternatives. What shall I do?"

Hotchins's face was drawn. The web DeLaroza had spun was indeed awesome. Had he been a mere dauphin in DeLaroza's grand scheme? The fear of deceit had lain deep in Hotchins's subconscious for years. Now the knowledge of it was like a smoldering fire that could either be fanned to life by his conscience or smothered by his avarice.

"The pluses and the minuses," he muttered aloud.

"Ah, yes, the pluses and the minuses."

In the end Hotchins knew he had no choice. When he stripped away the emotional considerations, as he always had, as he always would, it came down to the simple formula. The pluses and the minuses.

"Well?" DeLaroza said.

"Do . . . what you think . . . is best."

"No. You are the one who makes the decisions. Nobody pulls your strings, is that not correct? So, tell me. Say it, Donald."

He shook his head.

"Then we shall let nature take its course?"

"No!"

"No? Then tell me, what shall I do?"

Hotchins lowered his head like a child.

"Just take care of it."

"*Say* it," DeLaroza demanded.

But Hotchins just shook his head again. He tried to say it but the words crumbled in his mouth like ashes. The moment of reckoning had passed.

23

The lingering stench of death, the bitter smell of cordite which seemed to hang obstinately in the air, the rancid, salty odor of dried blood, the oppressiveness of the closed room, was overwhelming. Sharky leaned against the door, staring at the pockmarks in the wall, the brown stains streaking down to the floor. Faltering images played at the back of his mind, images he wanted to forget but needed to remember.

He was close to exhaustion. His bones ached; his lungs hurt when he breathed; his vision was fuzzy, his mouth dry and hot. He went into the kitchen, found a Coke in the refrigerator, and sat down at the kitchen, table to drink it. He decided to start in the kitchen as long as he was there.

He took a legal pad and a felt-tip pen out of the small briefcase he had brought with him and wrote the word *kitchen* on the top line. Under it he would list anything that seemed incongruous with its surroundings.

The room was neat, tidy, sparkling clean. The countertops were bare except for an antique wine rack in one corner, some appliances, and a paper sack with two wineglasses and a corkscrew beside it on the counter near the sink. He checked the garbage pail. It was clean enough to cook in. Next he checked the paper bag, using his pen to spread the top open. There was a bottle of wine inside and a sales slip. The wine had been purchased the previous day from Richard's Fine Wines. It cost eighteen dollars.

He started his list:

Counter: paper sack.
Bottle of Lafite-Rothschild wine, value $18.
Two wine glasses.
Corkscrew.

During the next two hours Sharky carefully analyzed each room in the apartment. As the list grew his adrenaline started pumping again, warming the aches away, providing a second wind. When he was finished, he went back to the kitchen and started a new list under the heading *Significant.* When he finished the list, he sat back and smiled. His eyes had lost the dull, glassy look of fatigue. He smacked his hands together and said, *"God damn!"* aloud and reached for the phone, pacing the length of the cord while it rang half a dozen times.

"Yeah," Livingston said hoarsely. For a moment he was completely disorganized. He could not remember what day it was or where he was.

"It's Sharky."

Livingston opened and closed his eyes several times and cleared his throat.

"Yeah?"

"Can you get over here?"

"Where, man?"

"Domino's apartment."

"Oh, yeah. Well, uh, what time is it?"

"Hell I don't know, it's . . . a quarter to six."

"Shit, I've only had two hours sleep."

"Arch, get over here fast."

"You got something?"

"I got enough to wake you up real good, man. Get it over here fast as you can."

Livingston was awake now. "On my way, baby, on my way."

He jumped off the bed. He was wearing shorts and a tee-shirt. He pulled on a pair of corduroy Levis and slipped on a plaid shirt and strapped his hip holster to his belt. On the way out the door he grabbed a fur-lined jacket. It took him fifteen minutes to get to Domino's apartment.

"Okay," he said as Sharky opened the door, "what you got up your sleeve now?"

Sharkey led him into the kitchen. He had made a pot of coffee and he pushed Livingston into a chair, shoved a cup of coffee in front of him, and sat down with his legal pad.

"What I did," he said, "I washed the place from top to bottom and I made a list of everything that was even slightly out of the ordinary. Stuff like keys on the living-room table, suitcase on the floor, bottle of wine on the kitchen cabinet, everything. Then I went back over the list and made a second list, only this time I only put down stuff that seemed to relate."

"Uh huh," Livingston said.

"Okay, here's what I got:

"Item: An eighteen-dollar bottle of wine on the kitchen counter still in the bag, two wine glasses, and a corkscrew. The wine was purchased yesterday. There are six bottles of wine in that rack over there, including a bottle of Lafite-Rothschild.

"Item: Keys on the coffee table in the living room. Six keys altogether. Two go to a General Motors car, two look like regular house keys, and one is a safe deposit box key. The other one was not on the key ring. It fits the door to this apartment.

"Item: A beat-up Samsonite one-suiter on the floor beside the bed, pushed back against the wall. The stuff in it is messed up, all pushed over to one side. It contains a tennis dress, sweat socks, underwear, no toilet articles, no make-up.

"Item: The luggage in the closet is all Gucci. Worth a fortune. Not a scratch on it."

Livingston looked up, the coffee cup forgotten in his hand. Sharky went on.

"Item: A blue and white windbreaker hanging in the closet.

"Item: One yellow negligee on bed, spread out very neat.

"Item: One small leather case filled with make-up on the table and a Lady Schick electric razor. In the bathroom there's another electric razor. An Osterman, also for a lady.

"Item: No purse on the premises, no bank book, no address book."

Livingston lit a small Schimmelpenninck cigar and twisted the legal pad around so he could read it. "Well, that's a nice job, considering you musta done it in your sleep, but what're you drivin' at?"

Sharky chuckled. "Okay, follow me on this. If Domino was going on a trip, why did she go out and spend eighteen bucks for a bottle of wine when she had one in her wine rack? And why was she getting ready to open it? You don't open a bottle of wine like that unless you plan to drink it all. So why open it if she was going to

leave? Second, there's the suitcase. Look in the closet.
She has three pieces of gorgeous luggage in there. Why
would she carry that old beat-up job in there? Also look
around here, Arch. The place is neat, neat, neat. Look
in the suitcase. All the clothes are shoved to one side.
But the negligee is spread out very prim and proper.
Also the traveling case of make-up and the electric razor. Why two razors? And the windbreaker in the
closet? It's the only jacket in there. All the rest of them
are in the hall closet. Don't you see it, Arch? She wasn't
packing to go anywhere, she was *un*packing. She took
the make-up case and the electric razor *out* of the bag,
that's why the clothes were mussed up. And she put her
windbreaker in the closet. She was planning to put the
negligee *on*, not pack it. The apartment key wasn't on
her key ring because it wasn't here. It was loaned to
her . . . by Domino. Domino has a Mercedes, these
keys are for a GM car. Don't you see it, Arch. Domino
was out of town and the dead lady was staying in her
apartment. Scardi killed the wrong person."

Livingston looked down at the list. He was still skeptical. "You're reaching, baby. I mean, some of this
makes sense but . . ."

"No purse. No bank book. No address book. Where
are they? They're not here, because Domino took hers
with her and the woman Scardi killed *didn't* bring
hers."

"You're moving too fast for me."

"I had to make sure, Arch, so I went down to the
parking lot and I started checking those GM keys in
every General Motors car down there. I checked fourteen before I found the one the keys fit. A seventy-five
Riviera. This was under the seat. She must have forgotten it."

He slid a woman's wallet across the table to Livingston who opened it and stared at the license behind the plastic window.

"Je-sus Chee-rist," Livingston said softly.

"I've never seen her before, but I'll bet you have."

Livingston looked at the photograph on the driver's license and nodded.

"Tiffany Paris," he said.

"Scardi hit the wrong woman, Arch."

"Maybe. Or maybe he was after Tiffany all the time."

"It's possible, except for one thing. Scardi'd been snooping around here for a couple of days. It took him a while to luck into the Jackowitz set-up. So unless Tiffany made her plans several days ago to spend Friday night here, he wouldn't have known she was going to be here. And if he didn't know she was going to be here, he was after Domino."

Livingston jumped up and began pacing the room. "Sure, it makes sense that way. Domino left here yesterday morning. Then Scardi went into the Jackowitz place and started watching the apartment. When Tiffany came in, he came across and cut down on her the minute she opened the door. She was backlit. And she and Domino are about the same height."

"And the same coloring."

"And if Scardi hit the wrong woman, he'll be back when he finds out. He's gonna finish it up right. I mean, his kind don't fuck up a job and walk away from it."

"Remember the ears in the box he gave Luciano?"

"What we gotta do, we gotta find the lady and stash her someplace safe, someplace they can't find her. Then stake this apartment out and hope he comes back again."

"Or track him down first."

They both heard the sound at the same time, a grating of metal on metal. Someone was putting a key in the lock. Sharky vaulted out of his seat, pulling his automatic from under his arm, rushing from the kitchen toward the door. Livingston was right behind him, clawing for his .38. Sharky was six feet from the door when it swung open. He stopped, dropped into a crouch, and aimed the gun with both hands.

The door opened and he was face to face with Domino Brittain.

She looked at him, down at the gun, back at his flattened nose, and she raised an eyebrow.

"Something wrong with my elevator?" she said.

———————————

Sharky lowered his gun and sighed with relief. She did not move. She stared back and forth at the two detectives until Sharky took out his wallet and held it toward her, letting it flop open to his shield and I.D.

She looked at it, then leaned forward for a better look and stared over the top of it at him.

"A cop?" she said.

Sharky nodded.

"You're a *cop?*"

Sharky nodded again.

"A real . . . live . . . cop."

"Detective," he said, somewhat embarrassed.

"Detective."

"Uh huh."

She looked at Livingston.

"Him too?"

"That's Arch Livingston, my partner."

"Pleased to meet you," Livingston said, but she had already turned her gaze back to Sharky. She shook her head.

Livingston sidled up to Sharky.

"You two know each other?" he said with more than a little surprise in his tone.

"We met."

"Oh, really?"

"We'll talk about it later."

"You better believe we will."

Domino stepped inside the room, but she could not see the wall, the open door blocked it. "Would one of you gentlemen like to get my bag?" she said, pointing to the Gucci sitting in the hall. "And then maybe we can talk about what you're doing in my apartment playing cops and robbers."

Livingston took the bag and leaning close to Sharky, said, "She's a cool one, buddy. But I guess you knew that already, right?"

"I said later," Sharky muttered out of the side of his mouth.

Domino was standing very close to Sharky, and she looked at him and said, "Now what was this about working on the elevators?"

"Sorry about that."

"It's a pretty good act."

He wanted to keep up the banter. He liked it and he liked her and he was grateful that she was still alive, grateful to be close to her again. He knew too that she was smart enough to sense it. But he had to change the subject and he dreaded what was coming.

"Domino," he said seriously, "who stayed here last night?"

"Are you grilling me?—is that what they call it?" She was still trying to keep the conversation light and Sharky was having difficulty making the transition. She looked past him, at the open door, and began to sense that something bad had happened here and then he stepped back and pushed the door shut and she saw it, the splattered blood stains, the pockmarks on the wall, and it began to register, first in her widened eyes, then her strangled cry. "Oh, my God!"

"Was it Tiffany Paris who stayed here last night?" Livingston said.

"I-I-I-I . . ." she stammered.

"Easy," Sharky said.

She thrust her fist against her teeth and turned away from the ghastly wall. The blood drained from her face and for a moment Sharky thought she was going to faint. He put his arm around her and as he did she began nodding very slowly.

"Arch," Sharky said, "there's some brandy in the dining room."

"Right."

"I'm sorry. I should have warned you but . . . I, uh . . . didn't know what to say. Tiffany was here last night, right?"

"Y-y-y-yes." She looked up at him and her face began to go, first at the corners of her mouth, then the tears welling in her eyes. She started to ask a question, but the words caught in her throat and she choked. Livingston brought a pony of Courvoisier and handed it to her, but she did not take it, she kept searching Sharky's face, hoping her fears were wrong.

"I'm sorry," Sharky said, "she's dead."

The tears came and she began to sag, weak-kneed, against him and he led her to the couch and sat down beside her. She covered her face with her hands, her fingers pressing against her eyelids, trying to control her feelings. Finally she broke down and began to sob.

"H-h-h-ow . . . d-d-did . . . ?" she said and then stopped speaking. Sharky handed her the brandy. "Here," he said, "try this."

She took a sip and gagged.

"I h-h-hate brandy," she said.

"Look," Sharky said, "I know how you must feel right now, but this is very important. When did Tiffany first know she was going to be staying here?"

Watery, bloodshot eyes peered over her trembling hands.

"I . . . decided on the spur of the moment to go to Savannah and . . . see some friends so I . . . told her she could . . . stay here for the night."

"When was this?"

"Yesterday morning."

"What time?"

"I had an early hair appointment at Raymond's on Piedmont Road and I called her after I was through. I guess it was about . . . ten-thirty. We met at Houli-han's for lunch and I gave her the key. Then I had to leave to catch my plane."

"So she had no idea you were leaving town until ten-thirty yesterday morning?"

"That's right."

"That does it," Livingston said. "We gotta get her outa here and fast. I'm gonna make a phone call." He went into the bedroom.

"What's he talking about?" Domino asked.

"Are you okay now?"

"I guess. I don't know. Why . . . what happened to Tiff?"

"She was shot. About eight o'clock last night."

Domino stared back toward the door, the full horror of what had happened working on her features. "What happened? Was it a hold-up?"

"No, it wasn't a hold-up and it wasn't an accident. But . . . we think the killer made a mistake."

The horror in her face turned to shock. "Mistake?"

"We think . . . we're almost positive . . . that he was after you."

"Me!"

"She was shot by an ex-Mafia assassin named Scardi. Angelo Scardi. Does that name mean anything to you?"

She shook her head and then said, "Mafia?"

"How about the name Howard Burns?"

"No, no. Neither of them. I've never heard either of those names before. What do you mean, Mafia?"

"This Scardi was a Mafia killer. Someone hired him to kill you. He came here last night and got Tiffany by mistake."

She was more controlled now, the shock and horror replaced by confusion and doubt. "Why?"

"We were hoping you could answer that."

"Well, I can't answer it," she said and anger crept into her tone. "And I don't think you know . . . how do you know that?"

"This Scardi's a real pro. He's been planning it for several days. Don't you see? If Tiffany didn't know she was coming here until yesterday, it had to be you he was after. And he'll try again. He's not the kind who'll settle for a mistake. That's why we've got to get you out of here."

She shook her head violently. "No, I won't be forced out."

"Forced out? We're not forcing you out; we're trying to save your life."

Sharky understood her dilemma. Too much had happened for her to fully comprehend or accept.

"Just trust us, please. Believe me, you're in great danger as long as you stay here."

"Trust you?" she said. "You've already lied to me . . . that ridiculous story about the elevator. Now all this."

"I'm sorry about that. There won't be any more lies, believe me. Now will you please throw some clean clothes in your bag so we can get out of here?"

"I want to call somebody," she said.

"What do you mean, call somebody?"

"I mean, call somebody I know. I don't even know

you. I don't know him. One minute you tell me you're one thing, the next minute you're something else. Now you want to drag me off somewhere. For all I know, you two may have killed Tiffany. Or maybe she isn't even dead. God, I don't know what to think."

Domino's confidence was returning, the self-assurance, the impudence. Her shoulders seemed straighter, she held her chin up high, but with all the straining for composure there was still fear in her eyes. And Sharky's relief at finding her alive was beginning to turn to anger. He was tense and frustrated and his nerves tingled with lack of sleep. He recognized a volatile situation building up and he had to move to stop it. He stood up and taking her by the arm led her to the window and pointed to the other tower.

"See that apartment up there on the corner? That's where he waited. He's like a cobra. No conscience. He's killed fifty people. *Fifty* people! He killed a man and cut off his hands so we couldn't identify the victim. He found out those people were out of town and he broke into that apartment and he sat there all day, very patiently, waiting for your lights to come on and when he saw them he came over here and he rang the bell and when Tiffany opened the door he blew her head off with a double-barreled shotgun. She was dead when she hit the floor. We couldn't even identify her. We thought it was you. Now pretty soon he's gonna find out, see, that he made a mistake and when he does he's gonna come back, because that's what he's all about. He's out there someplace, in the dark, waiting. Maybe he knows already. Maybe he's up on the roof, watching us right now. Or waiting in the back seat of your car. Or maybe just outside the door there—"

"Stop it!" she cried.

"Am I making my point?"

"He's right, you know," Livingston said from the doorway. "You stay here and you might just as well hang a target on your forehead and sit in the window waiting for it to come."

"Ohhh." She shuddered.

"We're not doing this for effect," Sharky said. "We want to keep you alive, Domino, and not just because it's our job. I like you. We thought . . . we thought we lost you once. We don't want it to happen again." He turned to Livingston. "Are we set?"

Livingston nodded. "The place is safe and comfortable. Clean. It beats the hell out of a pine box."

She held her hand up and stopped him. "All right. That's enough. I don't understand any of this, but you've convinced me."

She got up and went to the bedroom. "May I change? I've been in these clothes all day."

"Keep away from the windows," Sharky said.

"Will you stop *saying* things like that!"

"I'm not trying to scare you," Sharky said. "I mean it. Stay away from the windows."

"Where am I going?"

Livingston said, "I'll tell you when we get there. The less you know now, the better."

She went into the bedroom and closed the door. She leaned against the dresser and saw Tiffany's suitcase and the tears started to come back. She shook them off. She looked at the window and suddenly it was no longer just a pane of glass—it was an ominous threat. A sense of danger crept over her and she suddenly found it hard to breathe. She opened her own suitcase, threw the dirty clothes on the floor, and aimlessly, thoughtlessly put clean things in their place, then changed into jeans, a checkered shirt, and boots. And all the time the questions gnawed at her.

Why? Who?

But that only made it worse. She turned her thoughts to Sharky and she felt strangely reassured. She felt a link to him, a lifeline that tied them together. Her lifeline. Her danger was now his danger and because of that she sensed a new strength in him, something she had not felt before. *A cop*, she thought. And that was far more appealing than an elevator man.

How much did he know? About her? Tiffany? Did he know about Donald? And Victor?

She would have to tell Donald. He was certain to find out about the shooting and he might do something foolish. He was capable of such a thoughtful gesture, but he could not afford to be linked with this. The least she could do was call him, tell him she was all right, tell him to keep out of it.

She went back to the bedroom and stood beside the phone, remembering Sharky's reaction when she had threatened to call somebody.

Oh, hell, she thought, *it can't hurt to put his mind at ease. He had his own problems; he didn't need any of hers.* She picked up the receiver and quietly punched out his private number, a phone by the bedside in his suite that only he answered. It buzzed several times while she watched the door, fearful that either Sharky or Livingston might come in.

He isn't there, she thought, and was about to hang up when he answered. His voice seemed strangely cold, suspicious. "Hello?"

"Listen to me, I haven't much time. A terrible thing happened. Somebody was killed in my apartment."

A pause. Then: "Where are you?"

"Don't worry about me and don't get involved in this. I'm going to be all right. A cop I know named Sharky is taking care of me."

"Where are you going?"

"I don't know, but I'll be safe. Can't talk anymore. Goodbye."

She put the phone down very softly.

In his suite, Hotchins stared at the buzzing telephone for a moment and then slowly replaced it.

"It was her," he said.

"Where is she? Is she at home?" DeLaroza was standing beside him.

"Yes, but the police are into it now. Apparently they're taking Domino into protective custody."

"Who? I need a *name*," DeLaroza said.

"A cop named Sharky."

DeLaroza sighed with relief and then smiled. "Excellent. Now you can go back to the others. I'll handle this."

24

At thirty-four Hazel Weems had begun to show the hard lines of a hard life. She had grown up in the South Georgia cotton country and had started to work in the fields when she was seven. Her father, a sometime preacher, sometime fieldhand, had sent her to live with an aunt in Atlanta when she was fourteen. It was her father's intention to give her a chance at a decent life, but the aunt had turned out to be an alcoholic who drank up the ten dollars a week that was sent for Hazel's upkeep and who frequently beat her in a drunken rage.

On one particularly brutal night neighbors had called the police and one of the investigating officers was Duke Weems, a kind, sympathetic ex-football coach who was twenty-five years older than Hazel. Soon after the beating Weems found her a foster home with a West

End grocer and after that was a frequent visitor. After two years of courting they were married. Hazel was seventeen and Duke was forty-two. Two years later he dropped dead of a heart attack chasing a purse snatcher through Five Points.

A year after that Hazel passed the police examination and was inducted into the force as a meter maid. It took her seven more years to make the regular force and another two to become a third-class detective, one of the first women investigators on the force.

Duke's ex-partner, Arch Livingston, had talked Hazel into taking the police exam and had worked tirelessly with her to prepare her for it. It was Livingston too who had fought to get her transferred to the uniformed squad and then badgered his superiors until she was permitted to take the exam for detectives.

If Livingston had asked her to cut off her nose and send it to him for Christmas she would have done it.

She lived on the South Side of Atlanta in a predominantly black neighborhood, her small, tidy two-bedroom house the kind they once called a bungalow. There was an island at the end of her street that was pruned, plucked, and planted religiously by the Parton Place Garden Club. Hazel was not a member.

Hazel met them at the door and sized up Domino with the eye of a widow studying a prospective daughter-in-law. No hat, a roughhouse shearling coat, blue jeans, and scruffy boots. She liked what she saw.

"These two ain't bullying you, are they, honey?" she said, steering Domino into the house.

"I'm not sure yet," Domino said and smiled.

"If they give you any shit, you just tell Hazel. I've known this one since he was a rookie directing traffic on Five Points and this one here, I've just seen him around, but all he's good for is raisin' hell and drivin' the captain bughouse. You caught yourself quite a pair, lady. I'll put some coffee on."

"I'll help," Livingston said and followed her into the kitchen.

"Look here, Hazel," Livingston told her. "I got you fixed up with a room at a first-class hotel. Just for a couple of days. Won't cost you a dime."

She turned on him.

"Move outa my own house! What the hell you talkin' about? You got free board. Why don't you go to the hotel?"

"Too much traffic. Too public. This lady's on somebody's hit list."

"What did she do?"

"I don't think she knows. And that's for real. I don't think she can tell us, 'cause I don't think she's figured it out herself yet."

"Well, anyway I ain't goin' to no Lysol-smellin' hotel. What the hell, Archie, I ain't the Avon Lady; I'm a cop just like you. If there's trouble, I'm as good as anybody else downtown. Don't come at me with that macho shit."

"It ain't macho shit, lady. We're gonna be in the middle of the goddamndest interdepartmental ass-hittin' you ever saw. You want to get caught in the middle of that?"

"Between you and who?"

"Right now I'd say between us and Riley and Jaspers and D'Agastino."

"God *damn*, you do things in a big way."

"You get my point. You get out and when it hits the fan all you got to know is that I asked to use your place for a cover for a coupla days."

"It ain't any of my business, Sergeant, but ain't you been in enough shit through the years? You got to stick your foot in it again?"

"Ain't my gig, this time. I come along for the ride. He's a young fella. Needs all the help he can get."

"Good. In that case I'll just buy a ticket and jump aboard, too. Now get outa my way while I make some coffee."

_____

Sharky carried Domino's suitcase into the guest bedroom and put it on a chair near the door. The room, modest but comfortable, was quite a contrast to Domino's apartment.

"Is the place okay?" Sharky said.

"It's fine," Domino said. "What a nice lady she is but . . . why is she doing this for me?"

"She's doing it for Arch, although if she didn't like you she probably would have thrown us out. She's a detective. Her husband was one of the first black cops in the city. He died a couple of years ago."

"How sad. She seems so young to be a widow."

"Yeah, well, that happens."

"Is that the way you think? 'Oh, well, it happens'?"

"I can't imagine what it's like to be married to a cop," Sharky said. "I suppose there are realities you either accept and live with or you end it."

"Or it gets ended for you," she said.

"That, too."

Domino sat down on the bed. "I'm tired," she said.

"There are a couple of more questions . . ."

"I thought it was going to be my turn next," she said.

She stared at him, boring in with those green eyes, and Sharky felt the back of his neck warming up. He was moved by her vulnerability and her spirit. He would like to have said something to her but he was afraid it would come out wrong. Instead he said, "You want to know about the elevator, hunh?"

She nodded.

"I could lie about it, you know. I'm very good at that. It's something you learn on the street."

"Oh, I know how good you are at it. You sucked me in beautifully. But I thought we could make a fresh start—and both tell the truth this time."

"Okay. We were bugging your apartment. I was monitoring the tapes."

There it was, quick, to the point, and probably deadly. But her reaction surprised him. She wasn't mad or indignant or even embarrassed. She simply looked at him rather whimsically and said, "Why?"

"Did you know Neil Dantzler and Tiffany were involved in blackmail?"

"I don't believe that."

"Oh, you can believe it. That part we're sure of. They shook down a Texas oilman for fifty grand."

"Tiffany?"

Sharky nodded.

"Then it was Neil. He made her do it. She wasn't like that."

"It doesn't make any difference. They did it."

"And you think I was part of it?"

Sharky shook his head. "Nope, don't think that at all. But we had to find out for sure."

"And, uh, how many of these bugs did you have in my place?"

"Enough. I could hear everything in that apartment but the plants growing."

"How long were you, uh, up there?"

"Long enough. Since that night Confucius came to dinner."

"Ohhh." She sucked her bottom lip between her teeth and looked at him and then shrugged. "What can I say?"

"You can tell me who he was. That's one of the ques-

tions. We've got to start someplace. *Some*body wants
you dead."

Victor? she thought. *It couldn't be him. And revealing his name might eventually involve Donald, possibly
destroy his career for nothing.*

"It wasn't him. He's from out of the country. Germany. He went back to Europe the next day."

There, that was easy, she thought, *as long as he
doesn't lean on it.* She changed the subject.

"Would it help my image any if I told you I'm going
to retire?"

"It won't change anything," Sharky said softly. "Hell,
I'm not here to judge you. What you do is your business."

She cocked her head to one side and smiled. "Do you
mean that?"

"Sure. We're being honest, remember?"

"Thank you."

"I felt like a goddamn eavesdropper anyhow." He
hesitated, then changed the subject. "You're sure you
never heard of Angelo Scardi or Howard Burns?"

"Who is this Burns?"

"It's Scardi's moniker . . . alias. Scardi was very
big in the news about seven years ago."

"Oh, hell," she said, "seven years ago I was seventeen and living in Mudville, Utah, and all I cared about
was Warren Beatty and rock and roll."

"Then he's just the trigger. Somebody else wants you
scratched and that's the somebody I want."

"It sounds personal."

"Well, it got that way . . ."

"Why? Because of me, Sharky? Because you thought
I was dead?"

"Uh, I . . ."

Livingston saved him.

"You gonna be okay?" he asked Domino.

"Yes. And I thank you."

"Sure." He turned to Sharky. "I'm gonna check in with Friscoe but I'm not givin' him this number. I'll set up a phone drop, have him leave a number. For now I'd like to keep this place between the four of us."

"Good idea," Sharky said. "What we should do, I can stay here with her. You meet the Machine someplace and fill them in. Everybody needs to know."

"Right. Be back in a minute." He went in the other room to make the call.

Sharky moved the suitcase off the chair and dropped into it like a sack of cement.

"You look like something out of a horror movie," Domino said. "When's the last time you were in bed?"

"I forget."

"Come here."

"If I lay down on that bed, I won't get up until Easter."

She looked at him and mischief played at her lips. "Wanna bet?"

Sharky thought about it. He wasn't too tired to think about it. Then she held out her foot. "Would you mind helping me off with my boots?"

He went over, turned his back to her, and took the boot by the instep and heel and pulled it off. She watched him and when he had pulled the other one off, she said, "Anybody ever tell you you've got a beautiful ass?"

Sharky turned around and looked down at her. "That's supposed to be my line," he said.

"Oh, piffle. Haven't you heard? Times are changing."

Livingston called to him from the other room and she sighed.

"Saved by Ma Bell," she said ruefully as he left the room.

Livingston handed Sharky a slip of paper with a phone number on it. It was a drop, the *P* in front of the number indicating a phonebooth.

"You got two urgents from The Nosh," Livingston said. "The first one was at six ten, the other one about ten minutes ago. He says he'll be at this number until seven thirty."

A warning bell went off deep inside Sharky, but he didn't stop to analyze it. It was seven thirty already. He grabbed the phone and dialed the number.

25

The apartment houses along Piedmont Road facing the sprawling inner city park were a tawdry souvenir of more elegant times. Once, near the turn of the century, the park had hosted the International Exposition and on one brilliant afternoon John Phillip Sousa had introduced "The Stars and Stripes Forever" before an assemblage that had included the President of the United States. But the grandeur of Piedmont Road was long gone. The lawns in front of the apartment buildings had eroded into red clay deserts infested with old tires and broken bottles. Behind paneless windows covered with old blankets derelicts of every kind huddled together in the agony of poverty, cooking over cans of Sterno or, worse, drinking it to forget their lost dreams.

The Nosh sat huddled behind the wheel of his Olds watching one of the battered apartments up the street.

He was getting nervous, even a little scared. He looked
at his watch. Seven thirty. Time for the meet. Why the
hell didn't Sharky call?

He reached under the seat, got his flashlight, and
climbed out of the car. And then, with blessed relief, he
heard the phone in the booth ring.

He caught it on the second ring.

"Hello."

"Nosh? It's Shark."

"Hey, man, I was gettin' worried. I'm runnin' outa
time."

"What do you mean, runnin' outa time?"

"I got this weird phonecall about six o'clock, Shark.
Guy tells me he can identify the voice on the tape.
'What tape?' I says and he says, 'The Chinese tape.' So
I says to him, 'I don't know what you're talkin' about'
and he says, 'Don't be dumb—the one from Domino's
apartment' and then he tells me he can identify the guy
on the tape for a hundred bucks, but I gotta come to
this apartment on Twelfth and Piedmont alone before
seven thirty. So I argued a little, you know, told him I
ain't goin' no place alone and then he says I can bring
you along."

"He said me? He said my name?"

"Yeah. So anyways, I went by Tillie the Teller and
got a hundred bucks and I'm here now, right up the
street from . . ."

"Nosh, don't move. Get back in your car and wait
right there. I'm on my way."

"But he's gonna leave at seven thirty and it's—"

"Nosh, you're not listening! Don't go near the
fuckin' place. Stay there. Wait for me, okay?"

". . . Well, okay . . ."

"Nosh?"

"Yeah."

"You stay there, you hear me?"

"Okay."

"Gimme fifteen minutes. I'm leaving now."

The Nosh hung up and stepped out of the phone-booth. He paced back and forth in front of the car for several minutes, watching the building.

He ambled up Twelfth Street to the front of the building. There were no lights. The street was black, the streetlamps broken or burned out.

If the canary splits, The Nosh was thinking, *I can at least nail him when he comes out.*

Paint curled from the windowsills of the three-story building and broken windows stared bleakly out at the dark street. Here and there lights flickered dimly behind old blankets.

The pits. The absolute pits, thought The Nosh.

He stood at the doorway, waving his light around, checking it out.

A furry night scavenger dashed from the doorway into the sanctuary of the bushes. It crouched there, peering out, its amber eyes glittering in the beam of the flashlight.

The Nosh stamped his foot at it and the creature ran off up the street, its ugly hairless tail dragging behind it.

He turned the light back to the doorway and approached it. The front door was gone. Inside was a small vestibule.

The inside door was propped open by a cement block.

The vestibule was a litter of empty wine bottles in brown paper sacks, broken glass, crushed beer cans. Someone had dropped a sack of garbage down the stair-well. It lay just inside the main door, a splash of refuse, well nibbled-over.

The Nosh shuddered.

There were sounds inside the building, but he could not believe that people actually lived there.

Night creatures scurried into cracks in the wall. A twenty-five watt bulb cast dim shadows on the stairwell, which smelled of rotten carpeting and sour cooking. The Nosh patted the tape in his inside pocket for reassurance and stood at the bottom of the stairs. High up, toward the third floor, the hallway lights were burned out. Somewhere in the building a radio blared static and country music. A child was crying behind one of the doors.

At first he hardly heard the voice. He thought it was the radio or something moving in the shadows or his imagination. He looked up into the darkness.

"Abrams . . ."

A whisper, barely audible.

He went up a couple of steps and listened.

Nothing.

He looked at his watch. Another five minutes and Sharky would be there.

"Abrams . . ."

The Nosh looked up again and pointed the finger of light into the blackness.

"Down here," he said.

Nothing.

He went up to the first floor. The child stopped crying and started to laugh. A woman's nasal voice joined Dolly Parton on the country-music station. The Nosh felt more secure. How could there be any danger in a building where children were laughing?

He went to the second floor.

"Up here, Abrams . . ."

"Who's there?"

Silence.

The stairs groaned with age as he climbed to the third floor and stood at the head of the steps in the darkness, probing the dark hallway with his light. Apartment 3-B was at the end of the hall, the number painted sloppily on the door with house paint. He walked slowly toward it and stood outside the apartment.

"Hello?"

Nothing.

He pushed the door open. It swung slowly on aged hinges. The apartment had a long central hallway ending at the living room with bedrooms off the corridor. No lights. A tremor rippled along The Nosh's arm and across his back and he shook it off. He took a few nervous steps inside. Broken glass crunched underfoot. He was walking with his hand against the wall, following the beam of his flashlight. He passed a doorway to his right and turned toward it, swinging his light at the doorless opening.

Then he heard Sharky, out on the street, calling to him:

"Nosh!"

Thank God. He turned back toward the main doorway of the apartment. It was then he heard the movement in the room. Instinctively he dodged to his right and crouched at the same time. But it was too late.

He saw the blinding flash before he heard the dull, muffled explosion. The shotgun boomed in his face. Two barrels, shattering the quiet of the hallway with their silenced *thunk, thunk!* For an instant the corridor was lit by the ghastly yellow-red exhaust flame as the gases burst from the ugly barrels. The heat from the gas shattered The Nosh's glasses, scorched his eyes, and the pellets tore into his face and chest. He was blown across the hallway into the wall. Pain chopped through the side of his face and tore at his shoulder. His feet flopped helplessly inches above the floor and he seemed to hang there for an instant before he fell.

He saw a figure dart through a doorway. It seemed miles away. His foot was kicking the wall convulsively and he thought, *I should stop that.* But the effort was far too great. His reflexes went wildly out of control.

He pushed himself into a sitting position, his one leg bent behind him, still kicking, and fell against the wall. He was vaguely aware that his life was leaking out of him, forming a dark pool at his feet. His hand was shaking, but he managed to work his wallet out of his pocket and threw it aimlessly into the main hallway.

"P-p-p-police," he stammered at nobody. "P-p-p-police . . ."

And then with all the fading strength he had left, he screamed:

"HELP M-M-M-M-E-E-E-E. . . ."

26

Sharky had taken only a moment to tell Livingston he had to leave, that he was worried about The Nosh, and to tell Domino he would be back shortly.

He drove like a maniac across the city, speeding through red lights, cutting through filling stations at intersections, his hand on the horn all the way. Pedestrians fled for their lives before him. He spotted The Nosh's Olds from a block away and screeched in beside it, but he saw it was empty before he even stopped. He jumped out of the car, looked up Twelfth Street.

Darkness. The wind rattled old fences and dead tree limbs.

Which apartment? Where was he? Sharky's heart was pounding so hard he could hear it, like a pump in his ears. He cupped his hands and yelled:

"Nosh!"

And a moment later he saw in the upper floor window across the street the hideous yellow-red flash. *Oh Jesus!* He grabbed his flashlight and ran across the street and into the apartment house, his automatic ready. The he heard the terrible scream:

"HELP M-M-M-M-E-E-E-E. . . ."

Sharky charged up the stairs, up to the third floor, his light leading him on. When he reached the top floor he stopped, looking at the open door at the end of the long hall. He heard something thumping inside the apartment, like someone knocking on the wall. He moved cautiously down the hallway and then the light picked up the glitter of gold on the floor. A gold detective's badge.

"Nosh!"

He ran to the doorway of the apartment, saw the flashlight on the floor, its beam fixed on a foot that was jerking spastically, kicking the wall over and over again. He flashed his light on The Nosh's face. Abrams was leaning against the wall. The side of his face was blown away and his mouth was crooked and bloody. His jaw was torn loose at one side and bits of glass sparkled on his cheeks. There was a jagged, gaping hole where his shoulder had been and blood spurted from a dozen wounds in his chest.

Sharky jammed his gun in his belt and dropped on his knees beside the little man.

"Nosh. Jesus, Nosh, hold on. I'll get somebody. Can you hear me, buddy? Hey, c'mon Nosh, nod. Blink your eyes. Do *something!*"

"I . . . grahg . . . largh . . . agha. . . ."   The Nosh's voice was an ugly croak stifled by the blood that filled his mouth and overflowed onto his chest. He began shivering violently and Sharky pulled off his jacket and threw it over him.

"C'mon buddy, hang in there. I'm gonna find a phone, okay? Shit, man, don't fade out on me now."

The Nosh's eyes rolled in his head. He looked up at Sharky without recognition. His eyes were turning glassy.

More blood surged up from his chest and filled his mouth.

He was limp. His head lolled against Sharky's chest.

"Nosh!"

Abrams looked up again. His face seemed to sag. The skin grew loose. He was turning gray. His eyes were no longer focusing. They began to cross. There was a clatter in his throat and then his eyes rolled crazily and turned up into his head.

"*No . . . c'mon . . .*"

Sharky's attention was riveted on his dying friend. When he heard the sound behind him, it was too late. The knife edge of a hand slashed into the back of his neck and he was thrown over The Nosh's body, the pain from the blow stunning him as he lurched into the wall. He twisted as he flew forward, swinging one leg in a wide arc in the darkness, kicking blindly, feeling it hit something soft, sinking deep into human flesh. He kept rolling, away from the wall and into the dark hall until he was stopped by two legs. He swung his knees under him, balled his fist, and shoved himself upward, driving his fist between the two legs until it slammed into a crotch. He grabbed in the dark, his hand closing around the unseen figure's genitals, and he jerked him forward. A toe found his back and buried deep just over the kidney and Sharky roared with pain and rage and twisted back in the other direction, swinging his fist in the dark. He missed, took another blind swing, and missed again, then remembered his gun and pulled it from his belt, but he was afraid to fire. He was disoriented in the dark, afraid he might hit The Nosh. He sensed movement all around him. A fist hit his shoulder and bounced away in the darkness and he rolled again, toward the main hall, away from the activity.

The beam from one of the flashlights swept the hallway, found him, and Sharky spun around, half sitting, and fired an inch above the light. The flashlight spun crazily in the dark, hit the floor, and shattered. There was a groan in front of him, the sound of a body hitting the floor.

A foot crashed down on his ankle and the pain stabbed up his leg. He swung the gun, trying to imagine his assailant there, in the dark in front of him, and raised the gun, but before he could get another shot off, a foot kicked his wrist, knocking his arm straight up. The gun flew out of his hand and clattered away in the darkness. Another foot slammed down into his stomach. Sharky gasped, grabbed the leg, and twisted hard, pulled himself up to his knees, his fury turning to blind hate. He wanted to hurt them, these unseen figures striking at him in the dark, to kill them.

And then a fist as hard as a gauntlet smashed into his temple and his brain seemed to explode. The floor tilted insanely under his knees and he floundered, trying to catch himself, to stay up. Another fist slammed into his neck and this time the pain could not be ignored. It fanned out through his body like an electrical shock. His hands went numb. His back gave out. He jackknifed and fell forward and it seemed forever before the floor came up to meet him.

The sounds around him were echoes that grew fainter and fainter. And then there was only the darkness.

27

Sharky stirred and turned over on his back, but his foot was caught on something and he stopped. He tried wiggling it and felt the bite of a rope in his ankle. He was tied to something. He opened his eyes and his vision strayed crazily around the room. Nausea swept over him and he closed them again.

Pain mushroomed into his neck and temples.

He closed his eyes and lay still. He felt like he was moving, rocking back and forth.

I'm still dizzy, he thought.

Then he heard a weird scream, a sorrowful cry that seemed to echo over and over again, raising the hair on his arms.

My God, he thought, *what was that?*

It came again, a mournful shriek that died slowly and was answered a few seconds later by another echoing from farther away. He recognized the sound. It was a loon, lamenting insanely in the night, its demented love call answered by its mate.

A loon? He lay there sorting out the sounds around him. They began to make sense: ropes creaking, boards groaning, the rhythmic slap of water against wood somewhere below him. It was a boat.

He opened his eyes and blinked, trying to clear his fuzzy vision. The room was shadowed, lit only by a lantern that swung in an easy arc overhead. He lay hypnotized by it until the nausea returned. He gritted his teeth to keep from vomiting and turned his eyes away from the light.

It was a small room, a cabin, and he was lying on the lower bunk of a double-decker. One side of the room curved in and there was a porthole in it. Facing it, on the other side of the cabin, was a hand-carved latticework partition which separated the room from the hall. The door was heavy and made of some kind of dark wood, rosewood or mahogany. The far side of the room, opposite the bunk, was dark. The lantern shed a small pool of light over a table and chair which sat in the center of the cabin. He smelled pork cooking in garlic.

In the darkness opposite him, a cigarette glowed briefly. He concentrated, trying to make out a shape, a form of some kind in the shadows but he could see nothing.

Then he remembered The Nosh.

God damn them. God DAMN them!

He fought back tears, but they came anyway, dribbling down the side of his face, and he reached up and wiped them away.

"Well, welcome back to the land of the living, Mr. Sharky," a voice said from the shadows.

He squinted into the darkness.

"Oh, don't try to see me," the voice said. "It's much too dark. It will only strain your eyes."

It was a big boat, too big for the river. Then the loon cried again and Sharky thought, *I'm on the lake. Seventy miles from Atlanta.*

A voice he did not recognize, hoarse and trembling with fatigue, said:

"Where's my partner?"

My God, he thought, *was that my voice?*

It was a weak, whining, nasal voice and Sharky hated it.

"Unfortunate," the voice from the darkness said, "but the sacrifice was necessary."

The rage built inside Sharky like a tornado in his gut. But he held his tongue. Nothing more would be accomplished with dialogue. Escape was the only thing he could think about now. *Concentrate on it,* he thought. There will be a way. *There will be a way.* He looked down at his foot. It was lashed tightly to the foot of the bunk. His jacket was stained with The Nosh's blood. The fire roared inside him again.

Let me take one of them out. Let me watch his eyes when he goes, the way I watched Larry's eyes.

"*Hai,* Liung," the voice in the shadows called out and the door opened. Three men entered. They were Orientals, short and lean, their faces wide and hard, their noses broad, their eyes beads under hooded lids. They wore white tee-shirts, the cotton molded around hard muscles and taut, flat stomachs. One of the three had a scorched hole in the shoulder of his shirt and a bloodstain down one side. Sharky could see the bulge of a bandage under the shirt.

Sorry it wasn't a couple of inches lower and an inch to the left, you sorry son of a bitch.

Another one had a splint on his forearm.

Sorry, Nosh, sorry I didn't do better.

The one with the splint on his arm stood near the door, his arms at his sides as the other two approached the bunk, untying his foot and dragging him to his feet. His knees buckled and they pulled him upright. His vision wobbled. The room went in and out of focus.

From the shadows, smoke curled like a snake, twisting into the heat from the lantern. Sharky concentrated on the corner, letting his eyes grow accustomed to the darkness.

"If you're trying to build a mental image of me, forget it," the voice said. "It's much too dark. And there's no need to say anything to my three friends. They don't speak English. In fact they rarely speak at all."

Sharky said nothing. He continued to stare into the dark corner of the room.

"You can save yourself a lot of time and pain if you will simply answer one question for me," the voice said. "That's all we're here for. A simple sentence will do it, Mr. Sharky. Where is the girl?"

Sharky said nothing.

"Where is she? Where is Domino?"

Sharky continued to stare at the glowing tip of the cigarette.

"All I want is the address."

Sharky moved slightly toward one of the Orientals and then quickly twisted the other way, snapping his arms down toward his sides. As he did, the two Chinese exerted the slightest pressure on the nerves just above each of his elbows. Pain fired down Sharky's arms to his fingertips and both arms were almost immediately paralyzed.

"Don't be foolish," the voice said. "They can paralyze you with one finger—and they will. That was a simple exercise. The feeling will return to your arms in a minute or so. The next time they will be more persuasive."

Sharky felt the numbness begin to subside. His arms felt as though they had fallen asleep. They tingled as the feeling returned. He shook his hands from the wrists and flexed his fingers.

"You see what I mean? Now can we make it simple, Mr. Sharky? Or will you require more complicated tricks?"

Sharky still did not talk. He peered hard into the shadows. Was it Scardi? The tobacco was brash and smelled rancid. Sharky concentrated on that for a few minutes. *English cigarettes,* he thought. *But his accent is American.* Sweat beads rolled down his face and collected on his chin, stubbornly refusing to drop off.

Gerald Kershman, the man in the shadows, was becoming annoyed.

"Stop staring over here," he said. "I find it irritating."

Sharky stared stubbornly at the corner.

Kershman said something in Chinese and one of the men holding Sharky reached up with a forefinger and pressed a nerve beside Sharky's right eye. The pain was literally blinding. The vision in the eye vanished. Kershman chuckled. He felt a surge in his testicles, a sensual thrill. He was growing hard watching Sharky's ordeal. Secretly he hoped Sharky would prove difficult, that the torture would get more intense, and he began to tremble with excitement at the thought. He dropped his Players cigarette on the floor and, turning his back on Sharky, lit another. Then he said:

"Time is of the essence. You will give up the information. It's really just a matter of time." Then, sharply: *"Pa t' a k'un tao chuo tze."*

The two Orientals jerked Sharky to the chair and forced him down into it. There were two straps attached to each arm and two others mounted on the table. They strapped his arms to the chair, leaving his wrists and hands free, and shoved the chair against the table and fastened the straps on the table over the back of each hand, tightening them until he could hardly curl his fingers.

"Before we proceed any further, perhaps I should explain a little about the three Chins. They are members of one of the oldest Triads in Hong Kong, Chi Sou Han. Since the twelfth century the oldest male of each of the three families of Chi Sou Han has been taken from his mother at birth and trained to be the ultimate warrior. Their discipline is beyond the comprehension of the western mind. I have seen one of these men stand in a *crouch* for ten hours without a falter. They endure the most excruciating pain in silence.

"They are experts in *tai chi ch'uan,* karate, and judo. They communicate through the use of body movements and they use only two weapons—their hands and the *yinza.* Are you familiar with the *yinza,* Mr. Sharky? *Da yu'an p'an!*"

The man near the door with the splint on his arm moved with fluid grace, twisting to his right from the waist up while his right hand swept past his belt and swung up shoulder high. Immediately, without breaking the continuity of the move he shifted his body in the opposite direction, flicking his wrist sharply as he did. There was a flash at his fingertips, a glint in the air, and a steel disc the size of a silver dollar ripped into the table so close to Sharky's hand that he could feel the cold metal. It had twelve steel barbs an inch long around its perimeter.

"An ancient weapon, Mr. Sharky, and far more accurate than a bullet. Chi Sou Han are also famous throughout China for what we would call in English *The Perfect And.* The art of torture. The most effective sample of The Perfect And is the Ordeal of the Fifth Finger. It is used to persuade the most obstinate subjects only.

Very simply, a joint is cut off a finger every eight hours beginning with the little finger. Five fingers, five days. The Chi Sou Han claim no man has ever resisted them beyond the thumb of one hand."

Terror seized Sharky. He was drenched in his own sweat. He lowered his head, staring down between his hands. He tried to curl his fingers but his hands were strapped too tightly to the table.

Kershman said, "For the last time, where is Domino?"

Silence.

Kershman's pulse thundered and he said, *"Nung hao la."*

The Chin with the splint on his arm stepped from the room for a few moments and returned carrying a small hibachi only slightly larger than his hand. It was filled with glowing coals. He placed it on the corner of the table. In his other hand he held a sharpening steel and a dirk, its tapered blade about six inches long. He stood close to Sharky and slashed the knife blade down the steel several times, the blade ringing as it clashed, steel against steel.

Sharky clamped his teeth together.

They're so proud of silence. I'll give them silence.

Sweat ran into his mouth and he spat it out.

The man with the knife put the sharpening steel on the table and turned toward the shadows.

"Hai. Tuo ch'ung la," Kershman said. He stepped forward a bit, his eyes shining with anticipation as the Chin stuck the point of the knife into the table beside the first joint of Sharky's little finger. With one swift downward chop he sliced off the end of the finger.

Sharky stifled the scream in his throat. It swelled there, hurting his tongue. He was shaking hard, but he held it in.

The Chin placed the blade over the coals until it was

red hot and then held the edge of it against the stump of
Sharky's finger. It sizzled. The room filled with the
smell of burned flesh. Sharky stifled another scream,
only this time it did not die. It was a squeal trapped
behind his lips as pain triggered the nerves to his brain.

He stared at the bizarre sight of his fingertip lying on
the table.

My God they did it, he thought. *The bastards cut off
my finger.*

And he fainted.

———————

He awoke with his pulse throbbing in his ruined finger. Every movement of the boat, every sound, seemed
like a knife jabbing into it. He used the pain, thought
about it, let it clear his head.

He lay motionless, listening. Above him, on what he
assumed was the deck, there was movement. At least
one of them was up there, maybe all four. He tried to
separate the movements, but that was impossible.

There was another sound from somewhere down below to the right of his prison cabin. He tuned in on it.
The nasal voice. The whiner. Talking. Hesitating. Talking. He was on the phone, reporting to someone.

Sharky thought about escape.

*How? Where would I go? Where am I? What the hell
kind of boat is this?*

*Immaterial, stupid. Get out first, then worry about
where you are.*

He focused his thoughts on escape. He thought about
weapons. The knife was still on the table and he was
tied by only one leg. The bastards were confident
enough. But when he checked the knot he knew there
was no way to untie it with only one good hand.

Anything else?

Jacket? No. *Shoes?* Hardly. *Nothing in my pockets. My belt?* The BELT!

It was a wide leather belt with a large, heavy, square brass buckle he had bought at the flea market. It would hardly make a dent in the skulls of Winkin, Blinkin and Nod, but Whiny Voice, now there was a possibility. He had to get him in close.

He had to make the miserable bastard show his face. But then what? He thought about the three Chinese with their little steel discs. *Careful Sharky.*

The thinking tired him and he closed his eyes and rested. He heard someone in the passageway. He turned his head toward the door, lying with his eyes half-closed, watching the door as it swung open.

The man standing there was short and fat, wearing a rumpled gray suit with the jacket open. His belly sagged over his belt. Thick, obnoxious lips, jowls, frog eyes. So that was the body that went with the voice. Sharky felt better.

Then he saw the 9 mm Mauser jammed down in Fat Boy's belt.

Kershman stared down at Sharky with contempt. De-Laroza had just chewed Kershman out. "Five days, hell. I want the answer before morning."

Kershman had felt humiliated.

He called out to Liung and the Chin with the splinted arm came down from the deck above. A moment later the other two followed.

All three of them are outside. Good.

Kershman handed Liung a tube of smelling salts and nodded toward Sharky. Sharky closed his eyes, feigning unconsciousness. He felt his foot being untied. Then the sharp odor of amyl nitrite burned his nose and he involuntarily jerked his head to one side.

"Wake up," Fat Boy said, back in the shadows now. "Time for round two."

They pulled Sharky to his feet, shoved him into the chair, and strapped him down. He felt like a rag doll in their hands.

"Look at you," Fat Boy said. "How much longer do you really think you can hold out? You're a wreck."

Sharky did not answer.

"I ask you again, where is the woman?" Kershman was almost screaming.

Sharky kept his teeth clamped shut.

"Where is she?" Kershman said and there was an almost feline quality to his panicked tone.

Somebody's putting the heat on him.

"You're a fool," Fat Boy screeched. *"Jaw sao."*

Liung picked up the sharpening steel and the blade rang across the rough metal. It grated Sharky's nerves, turning them raw. His finger began throbbing from anticipation. Fear was a lump in his throat.

The Chin stuck the knife point into the table next to his finger and waited.

"Kan ni ti ch'ua pa," Kershman said.

This time Sharky was more aware of what was happening. He heard the knife slice through bone and gristle a second before the pain stabbed up his arm to his shoulder. The cabin whirled around him and he groaned into his clenched teeth, stifling his agony. The finger was already numb when Liung cauterized it.

Sharky slumped forward, let his body go limp, felt them unstrap him, drag him back to the cot, and drop him on it. They tied his leg.

———————————

He was going to pass out again, he could feel himself slipping into that dark pit. He thought about The Nosh and the anger sustained him for a few minutes. He began to slip. He thought about Fat Boy, about his Mauser stuck there in his belt. That was good, that helped, but then he began to drop off again.

He thought about Domino and that was fine. Was she worth all this? The answer came back instantly. Yes. And how about the tape with the Chinese orgy? It was clear now. The man trying to kill her was with her the night he had been monitoring her. Why was she protecting him?

The worst of it passed and Sharky's mind began to clear again. His hand was a pulsating lump at the end of his arm. He tried to ignore it, to concentrate on Fat Boy.

There has to be a way to get the little asshole in here.

There is stupid! The slant-eyed bastards are the answer.

They don't speak English. Fat Boy speaks English. He has to hear you, right?

Right.

He rolled over with his back to the door, and reaching down with his good hand, he undid the belt buckle and then slowly, inch by inch, he slipped it through the loops. The belt fell loose and he relaxed a minute.

He was lying on his left side. The only way to get any leverage and keep his back to the door was to swing the belt with his crippled hand.

Jesus!

He pressed the end of the belt into his palm and, gritting his teeth from the pain, held it in place with his thumb. With his left hand he slowly wrapped the belt around his fist until about six inches were left. The heavy brass buckle hung on the end of the belt like a ball on the end of a mace.

One shot, kiddo, that's all you get. And don't forget Winkin, Blinkin, and Nod. They ain't gonna be hanging around sipping tea.

One thing at a time.

He had one shot and he had to make it good. If they got the belt, he was dead.

There was movement on the deck above him again. Winkin, Blinkin, and Nod were probably up there, doing their homework. Fat Boy was on the phone again. His voice was up a notch. More panic.

There were eight shots left in the Mauser, counting out the one he had used in the dark.

Two each for Winkin, Blinkin, and Nod.

One for Fat Boy.

One for the rope.

Go for it, kiddo. Go for the bomb. The clock's running out.

He heard Fat Boy hang up the phone. He was coming down the passageway. Sharky rolled over almost on his face. He slid one knee up under his leg.

Fat Boy was at the door. He was coming in.

Sharky moaned.

Fat Boy edged a little closer.

He groaned again, a little lower.

Fat Boy moved in.

"Help me," Sharky said, almost in a whisper.

From behind him he heard Fat Boy's voice, close to his ear, "The address, Sharky. Where is Domino? Tell me and I'll help you."

A little closer, Sharky thought. *A foot or two.*

"Domino?"

"Damn you!" Fat Boy said leaning closer, his lips wet with saliva, his frog eyes bulging with anger.

Sharky hunched his shoulders and with a massive effort, he rolled over, straightening his arm. The buckle snapped at the end of the belt. The belt whipped in a full arc and whooshed into the side of Kershman's nose. It burst like a raw egg. The bone shattered. Blood gushed out like water from a pump. The fat man

screamed in pain, his eyes bulging with horror as he saw
Sharky reach out and grab at his belt.

Sharky's fingers felt the butt of the gun, but the fat
man was reeling backwards. He clutched at it frantically, pulling it loose, but it fell from his hand. Sharky
lunged off the bunk to the floor and grabbed the automatic as Kershman grappled with the chair to keep his
balance.

Sharky could hear the Chins coming on the run. He
grabbed the gun, held it at arm's length straight up at
Kershman, saw the fear in his bleeding face.

"Please!" Kershman screamed as Sharky fired. The
bullet tore straight up through his chin, his mouth, and
into his brain. He went down on his back, his face
frozen in terror.

Sharky whirled, still holding the gun at arm's length,
held it an inch from the knot around his ankle, and
fired again. The heat from the blast scorched his ankle.
The rope disintegrated.

Liung swept through the door with the grace of a ballet dancer, his arm whipping up from his belt, the glint
of steel in his fist. Sharky fired, saw the disc sparkle
toward him, felt it rip through the top of his shoulder
and thud into the wall behind him. The bullet tore into
Liung's chest, jolted him, but did not stop him. He kept
coming, his hand swept to his belt again. Sharky felt the
Mauser jump and roar in his fist. He shot Liung in the
stomach. The Chin made no sound. Blood spurted from
both wounds. And he still came.

Jesus, it's like shooting an elephant!

His kneecap, idiot, his kneecap.

Sharky lowered the pistol and shattered Liung's kneecap with the next shot. He wobbled and fell straight forward, reaching out and grabbing Sharky's ankle. Sharky
thrust the Mauser an inch from Liung's temple and fired.
The Chinese died without a sound.

Five shots.

Three left.

He was on his feet when the second Chin charged the door. Sharky stepped over Kershman's body and tilted the table on end, dropping behind it as the Chin flung out his hand and sent three steel discs into the tabletop. Sharky raised on his knees and squeezed off a shot straight into the Chin's face, but he was moving too fast. It hit the corner of his jaw and tore half his ear off.

Two left.

The Chin leaped at him, kicked the table, split it in two as Sharky rolled over and slammed his back into the side of the bunk. The Chin rose over him, his hand raised, the fingers ridged, and started to chop down on him. The gun roared in Sharky's fist and the Chin's left eye exploded. He plunged over Sharky's head and died face down on the cot.

Sharky spun toward the door. The third one was there, his hooded eyes gleaming through the latticework, not six feet away.

One shot left.

Sharky swung the gun out, holding it with both hands, the belt still dangling from his ruined hand.

The Chin whirled and was gone. Sharky was on his feet. He jumped to the doorway and swung into the passage in time to see his adversary leap through the hatchway to the deck. Sharky ran to the bottom of the hatch ladder and stopped. He listened.

Nothing.

The Chin too was motionless. He had jumped up on the cabin roof and was poised there, over the hatch, every muscle tensed, his fingers curved in a classic karate pose. Waiting.

Sharky peered through the hatch and checked out the afterdeck. The Chin was not there. There was no place to hide. Against one railing there was a large emergency box. Two fuel tanks on the stern. Nothing else.

He looked overhead, wondering whether the Chin was up there. He had one shot left and the Chin had God knows how many of those whatchamacallit discs.

Sharky could take a chance, run out on the deck cowboy-style, and try to drop him with a John Wayne shot.

Suicide.

He had to get in close, put him away with one shot.

The Chin crept toward the bow of the boat, moving as soundlessly as a puff of smoke.

Sharky reasoned that the longer he waited, the slimmer the odds were. The Chin was trained to be patient. He could outwait Sharky until they were both too weak to walk. Sharky's patience was already running thin. If he missed with his last shot, the Chin could kill him with his big toe. He looked at the emergency box. Perhaps there was something in there he could use as a weapon. An ax, anything.

His finger began to throb. His nerves were screaming.

Go for the box. If it's empty, take your best shot and go overboard. Maybe the son of a bitch can't swim.

Sharky climbed to the top of the hatch ladder, hesitated for a moment, and then ran toward the emergency box. He looked back over his shoulder. The Chin was walking on the roof in the other direction, maybe sixty feet away. Sharky slid up to the box and flipped open the lid.

The Chin came after him like an antelope.

Sharky did a two-second inventory. Blankets, life preservers, flare gun, water bottles, radio . . . flare gun! He grabbed it and snapped it open. It was loaded.

The Chin leaped off the roof and landed running.

Sharky had to slow him down. He swung the pistol over the edge of the box and aimed at the biggest target he saw, the Chin's chest. The Mauser roared and Sharky heard the bullet thud home. The Chin was knocked sideways. He fell, sliding past Sharky into the stern railing.

Sharky's hand was shaking, his eyes were fogged with pain. He saw the Chin jump to his feet and he pointed the bulky flare pistol at him and fired. The flare spiraled out of the short barrel with a *chunk*. The Chin twisted as he fired and the blazing flare streaked across his chest, scorching his shirt, and ripped into the valve of one of the gastanks. The nozzle blew off, releasing a flood of gasoline. The gas hit the blazing flare and burst into flames. The Chin, distracted by the sudden fire, turned for an instant and as he did Sharky fired again. The second flare hit the Chin in the chest, shattered his ribs and lodged there, knocking him backward to the railing. He floundered there with the phosphorous flare shell sizzling in his chest and then plunged backwards into the lake. Sharky looked down into the dark water at the flare, still burning fiercely, its bubbles boiling to the surface, bursting into puffs of acrid smoke, as the Chin sank deeper into the lake, the glowing shell growing smaller and smaller.

A moment later the tank went.

The explosion knocked Sharky halfway across the deck. A ball of fire roared out of the ruptured tank and swept up into the mast and furled sails of the junk. The sails burst into flames.

Sharky ran from one side of the junk to the other, looking over the side. The motor launch was lashed to a floating pier.

The keys. Fat Boy had to have them. He raced to the cabin and leaped down the stairs. Kershman was still lying on his back, his crazed eyes staring at the ceiling.

Sharky ran the fingers of his good hand through the pockets and found not one but two sets of keys.

The other gastank blew up. Fire spewed out along the deck and poured through the hatchway. Sharky ran down through the main cabin and up the bow hatchway. He went over the side and dropped down to the pier.

The junk was burning like a piece of scrap paper. Bits of flaming sailcloth drifted out over Sharky's head and hissed into the lake. He tried the keys and finally found one that fit and cranked up the launch, jamming the throttle forward and twisting the wheel away from the blazing junk. The launch roared out into the lake, tearing the pier to pieces as it went.

Sharky did not look back. He flipped on the night lights and headed off into the darkness.

The high energy from the fight and the cold wind biting at him kept him alert. He found the main body of the lake and drove maniacally down its winding byways, keeping in the center of the lake to avoid debris along the shoreline. It was almost an hour before he saw the green light blinking on the end of the marina dock.

He pulled alongside and got out, tying the front of the launch down. It was easy to find Fat Boy's car, at that time of the year there were only half a dozen cars in the lot. He cranked it up and sat huddled in the front seat. A wave of dizziness shook him. *Hell,* he thought, *I've come this far, don't let me pass out now.* It passed and he flipped on the heater switch, slammed the gas pedal to the floor. The car screamed out of the lot.

He drove the seventy miles back to Atlanta in less than an hour.

All the lights in the house seemed to be on. Livingston had the front door open and was standing just inside it, his gun out, before Sharky got out of the car.

"Hold it right there," he yelled.

"It's me—Sharky."

"Sharky! Goddammit to hell, where you been? Where's The Nosh? What—"

Sharky reeled into the light from the doorway and Livingston swallowed the rest of the sentence.

"Jesus Christ, what happened to you?"

"You're not gonna believe me when I tell you. Is she all right?"

"Sure she's all r—"

Sharky stormed past him and into the house. Domino was coming out of the bedroom, her eyes puffy from lack of sleep.

"Oh, thank God," she said and then her face registered the shock as she saw his burned-out eyes blazing with pain and fury, his cheeks mottled with a two-day growth of beard, his shoulder ravaged and bleeding, the torn edge of a bloody rag hanging from his fist.

He stood in front of her, his body shaking from hypertension, fatigue, and anger.

Livingston kicked the door shut and put away his gun.

"What the hell happened, Shark?" he asked.

"The Nosh is dead," Sharky said. "They got him the same way they got Tiffany. Sawed-off shotgun . . ."

"I gotta call Friscoe right now. They been lookin' for you two all night."

"Don't call anybody yet."

"Where have you been?" Domino said. Tears were building up in her eyes.

"Where have I been? I'll tell you where I've been, lady. My best friend was ambushed. I been beat up, kidnaped, hauled out to a goddamn Chinese junk in the middle of the lake, had my finger chopped off by three wildass Chinamen. I've killed four people, blown up a boat, stolen a car. Shit, I've had a *great* night! And you know why? Because they want *you*, that's why."

His eyes danced crazily in his head.

"We've got to get you to a hospital," she said.

"A hospital. Shit, I don't need a hospital. I need answers. Who do you know has a Chinese junk? Who do you know has Oriental assassins doing his dirty work? Who do you know digs *Chinese orgies?* Your pal, Confucius, that's who. You lied to me. Told me the bastard went to Europe. Why? Don't you see it? He's the one behind it all, the one who's trying to kill you!"

He ripped the bloody bandage off his hand and held it out in front of her, the burned stump of his finger a foot from her eyes.

"Look at it. That's what they did to me."

She moaned and turned her face to the wall. He grabbed her by the shoulder and whirled her around. "Look at it. Don't turn your face away from me. That's what your life cost. That and a little guy who never hurt anybody in his life and ended up on a stinking tenement floor with his face blown off. And Tiffany, what about her?"

"Please stop," she cried.

"*Me* stop? These are the bastards you're protecting."

"Slow down, Shark," Livingston said, moving closer to him.

He turned to his partner and said, "The crazy thing is, we had it figured right, Arch. We were right on it. Scardi, the rip-off in Italy, Scardi's connection here. We had it by the ass." Then he turned back to Domino. "And we would've tied it up if you hadn't lied to me."

"No . . ."

"Bull*shit*. You told me that creep went to Europe, that he couldn't have had anything to do with it. If you had given me his name, leveled with me, The Nosh would be alive now. We could have taken the son of a bitch last night. But I trusted you. You told me . . . I believed you. Should have known better. Should have . . . Goddammit, are you so much in love with him that you're willing to—"

His fury exploded and he lashed out at her with the back of his good hand, slashing her across the face with such force that it knocked her back against the wall. Livingston grabbed his arm.

"C'mon, pal, you're acting like a jealous lover, for Christ's sake."

Sharky leaned against him. His hand was throbbing and he had a splitting headache. *Was that it, was he jealous?* He shook his head violently.

"No, nothing like that, nothing like that. Too many lies. Nobody's what they seem. All lies!"

"Shark, I gotta get you down. You need—"

"I need Scardi. And the motherless son of a bitch that brought Scardi in. I want them and if we can't take them legally, I'm gonna rip that cocksucker's heart out with my bare hands. *I need to get even!*"

He had turned back to Domino, glaring at her. Here was a Sharky she had never seen before. Gone was the roguish smile, the rough charm. In its place was a raw power that frightened her. Stripped of any elegance, finesse, cleverness, or caution.

He leaned against the wall, his knees shaking, turning to mud, his body wracked with chills, his mind teetering on the edge of insanity and bent on destruction, his strength coming from an almost carnal need for vengeance. The room began to swim around him.

He looked back at Domino.

"Who did you tell?"

"W-w-what?"

"Who did you *tell?* You told somebody about me.

That's how they knew. They were after me, goddammit. Don't you get it? They suckered me by setting up my best friend. They told him it was all right if *I* came with him. Not Arch, not Papa, or Friscoe. *Me*."

He jabbed his wounded hand at her. "You blew the whistle on me. You gave somebody my name."

He was shaking almost uncontrollably and he began to sweat again.

"They were gonna cut them off. Those crazy god-damn monkeys were gonna cut all my fingers off, one at a time, until I told them where you were. Can you believe that, hunh? Cut off all my fingers. Now *what's his name?*"

"Please," she said. She was crying hard. "Please, let us help you."

"Only one way to help me. Gimme the name. Just say it."

His fingers pressed into her arm.

"DeLaroza," she whispered. "Victor DeLaroza." It was all happening too fast. *Could Donald also be part of it? Of course—he had to be.* It was Donald she had given Sharky's name to, not DeLaroza. And yet, could there be an explanation? She needed time, time to reason it out.

Sharky began to sag, like a drunk losing control. It was almost an anticlimax, hearing it. "Shit," he said inanely. "Wouldn't you know it? I never even heard of the motherfucker." He looked at Livingston. "You gotta promise me, Arch, *promise* me you won't go after them without me. Tell Friscoe, tell him nobody's stealin' *my* melons this time."

"Sure, Shark, just take it easy."

"Promise me, damn it."

"I promise."

"Don't let him flush it at roll call. Make him hold off, okay?"

"Right."

"All I need . . . see, I need . . . couple hours sleep. . . ."

He took a step toward Livingston and his legs went. He sagged into the black man's arms.

"Shit, where's everybody going?" he said and passed out.

When Sharky awoke the first time, Twigs was sitting by the bed with his black bag open, taking his blood pressure. Sharky looked around the room and it was filled with fog. Vaguely, faces appeared and disappeared through the mist.

"What the hell you doin' here, Twigs?" Sharky said. "Am I dead?"

"Not quite. But I can't remember anybody recently who tried any harder."

"I'm okay. Just, uh . . . just . . ."

"Tired?"

"Yeah, that's it."

"Sure, just a little tired. In a state of shock. Blood pressure reads like a basketball score. Nothing at all."

He took a hypodermic needle out of the bag.

"Whatcha gonna do?" Sharky said fuzzily.

"Antibiotics. Also got to get a little snooze juice in you."

"Doandothat . . . gottastay . . . wake . . ."

"You got someplace to go at five in the morning?"

"Nawbdystealm'melons . . ."

"Sure."

"Arsh . . ."

"Right here, buddy."

"Doand . . . nuthin . . . outme. . . ."

"Right."

"Is he going to be all right?" Domino said.

"He's got the constitution of a horse. Didn't lose as much blood as I thought. Just keep him warm so he doesn't go into shock. If he makes it until noon he'll live forever."

"I'll keep him warm," she said.

He felt the needle enter his arm, felt the warmth from its fluid flooding his body. The room did a little dance for him and he faded out again.

He was dreaming. A crazy dream without form. Faces floated in and out of focus. The Nosh. The fat man on the junk. And Domino, like a face looking at him through smoke. He was on fire. And then suddenly he felt cold and began to shiver.

"It's all right, it's all right," she said, and he opened his eyes. There was only one light in the room, a lamp in the corner. He had a hard time separating light and shadow. Another chill passed over him.

"Easy," she said. She was talking softly and he felt her hands moving over his body.

"Cold," he said.

"It's alcohol," she said. "I'm trying to break your fever."

His lips felt scorched and his throat was like dust. He could hardly swallow.

She put her hand under his head and lifted him halfway up and held a glass of cold water against his lips. He gulped at it.

"Not too much," she said. She reached over to the night table, to a bowl of ice cubes, and wrapped one in a washcloth, holding it against his lips.

"Just suck on it," she said, and lowered his head back to the pillow.

She poured more alcohol in her hands and spread it

on his chest, moving her hands easily and lightly over his hot skin.

He closed his eyes. The fire was going out. He could feel it leaving his body.

"Hey," he said, without opening his eyes.

"Hey," she said back.

"Sorry."

"For what? Saving my life?"

"Slapping you. Dumb move."

"Please, it's all right."

"No. I think. . . ."

The words drifted off, as though he had fallen asleep. She touched his cheek, then his forehead. He seemed cooler. She started to move away but his fingers closed on her wrist.

"I thought you were asleep again," she said.

"No. What I think. I think maybe it was jealousy."

"Sharky, you don't—"

"You gotta understand about The Nosh. He shouldn't have even been—"

She put her fingertips to his lips.

"Don't please. Arch told me about him. I'm sorry. I'm so very, very sorry."

Tears flooded her eyes and she turned her face away from him. Her throat started to close up and she knew it would be difficult to say any more.

"Point is, gotta stop them, okay?"

"Oh, yes." She leaned back toward him and the tears dribbled down her cheeks and fell on his chest. He opened his eyes and looked up at her. Then he reached up and brushed them away with his thumb.

"Don't."

"I want to tell you about it. You have a right to know. It was like"—she swallowed and wanted to stop crying but the tears kept coming—"it was like . . ."

He pulled her gently down until her cheek lay against his chest. The tears poured down over him.

"He was very good to me. For a long time. And I felt . . . I couldn't believe he could . . . could . . ."

"All I wanted was the name. What happened . . . what was between you . . . none of my business."

"But I want it to be."

"Baby, I don't care."

"Oh, God," she said. "I just want it to be over. I want it to be over with them. I don't want to see Neil again. I—"

He rubbed her neck with a weak hand.

"Soon."

And he fell asleep again.

———————————

The room was dark. She had turned out the light. He reached over and felt her beside him and sighed.

"Do you need anything?" she said.

"Feeling better," he said. "Just pooped. What time is it?"

He felt her hand cross his chest and she moved close to him. For the first time he realized they were both naked. He put his hand on top of hers.

"Don't worry about the time."

"You feel good. Soft. And warm."

He felt her cold hand on his forehead.

"You've still got a little fever," she said. "But it's going down."

"Yeah."

She moved her hand on top of his and closed her fingers around it, squeezing it. Her head moved closer to him. He could feel her hair against the side of his face and he moved it closer to her.

"Thanks for taking care of me," he said.

"Ummm."

"I, uh . . ."

"Shhh."

"No."

"Go back to sleep."

"I want to tell you. I, uh . . . before I flake out again. About The Nosh. It's okay. Everything just got screwed up."

"Please. Go to sleep."

"Yeah. That time in the market, when I first talked to you, I, uh . . ."

He moved his head closer to her, and lying there in the dark, he began to drift again and a moment before he fell asleep he said, "I love you."

A light awakened him the next time. It was a thin shaft coming from the bathroom. He held up his wrist, but his watch was gone. Water was running. He stirred, reached out for Domino, but she was gone. Then he saw her, standing naked in the doorway of the bath, a washcloth in her hand.

"Your fever broke," she said. "I'm just drying you off."

She came to him, sat beside him, put the cold cloth on his forehead. She leaned over him, her breasts crushed against him. She kissed his throat, then his dry lips. Then she slipped into the bed beside him.

The shot was wearing off. Sharky forgot the pain in his hand, the fever, how tired he was. He put his arm around her and kissed her and she reached around and stroked his back and slid her hand down over his buttocks and drew him against her.

She smiled. "I think you're recovering," she said.

"If I'm not, this is as good a way to go as any."

"Better," she said.

She slid her leg up over his hip, moved her hand

around her back and down between her legs and touched him, stroked him, held him against her, and began moving slowly back and forth.

This time Sharky didn't fall asleep.

———————

"What time is it?"

"Four thirty."

"How long have I been laid out?"

"That's a terrible way of putting it."

"Yeah, right. How long have I been knocked out?"

"Almost twelve hours. How do you feel?"

"I think I may be able to get up."

"You did okay a few minutes ago."

"I mean on my feet."

"Okay, want me to help?"

"I need a shower."

"I gave you an alcohol bath for the fever. You smell like a baby."

"Need a shave."

"I shaved you."

"Need some decent clothes."

"Arch went by your place and brought some over."

"I sure rate, don't I?"

"Um hm."

"How about Friscoe? Papa?"

"They're waiting out there for you, in the living room."

"Are we still in the ballgame?"

"Do you think Arch would break a promise to a sick friend?"

"Tell them I'll be out in a minute."

———————

They assembled in Hazel's living room. All of them looked better. They had cleaned themselves up, had a little sleep, and recovered from the initial shock of The Nosh's death.

Sharky was wearing his only suit, a tweed, with a fawn-colored shirt and a dark brown tie.

"How come you brought my Sunday suit?" he asked Livingston.

"You're going to a party."

"A party?"

"We got a plan," Friscoe said.

"A plan?"

"You got a little catchin' up to do there, Sharky," Friscoe said. "First off, this DeLaroza ain't your every-day garden variety squirrel, know what I mean? I mean, this guy's big potatoes. He's powerful. He's got half the world by the ass. He's untouchable. And he's Siamese twins with Donald Hotchins."

"The senator?"

"Who's about to announce that he's running for pres-ident," Domino said.

"Jesus! What did we get into?"

"Well," Friscoe said, "that depends. On the one hand, we may come out with the roses. On the other hand, we may come out with our foot in a bucket of shit, pardon the French, ladies."

"Somebody catch me up," Sharky said. He was still feeling weak, like someone who has slept too long.

"Okay, I'll do the honors," Friscoe said. "First, see, we know we can pin Scardi to the Tiffany killing if we can collar him. Also The Nosh. Although we ain't found him yet, I think we can peg that one on him too because of the m.o. By the way, I scored a few baskets myself last night. That fag movie actor was makin' the bets at the Matador Club? Nailed *his* ass, too. Had him under the lights all fuckin' night, pardon the French, la-dies, and about nine this morning he starts singin' like Frank Sinatra. What it was, see, he was puttin' down bets for this guy Kershman who works for DeLaroza. A big shot. So we get our hands on this Kershman, we may be able to tie the can to DeLaroza's tail. Incidentally, there's another tie-in. The car you pinched to come back here with is registered to this Kershman."

"You got a description?" Sharky said. "What's he look like?"

Friscoe took out his notebook and flipped through several pages. "Here we go. Five-seven, two-ten, getting bald, slobby-lookin' guy, according to this actor. The actor, Donegan, he does the gay joints, picks up fresh meat, and delivers it to this Kershman's door, for which he gets paid more than you and me together. How do you like them apples?"

"I think we may have a little trouble as far as this Kershman's concerned," Sharky said. "If it's who I think it is, he's at the bottom of the lake with a hole in his head."

"He was one of them?" Livingston asked.

"A guy who fits that description was running the show. A real pig."

"Neat," Friscoe said. "See, the problem is, right now we ain't got diddly shit to tie this DeLaroza to *any*body. Everything we got, okay? is circumstantial. We know he knew this guy and that guy and he was here and he was there and he owned this and that and the other things. But nothing we can hang our hat on. Unless we grab Scardi, see, and he sings, DeLaroza's walkin' free from where I'm sittin'. He's, like, once removed from everything that came down."

"Who owns the junk?"

"DeLaroza's corporation. But he can always lay the whole thing off on Kershman. We need corroboration somewhere in here."

"Who did you tell about me?" Sharky asked Domino.

For a long moment they stared at each other. Domino felt his eyes burning into her soul.

"Donald Hotchins."

Sharky whistled. "So he's in it, too. And he's running for president?"

"Yeah," Friscoe cut in, "but also, shit, pardon the French, ladies, see, that's another thing, it's like a goddamn Chinese wastepaper basket. Domino was with Hotchins the night Tiffany got snuffed. Obviously he didn't know what was comin' down at that point. He must've got into it, see, after he got back."

"You were Hotchins's mistress?" Sharky said to Domino.

"Kind of."

"Neat company you keep."

"The pits," she said.

"Has anybody figured out why they were after you?" Sharky asked her.

Livingston said, "We got a couple of ideas. The way we put it together to here, Corrigon must've got on to DeLaroza some way. How, we don't know. Domino thinks the hit may have happened in front of DeLaroza's building and she saw Scardi putting Corrigon's stiff in a car. It was Halloween night, so the time jibes."

"I think it was more than that," Domino said. "I think they were afraid of me because of my association with both of them."

"So, where do we stand?" Sharky said.

"Where we stand, we ain't got nothin' on DeLaroza. We can put Scardi under if we can collar him. Hotchins? So far all he did was blow the whistle on you and fuck around a little. Sorry about that, little lady, but you know what I mean there. Anyways, we can't get to DeLaroza right now and if we turn this case over to that retard Hanson, he'll shit purple apples. The case'll flush and DeLaroza and Hotchins'll walk. We got to tie these three bastards together and make it stick."

"We got a plan," Livingston said. "Actually it was Domino who came up with it. DeLaroza has this amusement place inside his building. From what we hear it must be something. It's been on the TV news all day today. Tonight's the grand opening, a costume thing, see, with the big shots goin' formal. Now, supposing Domino shows up there. She has an invitation, so getting in is no problem. And maybe when they see her, they'll make a move against her."

"This was your idea?" Sharky said.

Domino nodded.

"It's too risky."

"That's what we all said."

"Thing is," Friscoe said, "if Kershman is out of it like you say—that leaves us in the shit pile with no fly-swatter. And if they get smart and get rid of Scardi, we can't stick them for even runnin' a stop sign. The best we can do, we go to Jaspers, lay it all out for him, give it to the Feds, and hope to hell they can make something out of it."

"No way!" Sharky snapped.

"So, her idea's the best thing we got goin' there, Shark," Friscoe said. "After tonight our string's run out. We're on borrowed time right now. Anybody tumbles to that junk, Abrams's body turns up, school's out."

"So what are we gonna do," Sharky said, "just stand around and hope they make a move?"

"We freak them," Livingston said.

"How?"

"I'll let them see me, then duck back in the crowd," Domino said. "If I do it often enough, they'll have to do something. I'll be in costume and you'll be in your Sunday suit with a little mask on. It'll be kind of fun."

"Fun! These people don't play for fun."

"Right," Friscoe said. "And judging from some of their moves the last few days, they ain't afraid to take big chances. Sharky, you stick to her like Elmer's glue. We'll have you wired, and Arch and I will be in the lobby if anything breaks loose. Papa's gonna try crashing the gate so he can back you up. Anything happens, we'll be in there like the fuckin' Marines."

"I don't know . . ." Sharky said.

"Well, let's make up our minds, troops, because we got about two hours to show time. After that, it's give it to Jaspers and collect unemployment."

29

Enormous arc spotlights swept back and forth in front of Mirror Towers, their beams reaching up into a clear, star-filled sky. Live TV cameras rested on tripods beside a red carpet that stretched from the curb in front of the building to the blazing entrance to *Pachinko!*

Celebrities had started arriving at six for a private cocktail party in DeLaroza's penthouse. The regular guests had begun arriving even earlier and now they began filing into the four elevators for the trip to the magic gates of the amusement atrium.

Newsmen crowded around Donald Hotchins as he got out of the black limousine. His wife, Elena, remained in the back seat as usual, waiting for the furor to die down. She hated the public spectacle, hated the press, hated everything about politics.

Hotchins seemed the perfect politico, his longish

blond hair flopping casually over his forehead, his broad smile radiating sincerity. He seemed even taller and more handsome than usual in the elegance of a tuxedo.

As he got out of the car into a volley of popping flashbulbs and a phalanx of microphones, all thrust in his face, DeLaroza moved through the crowd of reporters to shake his hand.

"Is it true, Senator, that you're going to make an announcement later this evening?" one of them asked.

"Well, why don't we wait for a little while and see?" Hotchins said, still grinning. "By the way this is Victor DeLaroza. You ought to get to know him. You'll be seeing a lot of him in the future."

"So you are going to be making a statement then?" someone else asked.

"Wait another hour or so," Hotchins said good-naturedly. "I've never missed a deadline yet."

The press contingent laughed and moved back as the senator helped his wife from the sedan. She smiled coolly at DeLaroza, who nodded back, and then led the Hotchinses along the red carpet toward *Pachinko!*

She appeared older than Hotchins, a stunning woman, tall and straight, although somewhat stern-looking and formal. She had silver-gray hair and the kind of features the magazines sometimes call handsome. She was wearing a glittering white gown and a full-length lynx coat.

As they approached the entrance Hotchins saw through the crowd a woman standing near the doorway, her face inscrutable behind a waxen full-face mask with high, bright-red cheekbones and a thin slash of mouth. She was wearing a gold full-length mandarin dress with a blazing red sun in the midsection and her eyes seem to follow him through the slanted cutouts in the mask. He looked back as he entered the building. There was something disquieting about her.

"So that's the pair," Sharky said, as the Hotchins party boarded one of the bullet-shaped elevators to be whisked up to DeLaroza's penthouse.

"He looked back at me," Domino said, her voice muffled by the mask. "I was afraid for a minute he might have recognized me."

"Maybe the gown attracted him," Sharky said. "It's gorgeous."

"It came from Hong Kong," she said.

"Now, why doesn't that surprise me?" They entered the lobby and mingled with the crowd waiting for the elevators to *Pachinko!* They were a strange couple, Sharky in his tweed suit and black eye mask, Domino in the shimmering gold gown, with the eerie waxen disguise covering her entire face.

"You sure you want to go through with this?" Sharky asked.

"Too late to stop now," she said. "Besides, I have a little getting even to do myself."

The elevator opened at the top of Ladder Street and Sharky and Domino stepped out into a carnival of sight and sound.

Several hundred visitors had already arrived and the enormous atrium was crowded. Jugglers roved the steps of Ladder Street, tossing fire sticks back and forth. Music seemed to swell from every doorway. Traveling hucksters offered postcards and trinkets. The smell of barbecuing chicken and ribs drifted up from the food stalls.

"Look for Papa. He should be close to the top of the steps," Sharky said.

The place made him nervous. Too big. Too many

people. It was more dangerous than he had imagined.

Papa was standing in front of the first food stall, nibbling a rib. He was not wearing a mask.

"Have any trouble getting in?" Sharky asked him.

"Naw. I could crash a kindergarten party and get away with it."

"Where's your mask?"

"There's some things even I won't do for the department."

"The place is bigger than I thought," Sharky said.

"Worry you?"

"A little."

"Not me. Easier to keep an eye on her. Harder for them to spot you."

"Maybe you're right."

"You feeling okay?" Papa asked.

"I'm fine." Only Domino knew that they had stopped at Grady Hospital on the way to the opening, where Twigs had given Sharky a shot of speed. "You gonna become a junkie now that you're off the Narcs?" Twigs asked him. "I just want to stay awake tonight," Sharky had answered. The stuff was good. He felt strong and alert and his maimed finger was just a dull ache at the end of his arm.

"You got everything down pat?" he asked Domino.

"Sure," she said.

"Remember, if I tell you to do anything, do it. Don't ask questions, I may not have time to explain."

"Yes, sir," she said and threw a mock salute.

"And knock that shit off too, pardon my French, ladies."

"I think Friscoe's cute," she said.

"He's as peaceful as a split lip," Papa said.

"We'll go to the bottom of Ladder Street, check out the radio mikes. Could be a lot of interference in here. Put your hearing aid in your ear."

"It's uncomfortable," Papa said.

"Put it in anyway. Let's be ready when they get down here."

———————————

Friscoe and Arch were outside, standing apart from the crowd in a doorway to keep out of the wind gusting from the plaza. Sharky's voice came over the walkie-talkie loud and clear.

"This is Vulture One to Vulture Two. You read?"

"This is Vulture Two," Papa answered. "Loud and clear."

"Vulture One to Nest. We coming in okay?"

"You're coming in clear," Friscoe answered. "What's it look like up there?"

"Bigger than the Astrodome," Sharky answered. "The place is unbelievable."

"Well, enjoy. It's colder than . . . uh, it's very cold down here."

"Okay, let's stay loose. They ought to be here any minute."

———————————

In the crowded penthouse Hotchins eased DeLaroza out on the balcony.

"What about Domino?" he asked.

"Nothing. I have not heard from Kershman all day. But then, it has been quite a day, eh? Besides, this Sharky was proving more stubborn than we planned."

"I'm worried. If she's in police custody they probably know everything by now."

DeLaroza smiled confidently. "Do not fall apart now. What does she know? Nothing. Relax. Enjoy yourself. Within an hour we will have disposed of another problem—and given the police their killer at the same time."

"I hope there are no more mistakes," Hotchins said.

"I don't make mistakes," DeLaroza said vehemently. "I correct them."

"I hope you do," Hotchins said, and went back to the party.

DeLaroza walked along the balcony to his bedroom and took the private elevator down to his office. Chiang was waiting for him.

"You know how to accomplish this?"

Chiang nodded.

"Remember. He is fast and deadly. Forget his age. He hears like a rabbit and strikes like an asp. When you move, do it quickly. You will not have a second chance."

Chiang nodded again.

"Do not move the body until everyone has left. It would be dangerous with all these people about."

"*Hai.*"

"*Joy shan.*"

"*Dor jeh.*"

He moved silently out of the room. DeLaroza returned to the party and began herding the guests toward the door.

"All right," he said. "It is time for *Pachinko!*"

In the guest suite Scardi was painstakingly painting a clown face over his own features. He had been cooped up too long, first on the junk, then in this fancy prison cell. He had to get out, hear people, feel like part of the human race again. This would be perfect. He was wearing an outrageous clown suit, red-and-white striped with large red wool buttons. With his face painted no one could possibly recognize him and so he felt safe going to the opening.

He had finished applying the white chalk base and

the blue mouth and was painting large, round eyes when the door chimed.

It startled him. He slid open the top dresser drawer and eased out the .22 Woodsman. He held it down at his side as he went to the front door and peered through the viewer.

That damned Chink.

The Chinese was holding a silver tray with a bottle of red wine, a glass, a corkscrew, and a note. He opened the door. The note was addressed to Howard and he took it to the bedroom to read it, keeping an eye on Chiang in the dresser mirror as he did.

The note said:

> Have a pleasant evening. The wine is on me.
> Victor.

Damned white of him. He returned to his task, leaning over the dresser, close to the mirror, as he completed his makeup. He kept watching the Chinese.

Chiang was twisting the corkscrew into the bottle of wine and as he popped the cork out, the bottle slipped from his grasp. He snatched it up quickly, but several ounces gurgled from the neck, splashing down over the carpet.

"Shit! You clumsy fuckin' slant-eye!" Scardi snapped. Chiang entered the bedroom, bowing in apology and pointing toward the bathroom.

"Keep away from me," Scardi snarled. He stood near the dresser, his hand beside the .22, as Chiang pointed toward the bathroom and rubbed his hands together.

"You wanna towel, you ignorant gook? Go ahead. I ain't cleaning up your mess for you."

Chiang went into the bathroom, took a towel, and held it under the cold water and then began to wring it out. As he squeezed out the cold water he reached up into his sleeve with two fingers and drew out a thin steel tube about five inches long. It was no thicker than a pencil. He pressed a button on its base and a pointed shaft that looked like a short icepick shot from the handle. He held it under the towel and started back.

Scardi was still leaning over the dresser when he heard the faint click from the bathroom. He almost let it pass, but then it ran back through his mind, an instant replay of the sound, and the memory of it rushed back at him from the past.

A switchblade. The fuckin' Chink had a switchblade!

He grabbed for the Woodsman as Chiang came out of the bathroom, let the wet towel fall to the floor as he entered the bedroom, and took a single swift step toward Scardi. His arm arced from the waist, swept up toward Scardi's chest, the steel sliver gleaming in his fist. Scardi moved quickly, made a feinting move to the left, and then reversed himself and fell sideways, swinging the .22 up as he did.

The icepick was already committed. It missed its mark by six inches, plunging into Scardi's side low, just under the ribs, and piercing up deep inside him. The point stopped an inch from Scardi's heart.

Scardi screamed and jammed the pistol into Chiang's neck. He fired and the bullet shattered Chiang's Adam's apple, ripped through his jugular vein and came out the back of his neck. A geyser of blood burst from the wound.

Chiang staggered backwards, but Scardi pressed after him, twisting the pistol slightly, jamming it back in the wound, and firing again. The second bullet tore up through the back of Chiang's head and shattered his brain.

Scardi shoved the Chinese servant over backward on the bed, where he fell with his hands stretched out at his sides. Scardi shot him three more times, twice in the face and once in the heart.

The pain was like a hot needle deep inside Scardi's chest. He gasped for breath, reached down, felt the handle of the dirk sticking in his side, and pulled it out. He dropped the weapon on the floor and leaned forward, clutching his side, pressing in, trying to squeeze the pain away. He could feel it, feel the burning puncture sapping his strength.

He sat on the edge of the dresser, steadying himself with both hands. He examined the clown suit. He could hardly tell where the instrument had pierced the cloth. He went into the bathroom and unzipped the costume and examined the wound itself, a small, round hole beginning to swell at the edges. A pearl of blood appeared and winked obscenely at him. He carefully folded a washcloth and held it against the hole like a bandage and wrapped a towel around his waist to keep it in place.

He went back to the dresser. Pain came at him in waves, burning inside him. Sweat had begun to erode his makeup. Red tears etched their way down his chalky cheeks into the corners of his mouth.

The bastard, that filthy bastard, try this after all these years . . .

The fury raged inside him again, welling up, giving him new strength. His hate was a passion. For thirty years he had listened to DeLaroza bragging, flaunting their combined wealth, taking credit. For what? *For what?* The whole scheme had been his idea, not DeLaroza's. Scardi had invented La Volte. Scardi had gone in, done the legwork, taken the chances in the beginning. Scardi had set up the dummy hit at the lake, put the fix on Corrigon, arranged to transport the gold across the Alps into Switzerland.

It wasn't for me, he'd be nothin'. A fuckin' bank

clerk in Ohio someplace. Shit, he didn't even know he was a fuckin' thief until I saw it in him. A baby blue goddamn captain with no future.

He slipped the clip out of the .22 and replaced it with a fresh one. There were two more in the drawer and he put them in the pocket of the clown suit.

Got to stay up, he said to himself. *Got to stay on my feet long enough to find that fat bastard. Try to put the cross on me. Shit. Shit! I made him. Me, Scardi.*

"I made you, you fat gutless sonofabitch . . ." he screamed aloud.

He opened the small box on the dresser. Three red devils left. He popped two in his mouth and swallowed them without water.

An instant later they jolted him, setting all his nerves on edge, intensifying the pain in his chest beyond bearing. He put the back of his hand over his mouth and screamed again.

Then it was gone, replaced by the soaring rush of the speed. It cleared his vision, replaced the pain with a pure and driving hate. He snapped the silencer on the ugly snout of the Woodsman and slipped it inside the clown suit. Then he took his invitation and headed for *Pachinko!*

Scardi picked his spot carefully, with the same instincts, the same planning, that had kept him alive for forty-five of his sixty years in a business where death was as common as winter flu.

Several factors dictated his choice of position. First, accessibility to the victim. He wanted a clean head shot. The .22 Woodsman had a specially designed eight-inch barrel with a Colt-Elliason rear sight and a ten-shot clip. The weapon was deadly up to seventy or eighty yards. With the silencer Scardi knew he could probably get off two, possibly three shots undetected. One would be sufficient, two ideal.

Second, he checked the pedestrian traffic patterns, looking for a place he could get in a clean shot without a lot of people around.

Finally, he looked for an escape route. It would be

tough, escaping from *Pachinko!*, since it was accessible by elevator only. But there had to be a fire escape, a stairwell somewhere.

His *modus operandi* did not include trapping himself.

He stood on the balcony overlooking *Pachinko!* orienting himself, studying every inch of the place through pain-clouded eyes.

He was standing with his back to the western wall of the building, looking down into the atrium. To his left was Ladder Street, winding down six stories to the park's main floor, where it became the main thoroughfare of *Pachinko!*, ending at the gardens. To his right were the shallow pond and the Tai Tak Restaurant. In the far corner to his left was the entrance to the pinball ride and in the far corner to his right Tiger Balm Garden. Below him was the entrance to the underground Arcurion tour of historic Hong Kong.

There were three side streets in *Pachinko!* One was Prince Avenue, which ran perpendicular to the main street, starting at the foot of Ladder Street, and terminated at the giant figure of Man Chu, the robot who operated the ride. A second street, Queen Road, paralleled Prince Street near the gardens. A narrow alley connected them, the stores on its eastern side built up to the far wall of the atrium.

The alley was virtually empty. Few of the guests who jammed the spectacular complex had discovered it yet. Only two stores on the alley had been completed. One was a petshop about halfway between Prince and Queen. The other was on the western corner of the alley and Prince Street, a trinket shop with a stall in front.

Perfect.

Scardi guessed Hotchins and DeLaroza would come down Ladder Street, turn into Prince, and go to the pinball ride. They would pass within fifteen feet of the alley. From the corner, hidden by the trinket stalls, Scardi

could get off a couple of good head shots and escape
down the alley.

And then what?

He continued to study the far side of the atrium
floor. Then he saw the fire door. It was located on
Queen Street between the alley and the wall.

The fire door provided his escape route. Scardi also
reasoned that there would probably be an access door
from the playing field of the ride to the fire stairs. If
necessary he could enter the main floor of the ride and
escape through the tunnels that led to the first floor. A
risky trip, particularly for a wounded man, but an out
nevertheless in case the stairway itself was blocked by
police or security guards.

The wound burned deeply, but Scardi went over the
plan two more times in his head before he was satisfied.

Scardi smiled. He *was* satisfied. It was a daring plan,
but he had pulled off worse. And even if he didn't, he
was certain now that he could put a bullet in DeLaroza's brain before he died himself.

Hotchins had been introduced with glowing plati-
tudes by the state's senior senator, Osgood Thurston.
Hotchins's speech was short and to the point, a straight-
forward declaration that he was running for president
and running to win, for the guests had come to play, not
to listen to political speeches. The press would have its
chance at him later at the press conference.

Five minutes, that's all it would take.

He was halfway through the announcement when he
saw her the first time. A face in the sea of masks, staring up at him, smiling cryptically.

He floundered, lost his place as panic seized him. He
smiled at the crowd, regained his composure, and when
he looked back she was gone.

A moment later he saw her again, this time staring enigmatically from between the posters in a display in front of one of the booths.

Again, a few moments later, from farther down in the crowd.

He went on, losing track of what he was saying, flashing that smile, inventing lines, frantic to get it over with. For sixteen years he had savored the anticipation of this moment. Now it was here and he was seized with terror.

Domino was out there, in that crowd of masked revelers, taunting him.

He finished with relief, backing away from the podium, his bandwagon supporters crowding around him, raising his arms over his head. Lowenthal, Thurston, three governors, the mayor, five congressmen, a dozen state legislators, several bankers, and two of the nation's most powerful labor leaders.

The crowd was cheering wildly as the band struck up a furious version of "Georgia on My Mind." Flashbulbs and strobes blinded the dignitaries, and movie and television cameras swept the crowd, capturing its lusty reaction to their favorite son's entry into the campaign.

Only DeLaroza read the fear in Hotchins's eyes.

He pulled him aside after the furor had died away.

"What is the matter with you?" DeLaroza demanded.

"She's down there," Hotchins said. He was trembling.

"What are you talking about?"

"She's in that crowd. She's *leering* at me!"

"Who?"

"Domino. She's here. In this place."

"You are going to pieces. She would never take such a chance."

"I'm telling you, Domino is out there. She's trying to rattle me and she did it."

"Listen to me," DeLaroza said, "we have only to walk down that stairway and over to the entrance of the ride and get in that steel ball and then you will be finished here. I assure you, she will not be at the press conference."

"I'm not going down there."

"You are most certainly going down there. The cameras, the reporters, the public, they are all waiting for us. Everyone who sees you on television riding in an amusement park will identify with you. It is something everyone can relate to. You are not backing out now."

He grabbed Hotchins's arm and led him down into the crowd, bodyguards and security men forming a wedge through the mob, leading them down through the noisy bazaar.

They had gone a few steps when Hotchins saw the sketch. He pulled free of DeLaroza and rushed to the artist.

"Who is that?" he demanded, pointing to the easel. "When did you do this sketch?"

"Just before the speeches," the young artist stammered.

"Where did she go. Which way?"

The artist waved his arm toward the crowd.

"Out there somewhere, sir. She said she'd come back later and pick it up."

"What was she wearing?" DeLaroza demanded.

"Wearing?"

"What kind of *clothes* was she wearing?"

"Uh . . . I was concentrating on her face, y'know. Uh, gold gown. That was it, a gold gown. Big splash of red right here in the middle."

Hotchins remembered the woman at the entrance, the eyes following him from behind the impenetrable mask.

"It was her downstairs. I knew it. I knew there was something . . ."

DeLaroza was urging him along the stairs.

"Smile. Wave at the crowd. We are surrounded by guards. You have nothing to worry about."

"I have *her* to worry about!"

Like Scardi, Sharky too had devised a daring scheme, one designed to unnerve Hotchins, and it was succeeding. He and Domino had moved to the rear of the crowd. Now, as the spectators turned from the speaker's platform to walk down Ladder Street, they were leading the way into Prince Avenue. At the end of the street, the glowering figure of Man Chu waited ominously to send Hotchins and DeLaroza on the first official spin through the pinball machine. Photographers were jockeying for position and TV cameramen were eagerly setting up their tripods.

It had worked like a charm. Domino had put the mask on the back of her head and faced Sharky. Every time Hotchins looked in her direction, Sharky had turned her around facing him and then, the instant his eyes were averted, had turned her quickly back around, so that when Hotchins looked up again he saw only the expressionless mask.

They had moved through the crowd, trying the trick a dozen times or so, and Sharky was sure Hotchins had seen her at least three or four times.

Now for the cherry on the sundae. Hotchins and De-Laroza moved toward the robot. When the two were safely inside the steel car, with the guard rail snapped shut and the door secured, Domino would step out of the crowd and call each of them by name. The last thing they would see before plunging down into the dazzling interior of the ride would be Domino.

Sharky hoped they would try something desperate. As they started up Prince Avenue, Sharky lowered his head slightly and spoke into the microphone pinned on the back of his lapel.

"How you doin', Vulture?"

Papa's answer crackled in his hearing aid.

"Right behind them. Hotchins's flipping. May not work, but he ain't gonna sleep tonight."

"Stay close."

"Gotcha."

On the street below, Friscoe and Livingston stamped their feet and tried to control their excitement, waiting for something to break loose. They anticipated the unexpected and it was about to happen.

Scardi was in position. Waiting.

So far, so good. The alley was almost empty. Twenty, thirty people milling about.

The crowd was moving up Prince Avenue, choking the street from storefront to storefront. He could see DeLaroza's bald head and flaming red beard through the mass of people, moving toward him.

He checked the alley again. The people were beginning to move toward him, attracted by the noise of the approaching crowd.

At the far end of the alley a mime on stilts, dressed like Uncle Sam, stalked around the corner and started awkwardly toward him.

The wound was numb now. His chest no longer pained him. His life was ebbing away, trickling down his leg. He looked down at the clown suit, at the crimson stain, widening, seeping down over his hip toward his thigh.

He leaned closer to the wall, peering around the corner and over the stall of souvenirs. He slipped the last red devil in his mouth, waiting for its surge, suddenly feeling himself growing taller, more confident.

Come on, you bastard, just a little closer. He zipped down the clown suit and reached inside, felt the comforting grip of the Woodsman, drew it out, and folded his arms across his chest with the gun concealed, the snout pressed up into his armpit.

You pipsqueak little nothin'. A fuckin' G.I. that I turned into a millionaire. What a fool, to think you could kill the old pro.

The speed surged through his blood, cleared his vision. He checked out the people in the front of the crowd, looking for telltale signs. Cops. Bodyguards. Security guards. He could always tell them by their eyes, by the way they checked everywhere.

His gaze fell on the woman in the gold gown. She was walking straight toward him. He stared into her face. There was something familiar there. Did he know her? Was it someone who could identify him? He panicked for a moment, then remembered the clown face. Nobody could see through that clown face.

And yet . . .

He concentrated on the face again. She was twenty feet away, bearing down on him. He dipped into his memory and then it began coming to him. Slowly. A photograph. That was it, a photograph. A photograph he had studied for hours.

And then it hit him.

Domino!

Domino?

No. It couldn't be. She was dead. He had seen her face explode in front of his shotgun, seen her brains hit the wall. Domino was dead.

"You're dead," he muttered. He started backing away from her. "You're dead," he repeated.

Domino saw him before Sharky did, a terrifying sight. His face had dissolved, paint melting into a surrealistic glob of red and blue and chalky white. The ridiculous clown suit was stained blood red. His eyes were mad with fever. He was backing away from her. Saying something.

"Sharky?"

"I see him," Sharky said and stepped in front of her.

"He's saying something."

The crowd pressed them toward him.

"He's saying . . . Jesus, he's saying 'You're dead' over and over," Sharky said.

He looked hard into the crazed face, at the hawk nose, the pointed chin, the pig eyes. Then he saw the gun in his hand, the Woodsman.

"Jesus," he yelled, "it's Scardi!"

The clown turned and ran.

Sharky shoved Domino into the doorway of the store on the corner.

"Stay here. Put on the mask, don't let Hotchins and DeLaroza see you."

"But—"

"It's Scardi, don't you understand? He's all we need."

He yelled into the mike:

"Papa, the store on the corner of the alley. Cover Domino!"

"On my way."

"I've spotted Scardi!"

On the street the name shocked Friscoe and Livingston into action.

"Shit," Friscoe cried out.

"Let's roll," Livingston said.

Scardi ran down the alley, shoving people aside, plunging between the stilted legs of Uncle Sam. The mime teetered and plunged forward into an awning over the petshop, crashed through it, and fell on top of several cages. They split open and the alley was suddenly alive with yapping Maltese and Pekingese dogs.

Sharky charged through the madhouse, stepping over

the wreckage of the awning. Uncle Sam was struggling to his knees, his six-foot pantlegs straggling out behind him.

"You okay?" Sharky yelled at him.

"I would be if I could get these damn pants off."

Sharky went on, racing to the end of the alley. He stepped cautiously into Queen Street and looked both ways. The street came to a dead end at the wall on his left. To his right it was clogged with merrymakers. No sign of Scardi. He walked past the first few shops, looking in through the windows.

Nothing.

The bleeding clown had vanished.

Scardi stood inside the fire door for a few moments gasping for breath. He had caught a glimpse of a big guy in a tweed suit running after him. A cop? Some irate guest? He didn't care. He saw the door on the landing below, the door that led out onto the giant pinball playing field. His escape route.

He leaned against the wall and staggered down to the landing, pulled the door open, and stepped over the spring-loaded guard rail that surrounded the tilted board.

It was like walking into his own nightmare. All around him, reflected on the mirrored walls, the Mylar ceiling, were grinning Orientals. They towered over him, mocking him, strobe lights flashing from their slanted eyes, colors kaleidoscoping from their rubber bodies, electricity humming through the springs that wound around their bases. He was hypnotized by the fantasy garden, by the flashing lights, and he lurched crazily out among them like a somnambulist.

The upper part of the board was adjacent to the bottom of Ladder Street, separated from it by a wall of mirrors and plywood. Near the top over a narrow chute with bumpers on both sides, was the control booth for the ingenious ride. The operator, who controlled the speed of the ball, was too busy to notice the madman strolling through the maze of bumpers and chutes and tunnels. He had checked out all the controls. Everything was ready.

He picked up an intercom phone. "Okay," he said, "let 'er roll."

———————————————

From the safety of the trinket shop Domino and Papa watched DeLaroza and Hotchins climb into the six-foot steel sphere. An attendant pulled the guard bar up and locked it across their laps.

The press was having a field day, shooting pictures, ordering the candidate and the owner of the spectacle to wave, smile, shake hands with the mob that crowded around.

From deep inside the infernal machine, the operator pressed the start button.

The steel ball began its descent.

The crowd was cheering, lining up to be next.

The ball plunged down into the tunnel.

———————————————

Sharky had walked up Queen Street almost to the main thoroughfare and then turned and started back. Scardi was close by, he could feel it, sense the evil of the man. But where?

He walked back toward the end of the street. Then he saw the fire door, discreetly marked, camouflaged by shrubbery.

He ran down the street to the door, waited a moment, listening, drew his Mauser, and then, shoving the door open, jumped inside and cased the stairwell.

Empty.

Bloody footprints led down the stairs to the other door. He followed them, waited for a second, and pulled the door open.

A moment after the operator had ordered the ride to begin he looked up and saw Scardi, wandering like a lost child among the field of flashing bumpers.

"Hey, you!" he screamed. "Get outa here, you crazy fool!"

The bleeding apparition kept coming toward him.

"Oh, my God," he cried, "get outa there. The goddamn ball's coming!"

He snatched up the emergency phone.

Scardi shot him in the head.

The operator fell to the floor. Scardi could hear the rumble as the ball began its descent. It boomed out of the tunnel at the upper end of the game, spiraled around the giant playing surface, and rolled out onto the board, struck the first bumper, bounced away from it in a blaze of lights and clanging bells. It sped toward the top of the field, ricocheting off the guard rail into another bumper.

From inside the ball, DeLaroza saw the grinning face of Shou-Lsing, god of long life, grinning down at him as the steel car struck the springs around its base and bounced away, spinning around on its ball bearings, rolling toward another. It was picking up speed as it hit another bumper and another, jerking him and Hotchins from one side of the seat to the other. The ball sped past the control booth and he looked up.

There was no one in it!

"My God!" he cried out.

"What's the matter?"

"There's no one at the controls, no one to brake us."

The ball struck another bumper and reeled away from it, spinning on its axis, and rolled into one of the narrow funnel-like bunkers, slowing as it went through the tight passageway.

At the other end Scardi was standing in a dueling position, his side facing the ball, his hand held straight out, aiming his pistol at DeLaroza.

DeLaroza's eyes bulged as he saw the assassin standing there, waiting to kill him.

He released the catch on the side of the guard bar and jumped out of the ball. Hotchins, confused and dizzy, tried to follow.

Something hit him in the chest, knocking him back into the car. The guard bar snapped back, trapping him inside. Hotchins looked down at his shirt front, saw the tiny hole there, reached up very slowly, and touched it.

Blood spurted from the hole and cascaded down his dress shirt.

The ball rolled out of the bunker, struck another bumper, and bounded away amid clanging bells. Hotchins sighed and fell over sideways in the seat.

DeLaroza dragged himself to his feet. His ankle was twisted, the knees torn out of his tuxedo. He ran, limping, and ducked behind one of the bumpers.

Scardi was oblivious to the ball careening from bumper to bumper around him. It whisked past him, almost knocked him down. He had one purpose now. Nothing else mattered.

"Howard, for God's sake, listen to me!" DeLaroza screamed. He was backing up, trying to keep the bumper between himself and Scardi.

"Don't call me that!" Scardi cried out. "I ain't Howard. I ain't Burns. I'm Scardi. I made you. You hear me, Younger? You was nothin' but a dumb goddamn dogface. I gave you all this."

He stepped from behind the bumper and fired at De-

Laroza. The bullet hit the wall and one of the mirrors burst into dozens of reflecting shards.

DeLaroza turned and ran, aimlessly, dodging amid the grinning statues and flashing lights.

The pinball, totally out of control and roaring across the playing field, struck its last bumper, lurched over the floor, leaped the guard rail, and crashed through the wall.

The mirror exploded into millions of splinters. The wall shattered as the steel ball burst through it and rolled out at the foot of Ladder Street, struck one man and sent him reeling back up the steps, rolled over another, crashed into a shop at the bottom of the street and ripped through it, bursting out onto the main thoroughfare amid a shower of dolls, bracelets, and postcards.

The crowd scattered, falling over each other, as the antic pinball smashed through it, tossing people into the air like tenpins, ripping the marquee off the puppet theater before it tore through the wall at the edge of the man-made lake and soared out over the water. It plunged down onto one of the sampans, split it in half, and hit the lake, sending a geyser twenty feet in the air, before it finally rolled to a stop.

DeLaroza limped toward the gaping hole in the wall. Scardi aimed and shot him in the thigh. He fell forward, hit the springs at the base of a bumper, and was thrown like a rag doll almost to Scardi's feet.

The killer looked down at the battered DeLaroza. He calmly snapped a fresh clip into the pistol.

DeLaroza crawled to his knees. Across the floor he saw a man standing in the emergency doorway, watching the mad scene.

"Help me," he yelled. "Please, help me."

The man in the doorway yelled back to him.

"My name's Sharky. Hear that, DeLaroza? *Sharky!*"

DeLaroza moaned. He looked back at Scardi. The assassin was standing over him, grinning, aiming the pistol down at him. The gun thunked once, twice, three times, and the bullets tore into DeLaroza's chest. He screamed once and slumped forward, his head resting on its forehead in front of his knees, like a man in prayer.

Grinning maniacally, Scardi leaned forward and shot him again in the back of the head.

"Okay, Scardi, that's enough," Sharky said.

The mad clown turned toward him. Sharky stepped over the railing and started for him.

"Drop the gun, Scardi," Sharky called to him. "Police."

The word seemed to trigger Scardi's dying energy. He scrambled through the ragged hole in the wall, crawling through broken glass and splinters of plywood, out into the main floor of *Pachinko!*

He got up and, half-running, half-staggering, made for the opposite end of the atrium. The crowd scattered as he waved his gun madly at them, clearing a path for him. Ahead of him he saw the gates of Tiger Balm Gardens. He struggled toward them.

Sharky stepped through the hole and went after him, slowly, deliberately. There was no rush now. There was no place for Scardi to go.

On the stairs above him, Friscoe and Livingston saw Sharky stalking the frenzied killer.

Sharky saw them too and held his hand up at them.

"He's mine," he said coldly.

"Scardi?" Friscoe asked.

"It's Scardi," Sharky said, still following after him.

"You gotta take him alive," Friscoe yelled. "We need him."

"Not anymore," Sharky said.

Scardi stumbled into the gardens, rushing blindly away from his pursuer. He slashed through the shrubs and flowers, scrambling up into the protection of the rocks and crevices. He fell against the side of the cliff at the far end of the gardens, looking back toward the street.

The tall guy in the tweed suit kept coming. And coming. He was taking his time. Scardi fired a shot at him, half-heartedly, and it thunked harmlessly into one of the gates.

He turned and crawled frantically on his hands and knees, up, up, deeper into the crevices of the Tiger Balm. Every move now was agony. His sight was going. Every breath screeched through his tortured lungs. There was hardly enough blood left to sustain his frenetic flight.

Sharky walked into Tiger Balm Gardens, stepped over the fence, and followed resolutely after the mobster.

The silenced pistol spewed and dust kicked up in front of Sharky. He did not duck, did not dodge to one side or the other. He kept going, straight ahead, closing in.

Scardi dragged himself to his feet, backed away from him. His sight was almost gone. A vague shadow was moving toward him. He backed around a ridge in the cliffs and slumped against the rocks.

The unearthly shriek behind him was like no cry he had ever heard in his life.

He turned, looked up. A dragon loomed over him. Its mouth began to open.

Scardi screamed in pure terror.

The dragon's mouth opened wide and a river of flame poured from it, and enveloped him.

Scardi was a human torch, his clothes and body an inferno, his screams of pain as unearthly as the creature that had just incinerated him. He rolled back around the ridge, feet and hands thrashing madly.

Sharky shuddered and turned his back to him.

One shot, he thought. *One shot would put him out of his misery.*

Well, it was one shot Scardi would not get from him.

He started back down toward the gates. Scardi's screams followed him almost all the way down. Finally, they died away.

Domino and Papa came down the battered street toward him. She stopped a few feet in front of him.

"Are you all right?" she asked.

"Never better," he said and smiled down at her. Then he took her by the arm and walked to the edge of the lake. The stainless steel pinball lay upside down in three feet of water. Hotchins was hanging from the guard bar, his head and shoulders under water, his once handsome face distorted like a reflection in a funhouse mirror.

"So much for the next president of the United States," he said. "And that was the shortest political campaign in history."

———————————

The elevator stopped and they walked rapidly through the lobby and outside into bedlam. A dozen police cars had pulled up into the plaza, their blue lights whirling. A TV newsman was interviewing a woman who seemed on the verge of shock. An ambulance screamed around the corner and pulled in with its siren dying down to a growl. They walked past a crowd of spectators, some holding drinks from Kerry's Kalibash, staring up at the building.

Livingston and Friscoe were standing away from the crowd, talking intently with Jaspers who was jabbing the air between them with an icepick finger.

Sharky kept walking, holding Domino tightly against him. He had passed Arch Livingston and Barney Friscoe and Papa before The Bat saw him.

"Sharky!" he bellowed.

Sharky kept walking.

"Sharky!"

He was almost to the car.

"Sharky, goddammit, stop!"

He stopped, still holding her close to him, and looked over his shoulder at The Bat.

"What the hell's going on here? What the hell . . . I want some answers. Just who do you think you are, all of you? You're, you're . . ." He stopped.

Livingston came over to them. "You okay?" he said.

"I'm okay. I'm taking her outa here."

"Whatever," Livingston said and smacked him on the shoulder. "You run a hell of a machine, brother. Any time."

"Thanks."

The Bat snapped, "Now let me tell you something—"

Sharky cut him off. "No, you're not telling me a goddamn thing."

He started back toward the car.

"Godammit!" The Bat screamed. "You're through, Sharky! You hear me?"

But if Sharky heard, he made no response. He kept walking, past the police cars, past the crowd, away from the building, away from The Bat, away from the nightmare. The wind shifted and a cold breeze blew past them, carrying the carrion odor away from Sharky, blowing it back toward Mirror Towers and with it the hurt, the anger, the hate.

They got in the car and drove away.